PERFECT LITTLE LIVES

AMBER AND DANIELLE BROWN

PIATKUS

T0385375

PIATKUS

First published in the US in 2023 by Graydon House,
An imprint of HarperCollins Publishers
First published in Great Britain in 2023 by Piatkus

1 3 5 7 9 10 8 6 4 2

A CIP catalogue record for this book
is available from the British Library.

ISBN 978-0-349-43324-0

Printed and bound in Great Britain by Clays Ltd, Elcograf S.p.A.

Papers used by Piatkus are from well-managed forests
and other responsible sources.

Piatkus
An imprint of
Little, Brown Book Group
Carmelite House
50 Victoria Embankment
London EC4Y 0DZ

An Hachette UK Company
www.hachette.co.uk

www.littlebrown.co.uk

To everyone searching,
be honest with yourself,
answers are not always the truth

1

A FAT, HEAVY tear trickles down my cheek when I yank the final hair from my left areola, and it's not even twelve seconds after I exchange my tweezer for the disposable razor I grifted from Reggie's top drawer that blood is gushing down the inside of my thigh. I pause at the shocking appearance of crimson and immediately wonder if this laceration is punishment for being impatient or an indictment of my anti-feminism. Part of me thinks hustling to shave the stray hairs that still stubbornly sprout along my bikini line, despite the six agonizing laser removal sessions I've suffered through, is a reflection of how deeply I've internalized the particular brand of misogyny that says any hair below the brows on a woman is gross and revolting, and the fact that I'm doing this for a man, not myself, is in itself gross and revolting. I've also already chugged sixteen ounces of pineapple juice this morning, for obvious reasons.

The other part of me thinks it's complete bullshit, that being hyper hygienic and having a general disdain for visible body hair is simply considerate, because feminism and a preference for hairlessness shouldn't be mutually exclusive. I don't actually think Reggie has ever noticed the hairs on my tits, or even the splattering on my toes that I compulsively remove once a week, so in a way maybe I am actually plucking the hair from my nipples for my own aesthetic appreciation, not because of the patriarchy, and my feminism is not actually in jeopardy at all.

My dad used to get on me all the time for fixating on tiny, inconsequential details, a habit I no doubt inherited from my mom. But I really am torn about whether I should be judging myself or just owning the part of my personality that is unapologetically vain as I glance at my phone again to see if Reggie has gotten back to my three where r u and did u leave yet and you're still coming, right? texts, which is what I was doing when I slashed myself in the first place.

There is no reply.

No ellipsis to show he's typing.

I sigh because I can't remember the last time my thigh has felt even a trickle. Granted, the deep red liquid heading toward the marble tile is vastly less pleasant than the warm ropes that Reggie sometimes sends down my adductor, or wherever I request, but it's warm and sticky just like it, and in the most bizarre way, watching it drizzle down my skin turns me on a little. After checking my phone again to no avail, I bandage the nick on my leg and toss the razor, assuming Reggie is already packed in a subway car like a sardine. He is not ghosting me. He is not cheating on me. He just doesn't have reception and can't write back yet.

Another thing my dad is constantly grumbling about, usually while he scans the day's headlines in the *Star-Ledger* I bring him every Sunday, is how highly intelligent people can convince themselves of really dumb shit. So there's that.

I look myself over, naked except for the fresh bandage and the glint of gold around my neck, and wish I could see myself the way Reggie sees me. I notice the flaws first. The blemishes. The discoloration. The faded scars I still have from childhood. He notices everything he likes and never has time to consider that I could even potentially see a single flaw in my own body because his hands and mouth are always busy pawing and sucking before he has the chance. Well, that's how it used to be. Before Goldstein & Wagner claimed his soul. Now I think his perpetual delirium from the lack of sleep gives him a soft-focus gaze and that's why he thinks I'm so hot.

Most of my dresses are of the silky, shapeless variety, but the one I pick for tonight is also obscenely short, more reminiscent of a chemise than a dinner garment, something I would never wear out alone. But whatever I wear has to pull its weight tonight. My period is two days away and Reggie squirms even at the idea of a speck of blood. I'm virtually celibate five days every month because even bloody hand jobs freak him out, but he does run to Duane Reade without complaint whenever I'm almost out of tampons and always grabs the right box depending on my flow, so it balances out. He's put in at least ten hours at the firm today, but I'm totally down for doing all the work to get us both off, so yes, this is the dress, and I'm going to make sure he orders something light with plenty of green on his plate so he doesn't get the itis on the ride back to my place.

Still, as much as I am craving tongue and hands and a long, indulgent dicking down to sustain me while my ovaries wreak havoc, I would happily handle it myself once he's asleep and take a couple of hours of slow, deep conversation instead. A little shit talking, but mostly watching him eat, and laughing the way we used to back when we first met, when he was finishing the last leg of law school and had a fraction of the responsibilities he does now. I try not to romanticize the days when we were fresh and new, because it was fresh and new and so of course it was fucking romantic, but I'm human and can only look back on the inception of our relationship through a halcyon lens.

My apartment is a microscopic studio in a freshly gentrified Bed-Stuy, all I can afford on my own with my salary, which, five hundred miles toward the center of the continent, could get me a mortgage on a cute starter home. It can feel claustrophobic with more than two people inside it at once, but when it's just me here, it's perfect. The galley kitchen is at the front and my bed is made semiprivate by the two white open-shelf bookcases I have packed with too many books, some vintage with gorgeous, battered spines, most pre-loved before I got my hands on them. Reggie thinks I have a problem since I've lost count of how many I have and because I have dozens more books littered around the four-hundred-square-foot place. He had the nerve to toss around the *h* word once. I deadfished him that night, and he never used it again. Though if I'm being objective, there is barely a flat space that isn't occupied by at least one paperback, but that's only because I am an actual slut for an aesthetic floppy copy of almost anything. Reggie doesn't get it. He thinks hardbacks are supreme, and I think it's tied to the fragility of his masculinity somehow, especially since he's barely a recreational reader, which makes his opinion hardly justified. Then again, I'm a fiend for his dick when it's floppy too, so maybe I'm the one with a complex.

I run through my standard series of poses using my floor-length mirror to check how far I can lean over without flashing my nipples or my ass, and frown at my visible panty line. They're seamless, allegedly, but I can see the faint indent where they grip my skin beneath the delicate fabric of my dress. I step out of them and shuffle through my top drawer for a much less conspicuous thong, but then shut it empty-handed and decide that it's fine, Reggie has had a long week and it's only Tuesday. I'm sure he'll appreciate the surprise.

I'm ten pages away from knocking another contrived, predictable thriller written by a man that swears the narrative is feminist but comes off glaringly misogynistic off my TBR by the time I hear the jingle of Reggie's keys outside the door to my unit. I toss the book aside without dog-earing my current page, though I feel an instant pang of regret and swing my legs off the arm of my couch as I reach for my phone to see what time it is. It's been two hours since I gashed my leg. I wait for the door to fly open and brace myself to be seen, for his jaw to drop when he sees me.

But nothing happens.

Reggie doesn't push in. I don't hear that jingle anymore.

Before I fully convince myself that I'm suffering from hallucinations courtesy of my surge of pre-menstruation hormones, I straighten out my dress and cross the space to glance through the peephole and be sure. Reggie is on the other side, head bent over, his thumbs beating away at his phone's screen, whatever email he's writing taking precedence over our date. Envy erupts like a geyser inside me.

It's hard to stay pissed at him once I swing the door open and look him over without the distorting view of the peephole. His shirtsleeves are rolled up to his elbows, revealing his forearms that are corded with thick veins, the left one covered in a massive tribal tattoo I still don't know the meaning of. So slutty of him. His tie is loosened around his neck, but not all the way undone, and I can still smell the remnants of whatever soap he showered with this morning.

"Hey." He hasn't looked up yet. "Sorry I didn't hit you back. I was swamped."

I don't reply, will not dignify anything he says with a response until he properly acknowledges me and all the work I put in to look edible for him tonight. He finally hits Send and lifts his chin, a guilty smile tugging at the corners of his mouth. I don't know why, with all this pent-up anticipation, his double take at my dress still makes me blush, and I sort of resent that part of me. Though, at the same time, it feels good to be taken in like this.

"Thought you said seven thirty," I say, fighting to not sound too accusatory, but it's not much of a battle since the way he's checking me out is softening me right up like a stick of butter in a microwave.

His eyes are moving quickly, like they are being pulled downward by some invisible force. "This new?"

He reaches for my amorphous dress, his touch rough enough for me to worry about the preservation of its barely-there straps.

"Figured you'd like it," I say.

I would have much preferred an immediate and sincere apology for keeping me waiting, but I relinquish my simmering irritation and let him feel me up as I lean in to give him a kiss. He settles a hand on the small of my back, definitely wanting me closer, wanting more, but I pull away before he gets too distracted by the dessert and no longer has an appetite for the meal.

"So." I look for my purse. "Where you taking me?"

He smirks. "To the bed."

Which isn't far from where we stand, so very low effort on his part.

Before I can grab the strap of my Fendi Baguette dupe, Reggie shoves me into the wall, his long and hard suited body pressed against mine so tightly, I couldn't escape this hold even if I wanted to. I can smell the office on his skin and I can feel him. He's not hard yet, but I can't even remember the last time he kissed me like this, like we're on some kind of cheesy film set. Like kissing me is thrilling in that way it is when it's new and novel.

He wraps my legs around his waist, and I laugh against his mouth. "Reg…"

He pulls back slightly, but only to go at my neck like a carnivorous beast who hasn't managed to outsmart its prey in weeks. He knows every spot, every secret, and coherent thoughts and intelligible words are no longer possible for me to conjure. I have to grip the wall behind me in order not to completely liquefy. Asshole.

"Five minutes, then we'll head out," he mumbles between kisses, his pace quicker now.

"No." My breathiness embarrasses me. "You know you're oxytocin-sensitive."

Straight facts. Orgasms are like Ambien to him.

Reggie laughs, like really laughs, which is flattering but I'm serious. "Hey, putting me to sleep is the best compliment you can get."

He palms my ass like he owns it, then dives for my left nipple, doesn't even bother to push the thin cup of fabric out of the way, just sucks on my freshly pruned flesh through the satin, which is so wolfish, all I can do is bite down on my lip and watch as he squeezes the other one like he's juicing a grapefruit. I moan in pain, then writhe in pleasure, bounce from one end of the spectrum to the other in rapid succession.

"We haven't been out in like two months," I whisper, desperate to get him to calm down before we're both naked and fucking on the floor. I still have scabs on my knees from the last time we didn't make it to a piece of furniture after some horror movie we saw in some old theater in Brooklyn.

He makes a soft sound, my skin still between his teeth. "I know, but isn't this the whole point of..."

Shock hijacks the rest of his thought because his hand has gone up between my thighs and he's discovered my last-minute sartorial decision, but I know exactly what he was going to say, and he's wrong. The point of going out and sitting opposite each other in a booth, legs touching under the table as we gorge on food that's doused in too much olive oil and an even more alarming amount of salt, is to spend quality time together, the kind of slow-moving time we haven't spent together since he started at Goldstein & Wagner. Dinner isn't just a meaningless prelude to fucking just because we're in a relationship now. Of course, when we get back home we are going to fuck and bruise each other with love and call out to gods neither one of us believes in, but I want the conversation and the laughs and the flirting. That's what makes the sex even better. And there's still so much to learn about each other. So much more we can share fully dressed but stripped down to our most vulnerable selves that'll bring us way closer than a pillow-top mattress and a tube of lube.

This is what I should say. I should be brave and articulate exactly how him canceling our planned date makes me feel and why I still want to date him even though we're a couple. I should tell Reggie that even though I thoroughly appreciate that he literally can't keep his hands to himself, I'd much rather pick his brain before he gives me head. Because if we jump straight into it now, it'll make me feel like this—my body, my writhing, my moans—is more important to him than my thoughts, my jokes, my company.

I should.

But Reggie states the obvious before I can find the right words. "You don't have panties on."

He grins, and he looks so much like a little boy announcing this discovery that it borderline makes me feel like a perv.

I push his hand down and smirk. "You weren't supposed to find that out until we were at our table and there was nothing you could do about it for another two hours."

"Can't we just stay in tonight, babe?" The way he begs makes him sound as infantile as that grin made him look. "I just put in eleven hours at the office. I'm beat."

I know he's exhausted. I can hear it in his voice, see it in his eyes. But this is becoming a pattern. I've eaten dinner at restaurants alone so many times in the last couple of months that I told Reggie I wouldn't meet him anymore. He has to come pick me up like a chivalrous motherfucker now. That solved nothing except that I don't have to eat alone in public anymore.

No, I get to skip eating altogether because we never actually make it out. He either starts feeling up on me until I give in and help his tired hands get me naked, or blacks out as soon as he hits the part of my sectional that's not covered in books. I don't even bother calling up my favorite Italian spot anymore because I've bailed on so many reservations already, I'm afraid the hostess is gonna call me out and make me cry because I'm sensitive like that.

"Yeah," I say, making no question of my disappointment. "Whatever you want."

I push him off. Or really, he lets me push him off because he's sixty pounds heavier than me, but I can feel his regret as soon as I strut away. I don't give a shit about my neighbors whose ceiling is currently my stomping ground. The staccato of my stilettos soothes me like three ounces of Macallan.

I don't care about my period anymore. I don't even feel like being touched tonight. I'll just eat some saltines and faux cheese out of a can and get an early start on my monthly celibate stint.

"Ninety seconds," Reggie says, breaking the silence. "New record."

I pause, glancing back at him. "For what?"

"How fast I can make you mad at me."

Reggie follows me to the other side of my massive bookcase, where my frameless bed sits on a jute rug, swathed in slouchy white linens. I hate that just the sound of his zipper coming undone makes the small, intricate muscles in my lower abdomen clench. The metal clink of his belt is deliciously erotic too, but I yank off my heels and ignore the tempting symphony the sounds that Reggie undressing creates behind me.

"I'm not mad," I say, but I don't risk glancing over my shoulder again because I can hear that he has just stepped out of his pants. "I'm disappointed. We don't even talk anymore."

"Talk about what?"

He sounds frustrated already, and I can't help but yank my

body around to face him. The sharp movement sends one thin strap of my dress down the curve of my shoulder. "How work is going. Your family. Your friends. You."

"It's fine. Everybody's fine. I'm just tired as fuck." He works on the buttons on his shirt, then slips it off his shoulders. "I leave in the morning and it's dark. Come home, it's dark. It's a lot, babe."

And now I feel like a shitty person. He's right. He works overtime and never complains. He is the hardest-working person I know. This is probably the last thing he needs right now, my nagging. I should be more supportive. I want to hug him, but his head is bent over his phone before I get the chance. He checks his inbox before pulling off his undershirt, and I study his features, his full mouth and broad nose, lit up by his phone's incandescent bluish light.

"So you're not hungry?" I finally ask.

Tonight can still be mended.

"I ate at the office," he admits distractedly, his thumbs beating the screen softly in response to an email.

"Oh, I get it." I fold my arms across my chest and wait for him to meet my eyes, but he types away. "You forgot you were taking me out tonight, didn't you?"

He glances up, his expression now veiled in confusion that quickly morphs into regret.

It's not the first time. I shouldn't be surprised. This shit shouldn't hurt as much as it does, but it does.

"Did you even make a reservation?" I ask.

He stammers for a couple of beats, but I'm already crossing into the kitchen before a coherent word comes out because it's obvious his hesitation is the most honest answer I'm going to get. I yank open the freezer door and the urge to tell him to go to his own apartment to sleep tonight gnaws at me as I decide between the dairy-free pint of cookies and cream or the raspberry sorbet. He might have eaten, but I was warding off my appetite for him all evening and I'm starving. I have no patience to cook or even wait for delivery.

My dress is the kind that is as comfortable to sleep in as it is to wear out, so I throw myself under my covers without changing out of it and hunt for the page I was on in my book before his ass showed up. This only lasts a few moments. I quickly grab my Prada glasses from the nightstand so I can see without giving myself a migraine since I can no longer wear contacts because of the magnitude of my astigmatism, though I always feel self-conscious wearing them around Reggie. He has never complained, but even these stylish frames make me feel more frumpy dumpy than hot teacher. I'm not even a full scoop or two pages into the formulaic plot of my novel before Reggie is on his knees at my side.

"No," I say without looking away from the paragraph I've read three times and still haven't retained a thing from. He is not the kind of guy who prays, so I'm already anticipating his impending apology.

"I wasn't gonna ask anything," he whispers, the bass in his voice a stark contrast to the breathiness of his words.

"Then why are you on your knees?" I flick him a glance with a slight cock of my head, and his crooked side grin ruins me. I shouldn't be this easy.

"Okay, I lied."

Obviously.

He touches my leg, slides his long fingers toward the softest part of my thigh. I stubbornly move my eyes back to my page, but can't focus for shit.

"Wanna catch up over lunch tomorrow?" he asks. "There's this new spot by my office. Opened last month. Their cauliflower buffalo wings slap."

"Reg."

"Seriously. Had them last week."

I shut my book, but keep my thumb in the crack as a temporary bookmark and sigh. "It's okay. I get it. You're too busy to take a—"

"Not too busy for you."

The look in his eyes is so sincere, so earnest. But words are cheap. I dig into my pint with the tip of my spoon, but before I can bring the little mound I've carved out to my mouth, he takes the carton and my book in each of his hands. He discards them both before climbing onto the bed, his legs opened in a kneel around my closed ones.

"I was…" I glance at the book, and while I'm distracted by trying to remember what page I was on, he slips the spoon from my grasp too. "That's for work," I tell him in protest to this glaringly obvious attempt at seducing me into acquiescence. "I have to—"

"Lay back."

It's a command, not a request, and I can never oppose quiet authority on the spot, so of course I heed, sliding my glasses off as I do what he says. He licks his lips and my thighs clench in anticipation, the way he is so self-assured doing me in like always. I know exactly what is about to come now, and I hate how weak I am for it. I remove one of the super plush Euro-style pillows propped behind my back so I'm nearly flat and wait for the next command. It comes in a smooth whisper.

"Grab something to bite." He opens my legs and adjusts himself over me, strong and massive. "I don't want your neighbors messing up my flow this time."

This is how he gets me. Every single time. He makes me laugh, makes me forget why he pissed me off in the first place. I wanted to play mad at him until at least the morning, but here I am, showing my entire hand. I am full-on blushing as I palm around the bottom drawer of my nightstand for a wad of socks that will eat up the reverberations of my inevitable wailing. A few knocks on the wall is embarrassing, but manageable. That time the cops showed up was unbearably awkward, but it was my fault for ramming my arm into my lamp and shattering one of my picture frames on the wall. My brass light fixture wasn't the only thing I broke, just the only thing that made contact with anything other than drywall. When it's really good, I just throw things. And I have no idea why it helps, but it does. Reggie cracked up when I asked if I could get his tongue insured, like Tina did with her legs and Mariah did with her voice, but I'm still not sure if I was joking or not.

2

"UH-HUH," I SAY into my work phone. "Putting it in my calendar now."

I'm actually proofreading a draft of a review I just spent the bulk of my morning polishing up, but I hope I sound convincing enough because today is not my day to put in any actual effort. I barely comprehend what my boss even does, or what any of the execs in their messy offices anchoring this sprawling suite do, aside from pretending like they do a lot more than the assistants and lower-level account managers while getting better tax cuts than us, which is why I supplement my meager salary with penning freelance book reviews. For so long it's been as lucrative as a hobby, but recently the tables have slightly turned. I've been getting a steady stream of requests ever since my controversial rave review of a destined-for-the-midlist thriller by a debut Black author changed the trajectory of the book last spring and jolted it onto the *NYT* bestsellers list for eighteen weeks straight. It's not enough to quit this place because I'm still in the hole from all of Dad's staggering legal fees, but sooner or later the hustle has to pay off. At least, that's what Pinterest keeps telling me.

"Sure, I'll give you a buzz next week to confirm the details," I say, ending the call, then switch my voice back to its natural inflection. "Fucking incel."

I don't know why phone calls fill me with such irrational rage, and it's very stereotypically millennial of me, as is my paltry 401(k) balance, but they do. *Incel* might have been too harsh of a word for my very-married-yet-still-pervy client, but in my post-call fury, it feels justified and I slam my receiver into the cradle a little too hard. It crashes into the framed Polaroid of my mom, who is wearing the nameplate necklace that's resting at my clavicle right now. I slipped up once and forgot to remove it before my standing Sunday-afternoon visit with my dad and told him it was a replica, but it's the exact one from the photo. The one he bought for his wife on their one-year wedding anniversary. I'd contemplated replacing it with a sleek inscription of her name on my bicep so I could put the necklace back in the box where he keeps the rest of her things, but I didn't want to risk getting permanently inked with a potentially syphilis-laden needle. I'd already gotten a small inscription on the inside of my wrist with a quote from one of my mom's favorite books, but still couldn't bear not having a genuine piece of her connected to me at all times. So I swapped the real necklace for the look-alike, and now I am a liar.

"Bitch, I have a meeting to get to," Jasmine says, reminding me that I've been keeping her waiting in suspense for the last seven minutes while I took my call.

The bullpen is buzzing with post-latte, almost-lunchtime energy, but because my cubicle is tucked so far into the northeast corner, the roar is muffled to a soft purr. Jasmine is six feet tall, did not play basketball or volleyball in high school because her coordination is shit, sucked at track the one season she ran, was approached by a model scout when she was fourteen but turned them down because she prefers pages to pictures, and is the biggest literature snob I've ever met. Obviously, we vibed immediately. She has been waiting with bated breath for me to finish my call so I can fill her in on what happened after Reggie dropped down to his knees last night.

"Come on," she says, practically squirming in anticipation. "Was it at least good? Did he hold your hands while he did it? I love it when dudes do that. Makes me want to pop out back-to-back babies for him."

I don't immediately know why my instinctual urge is to lie, to tell Jasmine that over the last few months my man has become a banal lover, to bitch about how his tongue action was perfunctory and his stroke game was off. I almost have a fully fictionalized account of last night on the tip of my tongue, about how he eventually went soft and couldn't get it back up and had drool rolling out of his mouth before I could get off.

But the truth backhands me before the words can leap off my tongue, and paralyzes me. A lie would absolutely help me justify the hive of conflicting feelings buzzing in my gut. Confessing that Reggie is no longer satisfying my needs would make me feel like less of a shitty person for resenting the three orgasms Reggie gave me last night and secretly questioning whether or not I still see a crystal clear future with him in it. Because that's what I've been doing all morning, trying to justify these weird feelings of discontentment. At least if our sex life had tanked, I would have probable cause for complaining.

"I was misty-eyed by the time he came up for air," I tell her, jolted by the monotone of my own voice. "Did you see the way I walked in here earlier? I don't think all the feeling has come back into my legs yet."

She just stares at me. The lack of pitch in my delivery did not match the content of my admission. I think she is waiting for me to laugh, to signify that the dryness of my tone was intentional, that I am joking.

When all I do is shrug and sip my lukewarm smoothie, she scoffs. "Dude, do you know the last time I popped a squat over a guy's face?"

I shake my head. "I didn't mean it like that. I just…"

"You know what else I like?" Jasmine asks before I figure out how to explain. "When they sniff it before they start licking it."

And this is why I can only take Jasmine in small doses a few times a day.

The thing is, those three times Reggie made me come last night mean nothing when I think about the four hours—count them, *four*—he made me wait, all to renege on his promise to take me out. It's about the lack of emotional intimacy we shared, despite how much we shared our bodies. We couldn't have been closer while he rode me, sank so deep inside, whispering breathy hymns of praise into my skin as his sweat became mine, but Reggie still felt remote. He was there in body, but not in mind. He physically impaled me in the most transcendent way—it was almost spiritual, but there was this sheet of glass between us, this impenetrable wall of emotional detachment. I'd started to notice it a few months ago, but willingly ignored the signs, thinking I was being dramatic and blowing something minuscule way out of proportion. The fact that he didn't want to cuddle afterward was not something big enough to start a fight over. I thought he was just tired; worn out from the demanding hours of his new job, the pressure to perform and be everything he was expected to be. I wrote off the two times he couldn't get all the way hard as the stress finally getting to him, his overachieving side rearing its ugly, pointed head. I thought it was him. Now I'm realizing it might not have been him. It could be *us*.

"It feels manipulative sometimes," I say to Jasmine, and my heart pounds at the unadorned admittance. I've never been this kind of honest to Jasmine. We're office buddies, not *friends* friends. But the longer the words hang, the more I realize how true they are, how magnificent they are in their own darkness.

"I'm happy it's going well at the firm. He's worked his ass off for this, but…" I pause, pensive for a moment. "I just don't want to end up growing apart like my parents did."

"It was really *that* bad with your folks?"

I lean in for effect. "Before my dad got his corporate job, we lived in this tiny apartment. I was little, so I don't really remember it. But it only had one bathroom. So my mom would do her makeup in the morning while my dad was on the toilet."

"Like…"

"Coffee is like a laxative for him," I say, and her face scrunches up in disgust. "So yeah, that was literally the most intimate thing I ever saw them do."

"Okay, gross, but you and Reg are still getting it in on the regular, no?"

She asks that like us still having regular, satisfying sex puts us in the clear. Like our relationship is totally healthy and immune to dysfunction and dissatisfaction because we're burning calories under the sheets consistently.

I used to think like that too. I wish I could go back to being that cute little naive girl-woman who thought if what Reggie and I had was the opposite of what my mom and dad had, we'd be on track for forever together. I thought the sexlessness of my parents' coupledom was the bane of their marriage, but for the first time, I can see it couldn't have been. It used to be so obvious, so simple. A couple that sweats in bed together, stays together. But my parents *did* stay together even though they barely touched each other. They kept up a united front until the day she disappeared. Divorce was never on the table, as far as I could tell. All this time I thought sex was the glue, the eggs in the batter. But it must have only been the icing on top because their marriage never actually collapsed. Cake without icing isn't as sweet or as beautiful, but it's still cake. Icing without cake is nothing but useless sugar.

Reggie and I are all icing, no cake.

It hit me right when he pulled out of my mouth last night, as he closed his eyes and shuddered as if on cue, and my mind has been going haywire ever since.

"Don't tell me things are drying up between you two." She whispers like she is sharing a burgeoning conspiracy theory. "I thought you—"

"Nothing's drying up," I say, interrupting her, realizing she's taken my silence as confirmation. "We just don't vibe like we used to."

Her face twists. "What do you mean?"

"Like if we take out the sex, I don't think there's much left. I barely even see him anymore," I say, and as the words leave my tongue, they sting.

I've never admitted this to Jasmine. I've never admitted this to myself. It makes me feel awful to speak of him, of us, like that. But the truth is the truth no matter how it makes you feel. Fuck, I hate this. I should be so grateful to be with someone like Reggie. He has a great job, his own place with an actual couch and an actual bed frame with actual sheets and no baby mama drama. And I am. I swear I recognize how lucky I am, but my self-awareness doesn't change the fact that our connection feels grounded by sex and nothing else.

"All you have to do is hang in there a little longer," Jasmine says. "That ring will be on your finger before you know it."

"What, is marriage some magic Band-Aid? I don't want to *hang in there*. I want it to be like it…"

Like it used to be.

Or maybe it's always been this way and I've never noticed. Maybe the hazy mist of immediate attraction has worn off and now I can see what is really there, or the lack thereof.

"He's just busy with the new gig," Jasmine assures me. "Once he gets settled in, it'll go back to the way it was before."

I watch her for a moment, and I get her, but also, I know Reggie more than she knows Reggie.

"We're meeting at this spot near his office for lunch," I tell her, checking my desktop for the time.

"See? He's trying."

He is trying. I have to give him that.

I go into my purse and roll on some lipstick, press it in with my finger, then tap it on again. "We'll see. Gonna head out."

Jasmine hops onto my heels as I make my way through the suite toward the elevator banks. She is generous in her delivery of synthetic smiles to all our white colleagues we pass or intercept. I reserve my energy.

At the edge of the suite I feel my phone buzzing in my pocket, and for some bizarre reason I cannot comprehend, I answer it without considering the vaguely familiar number on the screen.

"It's Pia again," she says quickly, in lieu of a greeting, and I can't help but flex my jaw, more angry at myself for answering than her for calling for the umpteenth time. "Please don't hang up this time. I just want to—"

"I have nothing to say to you. What part of that don't you understand?"

"Listen, I'm moving forward with or without you, but I would much prefer it if it was with you."

If I had the kind of audacity this girl has, I would be rolling with billionaires, taking pointless trips in rocket ships like the Musks of the world instead of struggling to balance two demanding jobs, a long-term relationship and busting my ass to get my dad out of one of the oldest and most dilapidated correctional facilities in the country.

I part my mouth to light her ass on fire, something I regret not doing the first time she contacted me, but then I notice that Jasmine is still within earshot, heading to the elevators too to get to her meeting.

So much adrenaline surges as she mouths, "You okay?"

I'm not sure if I am, but I nod and force myself to flip back to my much gentler inside voice. Other people in the suite look over at us and the last thing I want is to cause a scene. "I wish you the best of luck with your project, but please do not reach out to me anymore."

I end the call with a pointlessly aggressive tap and Jasmine follows me out, no more questions asked, and it's such a relief.

I almost blew it. I almost backed myself into a corner that I've managed to evade for the last decade. All lies eventually unravel. The best way to keep a secret is to never allow people to know you are keeping something from them. At times it can get overwhelming—and on my worst days, debilitating—but it's practically become second nature, presenting this sanitized version of myself to my peers, my colleagues, the world. I've never spoken a word about Asher Lane to anyone. Not even Reggie knows the surface of my past. To everyone else I en-counter, my father is six feet under the earth, not in prison for capital murder. I am not the daughter of a merciless monster who slayed his wife in one of the quietest, safest, most wealthy suburbs in the nation. I am not the spawn of New Jersey's most infamous murderer, a heinous man who many wrote to the governor about, asking to have the death penalty reinstated immediately so my dad could be executed in front of a room-ful of witnesses who'd never seen him smile or heard him tell one of his circuitous stories about his adolescence in rural Vir-ginia. A modern-day lynching.

"Okay, I know you're weird about the whole *wife* thing," Jas-mine says, once we get past the main desk at reception. "But if you don't lock a guy like Reggie down, he's gonna trade you in for the first white girl who hasn't satisfied her BBD itch yet.

You know how they do. They fuck us for support, then fuck them for power."

"Not worried," I say, unfazed as I do something I should have done weeks ago when Pia first started badgering me, but absolutely after she expressed that the thesis of her documentary was getting into the mind of a convicted killer—block her number. "Reg isn't the mentally colonized type that associates success with whiteness."

Jasmine snorts. "You held his broke ass down throughout his last leg of law school. You deserve a Stonehenge-level rock. Matter of fact, he needs to hop on a plane to Greenland to properly ice you out."

"A sparkly piece of coal won't change the fact that I'm not a priority for him anymore."

"Fine. Don't come crying to me when he leaves you for some basic-ass Becky with good hair and no rhythm. Be looking like Quasimodo's ass when their man hits it from the back. Arch game weak as hell."

I smile at her, holding back a laugh. "They do always pick the plain ones."

We reach the elevators, and I push the call button to go down.

"Yo, if I got with a white dude, he'd have to be on his Hemsworth brother shit," Jasmine says.

"Facts." I shrug. "But they're all scared. Look at all the men here. Have any of them ever approached you?"

"No, but I always catch them staring."

"Exactly."

"Some of them are sexy as hell, but I just feel like fucking a white dude would be like, 'Let's role-play tonight.' And then he'd come back with a whip and a rope saying he's the master, and I'm his slave."

I laugh. "They're not *all* like that," I say, though I have never been with a white man.

"Maybe not, but even if he asked me to make him break-fast the morning after, I'd be like 'Bitch, do I look like Aunt Jemima to you?' But he can go down the block and fetch me an egg-white omelet, some avocado toast and an overpriced cappuccino with the heart in it. Reparations, motherfucker."

We both cackle. The elevator arrives with a cheerful ding.

Jasmine sucks her teeth. "How come when you call it, it al-ways comes right away? Because you're light-skinned?" She rolls her eyes. "Even the elevators here are prejudiced."

I laugh again and shake my head as the doors slide open. "I think there's some good white guys out there. Just feel like they wouldn't understand me, so..."

"Dude, you already got your Barack. Get your ass in there before I'm late for my meeting."

I slip between the doors with a smile that's not just leftovers from laughing. She's right. I got everything I hoped for, every-thing any girl like me could ever want. Technically, Reggie is going to be broke for the next few years until he pays off his student loans, but my man is gainfully employed, gorgeous, and isn't checking for any other chick. I hold up my phone and check my lipstick one more time, then start to text him that I'm on my way.

"Wait."

I look up and see Jasmine's arm dangling between the heavy metal doors, signaling for them to ease open again.

"Did you hear?" she asks, quickly glancing over each shoul-der to verify we are outside the earshot of our nearest colleague.

"Hear what?"

She steps in a tad closer and lowers her voice to a whisper. "Matt is considering both of us as Katrina's replacement."

The news hits me like a freight train; it's good news, of course, but just as much bad news. Katrina is a junior account manager here, and even though I've been on the firm's payroll for almost three years, I've never considered taking a promotion. I guess I've always assumed I would have outgrown this place before I was considered for a managing position. The salary boost wouldn't be astronomical, but it wouldn't be modest either; it would definitely allow me to get a savings account again and be able to get Dad a new, better attorney. I don't want to dedicate more time and energy to the hamster wheel that is surviving corporate America, but I also need the money in a way I've never needed money before.

Jasmine bounces away, and as the doors close, I feel imprisoned, like I don't have a choice in my future. Then I feel incapacitated by the avalanche of guilt that tumbles over me for even allowing the thought to cross my mind when my dad is locked in literal prison seventy miles away for a crime he did not commit. So of course I will fight for this promotion, so that this time when we file the habeas corpus petition, we don't get denied again.

My bra is squished inside my purse next to my can of Tic Tacs. It was a last-minute adjustment that I managed to pull off in the Starbucks bathroom after climbing out of that germy hole in the ground with all the other midday commuters.

When I step into the marble-clad lobby of Reggie's historic office building, the doorman smiles and asks me for my ID. As I'm reaching into my wallet, my phone buzzes in my hand. I slide my ID across the front desk, then answer it.

"Everyone's heading to the conference room now," Reggie says, before I can even speak, his voice a bit frantic.

"I thought you said you didn't have to go."

"It's not mandatory, but the other new guys are going. It'll look bad if I just dip out, you know?"

I struggle for a second. "Yeah. No, you should go." I sigh, trying to not let my feelings show. "Do you want me to bring you something? I can grab—"

"Nah. I probably won't even have time to eat."

"Reg, you can't just not—"

"Babe, you know I'd rather blow you than blow you off, but I don't wanna be the new Black dude who holds up the meeting. I'll text you later."

He drops the call before I can even tell him it's okay and I understand and have a good meeting or whatever.

I hate that by the time I take my ID back from the doorman and make it back over to the revolving doors my appetite has dwindled and I'm moving as if trapped in a stupor. It's just lunch, just another canceled date. Reggie is an actual lawyer now. I can't demand as much of his time as I could when he was still a student. Between adjusting to the new routine and dodging all the microaggressions from his homogeneous colleagues, he has a lot on his plate. He doesn't need his girlfriend complaining and draining even more energy out of him.

I still feel like shit, the rejection not just stinging but searing as I step through the annoying doors coated in fingerprints. It feels like I've been physically assaulted and I can't tell if my hurt is irrational or if my period is actually a day early and I just need a pound of something Swiss and dark and bitter.

I whip out my phone before I get through to the concrete and see that it's someone calling from a blocked number. After the call goes to voice mail, I unblock the number, then call Pia back, only because I realize there's something I forgot to say before. Still halfway through the rotation, I wait for her to answer, heat in my cheeks, in my palms. I barely know what this woman looks like. I googled her full name and found her website after checking out her boring Twitter profile. Beyond that bare-bones recon I did a couple of months ago, she's a complete stranger to me. I have nothing against her personally, but trying to come between me and my father? She needs to know she's messing with the wrong one.

She picks up on the third ring with a question in her "Hi, it's Pia," which I steamroll right past.

"You have no idea who I am or who my dad is. You know nothing but lies and you want me to help you spread them? Forget how offensive that is. It's insulting that you don't think I can see right through your bullshit. You pretend to care about the truth, but all you care about is fitting us into the narrative you've already settled on. You don't care about what me or my dad have to say, so why don't you just go into porn and exploit people who consent to be exploited? There's way more money in it anyway. Oh, and for the last time, my father is not a murderer, so you can respectfully *fuck off*."

I say all this without taking a single breath, without filtering a single thought, without realizing she has already hung up on me before the end of my diatribe. First there's fury, some residual anger from her calling again, some pent up from the last time she called, and new anger from her hanging up on me and leaving me to wonder where she tapped out. I almost give in to the urge to call her back.

Almost, because I'm too stunned by the tall, blondish guy I notice waiting for the door to come around, his head bent over as he scrolls on his phone.

Just from one glance I can tell his haircut cost more than my shoes. He's carrying a chopped salad in a brown paper bag with handles, the kind that costs twelve bucks minimum, so few calories for so much money. I usually never give his kind a second glance, much less a full-on gawk, but I come to a full stop when he finally looks up. Like not even a period, a fucking exclamation point. I watch this thoroughbred over my shoulder as he effortlessly struts his way to the other side of the revolving glass door and ambles into the lobby like he owns the place. Of course I know the odds of him having a financial stake in the building are absurd to none, but he's an able-bodied, cishet white guy. That's how they walk. They don't need to actually own the building to carry themselves like they do. They own the world.

What's a lone edifice to the entire fucking world?

He is so not my type with his impeccably tailored suit and lace-up Ferragamos, but I can't take my eyes off him and his beautiful clothes and perfect hair. He looks like money, and I can tell he smells like it too, a scent that's impossible to describe but we all know it when even a faint whiff wanders up our nostrils. I can feel how soft his hands are by just looking at the cut of his designer suit. A hard day's work is as foreign to him as skipping a couple of meals a week to make sure the lights don't get cut off is.

The thing is, I have felt his hands. Not on my body, not like that. But we have held hands more times than I can count, than I can remember. I thought I'd forgotten. I thought I'd successfully wiped my memory clear of all those times we shared, when the world was so much smaller but felt huge and life was so much simpler but felt grand. When the illusions that made life seem boundless and my future so sure were still intact.

I would have put money on me witnessing a supernova with my naked eye in my lifetime before crossing paths with Hunter Bishop again. Despite how hard I've tried to expunge him from my psyche, he has made appearances in so many of my dreams—most of them brutal nightmares—but I've never spoken his name to anyone. Not even Reggie. It would make him real again instead of an apparition of my buried past.

He is the same six foot one as I remember, but has put on a solid forty pounds at least, and even though his hair has also evolved from a starry-white platinum to a sun-highlighted golden brown, my heart skips too many beats to count because I'm certain it's him.

Just when I thought I had successfully obliterated all my memories of Asher Lane, there he goes, strutting past me like a complete stranger to remind me that they have only been lying just below the surface all these years, dormant. Capable of erupting and destroying this new me I've designed like miles of fresh magma from the pit of a volcano.

I can deal with Pia blowing up my phone, hounding me with incessant calls, attempting to get me to participate in a true-crime film about my dad's nonexistent involvement in my mother's murder. But seeing Hunter in the flesh like this, all grown up, alive and well—incredibly well, from what I can see—this is bringing another breed of Asher Lane memories bubbling to the surface.

Not the haunting kind.

Almost every memory my brain has held on to of Hunter is doused in an innocent kind of happiness I know I am incapable of ever feeling again.

3

"HEY, SORRY." HUNTER glances in my direction, but his gaze doesn't land directly on my face and quickly ricochets back to the navigation panel inside the elevator. "Didn't know you were coming up. Would have held it for you."

His voice fits him now. When it first changed and went down two entire octaves, it didn't match his sweet face, which I can see has hollowed out significantly since then. It sounded like a man much older than him had taken his lean body hostage and hijacked his vocal cords. Now the gentle rumble of his low-pitched voice complements his much hairier face, sculpted cheeks, thicker chest.

"Which floor?" he asks, because I am still standing outside the stall with my arm keeping the doors from shutting again.

He has already selected his floor, and his hand is positioned over the panel to select for me. There are a shit-ton of businesses in this building, but I know the one he has selected will lead him to Sachs & Marston, the law firm where his father made a name for himself decades ago.

In my immobility, he glances over at me again, lifting his gaze to my face this time. I keep my arm between the doors that eagerly want to shut him out of my life again and wait for him as his eyes brush over my eyes, cheekbones, lips. There is a promising pause, but then he meets my eyes again in question, like he is wondering if I didn't hear him. Or maybe it is just impatience, though he has always been much more forbearing than me.

"Well, this is embarrassing," I say, and I expect recognition to leap into his eyes. I can't really conceptualize what I must have sounded like when I was thirteen, and I know it must be drastically different from my voice now, but I was expecting something about it to be vaguely familiar to him, maybe something in my tone.

But he gives me nothing.

"Not sure where you're going?" he asks, angling his body toward mine, and I get a whiff of him. "Maybe I can help?"

On one hand, this makes me feel great, that my former best friend grew up to be a kind man. But on the other, more dominant hand, I am a cross between shocked and offended that the guy who lived on the other side of the hedges back in Asher Lane doesn't recognize me by face or by voice. I do, however, understand why twenty pounds, four years of running track and going from a training bra to a 34D is pretty hard to see past, but still, I am suddenly questioning my instincts. For a second, I absolutely doubt myself and consider the lofty idea that I am having some surreal experience like déjà vu, but not déjà vu, that this isn't actually Hunter Bishop, the boy who ditched AP calc to grab a freshly dry-cleaned plaid skirt from my closet and buy me my first box of tampons without complaint since I am the girl who got her first period in the middle of third period on a Tuesday and was too humiliated to go to the nurse's office, and also had no girlfriends to borrow one from.

There is a telltale trail of moles that starts on Hunter's left cheek and extends down his neck, shoulders and back, a galaxy of dark beauty marks, but just as I tilt my chin back so I can see over his collar and try to squint through his stubble for one of the marks, the elevator doors start to crash in on me again and this time he swings his much sturdier arm between them.

"It's just…" This is getting obnoxious, so I step in, and now we are only arm's distance apart. "Well, you still look the same."

"I'm…" He cocks his head and gives me another once-over, his gaze lingering on my hips for a beat and stumbling up past my boobs before making it back above my collarbone. "I'm sorry, but do we know…?"

His eyes lock on mine when his words dissipate. I can all but see recognition finally ricochet around his temporal lobe and send bolts of electricity up and down his spine as he studies my smile now through a new lens.

"Holy shit." It's a whisper, like I am a wonder. *"Simone?"*

There was the inflection, but it is not a question. He knows it's me. He remembers. The surge of energy coursing through his body is practically tangible. He wraps his long arms around me and pulls our bodies together, and when they collide I not only smell the zesty soap he must have used on his hair and skin this morning, I pick up on the softer, familiar scent underneath, the one I knew before Hunter went through puberty and started wearing too much of something that made him smell like a freshly opened bottle of Hendrick's.

He grabs me up so hard and so fast, my windpipe is crushed. He squeezes all the air out of my lungs, at least as much as necessary for me to lose my breath but not swoon instantaneously. He has always been bigger than me, stronger than me, but now he is man-big and man-strong. Humanity does not deserve dogs, but if there is anyone who gets close, it's the twelve-year-old Hunter who befriended me when everyone else teased and laughed and slung slurs at me, the only one who saw beyond our differences and stopped in the middle of the hallway to ask me if I was okay like he could somehow tell I was falling apart on the inside. But feeling him now, his muscles, the strange hardness of his body, it is clear: we are not kids anymore. Which is sad because that means we are also not friends anymore. We are strangers who were once practically inseparable, who had parallel experiences in the idyllic cul-de-sac we grew up in. We are not the same people we were before. Nothing is the same. For one, I arrived with two parents and left with one.

And maybe we come to the shattering realization that we are fully developed adults with pheromones and libidos and debts at the same moment, because just before I start to shift away, he abruptly pulls back. I see it on his face. It has just hit him that I am no longer flat-chested and streamlined, though he tries his best to hide it.

"Sorry, I..." He looks at me like he's surprised at himself, like he doesn't know what came over him either. "I didn't mean to—"

"No, it's okay. It's you."

He smiles. "And it's...you."

There is like seven seconds where neither one of us says or moves anything. It's not awkward, nowhere near as weird as I've always imagined it would be to see Hunter again, but somehow I cannot breathe properly.

"I don't know if it's an insult or compliment that I'm unrecognizable less than fifteen years later," I say with a smirk.

"To be fair, the last time I saw you, you were this high," he says, hyperbolically gesturing toward his hip, "about to start eighth grade."

I laugh. "I was definitely missing a couple things. God, I was such a late bloomer."

Of course, my words act as a cue and his eyes drop straight

down to my tits. He didn't mean to because they immediately jump back up to mine in earnest, but as soon as he realizes I witnessed him checking me out, he shifts away, chin tucked as his cheeks flush red, and I remember the look on his face right now is supposed to be the look on Reggie's face. My bra is in my purse. He must think I am a slut.

"No, you…" Hunter shakes his head. "I was just rushing. My head was…" His laugh sounds nervous, like he is about to burst from embarrassment. "I've got a big meeting upstairs in five, actually."

"Sorry. Duh. Not everybody's on their break just because I am."

"A break? What's that?" He gestures to the bag of takeout in his hand. "Gonna scarf this down before slipping into the conference room."

The doors start to squeeze shut again. He waves his arm to stop them even though he clearly shouldn't.

"So you…" I take him in again, his fitted suit, his silk tie, the kind of watch men don't buy to tell time but to show off how well-bred they are. "You really did it? You got your JD and everything?"

He shrugs. "Didn't really have much of a choice," he says, and I nod solemnly, knowing exactly what he means.

Scott Bishop had Hunter's entire life planned out from the day he spotted his tiny scrotum in the ultrasound machine. The teams he would join, the university he would attend, the degree he would get, the firm he would work for. The one he works for, of course. All Hunter had to do was acquiesce and follow the yellow brick road to Emerald City. It's the acquiesce part I was always afraid of, not because I wasn't sure he would be able to do it. Because I *knew* he would be able to do it.

"Are you still writing?" he asks, flipping the script on me. "How long have you been in the city?"

And now it occurs to me that he is the first person other than my dad who I've interacted with in the last several years who knew me before the braces came off, before my hair grew out past my shoulders, before I gave up on writing.

"Since college," I say, purposefully evading his first inquiry. "I do PR and freelance on the side."

"Freelance? Doing what?"

I part my lips to answer, but a paunchy guy in an ill-fitting suit brushes past me to get into the elevator hard enough to make me stumble back a step.

"Oh," I say, blindsided by the unnecessary collision. "Sorry."

The guy just stuffs his face with his bagel and hits his floor on the navigation panel with the tip of his phone.

"Bro, did you not see her?" Hunter asks him, and I barely react because this is the Hunter I know, the Hunter I love, or loved, always ready and willing to fight for me, not with anger but elegance.

This asshole just glares at him and takes a massive bite of his sandwich. "She's in front of the doors."

Which, as if on cue, start to close again, but Hunter wedges himself between them.

"Quick," he says as they slide open again to Asshole's annoyance. "Give me your phone."

I hand it over. He finds my contacts app right away and types in his number. When he hands it back and eases behind the doors, more people pile into the stall.

"Oh, Simone?" He waits until I look up from my phone. "Compliment. Definitely a compliment."

The doors shut on his smile, and I stand there for way too long, thinking what a coincidence it is that he and Reggie both ended up working in the same building. In a city with more buildings than trash cans, how ironic it is that I ran into him here, of all places, my future and my past colliding. And then I realize I am smiling too.

4

THE IRONY ISN'T lost on my dad when I tell him about running into Hunter. His grandest childhood dream was to live easy in the suburbs. He wanted the chirping birds, the sound of early-morning lawn mowing, the scent of freshly tumbled laundry and lilac trees permeating the neighborhood. But most of all he wanted to raise his own kid in a shroud of safety and comfort, the only things his parents were not able to provide him with, despite never taking a single paid vacation. But the pursuit of this sublime ideal, symbolic of the country's longest-standing myth, is ultimately what made him a permanent resident of an understaffed and overcrowded prison. The irony is not lost, yet manages to hover over us like a malignant cloud whenever we are in this heavily surveilled room and a pair of six-legged vermin boldly crawl by our meager feast of candy bars.

I stopped at his apartment on my drive down to Trenton to grab his well-loved copies of his two favorite Baldwin novels from his shelves. Some of the plants in the front room looked like they were a few days away from shriveling up and dying completely, which broke my heart because they're one of the first things he asks about every time I come here. He used to be so meticulous about keeping his pothos and ferns in exhibition condition, and even though I felt terrible for failing his plants, when I stepped into the kitchen the threshold gave, sinking almost an inch beneath my feet. That obliterated my burgeoning guilt and brought on the stress of having to problem-solve, yet again. Reggie has been helping me with the rent and sometimes I sneak into Dad's apartment to cook dinner and make him a plate. It's foolish and silly, but it always makes me feel a little better to do something we used to do together before he was trapped in this hellhole. I've already added reaching out to the property manager to fix whatever foundational issue is going on in the house to my running to-do list, but I'm so tired of having pretend dinners with my dad.

Someone took my mother from me and then the state took my father from me.

I will not rest until he's fully exonerated, and I need to keep his apartment in mint condition for the day he is released. But I am exhausted. And out of money.

"Good pedigree. Father's a judge," Dad says. He shoves a full inch of his Snickers bar into his mouth and shrugs as he bites off the head. "Not surprised. Hey, bring me another one of these, Sim."

I'm not sure if he's asking because I'm already up on my feet or because his leg is bothering him again. Ever since the fall a couple of months after Mom was killed, episodes of extreme pain ebb and flow, but he is a prideful man and doesn't normally ask for little things like this. It makes me worry that he's silently suffering through another intense flare-up. I hate the slight but immediately noticeable limp he's developed. Not because I find it grotesque or disconcerting, but because it's a constant reminder of yet another sacrifice he's made for me that

I'll probably never be able to repay him for. During the investigation, before they officially arrested him, he'd already lost his job and, foreseeing how the legal fees would drain all our accounts, he began painting houses on the weekends to make up for what my financial aid wasn't going to cover for my private high school tuition. He ended up slipping off a ladder while touching up a second-floor window. I would ask him how it's been, but I know he'll just tell me it's been fine.

We both do that, minimize whatever struggles we're going through ever since we buried Mom. Nothing will ever compare to the devastation of losing her.

I don't look at him as I head back to the table, Snickers in hand. Sometimes it is utterly crushing to imagine that you might not one day be able to give your parent the life you know they deserve after they've spent every waking moment trying to give you the life they believe you deserve. I know happiness is too much to ask of a man who has been through all he's been through, but I would gladly settle for contentment. All I want is for him to be freed from the prison that is worry until he is finally released from this literal penitentiary.

I hate that his last days of freedom were consumed by him being a minimum-wage slave. It is a parasite inside of me, the reality that I don't yet have a salary that can allow me to hire a piranha of an attorney who will get his next petition granted, a salary that could not only pay off all the debt we've already accrued from unpaid legal fees, but would also allow him to retire early. His days could be spent resting his leg and dedicated to taking care of his beloved plants and the stray kittens that keep popping up in his backyard, the ones he fell totally in love with at first purr while constantly swearing he wasn't a cat person.

"I'm not surprised he's a lawyer," I say, watching him twist the top off his soda. "I'm just surprised we ran into each other like that after all this time. In the *city*?"

My dad and I aren't gossipers, but this is different. This is Asher Lane adjacent. This is the exception of all exceptions.

"You said he went inside the same building where Reggie works?" Dad asks.

"Yeah."

"Think they're at the same firm?"

I pause. That's never even crossed my mind. I know Hunter. I know who Scott Bishop raised him to be and how absurd it would be to even entertain the thought that he's now some rebel who's working at a midsized firm that specializes in civil rights litigation when the red carpet was laid out for him to rise in the ranks at the kind of firm that consistently sees over a billion dollars in revenue a year.

"No," I tell him, referring to my recent research session in my head. "That building has more law firms than windows. Reggie's at Goldstein & Wagner, but Sachs & Marston is apparently in that building now too. They moved locations a couple years ago."

Dad nods, fills his mouth, then washes it down with a chug of soda. "So how's my man Reggie been?"

He's over our conversation about Hunter already, and I feel a clench of disappointment in my gut. I don't think he realizes how close we were. Or maybe he knows exactly how much we needed each other back then and it's why he'd rather not say another word about him. Our lives were so intricately linked back when we all lived in Asher Lane, the Bishops pretty much synonymous with the cul-de-sac, and it only brings back an onslaught of horrific memories for both of us.

Saying Hunter's name is the closest I've gotten to mentioning Asher Lane since our exodus. In the years we've been gone, we've pretended those five never happened. We don't talk about Mom either. I stopped going to therapy years ago, even though my last full-time gig had that good insurance that comes with reasonable co-pays, because every session came down to the therapist telling me that my current struggles were tied to my mom's death, and I was just like, *Bitch, tell me something I don't know.* And I can't remember the last time I heard Dad mention her name, though I come to visit him every Sunday, same time, no exceptions. It's the one steady thing that keeps us from getting too anxious like the way we were when everything changed and kept on changing until our life wasn't even a semblance of the one Dad built for us in Asher Lane. I still notice him flinching whenever his eye catches the golden gleam of my necklace. Mom's necklace. I don't know if it's because it's impossible not to picture her wearing it once he sees it on me, or if it's just seeing those six letters of her name strung together that rocks him.

I know Dad just wants me to forget Asher Lane, which means forgetting Hunter, so as he stuffs his mouth with a massive bite of chocolate, caramel and nougat, I answer, "He's good."

"No smile." Dad studies me, his now half-masticated bar in one of his severely calloused and perpetually dry hands. "What'd he do?"

"Nothing."

"What'd he do?" he asks, more forceful this time.

"Nothing."

"He must've done *something.*" He waits, and when I keep sipping my water, he stuffs the rest of his bar in his mouth. "Told you to bring him with you one of these days. Unless you're ashamed."

"Dad." I set my bottle down and watch him as he wipes his mouth with one of the thin paper napkins I got from the Chinese takeout I ordered last night.

"So how come you've never brought him down here?" he asks. "It's been almost a year."

The reminder takes me aback. He's right. In a couple of months, Reggie and I will have been together for an entire year. It both feels like it's been much longer and way shorter than ten months since our first night together, which we both, thankfully, decided was the unofficial start of our exclusivity. I start replaying that night in my head, the newness yet familiarity of his hands, the way he kept asking me if this was okay and that was okay, but when my mind jumps to the moment he asked me if I was about to come, I shake my head and remind myself that my father is inches away, watching me as he nurses his cherry Coke.

I sip my water, then shrug to hide how put on the spot this question makes me feel. "I just don't want to introduce you two until I know this is like...permanent."

I hate that I'm lying, I really do. The original plan was to tell Reggie about Dad's conviction after I figured out a way to retain a kick-ass attorney and get him out of here. Maybe there is some level of shame involved, but mostly it's fear, and it's been excruciating on both ends keeping them from each other. I know how badly Dad wants assurance that I'm doing okay, that I'm enjoying at least part of my youth. Sure, we've talked about Reggie, but I get why he desperately wants to see us together, in the same room, sharing the same air, glancing into each other's eyes. I've so badly wanted to gift him with the experience of sharing some of those moments. I just can't bear the thought of Reggie's first impression of my dad being the underweight, gaunt, grayhaired version of him that spends most of his hours confined to a forty-eight-square-foot space adorned by iron bars.

But at least I've had to feed my dad fewer lies. Reggie believes my routine Sunday trips to Jersey are to visit his grave site. I told him I only wanted to go alone because it was my chance to reconnect with him, which is true, but a prison is very different from a cemetery...or is it?

The truth is, it's just been easier to pretend he's dead than to share all the ups and downs of retaining a lawyer, then running out of money to keep them on board, being rejected from nonprofits who help wrongfully convicted people get their cases appealed. So many times I've wanted to ask Reggie for advice since he has a fresh JD, but I've had to bite my tongue and go down hours-long rabbit holes on Google to figure things out instead. I also didn't want my dad's conviction to scare Reggie away in the beginning. I know my father is innocent, but I didn't want that to be the thing that came between us.

"Permanence is an illusion." Dad's voice is suddenly low and solemn, and it makes me look him directly in the eyes. "I thought me and Evelyn were permanent."

Evelyn.

A moment of silence slithers between us.

I bow my head over the table, and even though I got myself a bag of Fritos from the vending machine, I can't bring any of the corn chips to my mouth, my appetite obliterated by him bringing her to the table so unceremoniously.

Dad became quiet after Mom died. Not just the way he is now as he too tries to force himself to finish his excuse for a meal. Quiet on a different level, not just in words but in spirit. It's like he wants to pretend she never existed. That way he doesn't have to remember how much she changed him, challenged him, saved him. For a long time, I understood this and went along with the gambit, but now it just feels violent to pretend the most important woman in both of our lives never breathed. Never cooked meals for us and took care of us when we were sick. The most I've heard her name from his mouth is when he has slipped up and called me by her name. He's been doing it more and more lately, but always immediately corrects himself and blames it on him nearing the edge of his diamond jubilee. But I think it's because the older I get, the longer I grow out my hair and lose the baby fat in my cheeks, the more I look like her in the one photo he keeps in his cell. Last year around Christmas, he didn't realize he'd done it and I didn't correct him because it was nice to hear him say her name without the immediate rush of guilt afterward. It almost felt like she was still here, and it made me wonder if it would have been easier grieving the physical loss of her had we not abolished her name all those years ago.

Sometimes I still forget that I don't have to pretend to not be sad anymore. I used to put on a front all throughout high school because I was afraid that my sadness would tip him over the edge. He was always so limp and heavy. Never angry. I never understood that. I kept waiting for the anger to ravish him, but not even a speck of indignation ever coursed through his veins. Not even after the autopsy was explained to us by an emotionless pathologist, and he learned that two lives were lost the night his wife was murdered, not just one. The life growing inside my mother too.

"Fine," I say, breaking the deafening silence, my heart pounding against my chest as I anticipate my own next words. "You wanna do lunch next week?"

"I don't want to force you if you're not comfortable."

"You're not forcing me."

"You don't have to. Forget what I asked."

"I want to. Reg is just crazy busy since he's been at G&W," I explain. "He gets up at five thirty every morning. I don't want to make him have to drive all the way back to the city from here. It's an hour and a half without traffic, as if there's ever no traffic. But it's fine. I know he really wants to meet you."

"Fine," Dad says, his voice resigned. "It's been…six years since I've seen a new face from the outside? It's a date."

He collects the wrappers from the two bars he eviscerated. I flash him a small smile and tuck his trash into my pocket. He doesn't smile back, but I know today was good for him. For the first time in years he has something to look forward to, and even though I'm terrified of what Reggie will say, the look in his eyes is worth it. Though it's hard to look at him and not notice the faint scars that linger from the lacerations he endured during his first few months here, I still also notice the smattering of freckles covering the bridge of his nose, something my mom often lovingly pointed out.

"You hear anything back from that lawyer?"

I regret mentioning to him that I had reached out to the Innocence Project. I got his hopes up, got him thinking we could have a lawyer work for him pro bono.

"They turned us down," I mumble, hating to be the bearer of bad news yet again. "Same thing. They need some kind of new evidence. But I'm gonna try again. I think I can—"

He lets out a big sigh. "There's no point."

"Dad—"

"Don't waste your time. You have more important things to worry about."

"Oh, really? What's more important than getting you out of here?"

"Hell, I don't know, Sim. Enjoying your life. Being young. Free."

"I'm not free until you're free," I say, getting a little louder than I mean to. "Sorry, but that's the way it is."

The silence is terse and heavy at first. Then it dissipates into regular silence, which almost feels peaceful.

We don't get to say much more before the thin, bearded guard heads over to politely tell me it's a wrap on our lunch. At the last second of our quick hug, part of me wants to tell him about Pia hounding me, about the film she's making, but I talk myself out of it. I'd love to tell him how I told her ass off, show him how every day I fight for him, his privacy, his peace. But it's not worth potentially upsetting him. Because the reality is, with or without our participation, it's still being made.

Sometimes I sit in my car in the parking lot to decompress, but today I shift into gear as soon as I shut myself in. I still have to wash, condition and braid my hair when I get home. I used to do it on Sunday mornings, but I stopped wearing my French braids to visit Dad because I noticed it was on those days when he would slip up and call me Mom's name the most. It was how she always wore her hair.

5

I WOULDN'T LET Hunter pay for the greasy lunch we're eating as we stroll through the south end of Central Park. Granted, we're eating out of brown paper bags, so it's not like it would have sent my card in decline, but I was the one who insisted we order separately. I'm pretty sure Hunter has assumed my preference for going Dutch hinged on some kind of radical feminist theory, but it didn't. I just so happen to suck at confrontation and I really don't want him to get the wrong idea. Back in Asher Lane, our small age difference felt huge and Hunter was the one who always took the lead, but now that we're both twenty-somethings, five years makes us more or less the same age, and I hope he's not offended.

Even some NYC natives have never been to certain parts of the park, but there's hardly a section I haven't been to. At one of my old temp jobs that had offices a few blocks away from the Grand Army Plaza entrance, I used to aimlessly walk around a new area of the park every afternoon to avoid having awkward, stilted lunch conversations with my coworkers in the break room. I didn't fit in there, and when I say this to Hunter, he almost asks me what I mean by this but stops himself. He nods, it clicking for him, and starts telling me more about his life, things that have happened during our time apart. I stop him when he tries to blow past his failed marriage.

"Hold up. Your ex-*wife*?" I scoff, shocked. "You think I'm just gonna let that slip by without unpacking?"

He inhales a breath through his nostrils and keeps it short and sweet. "I was married. It didn't work out."

"What does that mean? You cheated?"

He shakes his head. "Four years, never even slid into another woman's DMs." I stare at him with my mouth agape until he finishes swallowing his last bite. "Can't tell if you're impressed or in disbelief. Either way, I'm insulted."

"Think I'm...both?"

Done with his sub, Hunter tosses the bag and used napkins into one of the bins lining the pathway. I'm only halfway done with my sandwich, so he gestures to a bench before we pass it and waits for me to sit before joining me, a respectable distance between our thighs.

"I saw what my dad's cheating did to my mom, what it turned her into." He pauses, reflective, his voice serious now. "I could never be responsible for doing that to a woman."

I nod. I know Hunter is a good guy, but I can't help but think this is nothing more than a good sentiment. I know not all men cheat. My dad never cheated on my mom. I'm still weary when men talk like this, when such insurmountable proclamations about the future are made so casually, as if they are absolute. None of us really knows who or what we will become depending on circumstance, unanticipated hardship or success. I scrutinize Hunter's expression, which is morose and brooding like whatever emotional turmoil he witnessed his mother going through still has an effect on him.

I glance ahead at a woman breastfeeding a baby that's like two years old and think of Kate Bishop in a way I've never thought of her; as someone who has suffered, someone who has been lied to, disrespected and disregarded. It feels wrong to feel even an ounce of sympathy for the woman who once dressed her kid in blackface and called it Halloween and refused to care for her husband's dying mother, but I feel this nebulous softness pulling at me. Because that's the thing about Kate. She's made mistakes, but from what I've seen, it's never out of cruelty and instead just a result of her ignorance. She always means well, so I've always given her the benefit of the doubt. Though at what point does ignorance stop being a viable excuse?

"What?" Hunter asks, and I realize I've drifted.

I blink out of my brief trance and take a sip of my matcha before looking at Hunter over my shoulder. His stubble looks more intentional than it did last time, like he took some extra time shaving this morning.

"So your mom…" I pause, switching gears. "My dad still doesn't know."

He doesn't know the truth about his wife. His high school sweetheart. The love of his life. When Mom died, I realized I would be burdened with carrying the secret forever, but I honestly have not thought about what she did in years.

Hunter relaxes, lets his shoulders meet the back of the bench and runs a hand over his hair. "My mom knew there was another woman. She didn't know it was your mom, though."

His legs have opened a little more with his adjustment in posture, and I distract myself from the nagging curiosity to glance down at his crotch by taking a huge bite out of my sandwich. I don't want to be forced to judge the enigma of lumps and creases even though an instinctual part of me is tempted to make a quick assessment. I do it to almost every other guy I encounter, force of habit, but that's the bizarre thing. Hunter and I have recently met, yet we know so much about each other already. I can't appraise him like I would look at any other random guy without things getting weird.

When I look up, there is a pigeon, dappled and cooing, heading toward us and I'm grateful for the interference. But then the one becomes a handful of pigeons who have clearly sniffed out what's left of my sandwich, crowding around our feet in case I drop any crumbs.

"Okay." I glance at him. "I know we vowed never to bring this up again, but…"

He already knows where I am headed. Nods as he says, "Your mom was just about to leave my house. Nana was asleep upstairs. Dad got home from court early…"

"They were just going at it." The memory is as stunning as it was when it was happening before our eyes all those years ago. "Like…"

Our eyes meet, and our guilty smiles converge. This is the first time I've ever spoken about what we saw in Hunter's kitchen when I was eight and Hunter was thirteen and it seems like it's the first time he's ever spoken of it too. The vow we made never to repeat what we witnessed was our tame version of opening up superficial wounds and swapping blood.

"I know that should have been my mom," he says with a wry laugh. "But I'm so fucking glad I didn't have to see her like that."

"That would've been so traumatizing."

"Would have needed a six-pack."

I mock gasp. "We were kids."

"Of therapy sessions."

I laugh harder than him now and shove him in the shoulder. It's not with enough force to hurt him, but he wasn't expecting me to hit him and sways a little. He looks down at my hand on his arm and I move it away, but I still feel his gaze on me when I glance down at the huddle of pigeons flapping and waddling around our feet. I'm cruel and lift my sandwich to my mouth and take a hefty bite, but as I lower it, I see Hunter watching me as if judging me for not sharing with our uninvited guests. I might be projecting. Either way, I feel myself weakening, and the next thing I know, I'm breaking off a few pieces of bread and tossing them onto the ground. They all try to snatch up a piece at the same time. I glance over at Hunter and smile when I see that he is enjoying this as much as I am.

We just sit there watching the stubby birds pig out for a while, those primal sounds my mom and his dad made in the kitchen that day we walked in on them reverberating in my head.

"Are you ever just like...why, though?" I ask, glancing at Hunter. "Your mom's so pretty."

Kate Bishop is a five-foot-eleven, waiflike natural blonde designed to be admired. She is the kind of woman who was supposed to eventually take care of her much older husband, but refused to even help Scott care for his elderly mother when she got ill. I think of her svelte body, as thin and as lethal as a blade. Those electric green eyes.

Hunter shoots me a look and he doesn't even have to say a word.

"I know, I know," I say as his lips break apart. "Jay cheated on Beyoncé. But still. Your mom is..."

Maybe it shouldn't have come as such a shock—my mother, Hunter's father. If I had been older when it happened, maybe it would have been easier to foresee. My mom had retired from nursing a few months before we closed escrow on the mini mansion in Asher Lane. Dad was making twice his old salary with his new promotion at the bank and she wanted more time to spend with me. But a few months in, she was spending the bulk of her days at the Bishop house, looking after Scott's mother, whose advanced dementia was starting to hinder her ability to remember her own name. My mom was patient and warm and gentle, the antithesis to Kate, who was too preoccupied with upward mobility at her corporate job, or just enjoyed the time away from being a wife and mother too much to cater to his mom when she got home. I can see why Scott found my mom's willingness to care for the only parent he had left attractive. Of course, there must have been times where they ended up in rooms alone, shared moments that were emotional and intimate, but to disregard the nubile trophy he worked so hard to earn, the one he spent so much time and money augmenting and polishing and flaunting to his friends, for a fling with the neighbor?

"Yeah, she is," Hunter says, unable to deny his mother's beauty. "And I think when my dad met her he assumed everything on the outside extended to the inside."

I scoff. "Wow. That's deep."

I break off a few more pieces of bread from my sandwich and smile when I manage to get them to the pigeons who missed out on the first round.

"Come on," he says, sipping his iced flat white. "You never liked my mom either."

I hesitate.

He laughs. "Admit it."

"All I remember is how obsessed my mom was with her. I think she wanted to be her. Kinda. At least wanted what she had." I glance at him, and he's holding in a laugh and I realize what I've just implied. "I mean the perfectly manicured home, the nuclear family unit, a designated table to have dinner every night."

"But you two never really got close. She tried, but you always kept your distance."

I accept that with a nod, never having really thought about it but unable to deny it now that I've been confronted directly. I shrug, my eyes back on the birds. "I guess she came on a little strong sometimes. But I assumed it was because she wanted a daughter and we could do stuff that she couldn't do with you."

"Maybe," Hunter says, but it's clear he doesn't agree with me.

"To all the other families on Asher Lane, we were the Black family ruining the aesthetic, devaluing the properties. And my mom was just the help. But not to Kate. She saw my mom as a real person. She was pretty much the only friend she had within a hundred-mile radius."

I half expect him to deny this. But he doesn't. He just watches the pigeons for a few moments, and I watch him, wondering how come boys always get the long, thick eyelashes.

"It wasn't just my dad in that kitchen, you know," Hunter says, and I turn to him, my nude-brown lipstick staining the tip of the plastic straw between my lips.

"True," I say, though there are knots in my stomach and I hate the way this feels.

Hunter glances away for a second, then looks back at me with his head tilted slightly. "So why do you think your mom did it?"

"I don't know." I don't think I've ever truly considered this beyond mild speculation that she wanted a brief reprieve from her sexless marriage. "Maybe she was just bored. You know, with my dad."

He frowns. "Bored?"

"Men get bored all the time and cheat. Why can't a woman get bored and do the same thing?"

"Your dad was gone most of the time. Long hours. Out-of-state business trips every other month."

"Exactly. He worked like crazy." I think for a second. "Maybe your dad was just there at the right moment that one day and they slipped up."

"Maybe." He nods and sips, then asks, "But what about the rest?"

I pause. "What do you mean?"

"That wasn't the only time."

"What?" I lower my drink, hoping I've heard him wrong.

"Okay, I never actually *saw* anything after that, but that definitely wasn't the only time they hooked up."

He laughs because he doesn't know what this means and is blind to the chasm this opens. So many questions bloom in my head at once.

Maybe it wasn't the sexlessness of my parents' marriage that drove my mom to cheat, and it was her cheating that caused the sexlessness in their marriage. I think of Scott Bishop, the man, the husband, the father—but mainly the villain—and for the hundredth time I try to figure out what it was that my mom could have possibly seen in a man like him. Maybe it was his bottomless cruelty, his severity, that she found irresistible. Maybe with Scott she could be a submissive sycophant and not have to carry any shame for her hidden desire. Maybe what they had was purely a carnal thing and my mom never let herself think about the actual man she was opening her legs for.

"Then how do you know?" I ask, disbelief still buzzing through me. "How do you know it wasn't just that one time?"

"My dad wasn't that discreet. Heard some things. Late nights. Random business trips. The classics."

"Maybe it was someone else. Some other woman he was messing with."

"Trust me, it was your mom," he says, pulling his phone out of his jacket pocket to see who is making it vibrate.

"So what about your mom? Did she know about them too?"

For a second, he looks like he might regret sending the call to voice mail, then does it anyway. "Definitely not the whole time. I'd have to look at the dates."

I angle my head. "What dates?"

"She has this diary. My ex-wife saw it when we helped her pack up for the move. Flipped through a few entries. The part we saw she definitely knew he was sleeping with someone else.

I think it was like a year before you guys left, and when we caught them that was what, a couple years before that?"

For a moment I trip up on the fact that he said *my ex-wife*, the idea that he even has an ex-wife both preposterous and obvious at the same time, and then I nod. That means the affair lasted at least three out of the five years we lived there and all this time I had no idea.

"What move?" I ask, my mind jumping back to the part of his explanation that bumped me.

He sucks in a breath and takes his time blowing it out. "My parents split up almost two years ago."

"They're not on Asher Lane anymore?"

"Dad still is."

I run that over in my head a few times, then everything he's just told me. "When did it end? Your dad and my mom."

"I don't know."

"The diary didn't say?"

"I didn't read all of it. It was weirding me out, knowing her inner thoughts." He laughs awkwardly and shrugs. "Maybe when Nana died. Would have been hard to keep it up after that, right?"

I see where he's going. After his grandma died, which was a little less than a year before my mom died, there was no reason for my mom to go over to his house every day anymore. It would have been harder for them to maintain their affair without out a little orchestrated convenience.

But not impossible.

I think of the baby who never made it out of my mother's womb and instantly feel sick.

Hunter's phone buzzes again.

"Gotta get back?" I ask, disappointed as he checks the caller ID, because this is all finally starting to make sense.

He gives me an apologetic smile and then his rough cheek is pressed against mine. "I'll text you?"

"Yeah," I say, smiling through the sudden confliction I feel, completely thrown off by him kissing my face. "Text me."

By the time he steps away, my heart is racing. And maybe this is how it's going to be whenever Hunter is near me from here on out, because I don't know how I could ever be relaxed around the son of the man who killed my mother.

6

I'D ALWAYS THOUGHT of myself as a good person. A kind person. I never set out to hurt anyone. When I was young, I was always a good girl—responsible, honest, the one everyone could trust. I used to judge women who did what I was doing. I called them weak, pathetic, whores. I stripped them of their humanity and whittled their character down to a single action. Because what kind of respectable woman cheats on her husband with another married man? A middle-aged man with a wife and kid at that. I never thought I would be in this position, but there I was, and the truth was I couldn't stop. I didn't want to. Not yet.

And neither did you.

It started off very innocently. I was plagued by monotony, anxiety, a furious need to escape the prison of the life I'd willingly subjected myself to. My own mind and body. It's hard to understand unless you've been through it yourself, that kind of seething desperation. When you have been married for over a decade and your husband has not touched you in over a year, there is a switch inside you that goes off. You start to notice all the other men who have been noticing you. There is temptation. Specific glances are exchanged. You start to imagine what your life could be with someone else, at least for a while. Thinking of someone else is not a crime. You revel in this idea for a while, the fantasizing kind of the best part. And then finally you decide that, actually, you deserve to be happy.

Most people think it's always about the sex. It's about getting away with bad behavior, the thrill of it. But that was hardly the point. The sex was mediocre at best, mostly a physical incarnation of your built-up anger, the simmering resentment you had for your wife. I felt it while you were inside of me, the way you relentlessly took your frustrations with your marriage out on me. It was in the smallest moments, the little things you'd do. The way you would grab my hair or neck while I moved beneath you, a little too rough sometimes, usually around the two-minute mark, and as soon as you'd get a glimpse of my face, you'd loosen your grip, the recognition in your eyes almost like an insult. Or when you'd snap at me after I'd ask you a simple question and then quickly turn contrite and apologize like you forgot who you were talking to. You fucked hard. You fucked like a man drowning in his own self-loathing, who so badly needed to prove to himself that he was still, in fact, a man. It was like you worshipped me and hated me at the same time. You told me once, "If it weren't for you, I'd go fucking crazy," and I believed you. None of these things upset me. I understood because I was doing the same thing. That's why it *worked*.

You liked to call me up to meet at the hotel, the one closest to your office, and then complain about your wife for an hour. You lamented about how she spent three hundred dollars a month on coffee. How she had been nagging nonstop lately. How she was terrible in the kitchen and you would rather have eaten three-day-old leftover takeout than suffer through her clumsy attempts at cooking. This was one of your main gripes. You'd go on and on about how she was always doing really dumb shit, like once when the recipe called for a vodka sauce, she poured half a bottle of Absolut in the boiling pasta water and almost set the house on fire.

This is how it usually started, almost like foreplay. And while I understood your disgust, I was tired of hearing about how much you hated this woman. I could have told you to just leave her, but I didn't want that either. I liked that you were mostly unavailable, that there was someone to take up most of your energy during the day. I let you vent about whatever latest annoyance you had with her, because by the end you were all riled up and red in the face and sweating softly at the brow. It was so nice to see a man express some passion, and by the time you would take a breath and look at me, I would have already begun to undress. Usually, I made a show of it because I knew how much you enjoyed that part. I'd smile at you and you'd smile back. You liked this version of me and so did I.

Today, though, when you came in you didn't mention your wife at all. You were sheepish, tense, almost solemn. You dropped your briefcase by the door and tossed the book you were reading onto the bed. *Man's Search for Meaning* by Viktor Frankl. You called it one of the best books ever written and had read it several times. One of your favorite passages was, *Everything can be taken from a man but one thing: the last of the human freedoms—to choose one's attitude in any given set of circumstances, to choose one's own way.* You'd read it aloud to me on two different occasions. I found it corny, but you thought it was enlightening, inspiring.

As you ran your hands through your hair, gently pacing the room, I considered asking what was wrong, but it felt glib.

Mean even. I already knew the answer because with you it was always the same; your problems all led back to one source. I would have thought some of the stress would have been from your job, a big case you were working on, maybe. There were plenty of people who depended on you, who needed you constantly, urgently, but you'd never once complained to me about any of that.

"My mother just fucking went into hospice," you blurted out as I made my way across the room to greet you.

I didn't know what to say. I felt sorry for you. I really did. Your mother was dying and your wife was a narcissistic, entitled bitch. Your words, not mine. I stood there, awkwardly frozen in my silk bra and thong, waiting for you to continue, but you never did.

"Are you okay?" I asked, my voice soft.

"Yeah. I'm fine," you said without looking at me, raking a hand through your hair. "Sorry, I don't know why I just said that."

A moment passed, but you still hadn't moved from in front of the door.

"How was work?" I asked, just to fill the silence.

You sighed like just the thought of the day was enough to stress you out and shook your head a bit. "Do you really want to talk about work?"

"No," I said, biting my lip. I watched you walk over to the minibar and start to make yourself a bitter negroni.

"I thought so," you said, meeting my eyes purposefully. There was almost a smile, but not quite. You grabbed a glass and started to pour, skipping the ice, filled it halfway. First one, then a second. You handed the second to me and gulped yours. I did the same, a little slower than your pace, but still too fast.

You leaned against the wall for a moment, finding my gaze again. "Come here." You were no longer looking at my face, only my body, and that was all it took to turn me on. Sometimes just knowing that someone else wants you is enough.

I walked toward you and you took off your jacket. I pulled your tie loose, undid your belt while you watched in complete silence. And it was almost like our first time. The way you looked at me, the way you ran your hand through my hair so tenderly, so carefully, pressed your nose against my neck and breathed me in like just the scent of me is enough to satisfy you. But of course you wanted more. You told me this, like you always did, because you knew I loved it. You knew I needed it, to hear you say how much you wanted me. You took your time, whispered compliments as I pleased you, told me I was beautiful over and over like it was lyrics to your favorite song. I preferred silence because it was easier to detach that way, but you were always very vocal, very talkative, and I wondered if you were also this way with the wife. You fucked me against the bathroom door, then on the bed, kept moving me around like you couldn't get enough, and I kept up with you until you trembled inside me and held me so tight I thought you'd never let me go.

"Where did they make you?" you asked, catching your breath. "You're ferocious. Christ."

I laughed at your expression, at the sheer awe in your eyes as your warm body fell away from mine. You sounded as if it was truly our first time. You reached over on the floor for your pants and pulled out a pack of cigarettes. The pack was brand-new and you struggled a bit getting it open. I was surprised; I'd never seen you smoke before. You didn't seem like the type, but then again, we all had secrets, versions of ourselves we kept hidden from the rest of the world. After you lit up, you looked at me and grinned.

It wasn't until that moment that I thought of my husband. I could feel him lurking, disapproving of my presence. The way I looked. How much of a slut I was. And it made me smile, because for once I didn't have to adjust myself for him. I could just be me.

With you, I could just be me.

7

I CAN STILL feel the warmth and chisel of Hunter's cheek pressed against mine even though I am now in Reggie's shirt that is comically large on me, but also fits perfectly. I've been replaying our conversation so many times that I can no longer decipher what was actually said between us and what are simply hypothetical responses I have come up with to his casual but wild revelation that it was a full-on, yearslong affair between his father and my mother; not the isolated incident I've been convinced it was all this time.

Like so much of the past. How could I not have noticed my mother was sleeping with Scott for so many years? How could Hunter say those words to me and not realize the implication of them? There are so many overlapping questions flipping around in my brain at once, but mainly I can't stop wondering if I was the only one in the dark or if my father knew of my mother's horrible secret.

I was under the janky downpour of my shower when Reg-

gie keyed in a while ago. I thought he'd come in and slip behind me, so I waited for him to join me, but he went straight
to my fridge, stole the leftover drunken noodles I was saving
for tomorrow's lunch, and has been tucked into my bed with
his head bent over his laptop the whole time I've been detan-
gling and moisturizing my hair.

I'm halfway through my first chunky braid when I call out
to him from my bathroom. "Babe."

"Mmm?"

He sounds distracted, like he's deep in concentration, but I
need to make sense of my thoughts before I combust. Sometimes I want to demand more of him, but how can I demand
when I have offered so little of who I really am to him? He
knows my full name, but he has no idea what comes along with
the package I present to him every day. I have so very carefully
curated my memories and past experiences. I haven't done some
harmless light editing; I've created a full-on simulation and he's
bought right into the ruse. Because he trusts me. Because he
loves me. Because he would never suspect that I am capable of
such a level of deceit. How could he? He's fully convinced that
my mom and dad died in a horrific car crash and he respectfully never brings it up, so fortunately I haven't had to repeat the
lies too many times. Still, they gnaw at me in my nightmares.

"Are you done?" I ask. "Wanna talk about something."

I get no response, so I'm not surprised when I step out into
the main space and his laptop has his full attention. He's doing
that thing where he hears my voice, but is not taking in my
words. I know he's passionate about what he does, but balance.

"Did you hear what I said?" I ask, but end up just boring a
hole into the side of his head.

"Is it serious?" he asks, his mouth full of noodles. "Why you
looking at me like that?"

"Need to tell you something important, Counselor," I say,
the impatience in my voice betraying my annoyance. I usually

only pull that one out during sex when I want him to come faster, but it gets his attention.

"Chill. Here." He shuts his laptop and pats the empty space next to him. "What's up? Hit me."

I climb onto the bed and kneel next to him, then start on my second braid.

"Okay. I…" I take a breath and it feels like I'm getting naked for him for the first time all over again, except this time I'm not just baring my skin and all my scars; I'm sharing my past with him, secrets I buried so deep they practically feel like nightmares now instead of memories. "I haven't been honest with you."

"So you…lied to me?" he asks, sounding confused.

"Not exactly. I mean, yeah, I guess. Technically."

"About what?"

"A lot of stuff."

"Stuff like what?" I've captured his full attention now and I'm not so sure I like it. "Why are you being so vague?"

I hesitate, sucking in a breath for courage. "Promise whatever I say won't change things between us."

"Don't ask me that, Simone. Just tell me whatever it is you gotta tell me."

"I'm trying. I—"

"Who is he?"

I just stare at him, thrown. "What? There is no he. How could you even think that of me?"

"Then why the hell are you so chaotic right now?"

"Reggie, I didn't cheat on you. But I lied. About something. Really big." I steady myself with another deep breath, but it hardly makes me feel any more ready to come clean to him. "My dad isn't dead. My mom is, but she didn't die in a car accident. There was never any accident."

"So…"

"And I didn't always live in Newark, you know, before school.

Me and my dad only moved there after we left Asher Lane. We were in Golden Heights for five years. Until Mom died."

"Whoa, whoa, whoa. This is a lot."

"I know. I'm sorry. It'll start making sense soon, promise."

"So your dad is alive, but your mom really did die, just not in a car crash?"

"She was murdered."

"Asher Lane, that's— You really grew up in that bougie-ass cul-de-sac? I'm assuming this is all connected?" he asks, seeming frustrated, or maybe just overwhelmed.

"Getting there," I say.

"I don't get it. Who lies about shit like this, bro?" He jumps to his feet, a suspicious tinge to his words.

I can't blame him, but it feels so shitty. I don't want anything to change between us, but maybe I'm ridiculously naive to have even considered that as a possibility.

"Well, if it makes you feel any better, it's not just you I've lied to. I've lied to everyone about my past, who I really am, just...everything."

"You realize how weird this sounds, though, right?"

"Just let me finish." I stand up, have to pace to get the rest of the words out in a coherent way. "My dad was convicted of my mom's murder ten years ago. That's where I go every Sunday. To see him in prison in Jersey."

"Shit."

"But he didn't do it."

"Wait—"

"All this time I've been driving myself crazy trying to figure out who it could have been and now I finally have an idea. I mean, I *know* who did it. I just have to figure out a way to pro—"

"Hey, slow down. Run it back to your father being in prison."

I take in a breath and force myself to pace my words. "The cops did a half-assed investigation. I mean, to call it that is a joke. They had nothing, literally nothing against him. So they concocted some bullshit story about my dad killing her because why not, it's always the husband, right? They had their scapegoat and they ran with it."

"What do you mean?"

"We were the only Black family in Asher Lane, in all of Golden Heights. They wanted us gone and they got what they wanted."

"When you say *they*...who exactly do you mean?"

"Everyone. The neighbors. The police. The next-door neighbor is just the one who had the balls to actually do it."

"Are you saying—"

"I know this is a long shot, but hear me out. The physical evidence at the crime scene was moot. They didn't have a single fingerprint, hair follicle or blood speck that connected Dad to the scene. No DNA."

"Alibi?"

"Solid, but no one to corroborate it. He was alone."

Reggie nods for me to continue. "Okay."

"If he wasn't there, at the crime scene, that means someone else was." I'm aware of how rudimentary that sounds, but luckily Reggie is bearing with me instead of glancing at his laptop. "All this time I've been trying to figure out who it could have been. Some rando out for a thrill kill? A rapist who killed her because she threatened to go to the police after? Because no one wanted my mom dead."

"You sure about that?"

"Well, that's the point. I used to be."

"And now?"

"If the cops would have done even a shitty investigation instead of having tunnel vision on my dad, they would have found out about my next-door neighbor."

"Okay. Back to them."

"Apparently my best friend's dad had a long-term affair with my mom when I was little." I don't know why I'm whispering all of a sudden. It just seems too cliché to be real, too taboo to justify using my full voice.

"Your mom was smashing the dude next door?" His eyes are wide and hungry like I'm filling him in on some reality show plotline. "Can't believe you never told me any of this."

"I thought it was just a one-off. Didn't know it went on for years. Besides, I tried to block all this out," I say with a big sigh and give up on the lower half of my braid. "Anyway, her autopsy showed she was pregnant."

Reggie picks up his phone and taps it alive with his thumb. "Shit. Sorry. That's…"

It's tragic. It's unspeakable. I know the sentiment that Reggie is incapable of voicing, so I move along. "I thought it was a one-and-done thing. A slipup. But Hunter says it went on for years." I wait for a smoke signal. "You follow?"

He scrolls and frowns. "Not really."

"Reg, seriously. Stay with me." He looks up from his phone with a yawn and we lock eyes. "My mom was *three months* pregnant when she was killed. That's when she would have been down to the wire in making her decision on whether she was going to keep it, right?"

"True. Okay, now I got you. She would've started showing soon."

"And you can only wait so long before you can get an abortion."

He nods.

I nod too, then organize my thoughts. "So what if she wasn't carrying my dad's baby? What if she was pregnant with *Scott's* baby and had just told him about it and—"

"Shit, that's motive smothered in hot sauce. Scott is the next-door neighbor, right?"

"He's also a judge, formerly a prosecutor. Everyone in Golden

Heights knows him. No, reveres him. Ten percent gravitas, ninety percent ego."

Finally I have Reggie's full attention again, his eyes wide as he pieces everything together. *Cheating Husband Kills Pregnant Mistress to Avoid the Implosion of His Marriage.* It's classic. It's excruciatingly stale. It's also the answer to so many unanswered questions, the last piece of the puzzle I've tried to make sense of for years. I can't believe I never saw it. If the man Scott was as a husband and father is even a fraction of who he was in his career, murder wouldn't have been hard for him to commit. He is a man without a sliver of a conscience.

I slip Reggie's phone out of his hand and scoot close to him. "I had lunch with Hunter today, and he said his mom has this diary."

"Hunter?"

"Scott's son. He was my best friend. Really the only friend I had back then. That's why this is so weird."

"So your best friend growing up was a dude?"

Apparently, out of everything I've just divulged to him, the reveal that my best friend growing up did not have the same genitalia as me is somehow just as distressing as my father not being dead and my mother being murdered by my next-door neighbor.

"Is that all you got from that?" I ask, exasperated.

I slip beneath the covers with him and finish up my braid. Reggie's laptop is open before I even split my hair into the three sections I made earlier.

"I need to get my hands on that diary and see when the affair ended," I say, though I have no idea if he is even listening to me anymore. "If they were still seeing each other right before she died..."

"Whoa, whoa," Reggie says, and it makes me feel like a horse. He finishes typing something, then glances up at me.

"You know this is real life, right? Not a plot of one of those novels you're always reading."

I stare at him, incredulous. Obviously what I'm saying is pretty out there, but it's plausible and I've definitely read more absurd plots than this.

"You don't get it. I've been trying to appeal Dad's case for ten years," I say. "Ten years, and I finally have something that can help get us a lawyer who can get him exonerated. This is a big fucking deal."

"I'm not saying it's not. Just saying…" He pauses, choosing his next words carefully. "Just don't get your hopes up."

I cock my head. "You think I'm wrong?"

It's a dangerous question. I wait with bated breath for his response, which comes faster and harder than I anticipate.

"I think I barely know who I'm about to sleep next to," Reggie says, opening up an email to respond to.

That stings. Fuck, that stings.

But it's fair. And smart of him to avoid answering my question. I want to refute him, but I force myself to hold my tongue as he goes back to typing aggressively.

Once I've cursed him out numerous times in my head, and debate whether or not to tell him about Pia and that stupid documentary she's making, I roll onto my back, and tree-lined streets with their perfectly groomed lawns and matching mailboxes appear on the ceiling.

Asher Lane looks exactly like what it sounds like. Pretty. Safe. Like a woman who's been coddled and praised for being beautiful all her life though on the inside she is a cliché, shallow and empty.

And then I see the ambulances, that flashing red against the white. I hear the blare of the sirens, remember being forced to stay in a crappy hotel while Forensics searched the house after Mom was missing for twenty-four hours, then seeing Dad being cuffed. I remember visiting him at the holding cell, him being almost deathly quiet. The only thing he said the whole time was to please not cry, so I made sure my eyes stayed dry until I left. I remember moving to Newark and staying with my aunt who I'd never met, and who smoked crack in her bathroom with the sink running. All of our savings went toward his astronomical legal bills, and when I asked, he looked at me and told me everything would be okay. Even then, I knew it was a lie.

The feel of Reggie's lips on my neck snaps me back into the present, but as he kisses me and reaches under the shirt I stole from him, I feel Hunter's cheek against mine again and wonder if he knows. I wonder if Hunter knows who his father is and what he did. And if he does know, I wonder why Hunter asked me to have lunch with him today.

8

I HEAD ACROSS the Hudson to my aunt's house in Newark. It's an ugly house, tall and narrow and bubble-gum pink, impossible to miss. It's a two-family house, the first floor rented by a woman with four kids, the top two levels and basement belonging to my aunt. When I pull up, almost a block away, I see her light blue Camry in the driveway, a few kids playing outside on the front lawn who live next door. They disperse when they see me approaching the gate, hopping onto their bikes and speeding down the street. I stare at the house for a moment before climbing the stairs and feel no warmth toward it. It seems impossible that I lived here for over half my life, that this is where I used to call home. Really, it is just a shell, a place I came and left, and while I appreciate my aunt taking me in, it was always chaotic, and those moments are what I remember most.

I ring the doorbell and immediately hear a commotion on the stairs from inside. Loud, heavy footsteps follow and the door swings open. When my aunt's eyes settle on me, her face drops. She looks stunned. She quickly adjusts, forces a some-what amiable expression.

"Jesus, Simone. I thought you were the UPS man. I'm ex-pecting a package today." She pauses and looks me over. "What are you doing here?"

I shrug, offering her a smile, but it feels awkward as I do it. Like trying on a pair of jeans you haven't worn in years. "Just came to see you. Do you have a sec to talk?"

She's dressed in a gray sweat suit, barefoot and in her house glasses. I can see that she is in the middle of braiding her hair, most of it covered by a purple satin bonnet. She looks older than I remember, a few more lines around her eyes, the gray in her hair much more prominent, but then I realize that it's been at least five years since we've seen each other. We text from time to time, mostly around the holidays, but she has never come to visit me and I've stopped coming around as often as I used to.

The last time we spoke in person, things were not great. Somehow our conversation had veered toward my mom, as it often did, and I asked her respectfully if she could not bring her up every time we spoke because it was triggering for me. She didn't speak to me for months.

"Look, I'm happy to see you, but you've come at a bad time," she says, shaking her head, and I'm inclined to believe her ex-cept now she's avoiding my eyes. "Got a lot of running around to do today. Was just about to head to the Laundromat. My raggedy-ass dryer broke again."

"Oh." My eyes flutter and I try to recalibrate. I glance over her shoulder into the living room and everything seems just like I remember, only it's dark, the only light coming from the TV in the far corner. There's a pervasive burnt garlic smell coming from the kitchen, though I have never seen her cook a day in her life. "Well, I can try to come back a different time. I just thought—"

"No. You're here now," she says, waving a hand. She takes

a few backward steps and holds the door open for me. "Come on in. Sit down."

I step inside, not knowing what to do with my hands. She has never been a hugger. "Thanks. I can't stay long, anyway," I say, which isn't true, but more to put her at ease. "How's everything? You good?"

She locks the door, then secures the chain latch. "I should be asking you that. You never come round this way anymore. Something must be wrong. Do you need something? Money?"

"No, I'm okay." I sit down on the couch, brush away some of the cat hair covering the faded red cushion. "I just wanted to... I've been thinking about my dad's case a lot. He's up for his final appeal and you're the only person who I feel like might know something that could help me."

She frowns, confused. "Did you say his last appeal?"

"Yeah. The last petition was denied."

Her head shakes and for a second I think she may show some tenderness toward him for the first time, but then her frown returns. "You're wasting your time. I don't mean to be rude, but you are," she says, swatting a huge fly away from her face with her free hand. She takes a seat on the couch and her elderly gray cat leaps right up into her lap. I didn't even see him come into the room.

"Well, can we just talk?"

She sighs. "You know I don't like to talk about him in this house. I get it, he's your daddy, but—"

"I know. I know you're convinced he did it, but what if I told you I knew who did it and it wasn't my dad?"

She examines me for the longest moment. "If he didn't do it, who did?"

I take a breath, feeling the weight of my question and all of its implications before I even ask it. "Did you know that my mom was sleeping with Scott Bishop?"

She makes a face, like the idea is absurd, and I realize how little she truly knew about her sister. "Where did you hear that?"

"I saw them. When I was a kid. I never told anyone because I was… I didn't want my dad to find out. I'd always figured it was a onetime thing, but it went on for years, apparently."

She is still frowning, a hard, deep line etched in the center of her forehead. "Found out from who?"

"Hunter Bishop. The boy who lived next door?" She nods, remembering me talking about him, I suppose. "He knew about their affair too. We were together when we saw them."

This time her nod is hesitant, like she's taking time to properly digest the information. Then she shrugs. "Well, she never came right out and told me about it, but it doesn't surprise me."

I scoot closer to her. "Really? Why…why not? Did you see anything?"

"Chris was a stand-up kinda guy. Safe. Evelyn knew she had a sturdy, secure future with him, you know? She was never all that attracted to him," she says, shaking her head as if recalling some secret memory. "She married him because she thought it was the right thing to do. She wanted to have a family. She wanted you."

"But you never saw anything? You can't remember anything she said about Scott specifically?"

"Evelyn complained to me all the time. I should've picked up on it back then. It all makes sense now," she mumbles, more to herself than to me, and I can tell she's still thinking it over.

"What does?" I press gently.

Her eyes lock on to mine with an exasperated determination. "*That's* why Chris killed her. He found out about Scott and snapped. That fucking son of a bitch. All these years, I couldn't figure out why."

"But Dad never knew about Mom's affair. And the police report said it wasn't a crime of passion. They said it looked premeditated. That's why he got life."

"You know you can't believe anything any of them say. They lie. You know that."

"Okay, but what about the crime scene? The photos? Those don't lie. Everything was meticulously cleaned. Forensics said it had to have been planned down to the last detail."

"I should've fucking known," she says, her leg bouncing, and it's clear she is no longer listening to me.

"My dad didn't kill her, I'm telling you. It had to be—"

"Please, Simone. We've been through this." She nudges her gray cat away and heads toward the kitchen. The cat circles her clumsily with his atrophied hind leg. "I have a lot of shit to get done today."

I stand up and head for the door, push outside without looking back. In the car, I replay our conversation and think of all the moments where I went wrong, go through all the things I should have said, ways I could have handled that better, until my head is throbbing. As I notice that my fuel tank is on E, it hits me that the only real play I have is that diary. I need to get my hands on it. I just don't know how.

I think of Hunter and the way he looked at me and figure maybe there is a way.

9

I HAVE NEVER trusted anyone the way I trusted Hunter.

The worst part about all of this is that now I have to question everything. Even Hunter's intentions. Especially running into him the way I did at Reggie's office building.

I lean back in my chair and glance around the office, making sure no one has a special interest in me before I abandon my work. Jasmine catches my eyes for a beat. She's wearing her usual blazer-and-jeans combo, saying everything to Matt with a manufactured smile, but I highly doubt he takes it for anything but genuine. It's obvious she's putting in her bid to take over Katrina's accounts. That should be me, because clearly promotions here aren't strictly merit based; managers love a good ass-kissing smothered in baseless flattery.

I do a quick Google search to verify that the Sachs & Marston headquarters is actually in the same building as Goldstein & Wagner. It's a little disappointing when I realize our run-in was truly a coincidence and the two firms are actually housed in the same dark glass building. It means I have to ditch my theory that Hunter orchestrated our reunion after weeks of stalking me. It didn't really have legs anyway since I was the one who followed Hunter back into the lobby. If I hadn't done that, he would have gotten in that elevator like he does every day, and we never would have spoken a word. And there's no way Hunter could have known I was meeting Reggie for lunch that day.

I stayed up for hours constructing theories that only got wilder and more implausible as my delirium set in. No more assumptions. I need facts. I can't assume Hunter knows what his father did. Besides, he's the one who brought up the affair. He wouldn't have done that if he's aware of his father's secret. The dots are too easy to connect from there.

But then that makes me wonder how he could not have connected them himself. Is love that blind? Could the possibility of Scott being a murderer not once cross Hunter's mind simply because of how much he adores his father? If my father—

But my father would never. *Could never.*

I have forty-two emails to read through before my lunch break if I'm going to come close to finishing my task list before the end of the day, but instead of jumping straight into tackling them in order of priority, I grab my phone and call Reggie. The line rings five times, then goes to voice mail. I start to text him, but pause once I see all the unanswered texts I sent him this morning. I read them over, then clear out the text box and decide to call Pia instead. She answers almost immediately.

"I'm assuming this is either a butt dial or you calling to apologize," she says, her voice monotone.

I can't really gauge her mood, because I barely know her. She sounds a tad breathy, like maybe she has just jogged to catch up to an available taxi. Also, annoyed, and because she usually sounds much more upbeat and eager, I'm going to assume her annoyance is solely with me.

"Hi, Pia. It's Simone."

"Cool, and it's not 1973. Caller ID is a thing. Actually, pretty sure it's standard."

"Oh." I pause, blindsided by her sarcasm. "Didn't know if you saved my number or—"

"Is there a point to this call, or did you just want to talk shit again?"

"Look, I'm sorry if I seemed…" I take a breath, reorganize my thoughts. "I was just upset. Wasn't having the best day last time we spoke. Well, actually, we didn't speak because you hung up on me."

"What do you want? Me to tell you I accept your apology? Highly doubt that's what this is about."

I briefly wonder how she's perceived this, but shake my head and resign to contemplate it later. "I was actually wondering if we could grab coffee. Or something. I'll come to you."

"You'll come to me?"

"Yeah. Is there a spot you prefer? I don't really drink caffeine."

"Sounds tragic."

"Any morning works for me. Whatever's best for you."

She takes a beat like she's trying to process my offer. "What's with the change of heart?"

"Don't get too excited. I want to talk. Off camera."

"Then we can do that right now, can't we?"

I glance around the suite again. No one is within earshot if I half whisper, but it's not worth the risk. I step away from my desk and do a quick scan of the stalls before locking myself in the ladies' room.

"I've been trying to get my dad's conviction overturned for ten years," I say, when I'm confident the coast is clear. "We've been working with lawyers to prove the Golden Heights Police Department did a shitty investigation. They convicted him without a *single* piece of physical evidence. They locked him up and threw away the key because of two witness testimonies and because his alibi wasn't strong enough. But really they were just cleaning house. They didn't like that we were there and they took this opportunity to make sure me and my family never stepped foot in Asher Lane again."

"Am I having a really bad case of déjà vu or did we already have this conversation?"

"Do you want to just finish making your fallacious Oscar-bait film so you can launch your career? Or do you have even an ounce of integrity?"

"Now you're back to insulting me."

"No, I'm trying to get you to *hear* me."

She takes a second. "My only goal is to expose the truth. You can take that or leave it."

"If that's true, then you need to redo the thesis of your film. It should be about an innocent Black man held prisoner for ten years."

"And why would I do that? Because the murderer's daughter asked me to?"

I roll my eyes, my chest tightening. "Because my father didn't kill my mother. And I can prove it."

We meet at a Starbucks halfway between both of us. When I walk in, I scan the room for Pia, but no one seems to match the photos I've seen of her. There's a woman standing by the door, texting someone, but when I make eye contact with her, she makes a face, like she's worried I may be a stalker, then pushes out the door.

I secure the only free table left while I wait, and just as I'm pulling out a chair, a woman stops in front of me. I look up, and before I can ask, she sets her phone and large coffee down on the table, then takes a seat across from me. For the most part, she looks the same in person as she does online. She is taller than I expected, though, practically six feet, yet her air-dried, virgin brown hair hangs down past her hip bones. I can tell it's never been highlighted or overly damaged by heat. It looks healthy and clean, smells like peachy conditioner. She wears not a stitch of makeup—at least, not to the naked eye—a pat of concealer under her eyes at best and a dab of salve on her uneven lips, the bottom one much more full. She seems like the type who would prefer mint to rose as I do, and I suppose that goes with the whole dark academia-core she's got going on with her tweed pants, oxfords, and retro round glasses that I suspect are more for the aesthetic than medical necessity.

There is no greeting. Pia just jumps straight into it, says she needs to leave in twenty minutes and asks me to give her what I have. It takes me a beat to find my voice, and I try to play off my delayed response as a brooding consideration rather than nerves. She isn't the type to interrupt; she allows me to get all of my thoughts out in one fell swoop. When I finish, she takes me in for a moment, then sips her overly sweetened iced cappuccino.

"So everybody's wrong except you, right? The public, the judge, the jury, the police." Her brows rise and there is some amusement about her face, a sort of aloof smugness. It's clear that she's unimpressed. Also, that she thinks I'm an idiot unworthy of her time, but at least the feeling is mutual there.

I firm my voice. "The police didn't do their jobs."

"Golden Heights PD is one of the top divisions in the entire country," she says, as if she's very proud of herself for having just researched this fact, and I want to laugh in her face. Her ignorance is comical.

"Because until my mom's murder, the worst crime they had to deal with was white kids selling prescription pills to bored housewives."

"Pretty compelling," Pia says, taking an extra-long sip with her straw. "But you just bought me an eight-dollar coffee for nothing."

I watch her as she sets down the Venti cup. "What?"

"I appreciate it, but what did you expect me to do with a theory?"

"It's not a theory. It's the truth. Look—" I pause, then quickly switch gears. "Scott Bishop killed my mother."

A message pings onto Pia's phone. She glances down to check it, then quickly deletes it without reading it first. When her eyes meet mine again, there's a softness in them, a slither of pity, and I don't know whether to be offended or grateful. "My original offer still stands. You're welcome to present your side of things on camera and I will include it in my film. That invite extends to your father as well. But an unsubstantiated affair is as futile as hearsay." She starts to reach for her bag as she shifts back from the table, her chair screeching softly against the floor.

"I saw them with my own eyes."

She stops. "With all due respect, the two witnesses who took the stand during your father's trial claimed they saw him tossing her body into the trunk of his Mercedes."

"That's bullshit."

"It's just as feeble as your claim," she says, her eyes directly on mine, bright and still. "That's my point."

I take a breath, shaking my head as she grabs her phone. "I don't get you."

"How could you? You haven't asked me a single question about myself, my ambitions, my—"

"This isn't about you," I snap, and it isn't until I see her expression stiffen that I realize I've raised my voice.

Pia glances down at the table, tightens her grip on her cup, but doesn't lift it to her mouth. "Okay, you're getting upset."

"This is about my *father*." She opens her mouth to say something else, but I can't let her. "You don't understand. This is my *real* life. My dad's freedom. He's a victim of the system, not some subject for a documentary. I've been busting my ass to get him justice and now you come in and want to make money off his suffering? If that tainted juice is worth the squeeze for you, then I truly feel sorry for you."

I expect some kind of visible reaction from her, some hint

that maybe I've gotten under her skin a little, but her expression doesn't change. "What makes you think I want, or give a shit about, your pity?"

I let out a breath through my nose. I'm so done with this, so done. "What would it take for you to call this off?"

I hate that I sound so desperate, but that's what I am.

She frowns. "You mean scrap the film?"

"Yes," I say through clenched teeth.

"Hmm." She tilts her head, as if truly considering it. "Let me see if I can put this into perspective for you. I've been researching this project for the last three years. I had to jump through fire-rimmed hoops to ink a distribution deal with Netflix. I've already gotten over sixty hours of footage all supporting the state's decision and I have a handful of antsy investors who are anxious to see where their contributions have gone. Oh, and I'm on an impossible deadline."

"So pretty much nothing is what you're saying?" I ask, my voice flat.

She takes a long, self-indulgent slurp of her liquid crack. "If you got proof—real, in-your-face proof that Scott Bishop may have been the one responsible for your mother's murder—we can have another conversation. But my editor is expecting all my footage a week from tomorrow, so you might want to get to work."

I watch her grab her bag and sling it over a shoulder so that it lies across her body. "Is it that you don't believe me or you don't want to be proven wrong?"

"I'm a journalist." She smirks, as if harboring some greater knowledge unbeknownst to me. "Not a theist."

"Meaning?"

"Revising is part of the job. Like I said, my main concern is getting the truth out there. For some reason, you seem to be convinced that I'm some kind of amoral barbarian who wants to deliberately spread lies, despite being aware of an objective truth. If there's another story to be told, so be it. But a story will be told regardless."

She stands and I struggle to find my next words.

It's like I blink and she's gone. Poof. It doesn't feel real. Our conversation. The pressure she's just mounted on my shoulders.

There will never be justice for my dad. They took his freedom, his life, the majority of his sanity, right on the heels of his wife being murdered. No amount of restitution will replace the lost years, the damage the stress has put on his body, his heart. It makes it hard to keep fighting sometimes, this reality. But I think about the ripple effect getting Dad exonerated could create and that keeps me pushing.

When I get back to my desk, Jasmine is nowhere in sight. Everyone else for the most part is still enjoying the last leg of their lunch breaks, so I immediately call Hunter.

He answers on the third ring. "Simone?"

I can't tell if he is busy or confused, distracted or just thrown off, but the inflection at the end of my name betrays how surprised he is to have my voice in his ear. Or maybe he has a strong aversion to unsolicited phone calls like I do, and his anxiety is surging a surplus of adrenaline through his veins.

"Busy?" I ask, skipping over my greeting.

"You know us attorneys," he says. "Slackers."

"Sorry. I should've texted first. What am I, a boomer?"

He laughs. "I could actually use a quick mental break, so good timing."

There's a small pause, and I imagine he's shutting the door to his office or something because I hear a slight swooshing like he's in motion, the sound of metal clicking into place.

Hunter may be as far in the dark as I have been about what his father did, but that doesn't mean he's useless. There is no doubt, Hunter would very much like to fuck me. It wasn't just that on-the-cheek kiss; it was something more subtle than that but obvious at the same time. The way his eyes lingered on mine so many different times, like he had more to say but kept stopping himself. The way he watched me eat on that bench. The way his body was so tight next to mine, the way I could almost feel his restraint.

I have never been a calculating person, never been the type to pursue someone with the sole intention of manipulating them to get what I want with complete disregard to their feelings. But you only bury your mother's mutilated body once. Hunter is my only way back into Asher Lane, my only way of getting my hands on his mother's diary. I know what he wants, and if it makes me a bad person to use that knowledge to avenge my mother's death, then so be it.

"So, how are you?" Hunter asks, and it's like he actually cares to hear the truth, and it makes me consider the question instead of firing off a *good* or *okay* like I normally do whenever anyone asks me this question.

"Honestly, I never know how to answer that," I admit, giving up after a few seconds, my heart pounding, for some strange reason. "Do I just say *fine* so I don't burden you with my problems or do I be honest and tell you how I really feel?"

"Guess it depends who's asking," he says.

"So who is asking? I mean, I don't even know what we are."

"I think we're old friends. Only we're not *old* yet. But a lot has changed since Asher Lane, so…maybe we can get to know each other and become new friends?"

I like the sound of that. I'm smiling before I realize it. "I'm down if you're still the sweet guy I used to look up to."

"Trying to make me blush?"

"I meant literally."

He laughs again, and I remember this is one of the reasons I loved Hunter, how easy it is for me to make him laugh.

"Actually, you haven't changed at all," he says, correcting himself, and I can almost hear his leftover smile.

"Seriously, please tell me you're still that guy who would

write your neighbor letters because she had this obsession with getting mail but had no one to send her any."

"Ah, I completely forgot about that." He goes silent for a moment, but it's not weird because I think he's recalling the memories. "Jeez, we were so weird back then."

"Wish I could read them now," I say, trying to remember the things he would write to me.

"You know, I still have the ones you wrote me back."

My heart beats a little faster. "You're lying."

"They're at my mom's house. What, you threw mine away?"

"No, they, um…" And just like that, the momentum of our conversation stalls. I thought I was steering this perfectly. Then he has to go and get sentimental on me and ruin shit. I clear my throat. "They…they got lost when we moved."

"Oh."

I don't have to explain it any further. Hunter gets it. He may not have experienced the aftermath of the investigation and subsequent trial with me, but he understands how transformative that move was for me and my dad. We didn't just pack up a house and change zip codes. We became different people, skeletons of who we once were, stripped down to the marrow.

"Hunter," I say, hoping my voice sounds lighter. "What if we drive out together?"

I start to add *just me and you*, but that seems too on the nose. Obviously if we hit I-78 together we will be alone, and I really hope that sounds enticing enough for him to agree with what has to seem a little silly. They *are* just letters.

He pauses. "To Jersey?"

"Yeah, and read them together. This weekend. Why not?"

His hesitation is prolonged this time, and I feel like I just got kneed in the gut.

"I did it again," I say, wondering if I'd read the energy in Hunter's tense body next to mine on the park bench all wrong. "I'm imposing. You probably have a million—"

"No, I'm just..." He lets out a breath. "Not cool with Kate anymore."

"First-name basis. Wow."

"But she has been nagging me about stopping by, so..." I can almost hear him thinking it over. "I'll text you?"

"No pressure."

"Cool."

There's a long pause, and I assume we're each about to say why we have to go even though we really don't and hang up, so before it gets awkward, I say, "Wait."

"Yeah?"

"How are *you*, Hunter?"

He chuckles a little. "Not gonna lie. Had a shitty morning. This was a nice shift."

I smile and start to say something, but then I change my mind and end the call.

The rest of the day moves past me. Surprisingly, I complete my task list ahead of time and no one curses me out on the phone today. After I clock out, I walk to the metro station with Jasmine, who spends the whole time telling me about this dude who brought her back to his apartment last night to fuck and had four actual roommates and only one towel in the bathroom.

When I get off the R, a text arrives on my phone and of course it is Hunter. Do you want to drive or should I pick you up on Saturday?

My dirty secret: I hate driving.

You're from Jersey.

I know but it gives me anxiety. Don't judge me. I wait a second, then add, You can be my chauffeur.

Cool. What's your address?

10

I WOULD BE lying if I said I don't consider Reggie's in-unit washer-dryer combo as one of the cardinal benefits of being with him. I'm on my second load, my whites, so beyond ready for the simple splendor that is fresh, clean towels, but he is hung up on my pilgrimage back to Jersey with Hunter tomorrow. As irritating as this display of the frailty of his ego is, I know where it's coming from, so I don't let it bait me.

"Why are you making this about Hunter?" I ask, raking the dust from the dryer's lint trap with the tips of my nails while he sweeps the tile behind me. "This is about my mom."

"No, this is about *us*. I don't want you spending the night with some other dude. Especially not one I've never even met."

I glare at him over my shoulder. "You don't want me to, or you're telling me I can't?"

He straightens out and releases his grip on his broomstick. I've struck a nerve, the exact one I was aiming for. It's strange, this part of our relationship we're entering, the one where I can accurately predict how he's going to react to something I say. I've never been with any other guy for this long, so this is new and I'm not sure if I like it.

Before I reminded Reggie that I won't be in the city tomorrow night, I'd been enjoying myself as I watched him clean up the mess we just made in his kitchen with our takeout. He's been doing a ton of extra work for one of the senior lawyers at his firm all week and it must have slipped his mind because I'm sure I told him. He's been so swamped that he hasn't been over to my place in four days. And though he won't admit it, my confession not only stunned and bewildered him, but it has also rocked him somewhere deep. I've caught his gaze lingering on me multiple times in the last few days, in that way where I can tell he's fighting not to ask what's plaguing my mind. Even though I've revealed my secrets, I am now even more of an enigma to him. He thought he knew me, but my revelation only proved to him that there are more mysteries inside me, and I don't know if he trusts me the same. But my ovaries are finally done wreaking havoc on my skin and lower abdomen and just watching him partake in basic acts of domesticity has had me incessantly dipping my gaze below the drawstring of his gray sweatpants, searching for his imprint like I'm some kind of maniac.

I don't want to argue. I want to get rid of the friction between us with at least one of my orifices filled and then talk in bed about our greatest fears and other lofty shit until one of us falls asleep.

"How would you feel if I had a sleepover with one of my female friends?" Reggie asks, shifting to look at me directly.

If I answer right away, it will be a lie, so I turn back around and pretend to have a hard time sliding the lint trap back into the machine while I figure out what to say.

Reggie has never given me any reason not to trust him, but if the table was flipped and he told me about spending the night with his female childhood best friend, I would try to stop him too.

"Why can't I come?" Reggie asks, and I realize he's right behind me now. "You don't want me to meet your dad or something?"

I flip around so I can look up into his eyes. "No, babe. This has nothing to do with you," I say, and it feels so good to not have to contort the truth. "And Hunter will have me back for lunch on Sunday."

"His corny ass better."

He moves back to his broom to finish sweeping up our mess. I hop on his heels, suddenly envious and wishing he would grab me with such determination.

"So this is you being jealous?" I hoist myself onto an edge of the peninsula. "Because it's kinda hot."

He looks at me. "I don't mean to sound controlling and shit. I just know what a dude is thinking when his female *friend* asks to sleep over."

"I do too." I give him a smile and soften my face. "But you trust me, don't you?"

I don't wait for his answer, because I can't bear to see even a veil of doubt sheen his features. I fist his T-shirt and pull him down to my level. I kiss his neck and slip my hand down the front of his pants.

I'm such a fucking hypocrite. There I was, complaining to Jasmine about how transactional Reggie can make sex feel sometimes, how manipulative his prowess can feel, and here I am, sucking on his neck and cradling his balls so he will relinquish his valid hang-ups about me spending a weekend with another guy.

"You about to get yourself in trouble," Reggie warns with a groan so close to my ear, I shudder as the vibrations pass through my eardrum.

"What kind of trouble?" I ask, shuffling around in his pants.

"*Deep* trouble," he says, and I know he means it. I can feel him lengthening in my grip, filling out, so hard and ready.

"Is that a threat—" I bite into his soft, salty-sweet flesh "—or a promise?"

It's whatever I want it to be because Reggie lets the question remain rhetorical. He tosses the broom and pulls away my clothes one piece at a time as he backs me into his bedroom, the kind with two windows *and* a door, which he leaves open since we are alone, and I don't know why I'm wondering if Hunter has ever been with a Black girl when Reggie replaces his fingers with his dick, but I groan and call him *Daddy*. And even though the reverberation sounds like I'm overcompensating for something, it puts a smug smile on Reggie's face and he starts thrusting inside me faster, finally answering my question.

It was a promise.

All icing, no cake.

11

I HAD NEVER been a *nigger* until I stepped into Asher Lane, my mom holding my right hand, my dad holding the left. The small town we lived in before Golden Heights was even in the realm of possibility was four square miles with seventy thousand people crammed into it, but the Black and Latino community sheltered me from the ugliness that is explicit racism. But if returning to that haunting part of my past is what it takes to get the answers I need, to prove to Aunt Patrice that her brother-in-law is not a murderer, to finally retain an attorney who will be able to get Dad fully exonerated, to convince Pia to alter the thesis of her film, then it's a plunge I'm willing to take.

I step out onto the concrete outside my building and scan the block until I spot a low-sitting Audi pull up and idle at the corner. It's standard New York black, but in no way does it blend in with the ubiquitous Denalis and Range Rovers. I walk over to my rakish chariot without fuss because I have prepared for this. I washed my hair this morning so it smells like I am in a live shampoo commercial, then dabbed my most expensive perfume on my wrists and neck. My roots are still damp and I don't know if men can tell the difference between an expertly layered eau de parfum and an ephemeral body spray, but it's mostly for confidence anyway. My panties are full coverage and 100 percent cotton, but the smile I wear when I pull open the passenger door says they're of the high-cut, sheer lace, unmentionable sort.

"Hey." Hunter looks up at me, slightly startled. "That was fast."

He's wearing light-washed jeans with rips and slashes and a Henley that looks sculpted to his torso. The slim-fit suits I've seen him in didn't do the athleticism of his body justice, which is so much more in-your-face than the slim teenage jock physique I remember. He must still lift weights regularly, and as I look at him, I feel bad about the hash browns I gorged on as I diffused my hair.

"I told you I was coming down," I say.

"Women are never coming down when they say they're coming down. I would've gotten that for you."

It takes me a beat to realize he's talking about getting my door for me and I'm not sure how I feel. On one hand, it feels unnecessary and retrograde. On the other hand, it feels sweet and thoughtful.

"You can make it up to me by letting me use the AUX cord," I suggest.

"It's all yours."

I pretend to be wholly unaware of how dangerously close I am to flashing him when I split my thighs and tuck myself into his car. I also pretend not to notice how he shifts in his leather seat, despite the confines of his seat belt. I know that shift. That stir.

He takes my mini duffel that I have two outfit changes in and places it in the back seat, then gestures to my XXL sweatshirt that fits me like a dress, the hem barely reaching the middle of my thighs. "I thought you went to Princeton."

I was so busy trying to look hot-but-didn't-try sexy that I forgot to prepare something to explain where I would have gotten Reggie's Yale sweatshirt.

"Oh. No. Borrowed this from a friend."

I don't specify the nonexistent friend. Everybody wants somebody who other people want. If he assumes I have a male friend who recently let me borrow his clothes, it can only add to his attraction to me.

"Think you forgot your pants," Hunter says, gesturing to my bare thighs with his gaze.

"Pants are overrated."

He doesn't agree, but it's obvious he does by his smirk of approval.

"Don't worry," I tell him. "I'll change before dinner. Just want to be comfortable. Long ride."

"Cool." He motions to my seat belt. "Strap up."

I buckle up and check out the interior details of his car. It is dark and immaculate at first glance, so much more comfortable than my usual mode of transportation: the subway.

"Nice whip," I say, trying to sound aloof and cool, but then I'm pretty sure *whip* was not the right word.

"Can't take the Jersey out of me," he says, shifting his gear into Drive with a casualness I both envy and resent because I couldn't drive a stick shift even with a gun to my neck and I'll never own a foreign as glossy as this.

Once we're in the thick of traffic, Hunter smiles at me in a way that makes me think he knows my secret, that I have asked him to take me to his mother's house under false pretense, that I didn't ask him to drive twenty-eight miles to read old letters I wrote to him ages ago. He doesn't call me out. He asks if I'd like him to put the air on and roll up the windows, and I tell him I'm fine with the air blowing on my face as I google how to know if you're suffering from paranoia with my phone tilted away from his face in case he happens to glance over.

I haven't been alone with a guy who isn't my dad or Reggie in years and this is so intimate, being trapped in this confined space in such close proximity for the span of a good meal, a date. Except there are no distractions, nowhere to hide. We are technically still in public and therefore not *alone* alone, but there are still so many mistakes that could happen inside this mass of steel and fiberglass, so many things that could be said that could never be taken back.

I like the way Hunter drives. He steers mostly one-handed, his right hand always resting on his gear. He modulates between cruising fifteen to twenty miles over the speed limit, that sweet spot between modest and reckless, and keeps his eyes on the road even when he's asking me a question or responding to one of mine, which is reassuring and also gives me time to scrutinize him. The shave he clearly skipped this morning. How clean his neatly trimmed nails are. And he either doesn't have any degree of road rage or he is on his best behavior for me, because even when this Tesla cuts him off without signaling, he barely mumbles a curse under his breath.

"How did you know about Princeton?" I ask as he makes a right lane change.

Hunter flashes a guilty smile. "I googled you."

"Oh," I say, not expecting that or knowing how to reconcile this news quickly enough, so I deflect. "My nudes didn't come up, did they?"

At first he looks horrified, his eyes moving from the road for the first time, and I consider that I've read him wrong. Maybe he isn't into me in that way. Maybe he still sees me as his little sister and can't fathom me as a fully-fledged sexual being. Then he smirks and lets me know that he still gets my humor.

"So you single-handedly helped a debut author hit the *New York Times* bestseller list with *one* review. That's power."

I lift a brow. "Impressive recon."

"You don't have to be humble with me, you know." He adjusts his gear, making the manual thing look so simple and effortless, the way ballet dancers make leaping five feet in the air look graceful and elegant. "I knew you before you grew into your legs and got braces."

I mock gasp. "Is that shade? You're trying to say my teeth were jacked up?"

He was, and instead of owning up to it, he buries that truth in a laugh, and I join in because he knew me before the hips and the Accutane and the breasts too and I find it funny that he chose not to mention these things.

"Actually," he says, once our laughter dies down, "I was shocked when I didn't find a bunch of articles raving about this hot new bestselling author, one of Asher Lane's finest."

I stare through the windshield like we've just found out that the bridge we're crossing is out a mile ahead. Inert, unblinking, heart pounding like a hare who has just realized she's been spotted by a lioness. I haven't thought about writing in so long. Hunter is the only one I've ever shared that dream with. I thought he forgot about it the same way I did. And no one knows I'm from Asher Lane, so that tidbit would never make it in any hypothetical article.

"Is that still on the vision board?" I feel him flick a brief glance my way as he slows for the pileup ahead, but I don't meet his eyes. "Do you ever still think about publishing your own stuff?"

I lift one shoulder in a languid shrug. "I think about it in the same way I think about sipping Armand de Brignac on a yacht on the French Riviera. It's a fantasy."

Hunter has slowed at a red light and takes advantage of the holdup to study my face. I don't think I've ever seen so much disappointment veiling his features, but there's no denying what this is. His lips part, and I brace myself, but he doesn't say that thing I can tell is right on the tip of his tongue.

"What?" I ask, feeling something twitch inside me.

Hunter has a few kinds of hesitations, but they're all distinct. Sometimes he does it when he has too much new intel in his brain. It can take him a few beats to process and sift through it all. But I know which one this is without a doubt. I can still read him. This is the one when he pauses because he's afraid of hurting someone's feelings.

"Nothing." He offers a faint smile and glances through his windshield hopefully, but the light is still red.

"Come on." I don't know what is possessing me to do this. "Why'd you look at me like that?"

"Like what?"

"Hunter." I wait until he shoots me a quick glance. "I'm not a little girl anymore. I can handle it."

He acknowledges the last part with a slow nod as if he is coming to terms with it as we speak, then glances at the road again to see that he's in the clear. If he's disappointed in me, I want to hear him say it. Maybe it's slightly masochistic of me, but I'd rather it all be out on the table. It's not like his disappointment in me could compare to my own disappointment in myself anyway.

Hunter's foot eases up off the brake pedal when he says, "I was just wondering... Why put so much energy into helping all those other people's dreams come true and not your own?"

I wanted his honesty, pressed him for it, but I am still not prepared for his kind but blunt delivery. Fury hits me first, the unadulterated privilege one must possess to ask such a question so stark and ostentatious. I force myself to glare out my window because I know Hunter hasn't even considered the implications of what he's just asked me, much less the way he asked me. I also remind myself that he doesn't know how bad things spiraled for my dad and me after Asher Lane. He doesn't know of the roaches, the bedbugs, the food stamps, the evictions. The vortex of being poor in the third wealthiest state in the wealthiest country in the world. Still, even without that awareness, there is no way Hunter could compare him following his childhood ambition of becoming a lawyer to me not becoming a published author. Not when his father is one of the most venerable judges in the country and sent him to his Ivy League alma mater.

Just as the surge of anger dissipates, Hunter's voice pierces through the silence. "Sorry. I don't mean to be..." He pauses, and I wonder if he even knows what he's apologizing for or if he's just reacting to my reaction. "It's just the way you used to love books..."

Now he sounds sad and it angers me all over again.

"I still love books." It comes out with more of a bite than I mean for it to. "That's why I write about them."

"Yeah, but—"

"Writing my own stuff was just a pipe dream." I pause to stop my defensiveness from raising my voice. "Maybe I took myself seriously back then too, but once I started writing reviews, I realized I'm more of a reader than a writer. Besides, freelancing is helping me pay off my loans, my bills. It almost covers my rent now and I'm also up for a promotion at my day job, so..."

There's a beat, and then he nods. "I understand that."

"Do you?" I try not to laugh, but I can taste the derision that glazes my own words. "Because I don't think any decision you've ever had to make was predicated on the possibility of financial instability."

Hunter is the kind of boy—man, he's a *man* now—who's only ever had a pool of good and better choices to choose from. I bet his post-law-school lifestyle is still inordinately subsidized by his parents' astounding generational wealth.

"I'm not saying I can relate," he says, annoyingly unoffended. "I'm saying I understand."

The stubborn side of me screams that the difference between the two is so subtle, so nebulous, it's essentially absurd. But after I let his words simmer, I nod, if for nothing else but to maintain the peace. I start to angle my body toward the window and fold my arms in quiet defense. Then I catch Hunter easing up on the gas to let a Land Rover in and it's clear that if Hunter was a cat, he would be the kind to have bird friends. Not any bird. The bird that reminded him of the most vulnerable part of himself, the one who needed his care the most.

Fate and divine intervention is nothing more than poetic justice, wishful thinking at best, but if there is anything that gets me to doubt my firm stance that everything that transpires within this universe is a result of cause and effect, it's that Hunter and I were brought together for a reason beyond my conception. Cat and bird.

It's hard not to feel like our meet-cute wasn't orchestrated by gods or angels or some kind of metaphysical force when I think of who we would be now if we hadn't crossed paths. If it weren't for Hunter, I don't think I would have survived Asher Lane. The time I found my suicide note stuck to the inside of my locker attached to a four-foot-long piece of rope was almost my breaking point. The letter was penned by an anonymous classmate and stupidly signed by six others as if they were doing me a favor, putting in the labor of writing my last words for me so I wouldn't have to bother with the task. I could just get on with hanging myself. I recognized all the names on the bottom of the paper. Each signatory lived on Asher Lane. My dad cried when he read it. My mother showed up at the principal's home at eight in the evening. But Hunter was the one who held me and listened to me once my own tears finally ran out.

"Did I make it weird?" he asks, switching lanes.

"You're fine," I say, still looking out the window.

"I just remember you promising me that one day you were going to make me read the first book you published. Out loud. To you." He steals a quick glance at me, then returns his eyes to the road. "Payback, remember? For when I..."

He doesn't finish. He doesn't need to.

We both remember that promise the way the sun remembers to give the moon a turn to shine every night.

12

HUNTER WAS FIFTEEN when he controversially quit both the football and lacrosse teams on the same day. He made me swear to him that I wouldn't laugh at him as we rode our bikes to the library to sign him up for his first library card. I didn't tell my mom where I was going because I had to keep his secret, and she was starting to get weird about me spending time alone with him. He was almost as tall as his father and his voice was suddenly filled with bass, but she's a mom and didn't understand how pure what we had was back then. I didn't think of Hunter as a high school sophomore with a penis and he definitely didn't consider that I had an actual vagina.

Whenever I remember that promise I made Hunter, I think of the day I made him cry. I'll never forget that moment I had to watch my rock crumble right in front of me, can never shake how helpless and foolish and sorry I felt to watch the boy who rescued me so many times sniffle and heave and shake.

I was high on adrenaline after writing my first novel, and

since Hunter had been promising me for months that he would be the first to read it, I practically ran next door to let him flip through my loose-leaf-filled binder. I held the handwritten manuscript so close, I wouldn't even let my mom or dad read it because the honor belonged to Hunter. But he got busy with lacrosse, and then it was football season. And then he started inviting this big-tit blonde who he had the nerve to call his *girlfriend* over to his house every night after only seeing her for a week. That's when I freaked. I didn't mean to cry, but the tears just exploded from my eyes after I got done telling him how much him blowing me off hurt me. Then he was silent, just silent, and I covered my face and cried even harder, the mortification only exacerbating my tears. The pain morphed into anger and I ripped up my book, tore every page from my binder and eviscerated each one in front of him. By the time I was done with the last shred, he was screaming for me to calm down, but I wouldn't. I couldn't. I told him I was done being his friend and did everything I could to avoid him. It lasted a solid three weeks, the longest I'd ever gone without seeing him since moving next door to his house. He cornered me when I least expected it, showed up at my campus during lunch period looking so sad, so defeated, like someone who'd just come from putting his pet down. He said he missed me, told me it was making him sick to see me so mad at him, but I refused to speak to him. Until I saw the tears falling from his eyes. I heard them at first, in the way his voice trembled and skipped through a few words, but I couldn't believe it until they trailed down his face to his neck. He wouldn't wipe them. Just let them rain over his features. I'd never seen that side of him and his unbridled nakedness frightened me. He wasn't blubbering or hysterical the way I'd been when I cried in front of him. He was shockingly composed and only spoke in guttural whispers as he confessed his darkest secret.

Hunter told me that all he could see on the pages of my

manuscript was a jumble of letters and numbers floating on the pages, and trying to make out the words stressed him out to the point of actual nosebleeds. Books gave him anxiety and that was why he kept putting off reading mine. I quickly understood what he was telling me—he was dyslexic—but I didn't get how he'd made it into a thirty-grand-a-year prep school without help, until he reminded me of the arsenal of sports trophies in his father's den. Hunter finally wiped his cheeks with his sleeve as he told me the truth about where he got the slit in his left brow. It was the first time I understood why he had become so protective of me after I told him I was being slammed into lockers and dumped into trash cans.

It had been so long since Hunter had genuinely given reading some effort, and he'd never read for leisure, and couldn't conceive that reading for pleasure was even possible, so getting him back into it was rocky at first. Once he got comfortable, once he realized he could trust that I would never laugh, judge or rush him, he stopped apologizing when he made mistakes and the apprehension lacing his words faded away. As I listened to the new conviction in his voice whenever he read aloud to me, I realized his avoidance of my favorite pastime hadn't ever been about a profound lack of skill, like he'd been convinced it was. I wasn't teaching him how to read; I was simply resurrecting his confidence. He had been told so many times that he was incapable, defective, and he'd accepted it as truth, whether that false narrative was coming from his mom, his teammates or himself. We spent months and months huddled up together until it was Hunter who took the initiative to select a book for us to read together. I can't remember ever doing anything that intimate with anyone ever. Hunter was so vulnerable with me. He wasn't afraid to stumble, to stutter, to fail, to break down in tears of frustration in front of me. He trusted me profoundly, and that made me feel important. Watching him go on to ace his PSATs with an almost perfect score still remains the most fulfilling thing I've ever experienced in my life. By the time he was a senior, he was back on the lacrosse team, but was also devouring classics on the bus rides to his away games. He even called me in the middle of his prom to rant about the blandness of *Lord of the Flies* because his date was boring.

"I remember that too," I say with a shrug and stare out my window. "I was eleven. Things change."

He takes a few moments, then says, "Things change, but people don't. Not really."

I feel him glance at me, but pretend I don't.

"I just lost my passion to write after..." I blow out a sigh through my nostrils. "Everything."

He knows I'm speaking of my mother, and since death makes everyone weird, he concentrates on driving for the next few miles. "Do you really have nudes out there?"

I laugh, mostly relieved that we've moved on to something else, something lighter. "Asking as a lawyer or a friend...?"

He takes a second to think it over. "I'm...not sure."

"I've never taken nudes," I admit.

"Allegedly," he says as he pulls into a gas station.

I scoff. "You don't believe me?"

But he doesn't answer. He settles next to an empty station and pops open his tank. "Remember Simone Says? You used to make me do—"

"Crazy shit. You were a freshman getting bullied by a fifth grader."

He shrugs. "Because you were smarter than me. You could always figure out how to get me to do whatever you wanted. You probably still could."

His words slow down at the end and his gaze meets mine. For a beat it feels like this is One of Those Moments, and suddenly the car feels claustrophobic. I glance over my shoulder, pretending to be looking for the attendant.

"Probably still *are*," he corrects himself, clearing his throat. "Smarter."

I roll my eyes at his modesty. "You went to law school."

"As a legacy student."

I appreciate that he is self-aware and secure enough to admit it, but getting accepted into law school and passing the bar are still two very different things. He had a monumental advantage, but he still deserves his due credit for his accomplishment.

"Your dad's still at the courthouse?" I ask, realizing he has been probing into my life, and I have yet to show him the same courtesy.

He nods. "His entire identity is tied to that robe and gavel."

"Controlling people's fates," I say with a sigh, not surprised at all. "Would never want that responsibility."

I have much harsher opinions on his father, so many right in the pit of my throat, but I cap it at that. I don't want Hunter to know my true feelings toward his dad. Could make it tougher to get him to do what I need him to do.

An attendant comes up to Hunter's window, taps his knuckles on the glass. Hunter rolls it down and hands over his card. "Regular, please. Thanks, bro."

The smell is strong, so he rolls up the window while we wait. "So, how's your dad?"

"Uh, he's…hanging in there, I guess."

"Is he okay?"

I don't have enough energy to lie. Besides, there's no point in trying with Hunter. He'd see right through it. "Physically."

Shame strangles me as pity contorts Hunter's face. He goes quiet and pensive, appearing as if he's watching the meter calculate the cost of the gas, but his sudden discomfort is palpable.

"How have you managed?" he asks, flipping it right back to me. As I part my lips, I realize for once, I would rather discuss my dad being in prison than how I'm coping with it.

"I go see him every Sunday." I look through the windshield

as someone makes a terrible attempt to pull up in front of the gas pump and wonder how they got their license in the first place. But I still catch Hunter's subtle nod through my periphery.

"Must be hard," he says. "Seeing him in there. Like that."

I can tell Hunter would like me to elaborate, but this is all new to me. And I'm not sure I can articulate my feelings in a coherent way right now.

"I'm working on getting him out," I say, instantly regretting my words.

So many people believe my father slaughtered my mother. Shoddy evidence and all, the conviction speaks for itself. It's why I've always kept this part of my history under such tight wraps. I haven't spoken to Hunter since my dad's arrest. Before the police showed up at our house that night, Hunter had been on my side. He'd been one person who'd stuck with me despite all the gossip, the rumors, the bullshit, the lies all swarming the town, being plastered across TV screens at all hours of the day.

But things could have changed. The trial could have swayed him as it did so many others. Suddenly, I want to break out of this beautiful car and blow cash I don't have on an Uber to get me back across the Hudson.

"Have you appealed yet?" Hunter asks, and there's something encouraging in his tone. I can tell he's still with me, still believes in my dad's innocence. If I had the words, I would tell him how much this means to me.

"The first two petitions were denied," I manage to choke out instead. "But we're hiring someone new this time. Someone better."

An attendant taps on the driver's window again, this time to let Hunter know his tank is filled. Hunter waves at him, puts his car into gear, and we head into town. I glance out the window, grateful for the silence.

13

THERE IS A point where the houses start to become super-sized and immaculately manicured, sublime abodes with lush front yards, backyards with built-in pools, the overtly luxurious properties that are ubiquitous in this part of Essex County I thought I'd never return to, and my stomach roils.

"Everything looks exactly the same," I say, still taking in everything as if it is my first time.

Hunter glances at me before merging onto the off-ramp, and I realize I said that louder than I meant to.

"What's there to change?" he asks. "It's always been perfect here."

Perfect for people like him.

I relax a bit when I see that Hunter cruises past the turn for Asher Lane. Kate must be farther on the west side, which means I at least don't have to endure looking at all the houses I passed every day on the way to school, the twin brick Dutch

Colonials the forensics team parked in front of for days as they completed their inspection of our house.

"Shit."

Hunter looks over at me fast. "Forgot something?"

"Yeah, I'm empty-handed," I say, feeling slightly ridiculous for making it seem like there was some kind of emergency.

"What?"

"I can't show up to your mom's house for dinner without something," I tell him, keenly remembering how my mom always stressed the importance of bringing some materialistic token of appreciation whenever I was officially invited next door for dinner. "A bottle of overpriced wine at least."

"Trust me, Kate has enough overpriced wine."

"Then stop here. I'll grab some flowers."

Hunter doesn't protest. He turns inside the parking lot of Stegman's, the local grocery chain, and finds a spot conveniently close to the entrance.

"I'll be quick," I say, releasing my seat belt, and am slightly taken aback to see him following suit.

I almost tell him I'm fine, he doesn't have to accompany me inside, but then I realize he just might offer to pay. Considering the abysmal state of my checking account, I hold my tongue and make a note to send him a sweet text tonight after dinner.

Since the roses look slightly wilted, I go with a bouquet of hydrangeas and white lilies, remembering Kate's affinity for monotone floral arrangements. I turn to check with Hunter to see if there's anything he needs before I head to the self-checkout and freeze, my feet suddenly rooted into the ground like an ancient sequoia. I cannot speak, cannot believe the liveried figure is actually standing before my eyes. I can barely get enough oxygen into my lungs as he meets my gaze.

Ford Fitzpatrick.

The fraud who put my father in prison for life without a single regard for the truth. The man who orphaned me.

He was the lead investigator assigned to my mother's murder, and apparently he's now the county sheriff, according to the emblem on his uniform. I feel Hunter shift beside me, but I still cannot move or blink. Despite Aunt Patrice's firm deterring, I was in the courtroom when the verdict was read. Still, this somehow feels worse. Seeing him now, here, like this. I have never felt such a rush of pure, unadulterated anger. It's so palpable, it feels more than chemical. It feels physical.

A few years back I read that he'd suffered two minor heart attacks before undergoing a triple bypass. Somewhere deep down, I guess I've been hoping his body had finally succumbed to the stress his heart was under. But no, he is here in the flesh, one palm facing me, his large hand waving back and forth. I nearly combust, then remember Hunter, one step beside me. I peek over and see that he is returning Fitzpatrick's greeting. I know it's not fair of me to expect Hunter to view Fitzpatrick with as much disdain as I do, but this is the most distant I've ever felt to him, our feet less than a foot apart.

There are few men on this earth I regard as lowly as I do Scott Bishop. If anyone gets close, it's Ford Fitzpatrick.

Before the conviction, I mostly viewed him as another family man in the town who was doing the best he could, which is how I think most of Asher Lane saw him back then. But after my dad was thrown to the wolves, after he secured Asher Lane's most grisly murderer behind bars for life with no chance of parole, he became a larger-than-life hero. The man did more interviews than Barbara Walters that year, went on a press tour across the state for months.

As he closes in on us, taking Hunter's wave as an invitation, I notice he is carrying a get-well card.

"Hunter." Fitzpatrick's expression is warm, but more grimace than smile, or maybe my perception is skewing it. "Haven't seen you out this way in a while. How have things been?"

I don't know what comes over me when I grab Hunter's

hand. I'm shocked not only by this impulsive move, but how different his palm feels from Reggie's. For one, it's much softer, but it's also slightly larger. His fingers are slimmer, yet longer too. And he doesn't immediately return my grasp, not the way Reggie does.

"No complaints, no regrets," Hunter says.

"Good, good. And Kate? Jeez, she must be lonely in that house all by herself."

I hate how casually he mentions it, the fact that Scott and Kate no longer share a home, as if it's remotely his business. Then I remind myself that Fitzpatrick is no longer just a cop. He is a god to the people of Golden Heights. He is omnipresent and ubiquitous, and apparently all-knowing too.

Hunter mumbles something about his mother and then Fitzpatrick's eyes come to me, not so much in acknowledgment but as if to say it is my turn to matter, because I have the honor of receiving the attention of his gaze.

Then his eyes jump back to Hunter, the quirk in his lips now leaning more smirk than grimace. "Like father, like son. Your old man taught you how to pick them, huh?"

No, men like Fitzpatrick never disappoint. They are one and the same, misogynistic, callous motherfuckers.

"No, we're not…" Hunter glances down at where we are conjoined and shakes my grip away. "You don't remember Simone? She's…"

I'm not sure why he stops, but I assume it's because this is now as unpleasant for him as it is for me. I hope he regrets waving to this man. I hope as he's falling asleep tonight it plagues his conscience. But I don't blame him. He has more in common with Fitzpatrick than me. There is an immediate camaraderie among white men that even the past cannot penetrate.

Before I can jump in, recognition leaps into Fitzpatrick's blue-gray eyes. "What are you doing back here?"

The question is punctuated by a smile, but I don't return it.

At least it didn't take him as long as it took Hunter to put the puzzle together.

"Flowers," I say, shaking them a little. It's all I can do to not hawk all the phlegm in my throat right in that space between his eyes.

"Right..." Fitzpatrick says, obviously thrown by my short-ness as if he is one of my father's golf buddies and not his mor-tal enemy.

I glance at Hunter when I feel his hand against mine again. This time he's the one who grips me and pulls me along as he steps off, except he doesn't grab my hand. He takes the softest part of my arm with a little tug.

"We've got to get going," he says, tipping his head at Fitz-patrick. "Enjoy your night."

I'm a step ahead of him when he takes the flowers from my hand and tells me to head to the car while he pays for them, and the way gratitude rains over me, it feels like I am a desert and him orchestrating this escape is the first precipitation in months.

Before he gets the key back in the ignition, I apologize for grabbing his hand and he's almost offended as he profusely apol-ogizes for acknowledging Fitzpatrick, immediately taking full blame for the awkward encounter. I remind him that it was my idea to stop in at Stegman's, but it doesn't make him abbreviate his apology. He feels terrible and once again I feel protected in his presence, the way I felt when we were kids, when we had each other's back despite the world around us.

Leaving Asher Lane behind meant leaving Hunter behind too, so I never even entertained the idea of missing him. Once I moved in with Aunt Patrice, I had to completely erase him from my mental Rolodex, pretend like he never existed. But now I can't help but wonder what we missed when I went ghost, what we could have become if all my memories of him weren't fossilized in amber.

"He's running for mayor, you know," Hunter says, turning

out of the parking lot with one hand, and as if by sheer magic, the first residential property we slide by has a sign on a stake with Fitzpatrick's face on it asking me to vote for him for mayor of Golden Heights.

You can't make this shit up.

14

I STARE INTO my mother's eyes and almost hear her voice reverberating in the airy room, her tone slightly deeper than mine with a natural rasp that I always hoped I'd develop but haven't yet. Her smell comes back to me too, that sweet coconut scent of her hair mixed with the rich vanilla of the perfume she used to spray on her neck and wrists. Then I blink and remember I'm standing in front of the fireplace in Kate Bishop's formal dining room, the traditional kind of space that makes the meal we're about to all share feel high stakes.

I've only caught a glimpse of the woman who was married to the man who killed my mother, and she barely looks any different than she does in my memories thanks to a collection of tasteful lunchtime procedures. She is on the other side of the wall in the kitchen putting the finishing touches on the food, the room complete with two marble-topped islands as Hunter fetches a specific bottle of wine from the cellar in the basement at her request. She moves like a hummingbird from bloom to

bloom as she gathers the dishes. I can't see her, but I can practically follow her every movement because she's wearing heels
that create a satisfying staccato on the herringbone hardwood
floors. Her designer-soled footsteps come to an abrupt stop and
I hear a small curse slip from her lips. It makes me wonder if
she's broken a freshly gel-manicured nail or gotten a splash of
something on her daring all-white ensemble.

Hunter ducks in the room behind me and I instantly feel
more relaxed, his presence like the soft instrumental music they
play in spas. Just before I shift to turn away, I notice that the
photo of my mom and Kate out by the pool in our old house is
the only one on the mantel that isn't covered in a light veil of
dust. It's like it was just placed here, dug up from some random
box in the basement and set atop this surface crowded with the
other family photos.

"Hey," he says with a little bit of a smile. He seems slightly
nervous, but I can't figure out if he's on edge about seeing Kate
in a while or if he's merely feeling secondhand angst for me.

"Hey."

He angles the bottle of Cabernet Sauvignon. "It's a 2002."

"Sorry, I don't speak wine," I say, following him to the south
end of the table. "Is that significant or shade?"

"It's probably a two-hundred-dollar bottle."

"Then I'll be sure to sniff before I sip."

That makes him laugh. He sets the bottle on the table, then
gestures for me to sit. He waits until I cross my legs to pull out
his chair and I'm surprised by how close our legs end up under
the long stone table, considering how large it is. It looks like
it was imported straight from Italy and the tablescape looks fit
for a holiday feast or low-key wedding.

"All this for me?" I whisper.

Hunter matches my hushed tone. "You know her."

As if on cue, the staccato of Kate's footsteps resumes, and this
time the sound grows louder and louder with each step. She

rounds the bend with a smile as white as her sleeveless-blouse-and-skirt combo, two dishes in her hands. She's not wearing off-white. Not eggshell. Or ecru. She is swathed in pure white, looking as svelte and as imperious as a swan. Her heels are thin and nude, her diamonds of pristine clarity. From head to toe, she looks like she was ripped from a Chanel editorial. This is the way she dresses for dinner. In her own home.

When I was a kid, I was surprised to learn that Kate had a job. Not just any job. Not something frivolous like a data-entry clerk or some kind of part-time volunteering bullshit the other moms on Asher Lane prided themselves on. She had a full-time career most of the time we lived on Asher Lane, wore a suit and sensible heels and matte lipstick, and didn't have to ask her husband for a monthly allowance, something I always admired about her.

My mother was the housewife, which I could tell Kate secretly envied until she eventually abandoned her high-earning corporate role when Scott was appointed judge. Aside from Mom, Kate was undeniably the most beautiful wife on Asher Lane, the one with the most accurate semblance to a trophy, and Scott was constantly shipping her off to the West Coast to shine her up, a little nip, tuck, plump, inject. Plus, since she was so much younger than Scott, it just seemed like he married her to be an adornment more than a partner. Hunter was old enough to be independent by the time Kate left her job, so I never understood why she still never made it to a single one of his lacrosse games. All the other stay-at-home wives were at each one front and center.

"Need some help?" Hunter asks, but she quickly waves him off and disappears inside the kitchen again after setting down the plates.

I glance around the space while Hunter unscrews the cork on the bottle, his features tightened into concentration for a few beats. The house is undoubtedly smaller than their old one on Asher Lane, but no less grand. I recognize most of the furniture, everything too overdone and over-the-top for my taste, but carefully considered. The house is immaculate, the art on the walls so expensive it makes me a little spiteful. One piece is worth a month of attorney's fees.

Kate quickly comes back with two larger serving bowls, which Hunter helps ease onto the table right next to the flowers I brought. She sits down next to me, and now that I have a better look at her, the Botox in her forehead and the filler in her lips is obvious, but whatever else she has done to maintain her forever thirty-something glow is beyond my visual assessment. I force a smile when she catches my eye.

I know I shouldn't take my vitriol for Kate's ex-husband out on her, but part of me wonders how much she knew. Wives always know. Maybe not the whole truth, but enough to step in, yet so many of them enable or look the other way.

I watch as she fills her glass with the vintage red, a movement so well practiced, so second nature to her, it barely demands her full attention. Her eyes leave the glass while she's still pouring and she looks at me directly to tell me how beautiful I've become, how much I look like my mom, and the way she times the ending of her compliment to the pour of the wine, which is her assuring me that my mom would be so proud to see me as the woman I've become today, is impressive. I immediately thank her, and distracted by her sincere kindness, I instinctually decline the pour she offers me, then immediately remember I was supposed to play along and pretend to sip it throughout dinner. She hesitates, then looks to Hunter, who gestures for her to fill his glass, and I'm relieved. I didn't mean to be rude or make this awkward.

I survey the food she brought out. Fried chicken with not much color. Mashed potatoes with gravy, which look a little over-whipped. And corn bread. I'm about to make an assessment of this stereotypical menu she has presented, but then I see the salad and think that maybe I'm overreacting. I grab the tongs and put some of the tossed arugula and tomatoes on my plate, though it doesn't look all that appetizing.

"You know, I don't know if I ever told you this, but I went to school with an African American girl too," Kate says, and I'm not sure who she is talking to.

I look up from my plate and am taken aback by her smile.

"Black," Hunter mumbles after my eyes shift to his, desperate for an explanation of why his mother has randomly decided to point this out. "You can just say *Black*."

Kate coughs, lightly choking on the small sip of wine she swallowed, but it seems like one of those performative antics people do to break up the tension when things get excruciatingly awkward. When she glances up, a vague look of horror veils her well-done face.

"What?" she asks, but it's clear she heard him and is not confused and is still trying to bide time.

"It's what we say when she's not in front of us. Relax," he says, lifting his glass and draining it in one go. "It's not an offensive term."

I'm not a wine person, but I am cultured enough to know that wine is supposed to be delicately and intentionally sipped, not chugged like a cheap beer. I can't help but think it's some kind of proclamation, and just the thought tickles the edges of my lips. Whatever beef Hunter has with his mother, while it remains unspoken, it's clear and palpable. This could end up being quite an entertaining night after all.

"Simone," she says, shifting in her chair to face me. "Do you prefer I say *Black*?"

She genuinely sounds as if she's willing to do whatever it takes to make me feel comfortable, but I feel her looking at my face, my hair, as she waits for my response.

"Um, yeah, actually, I do." Kate's face doesn't change even in the areas that haven't been injected, so I add, "It's not like it's like saying the N-word."

It was meant to lighten the moment, but Kate doesn't pick up on this and takes me seriously, and I instantly regret my lousy attempt at humor.

"Of course it's not. I'd never use that word. Under any circumstances. Never," she says, and it is one too many *nevers* for me to fully believe her.

Kate stabs at the salad on her plate repeatedly, but peculiarly doesn't lift anything to her mouth. "Anyway, I went to school with a *Black* girl. You reminded me a lot of her when you all moved in next to us."

She lifts a piece of corn bread to her mouth with her fork, tines down, satisfied with herself.

I nod slowly. "Because I'm Black?"

Kate freezes like that was the last thing she expected me to say. "No. Because…" She pretends to be busy chewing, but I can tell she is stalling again because she can't think of any other reason I reminded her of her friend. "Not just because you're both…Black."

Kate reaches for her wineglass, drains half of the pour like it's liquid oxygen, and inside I am dying.

Hunter is already refilling his glass. "Why is this even relevant?"

"Hunter, I'm just trying to…" Her eyes flutter and she taps her mouth with her napkin. She is careful not to smear her lipstick or meet my eyes. "Pass me the chicken, please."

He hands her the serving platter filled with the wings. Kate helps herself to one, then proceeds to cut it with her fork and knife like it's steak.

I smuggle a laugh and catch Hunter's gaze, gesturing toward Kate with mine. He winces in embarrassment. Then I feel Kate staring at me, her utensils poised but frozen. I think she's caught me mocking her, but then I see tears bubbling to the surface.

"Kate, are you…?" I set down my own fork and search her eyes. "Are you okay?"

There's a beat, and then she blinks, seemingly popping out of the trance she's briefly slipped into. "I'm fine."

But it's obvious she's lying. If tears could be bright, hers would be. Big and bold and bright. She tries to blink fast and brush away more tears that start to fall with the tips of her fingers, but it seems like her efforts only produce more even faster.

"I'm sorry," she says, reaching for her glass. "Ignore me."

"What's wrong?" Hunter asks, not unkind but sort of impatient.

We both watch her take a sip of wine, but it doesn't have the effect I think she expected. Her tears gush out even harder.

"Nothing. I..." She catches her breath before it gets too far away from her, and when her eyes come to me again, I see that they settle on the lettered pendant hanging around my neck. "Your necklace. Your mom used to wear that all the time. I never saw her without it."

"Oh."

I touch it. I know it's there, but just resting the tips of my fingers on the precious metal makes me feel closer to my mother in a small but not insignificant way.

"I'm sorry for this," she murmurs, most of her voice lost to a gasp, and then she is wheezing and I am squirming in my seat trying not to do the same. "I didn't mean to... I just miss Evelyn so much..."

She commits what I'm sure must be an etiquette faux pas somewhere and lifts her cloth dinner napkin to her face, dabbing under her eyes before the foundation on her cheeks becomes streaked.

Kate's tears are copious and abrupt, and have totally disrupted the vibe of dinner, but it feels so nice to hear her name. Evelyn. Evelyn. *Evelyn*.

By the time Kate is back to breathing deeply and has a dry face, I've already followed suit and used my napkin to soak up my own tears. Hunter keeps his eyes on his lap, mostly, but once we grab our utensils again to resume eating, he touches my knee under the table, giving me a look like, *Are you okay?* I nod and smile, hoping it appears less faint than it feels.

He doesn't ask Kate. I glance at her as she resumes slicing her chicken with her fork and knife. She brings a chunk of white meat to her mouth, tines down, and I decide that not all wives know. Those are the kind of out-of-nowhere tears you can't produce out of sheer will. Kate has been grieving my mother as long as I have. It only makes my anger toward Scott multiply. He not only stole my mother's life, stole my father's freedom, ruined my childhood, but he also broke his wife's heart and forced her to mourn her best friend about five decades too early.

"Simone, you don't want any of the chicken?" I hesitate, so she goes on, "I know these can't compare to the ones Evelyn used to make for Scott's mom. She used this special season—"

"I wouldn't know. I'm vegan, so…"

"Oh." She sounds shocked, but there's no way she didn't know this. "So that must be why you never came over to our house for dinner."

Hunter scoffs and shakes his head.

"What?" Kate asks, and I wish we were already on dessert.

"You never invited Simone over for dinner," he says. "Literally never. It was always us going to their house."

Kate cuts her eyes at him, like *Whose side are you on?* Then she turns to me and smiles, but I can still sense the mortification bubbling underneath. "There was a lot going on at our house…with Scott's mother and everything. I didn't want her to—"

"Get in the way?" Hunter suggests just over his breath between bites.

"She was not *in the way*. I just didn't want her to…distract anyone," she says, and I cannot believe she thinks this is making it better. "She was very…needy. You know what I mean, right, Simone?"

Slightly caught off guard, I nod, less because I actually know what she means and more to avoid contributing to the level of tension suddenly crammed into this room. This is not what I was expecting when Hunter told me Kate would be making us dinner tonight and I almost want to tell him to fall back so we can just eat and get this over with. But I also understand where he's coming from and this has all been so illuminating. I never thought about why, when the six of us fused into a larger quasi-family and enjoyed a four-hour meal around a large chandelier-crested table, it was always at our house. But it's true. I never considered that Kate had a problem with me or my parents coming over. What is Hunter trying to say, that though Kate and my mom were practically inseparable, she didn't really care for me? Maybe the problem was my dad? Is he saying his mom's friendship with my mom was somehow superficial? And if he is, why does he feel compelled to point it out here and now?

"It's my fault, sweetie," Kate says, trying to remedy the blossoming awkwardness. "For not asking you for your preferences before you arrived. What kind of clumsy hostess am I?"

"It's fine," I say. "The salad's fine. Love the lemon."

I despise the lemon, but I'm positive I sell it even to Hunter, who is keenly aware of my aversion to citrus.

Still, Kate jumps up from the table like there is an emergency. "I can see what else I have that I can whip—"

"Will you relax?" Hunter is getting to the point where he can no longer hide his frustration. "She said she's fine."

Kate eases back in her chair like a child obeying a parent. She picks up her fork and stabs at one piece of arugula again.

It's silent for a while, and then Kate's voice pierces it, a whisper that manages to be both soft and harsh at the same time. "Why do you always have to do that? And in front of company."

Hunter stops chewing. Feeling his agitation, I put my hand on his arm, and he closes his mouth, then goes back to clearing his plate.

"Simone, you understand what I was trying to say, don't you, sweetie?" Kate tilts her head, and I can see her peach fuzz in the warm light above us.

I swallow, not appreciating how she wants me to choose between the two of them. "Well..."

"You know just as well as we do that the families on Asher Lane can be a bit...traditional in their thinking. When your parents came to tour the house next to ours, everybody whispered. For days. All they could see was an Afri—a *Black* family trying to lower the property values of our homes. But Scott and I were open-minded. Your mom and I had this instant thing, this familiarity, this chemistry. And we weren't the types to see color anyway. All we saw was—"

"You didn't notice they were Black?" Hunter asks, his annoyance almost tangible.

"And we didn't raise *you* to either," Kate says. She goes back to stabbing, her pace even more aggressive now. "I know it's not the politically-correct way to say it these days, but—"

"It's bullshit."

I glance at Hunter, surprised by how reactive he's being tonight, and all but hold my breath. It seems like it would be so much easier to just let these things go like I am forcing myself to.

"What was that?" Kate asks. "You know I hate when you mumble at my table."

Hunter moves to his feet. Crosses the room. And then he is standing over the bar cart. "There's no such thing as being color-blind. Give it up. It's embarrassing."

Hunter grabs a bottle of whiskey and pours himself a nice amount in an old-fashioned. I consider saying something, but then I don't. The intensity between them is so keen, I am nervous to even say a word.

"I'm *embarrassing*?" Her glass never drifts too far from her lips. "What else is new?"

They don't yell. They don't raise their voices a single oc-
tave when they fight. Every word is controlled to the point of
borderline insanity.

There is another opening, both of them quiet and avoiding
each other's eyes, but this is so uncomfortable to watch, I stay
silent. Hunter brings the bottle with him to the table and sets
it next to his plate. It is a statement.

"Here's an idea," Kate says, and I can already hear the derision in her voice. "Why don't we just eat in silence since everything I say is problematic?"

"I'm just tired of this shit. You—"

"Don't swear at my table."

"You think because you're this self-professed liberal, you're
one of the good guys. It's—"

"Jesus, will you stop attacking me?" she says, her hands press-
ing into her temples, and I am genuinely afraid that she is about
to crack like a tossed egg.

"I'm not attacking—"

"Hunter." I touch his leg and its warmth surprises me. "It's
okay."

Kate looks between the two of us, then with a clenched jaw,
slams her wineglass down hard enough to break it. The delicate stem collapses, surprising us all. Burgundy liquid splashes
all over her white outfit. Then she's on her feet, storming out
the room, and even this performative anger feels profound.

I'm not exactly sure what set her off—Hunter's brutal honesty, which seems like something she's not accustomed to, or
maybe it was how easy it was for me to get him to heed versus
how ineffective her attempts to rein him in have been. I wish
Hunter would have never started this, but I also think Hunter
is more confident when I'm at his side, especially in front of
her, and that warms me. My mom might have adored Kate, and
for all I know, those feelings were mutual. But my allegiance
has always been with Hunter and always will.

Once we're alone, I feel the weight of my hand on his thigh, and I remember touching him. His leg was the closest in reach, but now it just feels so inappropriate, so intimate to have touched him there. I pull my hand away and feel his eyes on me as he nurses his whiskey. Then he looks away, surveying the untouched food on his plate. He looks as if he has lost his appetite.

"Not that I didn't appreciate that," I say softly. "But time and place. You know?"

Hunter looks at me, then down at the brown liquid in his glass. I reach for it, and he doesn't stop me, but gives me an incredulous look. "You drink whiskey?"

"No." But I bring the rim of the glass between my lips and tip it back so that a good amount pours over my tongue. I do my best not to cringe as it goes down and explodes across my chest, but the burn persists longer than I expect it to and I almost start choking. "Wow."

He gently pats me on my back. "You okay?"

"Yeah." I reach for my napkin. "That is fucking terrible."

He laughs, which I anticipate, but then he kinda blushes and it surprises me. I set the glass back down and Hunter watches me for a moment. I return his gaze, inviting him to say what's on his mind.

He hesitates still, then removes his hand, which I forgot was even on me, and says, "Guess you don't need me to jump in the ring for you anymore, huh?"

There is a hint of sadness in his voice that catches me off guard and so all I can do is smile, but I think it conveys my thoughts perfectly. I don't need him to protect me anymore. I'm all grown up now and can throw my own punches.

15

THERE IS A collection of neatly packed boxes scattered around Kate's attic, some that seem to have not been disturbed since they were first brought up here. I've already spotted a few ones that I suspect contain books or items no one plans on using anytime soon. I kept an eye out while Hunter looked for the box containing the old letters I wrote him. Now I know exactly where I'm heading once the two of them are fast asleep tonight.

"'I know us girls aren't really supposed to believe in knights in shining armor...'" I glance up from my bubbly sixth-grader penmanship and see a closed-mouthed smile pulling at the corners of Hunter's lips. "'But you saved my butt today. I owe you. Whatever you want, just name it. It's yours.'"

I lower the letter in my hand and drop it down onto the pile of the ones I've already read and realize Hunter and I are lying in the same positions we used to back during our reading sessions in the library. Our backs are up against the wall, but he has one leg splayed out ahead of him with the other bent toward his chest, and I have both of my legs folded in front of me, the box of letters in my lap. The configuration used to be conducive to me watching over his shoulder as he read, and now it just feels instinctual. Sometimes I would even rest my head on his shoulder and doze off to the sound of his voice, and he'd keep on reading until he reached the chapter goal for the day.

"Did I ever pay you back?" I ask, tilting my head and squinting as if it will help me recall the lost memory.

"You never had to, Simone."

I smile at his smile, which is still not showing teeth, but has made it to his eyes that have dilated in the dim lighting, which make them look soulful and heartbreaking.

"I can't believe that girl said your hair felt like pubes," Hunter says, his eyes on my hands as I flip through the unread pile. There have to be three dozen more letters in here.

"Can't believe she clipped my entire braid." I shiver at the memory of seeing twelve inches of my hair being shoved into my hand by a sneering crowd of seventh graders. "It took years to grow back."

"You wear it out all the time now?"

I look up and see his eyes roving my shoulder-length curls. After those assholes chopped off my braid, my hair was too short to do anything with it except cornrows or a mini fro, and I opted for the cornrows. I was terrified of wearing my natural curls to school. There was always someone touching it without my consent to satisfy their curiosity of what my springy coils felt like, someone to shift it out of the way because they couldn't see around my hair to the chalkboard. One of my teachers even made me move from the front row to the back because it was *distracting to the other students*, then penalized me in my progress report for *not demonstrating an eagerness to learn*. That's when I told my mom I wanted braids. And then of course my pre-algebra teacher called my mom in for a meeting one afternoon to ask her if she could vary up my style because it was making some of the other students nervous. Upon elaboration, we learned my braids made me look like a *juvenile delinquent*, which I quickly realized was simply another euphemism for *nigger* on account of my mom refusing to explain it to me in the car. I begged her to let me straighten my hair, but she told me she wasn't going to let me ruin my curls just so I could assimilate to European beauty standards. While I thoroughly appreciate her adjudication now, back then I just wanted to pull a Willow Smith and shave my head completely.

"Yeah," I say, mindlessly tugging on one of the longest strands in the back so that it extends past my rib cage. "Unless it's wash day."

Hunter nods, probably remembering those Sundays when I would be cooped up in the house all afternoon long while my mom washed, conditioned, detangled, moisturized and re-braided my hair. "I like it," he says. "I like the braids too, but this is..."

He doesn't really know what word he is looking for, or maybe he is hesitant to say it, but I get his drift and am silently grateful he doesn't go through with the compliment. "Thanks," I say and hurry back to flipping through the letters so he doesn't see that I am starting to blush.

"Saint Benedict Prep was pretty rough, huh?" he asks.

"Nothing I couldn't handle."

"Yeah. You were a badass. You didn't even need me back then."

I look at him and my words come out slowly. "It was nice knowing I had backup."

I smile, and then he smiles, and then the room is too quiet. He gestures to the box of letters. "One more?"

I nod.

He grabs another folded piece of paper. Skims it. "Oh, shit."

"What?"

"This is the one you never read." He pauses, quickly skimming from beginning to end, and his voice drops. "You guys never came back home that day."

That day we fled Asher Lane with three laundry bags filled with all of our possessions. No luggage, no boxes. A day my memory has largely repressed.

"This is from you?" I take it and scan the long paragraph. It's definitely his gruesome handwriting. "Read it to me," I say, pushing it back into his hand.

I am aware of the gravity of what I am asking, so I'm not surprised when I see the lump in Hunter's throat bob as he swallows hard. Our eyes meet, and I give him a small nod to let him know he's safe. He is always safe with me.

He clears his throat and takes his time. "'This is so fucked up. Why do bad things happen to good people? I wish there was something I could do. These fucking cops in this town are useless.'"

He pauses, and at first I think he is caught up in the memory, catapulted back to the moment when he penned these words, but then I see he is reading ahead, making sense of all the letter before forging on. It has always been harder for him to decode handwriting than typeface, so I don't take this moment for granted. I know how much courage this takes. It has been so long since I've heard him read aloud. This feels nostalgic yet new at the same time since his voice is a full man voice now. Years may have gone by, and maybe parts of who we've become make us strangers, but it is obvious Hunter still trusts me in a way he has never trusted anyone else, and I almost hurl at the thought that he is related to the man who murdered my mother.

"'Anyway,'" he continues. "'I can't believe you're leaving. Makes me want to get out of here too. I'm tired of this place. But at least I'm out of here next year. Maybe when you finish high school we can get an apartment in the same building or something. I'll be in New York. You can go to NYU instead of Princeton. Just make sure you write me back when you guys get to wherever you're going.'"

This time when he pauses there is this weight of finality in his tone, and I know immediately that he is not struggling to make out words. He remains quiet, almost remote for a few more moments. I watch the wall, unblinking, wondering what that would have been like, me at NYU, him at Columbia. I envision how my life would have gone if we had reconnected sooner. Maybe we would have had an explosive falling-out or fallen in love or fucked each other's brains out.

"You never sent me your new address," he says just above a whisper, and I hear every word as loud as a crack of thunder.

I look at him directly and I want to touch him.

"You never wrote." His eyes are so honest and unguarded and obscenely blue. "You just disappeared."

I unfold my legs and turn on my hip so I can look at his face better. "It wasn't you. I missed you."

He nods, barely, and it hits me that I wasn't the only one who suffered from our abrupt move. I lost everything, my whole world as I knew it, the comfort of the past, the brightness of the future. But it has occurred to me for the first time that Hunter suffered a major loss too and his life didn't just bounce back to normal after we were gone.

The moment you realize you have caused someone emotional distress is so surreal. You want to deny it at first, you want to defend yourself, you want to tell them you never meant to hurt them. But it's all futile. What's done will always be done. Hunter is right. I knew his address by heart. I could have written to him.

"My dad didn't want me to even associate myself with Asher Lane anymore," I confess, hoping it's enough.

He nods. "Must have been hard. Must still be hard. No answers. No justice."

I let his words hang there, surprised that he gets how hard it is to not have any closure. I briefly think of my mother, desperately trying to understand how she could have kept her affair a secret all those years, because even just keeping my plan to find Kate's diary and out Scott Bishop is almost too heavy of a lie for me to handle.

Almost.

I'm already in his mother's house. It is too late to turn back now. I am going to find the truth no matter how many lies I have to tell.

I watch Hunter neatly stuffing all the letters back into the box. Then I smirk. "Lawry's."

He glances at me with his brows tilted toward each other like two lovers moving in for their first kiss.

"The seasoning," I say. "For the chicken."

He grins. "So you *did* know."

I nod, and he laughs harder than I expect him to, which makes me laugh harder than I have in a while.

"You know you don't have to do that anymore," he says.

"Do what?"

He gives me a look like I should know what he's talking about, but I'm lost until he tugs down on my arm so my hand is no longer shielding the lower half of my face.

"Cover your mouth…" His voice is so soft as his eyes settle on mine. "When you laugh," he says, and it's like he has carved open my chest and shone a light on the parts of me I thought I had hidden completely.

Our eyes lock and I immediately look away, the moment feeling too intense. I didn't even realize I still did that, but even with my eyes averted it's like Hunter can see every side of me and I'm not sure if I like it. For a second I do think about what he said, about how much I hated my teeth when I was younger, and then how uncomfortable I am when people tell me they love my smile because somehow I still don't believe them.

"I'm sorry about how I acted downstairs," he says, and I

glance up at him. He covers the box with the lid and just stares at it for a moment, unblinking. "You know the real reason she never invited you guys over, right?" He looks at me, but doesn't give me a chance to guess. "Your dad's Benz was more expensive than my dad's."

Again, I'm slightly thrown by Hunter's implication that the Bishops envied us, and I have to fight the urge to instantly rebuke it. "What?"

"Serious. How dare the Black family moving into the neighborhood have a sexier car? Guess Dad felt a little competitive. Not just with your dad, with everyone, but especially your dad. And my mom...I don't know...wanted to appease him." He shakes his head, shame rising in his eyes, but I don't hold his father's sins against him. It definitely follows the pattern, though, Kate acquiescing to Scott as if she were his pet instead of his life partner. Also, Scott being shit. It tracks perfectly, like a hungry wolf after a hare in fresh snowfall.

"Sweet ride, though," Hunter says, and now there's a dreamy quality to his voice. "Bet you look good whipping it around now."

I shift, picturing Dad's old S-Class sedan, its creamy beige interior, how he would constantly complain about the pricey maintenance. "Dad had to sell the Benz and the Porsche to cover the legal fees after they took away his job at the bank."

"Oh." I can tell he feels foolish for assuming there was even one element of our world that remained constant after the investigation. "But you see him every Sunday, you said?"

"We have a world-class lunch provided by the vending machines."

"Well, I'm glad he has you. I'm sure you're what's keeping him pushing through."

The sorrow I understand, but the wistfulness in his tone surprises me. Maybe he is not as close to his father as he used to be, which would make sense because he is nothing like that unrepentant beast.

I head down a dark path in my mind again, am wondering if Hunter does in fact know what his father did and this has caused some kind of rift between them, but my train of thought is eclipsed by Hunter's hand on my arm. He lifts and angles it so that he can better study the tattoo on the inside of my arm. The script is hand-drawn, and I can see him struggle to make out the words, his eyes moving left to right as he attempts to read it multiple times.

"'With the right words,'" I whisper, helping him out.

His laugh is as soft as my words, full of relief. "When I first saw this, I thought it was your boyfriend's name," he says, and it's like my entire body has just been dunked in Novocain.

Hunter knows about Reggie. He knows I am taken. I have no idea how he knows about him, but I've washed my hair and left my apartment without pants for nothing.

"My..." I shake my head, not sure if I should deny or attempt to explain. "My boyfriend?"

"Yeah. I mean, you're not married, clearly," he says, glancing at one specific bare, ringless finger. "But you're not single, are you?"

I am fully aware that this is where I am supposed to tell him that I *do* in fact have a boyfriend, but I don't know if I'll need Hunter after I find his mother's diary tonight, if I even find it, which if I don't, I will definitely need him again. I need to keep him as he is, curious. His lust is the only leverage I have, and I can't afford to lose it, not yet.

"You really thought I'd do something that gauche?" I ask.

"I don't know." He sweeps his gaze across the words again. "So what is it? What's it mean?"

"'With the right words, you can change the world,'" I recite from memory. "That's the full quote. It's from *Charlotte's Web*."

It is one of the first chapter books I had him read aloud to me.

"Oh, yeah," he says, and I imagine he is remembering this. "Didn't your mom love that book?"

"Yeah, she…" I pause, because just seeing flashes of her face, her eyes, her hands holding the book as she'd read it to me at bedtime is too much. And how am I supposed to talk about my mother to the son of the man who murdered her?

It is so quiet when Hunter takes my hand in his, so different from when I grabbed his in Stegman's, so much gentler that I can almost hear the tear break free and trickle down my cheek. This time I realize his hand is so soft, softer than mine, like raw cookie dough. It is shocking how natural this feels, how intimate, like we are both suddenly naked and exposed, and I struggle to recall the last time Reggie held my hand.

"She liked spiders," I finally manage, pleased that my voice only wavered a little. "Weird, I know. But she read it to me a million times. We had like four copies of it."

"You still have them?"

I shake my head. "It wasn't just your letters. A lot of stuff never made it to our new apartment."

He nods, his eyes down on his lap for a few moments. Then he is staring at my necklace. "She was a good person," he says, catching my eye even though I've been avoiding his. "Nana was an asshole to her, and she never lost it. Never stopped treating her like she was her own family. Not once."

I nod and look away because suddenly I don't see Hunter. I see Scott. I see how similar the twenty-something Hunter looks to the forty-something Scott I knew on Asher Lane. Suddenly, the resemblance is striking. Eyes, nose, height, build, even his voice sounds like the young Scott Bishop that seduced my mother.

And then stuffed her body in a trash bag once he was done using it for what he saw it worth.

The other reason I break eye contact with Hunter is because he wants to kiss me. I see it in his eyes, which have dilated even more now. He wants to take my face in his raw cookie dough hands and kiss me, slip into that treacherous territory that is closed-eye, open-mouthed kissing, that kind that moves you around the room in a haze, that makes clothes drop to the floor like burning wax, that makes forever flash in your head. He wants to feel on my body, all the places where I am concave and he is swollen, all the places I am protruding and he is flat, all the places I am soft and he is firm.

I force out a yawn as I reach my arms over my head.

Hunter watches me finish my stretch, then smiles a little. "Tired?"

16

I DON'T GO straight to sleep in the guest bedroom Kate shows me to, which she gave me a brief tour of, making sure to point out that the mattress is bespoke and organic. She's extremely attentive, showing me spare pillows with varying degrees of thickness, extra towels and a weighted blanket in the hallway linen closet. I wonder if she can sense that chasm growing up without my mother created deep inside me and is compensating for it, or if she herself now has a void she's constantly trying to fill, the one created by an empty nest. Either way, it feels nice. And part of me can't help but imagine Mom being pleased by us bonding again after so many years, even if only for a brief moment. She once suggested that I call her *Aunt Kate*, and though she was initially flattered, Kate said it made her feel matronly and it never stuck. Back then, our lives were so inextricably linked; we weren't just two neighboring families. Sometimes we were like a unit, a force.

Between the long drive and clumsy dinner, I'm mentally and

physically drained, and really want to just pass out without even undressing. But I still have a mission to complete.

I contemplate pulling up the photo of Michelangelo's *David* I have saved to my camera roll to eat up some time, the thick vein cording his right arm always doing me in, but once I go back and forth a few times on whether the walls are thick enough, I no longer have it in me to put in the effort masturbating to a two-dimensional muse requires. By the time Reggie responds to my thirst text, I've already devoured the first two chapters of an advanced reader copy of a dark academia suspense novel. When I notice it's midnight, I have a solid theory on who the campus killer is and figure the amount of wine Kate guzzled throughout dinner has to have taken reign by now.

I dog-ear my page and shut my book. The hallway is lined with doors, all of them identical and pulled shut, but also with carpet, so I am not as vigilant with my creep down to the slimmest door that leads to the next level up. I gently pull the door closed behind me and slowly climb the stairs two at a time so the opportunity for one of them to creak under my weight is reduced by half.

I start at the beginning and open one of the boxes as quietly as I can. The first one is full of books. A lot of old Danielle Steel and Nora Roberts. I've read most of them. And then I see some that are even more nostalgic, books that I used when I helped Hunter get comfortable reading. I flip through all of them, smiling at some of the covers and opening them briefly to smell the musty scent of the paper as I silently wish things could be as simple as they were back then.

I cross the room and go through more boxes. I stumble across a leather photo album that looks like it's from the nineties with its thick plastic pages. When I lift it up, a few loose photos slip out. I pick them up. All three shots are of Kate on the beach in cornrows and a blackfishing-level fake tan. Immediately, a part of me is livid, because white women get to wear blackness as a costume, and I do not, but then there is a small sound somewhere in the house, and I remember that I am snooping around someone else's personal things and need to hurry up. I put the pictures back, then dig around some more, and then beneath an old jewelry box covered in dust, there is a small journal and my hands almost shake.

I close the door and head back down to the second floor, and just as I'm about to push back into my room, I hear her voice peal through the darkness.

"If you're going to sneak into my son's room, maybe not get caught?"

There's almost a laugh lining Kate's words.

My heart skips a beat, but I flip around and manage to hide the diary behind my back in the near pitch-black darkness. "I'm not…"

Once I catch my breath, I still hesitate because though I'm not caught, I'm also not sure what to say to her. It's obvious she indulged in one pour too many at dinner and hasn't stopped boozing since. The snickering that follows her comment shows me she is being a bit unserious, but there's a level of consternation I detected in her tone that her subsequent laughter is failing to mask.

"This isn't what it looks like," I say, which doesn't sound convincing to my own ears even though it's the truth.

Kate takes a step toward me, and the almost-empty bottle of wine in her hand flashes in the dark. "It never is, is it?"

Instead of wasting my time convincing her I'm telling the truth, I reach for the door handle. It's better she thinks I'm horny than a snoop who was just creeping around in her attic.

"I'm pretty tired, so I'm just gonna—"

"Hope you're on the pill," Kate says, cutting me off, and I was so not expecting that, all I can do is stare at her for a moment, my lips agape. "Wouldn't want my son to end up pressuring you into getting an abortion."

I open my mouth. Close it. Open it again but the words still won't come out. I literally do not know what to say.

"Just looking out for you, sweetie." Kate blows a kiss and stumbles into her room at the crown of the hall.

I stand there unmoving until I hear her two doors shut with a whisper of a click and then make my way back to mine. Part of me wants to make excuses for her, to blame it all on the alcohol.

But the other part of me wonders if this is the true Kate Bishop. Insecure and insolent. Isn't alcohol nature's truth serum?

Maybe I don't know Kate the way I thought I knew her. Then again, maybe Hunter is right, and her husband's yearslong affair fundamentally changed her.

17

THUNDER AND LIGHTNING does to me what whips and chains do for some people. I can't tell if this early-afternoon rain is making Hunter as horny as it's making me, but this steady downpour that's making it look as if it's already dusk has so much dopamine and adrenaline pumping through me. I watch the meteorological aphrodisiac pound the window as he maneuvers us through the traffic heading back to the city, but all I can think about is Reggie giving me the same unrelenting treatment until I beg him to stop, then us snuggling up and talking lazily through the bad acting in a low-budget Netflix thriller.

Hunter is also a good driver in inclement weather. He is relaxed but cautious, and I can let my eyes shut for a beat without fearing we are suddenly going to hydroplane. I am still manning the speakers, which have been turned up higher on this drive back than on our drive out here because we haven't been talking as much. Hunter has tried to start up a conversation multiple times, but I have been dispassionately responding in a quiet, remote voice that sometimes I barely recognize, so it is not his fault. Whenever he says something that isn't a question but an observation that he is clearly hoping provokes a response, I am a computer chip that has overheated, malfunctioning from the inside, unable to be read. I'm here but not here.

The bizarreness of Kate's inebriated corridor tête-à-tête compounded with the anxiety that's been swelling ever since I got my hands on her diary and the terrible nightmare-filled sleep I got won't allow me to be affable. I passed out in the middle of reading the first entry, which was nothing but Kate complaining about Scott working so often. Her anomalous display of concern is what spawned the tumultuous sleep that finally released me with sweat pooled at my collarbone and dripping down my sternum.

So during this ride back to the city, I do my best to avoid Hunter's eyes, but every now and then he manages to catch mine, and I flash him a little smile that I hope is warm but uninviting. I still keep seeing Scott when I look at him for too long, especially his profile, which is pretty much copied and pasted from his old man. The eyes are what's different. Same hue, same deep-set broodiness, but Hunter's eyes have this soft openness that Scott's are missing.

Hunter didn't knock on my door this morning until slightly after nine and he was still in his sweatpants and white tube socks, hair an unwashed mess, sleep still crusty in the corners of his eyes, which made me feel better for answering the door without having even brushed my teeth. His voice was low and gravelly as he told me Kate was making us brunch and was expecting us to report to the massive kitchen island soon.

Brunch was lean and caffeine-free—egg-white omelets, gluten-free whole-grain toast, grapefruit halves and pulpy flutes of orange juice—but I could tell Kate had spiked her glass with something stronger. She avoided my eyes for the vast majority of the meal, but whenever we did meet gazes, she gave no indication that she had any recollection of our impromptu midnight run-in. Hunter offered to help her clean up the kitchen, but she shooed him out. We went in the back and watched the rain beat down on the pool. Hunter got giddy without warning, grabbed my wrist, then pulled his keys from his pocket, and before I knew it, we were back in his Audi, the engine idle as we stared at the empty public library. He hadn't clued me in on where he was taking me, so I couldn't remind him that the branch is closed on Sundays before he wasted gas and time that I could have spent poring through Kate's diary. We just sat there caught up in nostalgia for the better part of an hour, cocooned by the leather of his seats, blanketed by the kind of silence that feels whole. The rain slowed, stopped, then came back with a vengeance.

"Want to grab food when we get back?" Hunter asks. "There's this place in the Village—"

"I have lunch with my dad later. Don't wanna get too full."

"Right. It's Sunday."

Getting food is too much like a date, and I can't push off reading Kate's diary for another second. I need to know everything she knew about Scott and Mom.

Hunter quietly mans the wheel for the next handful of miles. I watch him for a few moments and feel bad for how short I've been since we've been on the road. I don't want to talk, but I also don't want to burn this bridge I've just started building with him.

"Confession?" I wait for him to switch off his blinker and settle into the inside lane. "I never saw you as the getting-married-super-young type."

He smiles, though he looks uncomfortable. "Me either. Guess I just got caught up. It's what my dad did…"

He shrugs as if it was that simple for him. And I guess it was. I don't know if Scott Bishop is Hunter's hero, but he definitely revered him, or at least his guidance, and it boggles my mind how someone as good as Hunter can be so blind.

"Everybody at my job is obsessed with getting a ring, and I always feel so left out," I say, and he chuckles.

"Your frontal lobe still hasn't finished developing. You have plenty of time to find someone to spend the rest of your life with."

"No. Left out because I'm not into it. Marriage isn't for me."

He makes a face. "Love the conviction you said that with, as if you've ever tried it."

I look at him and can't tell if I've offended him. "Not to take a huge shit on marria—"

"It's okay to shit on marriage a little. I mean, if my ex and I never got hitched, we'd probably still be together."

He doesn't really sound sad about it, more like shameful. I understand that. I wonder if he and his ex-wife had a big wedding with a guest list in the triple digits, if they bought property together, planned to have kids, had mundane fights about clumps of hair left in the shower drain and toilet seats left up.

"To me it's just an illusion of modern happiness," I say. "I'd rather actually be happy."

He considers that for a while. "My dad was going through his divorce when I proposed. Guess me proposing was kinda like me setting out to prove to myself that a good marriage could actually exist. And I failed just like him, so go figure."

Another shrug. I shift my eyes from him and stare at the windshield wipers. History repeated itself, but that was the least interesting thing from what Hunter just shared.

"Your mom initiated the divorce?" I ask, and I immediately cringe at how invested in this question I sound. I have to play this cool. I'm fucking this up.

"No. Why?"

I shrug, hoping it makes me seem nonchalant. "Just figured your mom would have been the one to file because of his..."

His infidelity.

"No," he says, getting it without me saying the word. "As long as they looked happy to everyone else, she was down to clean his underwear and cook his dinner. Dad would've had to do something way worse than cheat on her for her to leave him."

I nod, thinking of the optics. "Like ruin the picture somehow."

"Like completely annihilate it."

Traffic becomes more intense as we near the toll booth. Hunter concentrates on maneuvering through the mild chaos, which gives me a chance to catch up with my thoughts. Hunter said they divorced recently, so I try to come up with reasons after twenty-something years Scott would decide to finally leave his wife. Maybe he found someone else, someone even younger than Kate who was worth taking the plunge for. Maybe the answer will be in Kate's diary.

We don't realize we've left the umbrellas Kate reminded us to take from the bin in the foyer until Hunter pulls over to the curb a couple of blocks away from my apartment building. I insist that I'm fine, tell him he shouldn't walk me to my door because he'll be cold and itchy on his drive into Manhattan, but he hops out of his Audi with me, and by the time we're huddled up under the awning, we are both soaked to the bone and slightly breathless. His hair looks darker and the longest strands stick to his temples and cheekbones. His T-shirt clings to his torso. I can make out every contour, every ripple, and also his nipples, which only reminds me that he can probably see mine too, so I fold my arms over my chest, pretending like I'm cold.

It's not the first time we've been caught in the rain, but it's the first time there is expectancy in place of exhilaration. This is the part where I'm supposed to invite him up, tell him to take off his wet clothes and offer him coffee or tea to warm him up while I tumble dry his jeans and T-shirt. He's supposed to pat his hair and face and neck with one of my towels and smell me on the terry cloth, then realize it's not me he's smelling, just my detergent, but inhale deeply anyway because it's most likely the scent that's also on my sheets, and if he sniffs hard enough and closes his eyes, he will be able to imagine being in those sheets with me, nothing but fresh sweat and moans between us.

"So," he says, a glint in his eyes.

This is that moment. Since I'm obviously not going to invite Hunter up, this is when we are supposed to kiss goodbye, only the kiss turns into a sequence of kisses that deepen with each one and bring our bodies together. We are supposed to shiver from the rain drenching our skin, but the heat from our bodies pressed up against one another would combat that coldness, make us momentarily invincible to the elements. Hard and soft, tall and petite, we are supposed to fit together perfectly, like we've been engineered for each other's pleasure and convenience. And just when he draws back to finally give me a true goodbye, I'm supposed to pull him back and ask him to come upstairs, but we aren't supposed to make it to the third floor, where my unit awaits us. We are supposed to give in to the carnal pull between us, succumb to the magnetism right there on the steps like no one else is home. We are supposed to fuck passionately, desperately, making sounds of agony, doing our best to make up for all the years lost between us in a few minutes. It's supposed to be the kind of sex that makes us smile in the moment and tear up later when we're snuggled up in my bed still listening to the end of the rain thrum against the windowpane.

But I have lied and I would never do Reggie like that.

"What floor are you on?" Hunter asks, and I take a deep breath.

"Third. Last unit in the back."

"Decent view, huh? Want me to walk you up?"

"No, I'm fine. But thanks." I look up into his eyes and they look so dark, they almost don't seem blue anymore. "That was nice."

There's a small, almost imperceptible moment where I see him processing the subtle rejection. But he smiles anyway. This is Hunter. I don't know why I expected anything else.

"We should do it again," he says, then clarifies, "Not Jersey. Or my mom's house. You and me."

My eyes flutter, then drop down to my arms, which are still holding my torso. "Yeah, definitely."

"Dinner?"

"Text me."

But he lingers. Looking at me. Not wanting to leave, not wanting this to be over.

Then he laughs, and I can tell he is embarrassed, and part of me wishes I could rescue him. "I should…"

"Yeah," I say, but once I turn away to reach for the door, Hunter takes my arm, holding me in place. My sneakers are filled with water, my socks are soaked. It almost happens too fast for me to react, Hunter leaning down with his face angled so he can kiss my lips, but I manage to turn my cheek just in time. His lips stumble against my face. Then he pulls back, but I keep my chin down so I don't have to see the dejection on his face.

"I have to shower and get ready to drive back down—"

"Sorry, I…" He shakes his head, and I can almost feel his shame leap from his body into mine. "Tell your father I said hello."

I appreciate the smile he flashes before backing away.

I also appreciate the way his jeans cling to his quads as he makes his way back across the street to his car for way too long, and I feel like I've deceived Reggie as I climb the steps up to my unit, even though this is all merely a means to uncover the truth on my end.

18

I CAN'T PLACE where I am when my eyes pop open. Reggie is standing over me, so I assume he's just called my name or shaken me awake, but I can't immediately piece together why he looks so concerned, like a puppy I forgot to feed.

I glance around. I'm on the couch, legs curled under my butt. Then I see it. The book I was reading before I passed out. It all comes back to me in distorted sections, the third entry of the diary.

When Kate mentions Scott possibly sleeping with someone else behind her back the first time, it's not news to her. It's like she'd already been suspecting it for months, maybe even longer at that point, which was about six months after she quit her job. So my theory about her quitting her job coinciding with her becoming aware of Scott's shady behavior has legs. Maybe she thought if she was at the house more often and was less exhausted from the long office hours and daily commute into the city that she could stop him from straying.

The silly things us women think.

"What happened?" Reggie asks, and I can tell I'm still missing a piece or two.

"What are you...?" I grab my phone. "What time is it?"

I don't wait for him to tell me. I spot my phone and glance at the time, but I'm quickly distracted by the banner that lets me know I've missed four calls and six texts from Reggie all in the last fifteen minutes.

"We have to get there by two," he says.

I slap my forehead. "Shit."

Dad. How the hell did I fall asleep? I'm not prepared to wing this. Reggie is the first guy I'll be pushing forward for appraisal and I don't even know what I want. To impress my dad? His approval? I didn't even plan my outfit. What do you wear that pleases both your dad and lover and doesn't break prison rules?

"Why weren't you answering your phone?" Reggie asks. "I've been downstairs for twenty minutes."

I jump up from the couch and head over to my closet. "Why didn't you come get me sooner?"

"Thought you were just running late."

"When do I ever run late?"

I strip away my clothes and pull out three casual dresses. I toss the first one on the bed, then hold up two in the mirror before I decide on the right one.

"You okay?"

Reggie sounds concerned, so I decide to fill him in. "I got caught up in reading."

"You're always getting on me about working and now..."

I peek back and see him spotting the gently battered diary on the couch.

"Oh. That." He sounds surprised, like he doubted I'd complete my mission. "You got it."

But he doesn't know I didn't wear pants when I got in the car with Hunter and bypassed the perfect opportunity to tell him I have a man when we were alone and huddled up in his mother's attic.

Reggie walks over and picks it up, flips through the first half.

"I was nervous that Scott stopped sleeping with my mom after she died," I say, grabbing a pair of shoes from my top shelf.

Reggie looks at me, aghast. "Whoa, whoa, whoa. Run that back."

"No," I say, hearing now that it sounded like I was insinuating that Scott is not only an adulterer and murderer, but also a necrophiliac. "Hunter's grandma. After Hunter's *grandma* died."

"Shit. I was about to say."

I'm about to forge on, but then realize I've never really filled Reggie in on this part of my past. "My mom was a nurse before we moved to Asher Lane. She didn't need to work anymore, but Mrs. Bishop had advanced dementia. So she offered to help Scott with her since he was always in court and Kate was basically apathetic."

Reggie nods, and we're back on track.

"I was hoping it hadn't ended when she died because that would mean the baby was my father's. At least, more likely."

"And Scott wouldn't have had any reason to want your mom dead," Reggie says, still nodding.

"Exactly."

"But it continued after that?" he asks.

I nod. "The last entry is dated *one week* before Mom died. Kate was getting divorce papers drawn up. Look, her words…"

I flip to the last handwritten entry and point to the lower third of the page.

I'm serving him as soon as my attorney is done preparing the papers. That way the bastard can fuck his little cunt all she wants.

Reggie pauses. *"Little cunt?"*

It's the same reaction I had when I read it. Yes, my mother

was sleeping with her husband, but the *c* word was uncalled-for, even in a private diary. I have to also remind myself that Kate didn't know who she was writing about when she called my mother that name, but I wonder if she had, would her words have been even harsher? Would she have thrown in *nigger*? *Nigger cunt*. After years of friendship and neighborly camaraderie, as shallow or as superficial as it may have been, would my mom have been reduced to those slurs if Kate realized she'd been sleeping with her husband?

"But I thought you said she already knew the hubs was fucking around," Reggie says. "What made her suddenly file for divorce?"

I move close to him and flip around so he can zip my dress. "Hunter said Kate was willing to stay with Scott unless he did something that ruined the look of their perfect family."

"Oh, a light-skinned baby would've fucked that picture all the way up." He finishes the zipper and scans the rest of the page. "Did she mention the pregnancy in here?"

I shake my head. "Mom was only three months along when they found her body. She'd probably just found out herself."

He nods. "True."

If my mom's affair with Scott lasted until she died, there's no doubt: that baby was Scott's. That baby, that unborn life, is what stole my mom's life from me.

"After Mom found out, she must have gone straight to Scott so they could figure out what they were gonna do. Maybe he wanted her to get rid of it, and she wanted to keep it. Maybe they both wanted to keep it. Either way, Scott doesn't have a choice but to confess to Kate, and when he does, she flips, gets the papers drawn up, and that brings us to here," I say, motioning to the diary entry he's just read.

Reggie does the kind of slow nod that lets me know he's followed every word I've said and is still processing. And as my speculation hangs in the air, something else clicks. Ever since last night, I haven't been able to stop thinking about Kate being so concerned about whether I was on the pill. I still can't get past how she doesn't see that her son is not the kind of man who would force me, or anyone, to get an abortion.

I assumed Kate was trying to intimidate me into staying away from Hunter, trying to scare me away from her son by insinuating that he is only interested in me for sex. Now I see that's not why she felt compelled to have that bizarre talk with me. It wasn't just the cabernet binge she'd been on that loosened her tongue. She's been through this. Not exactly this, not physically. But she knows what her callous husband did and does not want history to repeat itself.

Now I understand exactly what Kate was trying to tell me, I see how she was trying to *help* me. Scott Bishop tried to force my mother to abort her baby because he knew better than to disrupt the aesthetic of their holiday card. When Mom refused, he took matters into his own hands and got rid of the baby himself.

"Scott got scared she would leave, so he did what he had to do to protect *the picture*," I say, using air quotes, and the way Reggie looks at me, I know he gets it now. He knows I'm onto something and this isn't just me turning real life into a mystery novel.

I expect him to throw around a couple of his favorite terms like *confirmation bias* or *logical fallacy*, but he doesn't. Still, being the lawyer that he is, he is probably thinking the same thing I'm thinking: How am I going to prove it?

I also lied to Reggie and told him I was a virgin our first night together so he wouldn't feel bad about not being able to get hard enough to do all the things he'd been promising he'd do for weeks. I'd actually been with two other guys, but the first time was way back when I was sixteen and this boy tried to stick his dick in my urethra and the second guy was my freshman year of college with this rookie firefighter who barely got the tip in before he hosed my rib cage down, which in the moment was tragic but in hindsight was the best-case scenario since he'd gotten whiny about using a condom. So in no way was I experienced my first night with Reggie, but it was also not my first rodeo. I figured it would take the pressure off him to perform and also showed I had no prior experience to compare him to. He said he was nervous. He was sweating profusely and had been stuttering over his words since we started walking back to his place from the Cajun restaurant he took me to. Maybe it was my fault, maybe me whispering at the table *I wanna do it tonight* five minutes after we opened our menus built up too much pressure. Even after I helped him get fully hard, he was still wound too tight. Now he was worried about hurting me, even more nervous about seeing blood. I told him my hymen was no longer intact due to me learning the splits at dance camp when I was nine, which is truthfully how that happened, and I legit saw some of the tension abandon his body as he laughed. The next morning while he made me tea and I washed my hair in his freestanding shower, I debated coming clean but decided against it, figuring it would be way more complicated to explain why I lied than to maintain the lie with any obligatory subsequent lies that took.

That is the only lie I haven't come clean to Reggie about. Until now.

It is not that almost-kiss Hunter initiated that is haunting me, or how long it took before I drew back and swerved, though I do feel bad that my reaction time was so delayed. What is gnawing at me is that I haven't told Reggie I intentionally let Hunter assume I am available so I could get him to take me to his mother's house, and have maintained the pretext since in case there is something else I need him for in my efforts to prove his father murdered my mother. It's technically an omission, but a lie is a lie is a lie.

Reggie and my dad erupt with laughter for the umpteenth time since we've been at our table. We are the loudest ones in the entire space, all the white people here to see their loved ones constantly looking over like there is some kind of minstrel show going on. It's the first time I've seen Dad laugh a full laugh since his arrest. I have Reggie to thank for that, and it only makes the lies taste even more sour.

I don't realize I've gone catatonic until I feel the heat from Reggie's palm on the top of my thigh. It is innocent enough, but I'm so glad my dad can't see through the metal tabletop. I am not the cool, irreverent girl who can handle her man groping her bare skin in her father's presence.

"You okay?" he whispers in my ear.

I see even more concern flash in his gaze when he feels how I involuntarily jerked at his touch. I nod vigorously, overcompensating, but I know he is probably still suspicious of my bizarre reaction.

"Just cold," I whisper, and if jackets were allowed, I'm sure he would slide his over my shoulders, which would make me feel small and delicate. Instead, he rubs my leg back and forth a few times, and the friction does help. When I glance up, I catch my dad smiling. A real smile, not just one left over from laughter, which stuns me. It's not the first, but it's the brightest one he's gifted me with since he's been here.

"So, Reggie," my dad says, setting his Coke down. "I like you. I like what I've heard about you. You've got a lot going for you. But what are your intentions with my daughter?"

Immediately, the air in the room is different. Reggie glances at me, panic in his eyes. Then his gaze is back on Dad.

"What?" I object. *"Dad."*

He's still jovial. "Let him answer."

"You guys just met two-point-five seconds ago," I say.

"It's fine," Reggie says, shooting me a small smile before taking a chug from his water bottle like we are suddenly stranded in the middle of the Sahara.

When he sets the empty bottle down and parts his lips, I realize my attempt to derail this line of questioning was not fueled by my impulse to rescue Reggie from being forced to go through the awkwardness of explaining his *intentions*. It's that I don't want to hear his intentions myself. *I'm* the one who feels awkward, not Reggie. He looks nervous, sure, but only because he's being put on the spot by the man who provided one of the X chromosomes that created the woman he'll be sharing a bed with tonight.

"Well, I can honestly say I've never felt the way I feel about your daughter." Reggie glances at me with a smile, and I hold my breath when he shifts his gaze back to Dad's. "I love her. I have no intentions of hurting her."

And now I understand why people claim *love* is a strong word. Its power, its magnificence, its weight crushes me and puts a tentative smile on my father's face. Reggie has never said those three words to me, not even when he is about to come like some men do. It is not that I don't believe them that makes my heart pound like I'm being attacked. It is that I do.

"Love ain't much," Dad says, lifting his drink. "What are you gonna do about it?"

The question nearly triggers my fight-or-flight response. It's a challenge, maybe even a dare.

So many parts of me violently reject the question. Why does something have to be done about love? Why can't love just be love? Why do we insist on caging it and limiting it to the confines of an antiquated institution? Has no one ever seen an owl behind bars at the zoo?

"Dad." My teeth are clenched, eyes wide.

He shrugs innocently. "I just want to know if the young man sees a future with you. A *serious* future. Or if he's just playing games." His gaze lands squarely onto Reggie's again.

"I do," he responds, sounding so confident, in full lion mode. "I see myself marrying her. With your blessing, of course."

It's all so formal, so retrograde, so suffocating. We've never discussed marriage or the future. I'm parched and drowning from the inside. I can't do this right now, not tonight. I want to figure out my next move now that I have Kate's diary.

"Well, you better start joining our Sunday meals," Dad says, lifting his bottle yet again, this time to signal a toast. "It's a tradition. A *family* tradition."

It's true. Even though I now have to question why my mother would always insist on showering before Sunday brunches after she'd come from helping Scott with his mother next door.

Reggie lifts his bottle and takes my free hand under the table as we all pretend the plastic makes that happy clinking sound multiple glasses make when they touch. My smile feels strained, but I don't think either of them notice. Reggie leans over and kisses me on the forehead, and the toothy smile on my father's face breaks my heart. He hasn't looked this happy since my mother was alive.

19

A COUPLE OF hours later, Reggie is already halfway naked, but my mind is still on the idea of him attending all my Sunday visits with my dad, the only face-to-face time I get with him these days.

"Sorry about my dad putting you in the hot seat like that," I say, tying my hair up with a scrunchie. "He just wants to make sure his only daughter is taken care of or whatever, especially while he's in there. You know how dads are."

Reggie shrugs. "Not really since mine never cared to meet me. But it's cool."

"Well, Dad also has this complex now because of everything that happened. He feels like he failed being a provider, which he didn't. But his feelings are his feelings and now he wants me to be with someone safe." I cringe at how that sounds. "Not like a seat belt. Like..."

"Six figures, 401(k) safe." His laugh is soft and understanding. "I get it."

It seems so anti-romantic when he puts it like that, but he doesn't sound put off by the idea like I was hoping he would. He slinks behind me and curves his arms around my waist like we're about to pose for our '90s prom photo. My nipples go hard at the slow, damp kisses he places on the nape of my neck.

"You know I meant what I said, right?" he whispers.

That's what I was afraid of.

I moan and pretend the kisses are what has inspired my hesitation. "Thought you said marriage isn't that important to you."

"That was when we first started hanging out. Before you got me hooked." He pauses and his voice gets more serious. "I mean, what am I doing if I'm not planning on making this official one day, right?"

I exhale a breath. "Yeah."

He circles around me and looks at me for real. He smiles, and I know he can't tell that I am lying. Because I'd essentially built our relationship on a huge lie, Reggie doesn't know when I'm not being honest with him, and it makes me wonder if I would be able to tell if he was being dishonest with me in such close proximity.

"I know things have been weird the past couple months, but once I settle in at G&W, it'll be the way we used to be and we can talk about all this more seriously, okay?"

"Maybe we should talk toni—"

But he steals my tongue so talking isn't exactly a possibility anymore and it's only a few moments before I feel how much he wants me, how much the prospect of me becoming his wife one day has turned him on.

He makes sure I am warm and ready for him by the time we are both naked, but once my face is in the pillows and his hands are on my hips, my cacophonous thoughts crowd my mind and I go numb to his rhythmic stroking, his possessive touch. It is like when you're at the dentist and you can see something being done to you, but your nerves are stunned, so your brain doesn't process the pain. There is no pain as Reggie builds momentum inside me, but there is also no pleasure. There's nothing. I've become one of those women I used to mock, just lying under him, inert, waiting for this to be over with. I panic for a second, becoming aware that I've been practically immobile since he's been inside me, worried that my indolence will render his erection limp and useless. But then I hear it. The guttural sound that escapes from the pit of his throat as his body shudders on top of mine.

He is still slightly breathless when he plops over onto his back. "Did you come?"

"Um…"

He stares at me, and I am so ashamed because I can immediately tell I am caught.

Reggie pushes up so his weight is on his elbows and his abs are contracted, all the ripples showing like he has been carved by a genius. "You were about to lie."

It is not a question. He sounds more shocked than angry. I am actually pretty surprised at myself too, but it's not like he has ever asked me this before. Maybe he is actually becoming more attuned to my emotions and can read my small hesitations better. Or maybe it's easier for him to spot the small lies yet still remain blind to the bigger ones.

"I…" I really don't see any other way out of this. "It's late."

"What?" He genuinely sounds baffled at my totally sensible excuse, and I silently curse whoever taught him about sex, who taught him to be such an egalitarian lover, because I just want this moment to be over, but at the same time I would very much like to send them a gift basket filled with expensive chocolate and juicy fruit. Maybe it was one of his brothers. He has two much older brothers.

"I know you have to get up early," I say, though I know it isn't enough.

Reggie shakes his head, not willing to hear any more. I am stiff with searing embarrassment, but he flips me on my back effortlessly and slides two middle fingers between my legs.

Sometimes I feel bad that I mostly prefer his fingers over his penis because I can only imagine the degree of damage that kind of truth could do to his ego. There is absolutely nothing wrong with his penis; it is beautiful, straight and just the right amount of thickness, but there is something more precise about his fingers, and I love that when he is moving them inside me, he is not fighting against the pursuit of his own pleasure. Mine is his only concern. When he glances up at me with this giddy smile on his face, I smile back, hoping it will absolve me from my guilt. He holds my eyes and tells me I am *so fucking beautiful* and it makes me want to suck on what is left of his erection until it is soft and spongy on my tongue, then keep sucking it until it is rigid like a weapon again, give him blow two times in a row so that the second time there is barely anything left and I can briefly be one of those cool girls who doesn't pull back when her man tells her he's about to come.

A distorted memory pierces my subconscious and rips me from a terrible car-brakes-don't-work dream hardly an hour after I dozed off. On one of my visits to see Dad in his holding cell while he was waiting for his grand jury hearing, he told me about a rumor that was going around. It was being whispered that Scott Bishop had popped in to have a word with the DA. I was too young to understand the significance of that at the time, but now I realize it's one of the pieces to the puzzle. Dad assumed Scott had gone to the DA to speak for him, to do his neighborly duty. He even mailed him a note thanking him once the trial was over, convinced it helped despite the conviction.

But Scott didn't speak for my dad. He went to the DA to

make sure he would not be considered a suspect. That could have meant saying something that would further implicate Dad or just making sure he was not implicated himself.

He went there to cover his ass, but Scott Bishop's tighty-whities are going to be pooled around his ankles once I'm done with him.

20

IT WAS SUPPOSED to be a onetime thing, but of course one time turned into two. Into three. Weeks passed. A few months went by. Every time we met things got more intense and it was around month three when my guilt had finally started to wane. Getting out of the car was always the hardest part. Sometimes I'd catch you gazing at me a little too long after I got dressed. I could feel it, you wondering what it would be like to leave your wife for me. I never said anything, and neither did you, because we both already knew the answer.

Still, you were always talking about leaving your wife, how you'd do it, what you'd say. I never batted an eye. You were strong and fearless when it came to your career, but in every other facet of your life, you were the type of man who talked instead of actually doing. It was more of a fantasy for you, a theoretical mental exercise that seemed to work like a placebo. You were too concerned about other people's feelings to ever put yourself first if it meant hurting someone else, even if they deserved it. That's why it took you so long to admit to yourself that you were attracted to me. You were afraid that if you admitted it, you'd be tempted to do something about it. You fought it for a while. Just the thought of you hurting your wife—even with all her faults—killed something inside of you.

You didn't need to worry. Your wife would never find out and neither would my husband. We were beyond careful. I wasn't stupid and neither were you. This was Asher Lane. People were well-groomed, professional. Conservative and judgmental and uptight. My husband's kind of people. Everyone talked. Rule number one, of course, was always use protection, no matter what, which we did. You told me you had gotten a vasectomy one year after your wife gave birth to your son, but I insisted. Crazier things had happened. We also agreed from the beginning that calling each other at home was unacceptable.

When your birthday came around, though, you seemed to forget all the rules. You turned fifty and it was as if suddenly you were looking at the totality of your life all at once and wondering where you'd gone wrong. I tried to calm you down. You told me you just wanted to be happy, you were tired of putting on a show for everyone else and just wanted to be free. You said you wanted to be with me. I tried to talk some sense into you, but you wouldn't listen. You were frantic, speaking over yourself, barely allowing yourself to get out the words. You began shouting. You said something about taking control.

"I can leave her," you said in your most stern voice. "I'll do it. Just say the word and I'll leave her." You were breathless, almost panting.

I pulled you back into the room and tugged at your clothes. Your neck. We kissed. My phone rang in my bag, but I ignored it. I moaned in your mouth and told you what you wanted to hear, that you made me happy, but that the time was just not right for me to leave my husband. I had to do it when the time was right. I pulled you to the bed. Sex happened. Afterward, you were much calmer, your head clearer. You turned to me and said, "Thanks," then pulled your pants back on.

I felt good. Powerful. You thanked me again on your way out the door, saying you couldn't believe how late it was already, that your wife was probably worried.

When I finally checked my phone in the car, I had three missed calls. All from my husband. I thought about calling him back, but I didn't want to talk to him now. He would only ruin the moment and I wanted to ride out this feeling for as long as I could. It felt as if I were floating, like I was in total control of the situation.

Eventually, I drove home, not because I wanted to, but because I had to. Before I could even step foot into the living room, my husband was on his feet, still dressed in his work clothes, shoes scuffing the freshly waxed floors.

"Hey," he said. "Where were you? I tried to call you but kept getting your voice mail."

His voice sounded severe, like he was truly concerned, and a part of me softened, because this was all I wanted. Some consideration, some hint that I still mattered, that I wasn't a ghost. That he still cared.

"Sorry, honey," I said, dropping my bag by the door. I didn't stop. "You know how I get when I'm at the gym."

I headed for the stairs, unzipping my jacket.

"I thought you didn't go to the gym today?"

"You know I go to the gym on Thursdays at six," I said at the landing, moving faster now.

He tilted his head. "I stopped by there earlier and the guy at the front desk said he didn't see you today."

I nearly tripped and fell back down the three stairs I'd climbed.

My heart pounded in my chest. "You came by today?" I asked, stalling, my mind racing in multiple directions at once.

"Yeah. A half hour ago. Wanted to see if you wanted to go out to dinner tonight."

I felt short of breath. I didn't know if he was testing me or not. I didn't know how much he knew. And what did he mean, go out for dinner? We hadn't gone out in at least a year. It felt like a trick. Suddenly, it felt as if everything was so close to unraveling and I wondered how he would react if he knew the truth.

My husband was not a violent man. At least, not around me. I'd never seen him hit someone or even raise his voice, really. There was that one time, though, when we were first dating and some drunk idiot bumped into me while we were out. His beer splattered all over my top. My husband had been at the bar getting us drinks, and when he came back over, I told him what had happened. That the guy tried to ask me for my number but ended up spilling his drink all over me. "Next time, come get me and I'll fuck the asshole up," he'd said, dryly. I laughed. I thought he was joking. But then he repeated himself, saying he was serious.

That might have been the sexiest thing he'd ever said to me.

I still couldn't see it, him ever hurting me, or anyone, not in that way. But every man had his breaking point. I didn't know what he was truly capable of. I could feel the tips of my fingers growing damp.

"I...got sick," I finally said, keeping my head down. "I never made it inside, was just sitting in my car for a while, hoping it would pass. Just decided to come back home."

He seemed not to pick up on my lie—he looked only concerned now, which made me feel a little bad, but relieved at the same time. "You okay? What is it? The flu or something?"

"No... I don't know. I just felt nauseous. Maybe I ate something bad. I had sushi for lunch. I think that was probably it."

"You should have called me. I could've come and picked you up. How do you feel now?"

"Better. But still a little out of it, you know. I just need to rest, I think."

"Want me to come upstairs with you?"

"No," I said, a little too quickly, and I saw it on his face, the way his eyebrow twitched the slightest bit. He didn't believe me. I could almost see the wheels turning in his head.

But then he looked away and cleared his throat, his expression resigned. "Okay. I'll come check on you later."

I forced a smile and headed up the stairs, feeling his eyes on me the whole time. I locked myself in the bathroom and hopped right into the shower. I turned on the water as hot as I could stand, dipped my head back under the steam and washed my face, my hair, every inch of my body, trying to remove every trace of your scent from my skin. I rinsed, then lathered up again. When I made it into the bedroom, a text popped up on my phone. Holler if you need anything. There's some Pepto-Bismol in the medicine cabinet.

It felt off. Eerie. The timing of it all. He was never this sweet, this thoughtful. I wondered if he knew. If he'd been following me somehow and he had found out the truth. Maybe he'd tracked my car.

I climbed into bed and thought back to the night we met, wondering what my life would have been like had we not made eye contact. If I never gave him the opening to come over and speak to me. If I said no when he asked me for my number.

He was so much different back then, more free-spirited, spontaneous, fun even. Tall and fit and confident, the kind of man who could sweep a woman off her feet and make every other man seem incompetent, a weak comparison. He wore tailored suits, asked how my family was doing whenever he'd pick me up for a date, wined and dined me, and never asked for head in the back of his car, which at the time I thought was pretty standard. That baffled me. My friends all agreed; he was "classy." We talked, we touched, we cuddled, but he was hesitant to make the first real move. I thought it was endearing, so different from every other man I'd been with. In my experience up until that point, men were overly eager, detached. He was the opposite. Affectionate. Attentive. Needy almost. He was never shy about showing the way he felt about me, used to reach for my hand when we'd be out, even if no one else was around. It was romantic, this compulsive little gesture. Almost like a tic, as if he couldn't stand the idea of us not touching, not being connected in some kind of way. I wanted him so bad, by the time we did sleep together, I already knew he'd be the one.

Things moved quickly after that. I was consumed, and so was he. We spent almost all of our free time together. Taking long drives down to the shore on the weekends. Sitting on the couch with our legs intertwined. Back in those days it was nice just to be in each other's presence, to be touching, talking, near. I laughed at all his jokes and I wasn't pretending. He proposed in front of my family after eight months, got down on his knee and did the whole bit. There was even a *speech*. The wedding was magical. His father loved me, called me the daughter he never had. He played golf less often then. He accompanied me to the grocery store just so we could spend more time together. He called me at work sometimes just to talk on his lunch break and we'd gossip about people at my job, who was fucking who.

Things started to change after I got pregnant. After the baby came. It started out wonderful. I loved the idea of being pregnant, of this soon-to-be person who was completely and utterly dependent on me. It gave me a new purpose, fueled every decision I made. I knew it would change me forever. I was ready. I enjoyed watching my belly grow, feeling the weight of my breasts as they filled with milk. I went shopping every chance I got, picking out blankets and knitted hats and teeny-tiny pink bootees. We'd agreed from the start to have the gender be a surprise, but I just *knew* I was having a girl. I felt it. I already had names picked out in my head.

My body changed more and more every day and I could feel that it wasn't just physical. And then once I gave birth, I knew I'd never be the same ever again. I loved being a mother. Seeing the amalgamation of both of us. Those big round eyes and full lips. Some of him and some of me.

I wasn't expecting my husband to change too. It was like I was no longer my own entity in his eyes, I was only a means to an end. I no longer felt like the woman I'd worked so hard to become. Independent, dynamic, capable—the opposite of my mother. I felt like someone's wife. A dutiful robot. And sometimes, a child. That's how he treated me, how he spoke to me, even in front of company, the neighbors, as if I were supposed to just go along with his every command without qualm or question.

I loved being with the baby, but after a while I grew bored. I needed to be around adults, I needed interaction with the outside world. I wanted to go back to work. But my husband wanted me to quit my job and become a full-time mother like all the other wives on the block because it "looked better." *It was the way things were supposed to be.* He also expressed his wariness of nannies, that he didn't trust some stranger around his baby. His mother had raised him all on her own and he wanted the same for his child. I suspected she was the one who pitted him against the idea in the first place. She'd never liked me or the fact that I worked in New York and made my own money. A lot of money. She was jealous, but I could never say that to him. In the end, I did it because I wanted him to be happy and I truly thought it was for the best. It made sense. I could always go back to work later, like a lot of women did. I trusted that it would work out, I trusted him. He was my everything. My best friend. My confidant. The father of my child. I thought I knew him. I thought I knew myself.

As time passed, he became more distant, more involved with work. He also became very secretive, and occasionally, very patronizing. He couldn't or simply wouldn't understand why I wanted to go back to work and was always admonishing me whenever I'd take interest in anything else besides our kid. We argued more. We fought like we'd never fought before. He hated that I'd yell and would stop talking to me for days on end, just to punish me. It was vicious. Just to avoid the fights, we talked less, texted more. He avoided being home and I started sleeping more, just to pass the time. We barely had sex, and when we did, it was brief, dull. This went on for months. Years. There were moments of reprieve, times when we would cuddle in bed like we used to in the beginning and fall asleep on each other's chests. Sometimes I'd leave the bathroom door slightly ajar while I showered and we'd talk through the crack while he got dressed. But these moments were few and far between. Most of the time I couldn't even remember the last time we'd touched, let alone said *I love you.*

Last year was the final straw. It was our fifteenth anniversary. Our child was no longer a child. I wanted to finally get back to who we were before the baby, before everything changed. I cleaned the house and cooked dinner—lasagna, his favorite. I had planned out everything I was going to say and practiced a few times in the mirror. When he got home he said it had been a long day and headed straight for the shower. I followed him into the bathroom, my feet silent on the tiled floor, the mirror already starting to fog up. He noticed me before I could open the shower door completely and stuck his hand against the metal.

"Can we do this later?" he asked. "Just need to clear my head, okay?"

I nodded and said nothing, his calm, steadfast dismissal of me like a knife in the back, driving in slow and all at once.

Of course, we didn't do anything later.

21

MAYBE THERE IS some kind of record, a text, an email, something that would prove that Scott tried to pay my mom to have the abortion and keep her mouth shut. I don't know how I could get my hands on this, if it even exists. I don't know if there is something Hunter is not telling me. I don't know if he knows more about his dad's affair with my mom. He was older, only a few years but at that age a few years makes a big difference. He could have seen things. Maybe not them actually fucking again. Other things.

Right now all I have is conjecture. Speculation. The only evidence I have to back up my theory is Kate's diary, which is currently in my lap but only confirms the affair. Before I reach out to Pia again, I need something that will get me to the murder, to Scott forcing my mom to have an abortion, to her refusing to have the procedure done and Scott getting rid of the problem in his unique way.

I only have two more days to figure out what else Hunter

knows without letting him know I'm investigating. I don't think I can get him to take me back to his father's house on Asher Lane without him asking questions I don't want to answer. The police never obtained a warrant to search their house because no one in the household was a suspect, so there is a possibility that I could find something in there that could prove Scott's involvement in Mom's murder, but I can't risk Hunter getting suspicious, so I'm going to have to come up with some other way to gather more intel.

The bullpen is starting to get loud as the cubicles fill up. I pause my audiobook, take out my earbuds, sit up straight and pull up an email draft in Outlook so it looks like I am on a work call when I hit up Hunter from my cell. I've already texted him a heads-up, and he answers before the second ring finishes. He sounds tired when he says my name, like he hasn't nursed his morning brew yet, and I try so hard to convince myself that those two small syllables didn't sound sexy under his gravelly modulation.

I didn't picture us doing small talk, but Hunter sounds genuinely interested in how my morning has gone so far. I answer him honestly, telling him that I woke up late and had to skip breakfast, and that on the train there was a guy standing next to me who kept accidentally rubbing against my ass every time the car jerked. His response to that is to tell me I was in his dream last night, and I have no idea what to do with that, so I start rambling about this absurd plot twist I just got to in the novel I listened to on this morning's commute. I expect him to zone out and throw in a few obligatory *wows* and *that's wilds* since it's what I've become accustomed to whenever I get overly bookish with Reggie, but he asks a couple of clarifying questions and even gives me a prediction of where he thinks the author is taking the story. It is the complete opposite of what I was theorizing and that makes me smile, affirmation that the book snob I converted him into twelve years ago is still alive in him somewhere.

"I can take my lunch whenever," I tell him, getting to the point of our call.

"Cool. I have a…"

His voice trails off. The pause is abrupt, so I imagine him looking up and politely gesturing to the person who has joined him in his office for them to give him a few moments. I have no idea if this is actually what causes the slight hiccup in our conversation, but it is reassuring to think this is the kind of priority I am in his life, to make a colleague wait instead of rushing me off the phone, so I go with it.

"Sorry," he says. He clears his throat, but when he speaks, his voice is still raspy. "I have a thirty-minute window between one and one thirty if you don't mind eating in my office."

Now I realize he was probably just looking at his schedule, and I feel a bit foolish.

"Whatever's easiest for you," I say.

"Cool. I'll slide you in." There is a pause. "Just sent you something," he says. "Text me what you want me to order for you."

My phone buzzes and a menu pops up. It's a vegan Mexican restaurant in Soho and I smile because I can't believe he remembered that Mexican food is my favorite. As I quickly scan the entrées, I think of his ex-wife. He probably spoiled the shit out of her, allowed her unlimited swipes of his black Amex. No matter how hard Reggie works, he will never be able to spend with the kind of abandon that Hunter can. He has no cushion. There are no seven-figure properties being left to him.

"Thanks, Hunter," I say, suddenly wanting to get him out of my ear, and not just because I've spotted Matt across the space. "Appreciate it."

"It's on the company," he says dismissively, and I simultaneously feel better and worse. Better because it means Hunter isn't actually buying me lunch and that seems like a lighter transgression. Worse because it reminds me how expendable I am to my own company. I'm not even worth having my lunch taken care of.

"No, I mean for making time for me," I say, though once the words are out of my mouth, I regret them.

It's true, I do appreciate him squeezing me into what has to be an intense day of meetings, calls, research and paperwork. But I hate that I keep comparing him and Reggie. Now all I can think of is how Reggie blew off our lunch date and how unlikely it is that Hunter will. It shouldn't matter. Hunter is clearly more established at his firm, and Reggie is doing everything he can to impress his new team while also working twice as hard for half as much. But it is impossible not to pit them against each other.

"Simone, it's me," Hunter says, and I know what he's trying to say—we're still friends, and as friends, it's nothing. I don't have to thank him for carrying out his friendly duties. But how can that be when we're totally different people? There is so much he doesn't know about me, about who I've become.

I end the call without saying another word.

"Damn. Reggie got you smiling like *that* in the middle of the day?"

I look up and see Jasmine hovering over me. I straighten out my face and tuck Kate's diary back into my bag. "That wasn't Reg," I tell her.

One of her microbladed brows goes up. "So who is making time for you?"

"Uh…" I can't even deal with her today. "Rachel in HR."

I can tell Jasmine isn't buying that, and I'm so stupid because I was using my cell, not the landline, so the suspicious look on her face is fully warranted, but luckily she gets distracted by a text.

"My sister is so aggravating." She huffs and hastily texts her back.

If Jasmine isn't complaining about her aggravating sister,

she's complaining about her annoying mother, discourse that is excruciating for me to endure, but I always smile and nod along as if I completely understand. Faking it in platonic relationships is less of an infraction, and it is better than Jasmine noticing how sad the conversation has made me.

"I always wonder if I was gonna have a sister or brother," I say, and I don't realize the words have slipped out until Jasmine looks up and cocks that perfect brow again.

"What?"

"Well, *half* sis—" I catch myself. "Nothing."

Jasmine looks like she wants to know more, but I am saved again, this time by Matt approaching my desk in his expected polo-and-chinos uniform that shows off his statement socks. Jasmine greets him, nearly inching down into a curtsy, and then he locks eyes with me from behind his thick-rimmed tortoiseshell frames.

"Do you have a few minutes for me?"

"Yeah, sure," I say, and then I'm staring at his crotch, not because I am remotely interested in whatever is there, but because his fly is down. It's completely open and I have never been so swiftly overtaken by secondhand embarrassment.

I expect him to step closer so people won't be privy to our conversation, but clearly I have misread the seriousness of his request because he leads me into his office and promptly shuts the door. The blinds are already down when I sit down in the chair he motions to. Suddenly, this feels like a confrontation and my mind is whirring because we're still months away from our quarterly progress check-in.

I don't know much about the man, so I am not quite sure how to read his tightly wound energy. I keep my distance between all of my colleagues, even Jasmine. Thank God he sits immediately after me so I don't have to endure any more unsolicited glimpses at his royal blue underwear.

"Listen," he starts, grabbing a pen from the cupholder on his messy desk and fidgeting with it with one hand. "There's no real way to ease into this, so I'm just going to cut to the chase. I know about your father."

His statement feels violent, only I can't decide if it's a threat or a warning.

I want to ask Matt what exactly he knows about my father. I want to ask him if he knows that my father is an army vet who was discharged with honor. If he knows my father had an 820 credit score and zero debt before he was sent to prison and probably made three times Matt's current salary—not including bonuses—before the investigation got underway.

But I know he's referring to his current incarceration status and so I say nothing. I brace myself for the next swing.

Matt remains mute, like he is waiting for my reaction.

"Does this change anything?" I finally ask, and it's all I'm willing to do to move this already cumbersome conversation along.

"Does this change anything?" he parrots, clearly attempting but failing to temper his incredulity. "It changes a lot, at least from my perspective."

"I don't understand," I say because I genuinely do not. I have not hidden this part of my past from him or this company because I was afraid it would be used against me.

I don't tell people my father is behind bars because they will inevitably get curious. They will open up a browser and see what kind of crime he's been convicted of, and once they not only find out it's a felony charge, but also that it's a life sentence for first-degree murder, they will see me differently and assume I've either not been nurtured properly or it's a nature thing, something in my genetics that links me to my father. I will no longer be looked at as an individual, but a composite of who I present myself to be and my father's conviction. I've hidden my past because I don't want to be probed by the questions. Because I hate that everyone who knows about the outcome of the trial always asks me about my dad and never my mom. They both got their lives taken from them, but only one has the chance to be resurrected.

"Simone—"

"It's not a crime to not disclose the incarceration status of your parent in a cover letter, is it?"

He shakes his head. "I was considering you as Katrina's replacement, but now I'm not sure if I should keep your name in the hat."

I can barely hold back a scoff. "That's discrimination. You can't deny me a promotion because my father is—"

"This isn't about your father. This is about your focus," Matt insists. "I see it's the ten-year anniversary since the trial. It must be heavy. Reliving what your father did to your mother."

I want to roll my eyes because I know he's only done surface-level research. He hasn't skimmed through any of the court transcripts or legal documents. He probably hasn't even considered my dad is innocent, or that I visit him every week.

I shrug, though all I want to do is bolt out from behind these four walls. "It's life. It's not a distraction."

"The workload is much heftier for this new role. The first few months are going to be especially taxing. I need someone who is focused and can jump straight in. Not someone who's taking calls while they're on the clock and preoccupied with…"

He doesn't know what word he's looking for, or maybe he's oscillating between a few options, desperately trying to figure out which one would be the least offensive.

"I can handle it," I say, keeping my response short and sweet so there's no room for him to hear the lie in my voice.

I do not want this promotion. I only want the increase in salary, and that's enough for me to fight for it. In so many ways, I've dedicated my life to getting my dad free, yet so often it feels like I'm barely doing enough. Like why do I get to enjoy even the smallest parts of life when he can't even enjoy a private piss or shower?

"I just need to make sure you know what you could be jumping into and are ready for it," he says, sounding more like his normal laid-back self.

"I am."

"All right, I'll keep your name in the running for now," he says, putting his unused pen back in its jar, and I sort of flinch because the last two words feel like a threat. "And don't worry. This stays between us. I'm willing to take your word for it, but I don't know how many others up the line I can convince."

I'm not fooled one second into thinking this is a courtesy he's extending to me on a personal level, simply because it's the ethical thing to do or because he in some way empathizes with me. I think what he really means is he doesn't want to have to defend his decision if he were to promote me. It probably also has something to do with the optics. This kind of news could spark the brand of press no publicly-traded company welcomes and Matt doesn't want the headache.

"Thank you," I say sincerely, so relieved this meeting is over. "Appreciate it."

"Absolutely. You're one of the anchors on this team."

I've never considered that Matt sees me as even remotely valuable here, much less an asset, but I can't think of a reason he would have to blow smoke up my ass right now.

He stands in dismissal, and against my will, my gaze jerks to his open fly again, and because I'm the most unlucky girl on the planet, he curiously follows my sight line and sees the disturbing sight I've been fighting for the past ten minutes. He quickly zips his pants, avoiding my eyes.

He stops me just as I grip the door handle, obviously not as embarrassed as I am for him.

"It must eat at you every night," he says, so softly I have to play his words over a few times to make out each one.

"What?"

"Your mom's in the ground and he gets to wake up every morning and breathe air into his lungs."

So many unspeakable urges I force myself to resist in this moment.

"We cremated her," I say, unceremoniously.

Then I shut the door to his office even though he always keeps it open and make a beeline for my cubicle.

It's not until I'm caught up on my emails that I realize I have no idea how Matt found out about my dad, my past, my secret. That should have been the first thing I asked. Or at least had him clarify what he was referring to when he indirectly accused me of taking calls on the clock. Reggie is the only person who knows the truth, but he wouldn't tell my boss. I rack my brain, trying to come up with scenarios that would make sense, most of them deeply implausible, until I think of her. Until Pia's full, Leonardo da Vinci face comes into my head.

She was the one I took a call with on company time. She's also the only other person who knows about everything, or at least thinks she does. She knows where I work too, but I can't think of a single reason why she would speak to my boss. It's not like I told her about the promotion I was up for. What could be her motivation? Besides, I apologized. We're on good terms now. Well, relatively good terms. We are by no means friends, but how would becoming my nemesis now benefit her? Is this a threat? Does she think telling my boss is going to make me cave and participate in her film?

I debate texting Pia, and as I open my messages app, I'm distracted by the time. I only have ten minutes to get to Hunter's office for our lunch date.

If I blow this promotion, I won't be able to start saving up again to retain the kind of lawyer we'll need to get an approval on this next petition, especially if I can't stop Pia from releasing her film that will disparage Dad's name all over again to a global audience.

I feel tangled up, buried so deep under responsibility and expectation. I've come clean on old lies only to have started new ones.

I wish I could be honest with Reggie and Hunter. Wish I could destroy all sixty hours of footage Pia has filmed and will eventually send to her editor.

Wish I could lay my head in my mom's lap and ask her what I should do as she twists her fingers in my curls.

I am usually intentional about showing receptionists respect. I worked as a temp for a handful of firms before landing my current gig. I know the hustle, the rampant thanklessness of the job. But this Saks-mannequin-looking chick perched behind the massive mahogany desk in the Sachs & Marston lobby is trying me. She was snotty from the point of my arrival, and I gave her the benefit of the doubt and assumed she is like this to everyone, but her negligence is starting to feel personal. If she takes another call before paging Hunter, I'm going to go full Illtown on her.

"Sorry," she says, placing her receiver down for the fourth time. "Who were you looking for?"

"Bishop." She just stares at me. "Hunter Bishop."

"Hmm. That name's not ringing a bell."

My impatience makes me want to grab the cup of expensive-looking pens from her desk and haul them at her forehead, but I tell myself she is probably new and hasn't memorized all of the attorneys' names yet. I see her consult a binder-bound directory and use a gel-manicured finger to help her scroll past all the *A* last names, the *B*s...

"Yeah," she says, double-checking the list. "There's no Hunter Bishop here."

"You mean like here right now?"

"I mean here at the firm."

"Maybe you're not looking in the right directory."

She looks at me as if to say she didn't get hired yesterday. The phone rings again and of course she reaches for the receiver with no hesitation. It's already fifteen past the hour, so I wander away from the desk and shoot Hunter a text.

I'm in the front. Receptionist isn't letting me back 🙁

He responds right away: Coming to get you now.

I glare at the brunette behind the desk and have to tell myself that deeming her chin-length bob as passé is purely a result of my bias. Her haircut is as flawless as her makeup. I can't deny how well put together she is, but I'll still get to shoot her a shady look when Hunter, who's probably the hottest lawyer here, comes out.

"Did you still need help?" she asks.

I don't answer her. My phone buzzes with another text from Hunter. I don't see you?

I glance around the space one more time. There's a massive orchid arrangement on the front desk, a woman talking on the phone by the door, people coming in and out of the doors, but no Hunter.

Another buzz.

Are you at suite 2300?

How embarrassing. I could have sworn the directory downstairs said this was the Sachs & Marston suite. I glance up to see what company I've actually stumbled inside and freeze. There's a sign right behind the flawlessly bobbed mannequin. Sachs & Marston.

I hurry out of the suite and press the call button for the elevator four times. I shift my weight from leg to leg, the suspense killing me as I wait and almost cause a head-on collision with two exec-looking types who step out of the elevator when it arrives. I apologize for my haste and feel one of them boring a hole into my ass with his gaze as I turn around in the stall.

I pause when I ease in front of the double doors leading to the law offices hosted in suite 2300.

Goldstein & Wagner.

This makes no sense. Hunter was supposed to follow in his father's footsteps, take the path of least resistance. He was supposed to earn his stripes at a private law practice like his dad did before becoming a piranha in a robe and gavel. Could Hunter really be making a relatively modest salary fighting for people's human rights at Goldstein & Wagner when his unrepentant father spent decades complicit in a system that methodically strips people, mainly people who look like my father, of the very thing Hunter is now advocating for?

I can't step in. I can't push through these doors and follow Hunter to his office and have lunch with him when Reggie is somewhere in that suite probably working furiously through his lunch break.

This whole time they've been working at the same firm. *The same firm.* I haven't actually done anything inappropriate with Hunter, but this is still a mess. There is so much potential for this to implode. I can only imagine how Reggie would react if he knew he had to work in the same suite as a guy who wants to fuck me, who I've given no inclination that the feeling isn't mutual.

A woman in pleated navy trousers and sheer-sleeved pussy-bow top pushes out of the doors, and I catch Hunter leaning on the reception desk in a slate gray suit, his eyes down on his phone.

I make sure I'm gone before he glances up. I bolt back to the elevators, but then I get too impatient and nervous that he'll come out looking for me, so I find the emergency stairwell and jog down a few flights of stairs in four-inch heels. I feel a text come in with a buzz when I push through on the seventeenth floor and call the elevator, but I don't glance at Hunter's message until I'm back outside.

He's asking me if I'm lost. I text him back, telling him I have to cancel our lunch.

22

I NEVER THOUGHT I'd see the day when I was barefoot in my kitchen, cooking for a man.

Hunter watches me from my couch, sipping the drink I mixed for him using a splash of the Hendrick's I honestly keep on my shelf for aesthetic purposes. There is some sporting event on the TV, which is on mute, but for some reason this all doesn't feel as regressive as I would have imagined. Maybe since he is not my husband and isn't sharing my bed tonight, and I am making this meal for him in apology and not out of duty, this isn't truly as Stepford as the visual might allude to. And I can't say I am not enjoying him sneaking glances at me as I make the sauce for the pad thai from scratch. Hunter is the type of guy who will eat anything, but I remember how much he loves the beautiful interplay of sweet, sour and salty. I had to rush out and pick up most of the ingredients from Trader Joe's after I clocked out, but I need to put in the effort so he doesn't distance himself from me after I bailed on him this afternoon.

I warn Hunter that I am replacing the umami with mushroom powder and a bit of toasted seaweed that will give the sauce its signature fishy taste, and he tells me he will be happy with anything because he is starving, and this is music to my ears. I am still nervous he won't enjoy my vegan version of his favorite meal, but I let him catch up with the score of the game he is intermittently watching while I hustle around my Barbie Dreamhouse–sized kitchen. I add a healthy squirt of sriracha to the sauce, a pinch of freshly grated ginger and a generous dollop of peanut butter. I peek up just in time to catch his smile of approval, and I am glad he now sees that I am going out of my way to please him.

"You didn't go to Sachs & Marston," I say, keeping my voice as insouciant as possible.

I move on to chopping up a scallion, which means I can't shift my eyes away from my knife and can appropriately avoid gauging his reaction to the tiny bomb I just dropped.

"I did, actually," he says, and I can detect that he wasn't anticipating this turn in conversation.

That pauses me. I look up from my blade, but he speaks before I get a word out.

"I put in a year there," he says.

I nod. "Then you left for G&W?"

I don't quite understand the laugh he releases as he shifts to his feet. "It was pretty awkward when S&M moved their offices a few floors beneath us. Definitely played elevator dodgeball for the first few months."

"But…" I shake my head. "Your dad."

"My dad."

"Did he flip when you told him you were leaving for G&W?"

"Nope."

My jaw goes lax. "You didn't tell him?"

"Nope."

Hunter gestures to the matchstick carrots on my cutting board. I nod, letting him know it's okay to steal a couple.

"And you just don't give a fuck?" I ask, watching him devour a handful in one go.

"It's my life. You should try it."

"Try out your life? Sounds...like a good time."

He finishes chewing, then watches me for a second. "Doing what you really want to do."

I drop my eyes and put my back to him. He steals a few more carrots while I shuffle around in the fridge for the garlic. "I told you," I say, not in the mood to get into this again. "I don't really want to write anymore."

"I didn't say anything about writing. You did."

I pause. I see what he just did. Cute.

I flip back around holding a bulb of garlic tight in my palm. I avoid his eyes as I peel off pieces and shove them into my overpriced but highly efficient garlic press.

"Come on, Simone. I know you. You might be all grown up, but that little girl who dreamed of people reading her book is still here."

I don't say anything. I am working tremendously hard to make it look like crushing garlic is a demanding task that requires grave concentration.

Hunter eases closer to me in his hard bottoms and lowers his voice to a soft murmur. "I know it's easy for me to say, okay? I know that. But you can do this. Even if you have to keep your office gig for a while."

I sigh. I know what Hunter wants. I'm sure in his head there is a scenario where I drop my defenses and hear him out, then work on a draft of my debut novel, which he will occasionally check in to cheerlead me on. And once it gets all too consuming, once the story demands hours and hours of my concentration every day, he tells me I can quit my day job and move in with him. I put in my two-week notice and he acts as my economic support until I sign my six-figure book deal.

This is his fantasy. Not mine.

I don't need or have any desire to be rescued. I've done just fine without him charging in on a noble steed. He could alternatively offer me an interest-free loan and it would be no different than the hundred grand Jeff Bezos got from his father to invest in Amazon, but I'm not looking for a sponsor either.

I know this isn't fair, but I'm not the one who imbued me with such pride or designed society to be so imbalanced.

"It might help," he says, pushing all the noise to the back of my head. "You know, work through all your feelings about what happened."

I start to nod, but I don't commit to it. I've read that a lot of authors write to work through trauma, but those are truly brave people. When I catch a whiff of danger, I run.

"Sorry I bailed on you earlier," I say, just to talk about something else. "I got randomly pulled into something."

"If anyone understands that, I do," he says with a laugh, and I appreciate him for not probing deeper.

I grab another knife from my floating rack and start hacking the white onion.

"Need some help?" he asks, and there is a joke on the tip of my tongue about him being incapable of doing anything except making a mess, but I resist it because maybe I'm being too presumptuous. Something also feels off about the timing.

"I'm making up for standing you up. You can't help." I point to one of the two bar stools on the other side of my tiny peninsula. "Sit."

Once I'm done chopping and slicing and mincing, I light the fire under my wok. Hunter loosens the knot in his tie and asks me if I've finished the audiobook I was ranting about earlier. I tell him I still have about an hour left, but quickly get verbose about another recent read he would probably like while he opens the top buttons of his shirt.

"It's about a former serial killer and a rookie detective going up against each other."

"Sounds dark."

"It's...provocative."

"Yeah, how?"

I mull it over while I add the bulk of the ingredients to the wok. "It talks a lot about how people who do good and people who do evil aren't that different. They usually want the same thing. They just go about it differently."

"And what do you think?"

I take a moment. "I'm not sure if I buy it."

I turn away from him so I can keep a close eye on my veggies and pretend I can't feel him staring at my ass.

"People who do evil are still human, right?" he asks.

"Yeah," I say, peeking back at him and seeing that he is now unbuttoning his right cuff. Something his father used to do when he came home. Hunter looks so much like him right now, or it could just be that I feel like I've subconsciously been talking about Scott in my summation of the book I'm reading.

"And don't all humans want the same things?" he asks, then adds, "Excluding sociopaths."

I toss that around in my head the way I toss my veggies in my wok, then glance back at him over my shoulder. "I guess."

My eyes drop to his now exposed forearms, and I can't help but follow the cord of one of his veins until it disappears on the back of his hand. And then I turn away and stay that way until I finish the food.

The pad thai is a little too sweet and a little too spicy. I am tingly with flattery when Hunter gets up and piles more on his plate seconds after he tastes it. I laugh because there is no way he can possibly eat that much, but when his bowl is empty again and he is still scraping, I am astonished, looking at him with this giddy smile on my face because people devouring the food I cook is my love language. Hunter looks like he wants to stretch out on my couch and rub his tight, flat belly. But he doesn't. He insists on loading the dishwasher for me even though I told him I could handle it.

When the moment feels right, I say, "I think they were sleeping together the whole time."

"What do you mean?" he asks.

"I mean it didn't stop—the affair didn't end until my mom was murdered."

I need to know if there is any chance that the baby my mom was carrying was not Scott's. My entire theory falls apart if it wasn't his baby.

"I don't know. I guess." He rinses out my bowl and adds it to the middle rack, which is wrong but I don't correct him. "I don't think my dad ever planned on ending it, that's for sure."

"So he had no regard for your mom? Did he even love her?"

Hunter thinks about it, then smiles and says, "How can a man be in love with two women at once?"

Bullshit. Scott Bishop did not love his wife. And even if he did, there is no way I am going to accept that he loved my mom. Everything I've ever known about him tells me that he is incapable of feeling such an emotion, much less expressing it with another person.

"He…" I stammer. "So you really think your dad…" I can't even say it. The words feel like a betrayal, even in my head.

"He liked having my mom around," Hunter clarifies. "He *loved* your mom."

Possession and love, two very different things.

I angle away in case I am making a face like I just took a fast fist to my solar plexus. There is no way to kill someone you love. Scott Bishop did not love my mother. Scott Bishop never cared about my mother. He used her and disposed of her in a literal trash bag when he was done with her, when she was no longer a benefit to his life. He fucked her after she spent all day helping his mother, serving him. Then he buttoned his pants, smoothed out his hair and played house with his wife like their home in Asher Lane was some plantation in the Bible Belt.

"How do you know that?" I ask, doing my best to keep my voice level.

"I just do."

I can't believe this, can't believe Hunter could be so naive to think his father was in love with his mistress. But it shouldn't surprise me that he can't tell the difference between lust and love. He can't even tell seduction from manipulation.

"So if your dad loved my mom," I say, "then why didn't he ever leave your mom?"

"Family over everything."

"What's that mean?"

I sidle up next to him and shift some things around in the machine. I can smell his deodorant or whatever he showered with this morning, that same intoxicatingly warm scent.

"My mom knew he was sleeping around," he explains. "And Dad knew she knew. It was an open secret that they weren't willing to break up the household over."

My nod is slow, my mind whirring. "For your sake?"

"I don't think they were thinking about me that much back then."

I nod, remembering what he said about maintaining the aesthetic. Hunter shuts off the tap, and I finish reorganizing the dishes inside the machine.

After I start it up, I look up to him. "Mom was three months pregnant when it happened." He doesn't say anything, doesn't even blink. "The autopsy—"

He nods abruptly. "I read it."

I swallow and force myself to forge on. "Do you think the baby was your father's?"

"I..." He pauses for a really long time. "Never thought about that. But yeah, guess it's possible."

I stare at him, unable to believe that he could have never considered that my mom was carrying his dad's baby after walking in on them fucking like that in the kitchen and knowing it didn't end there. Scott Bishop hadn't even taken the time to take her clothes off. It was passion. I didn't get that back then, it was just weird, but now I see it for what it was. Passion can be reckless. Dangerous.

I need a minute to think. "Be right back," I say, heading to the opposite end of my studio. "Wanna get out of these work clothes."

"Sure. Go ahead."

I disappear behind my bookcases and grab my favorite pair of sweats before slipping inside my bathroom. I replay our conversation over and over, but my head is still jumbled by the time I step back out. Hunter's back is to me, but it is very clear what he is doing.

Still, I ask, "What are you doing?"

Hunter doesn't have enough time to shut the top drawer on my nightstand. He flips around, raising the book he has just taken from it so I can see it clearly.

The ground falls away.

He is not holding one of my novels. He is holding a diary. Kate's diary.

"Why is this here?" he asks, and I'm thrown by the sternness of his voice because he is the one who has just violated my privacy, not the other way around.

I shake my head. "Were you going through my drawers?"

He swallows. "I was just…"

It doesn't click until he looks me over. The way his eyes take in the oversized sweatshirt and matching pants I've thrown on, it is obvious he didn't realize I literally meant change into something more comfortable, not something easier to rip off.

"Just what?" I ask, making no question of my impatience.

"I thought you wanted to…" He glances back at the drawer and swallows. "I'm out of…"

Condoms.

I should make him say it, but this is about as much second-hand embarrassment I can handle for one night.

"No, Hunter." I cover my eyes with a palm. "I was literally changing."

"I see that."

"We're *friends*."

"Are we?" he asks, jutting the diary forward. "Because it looks like you swindled me into taking you to my mom's house so you could steal her diary."

My mouth opens, but no words come out.

"Friends do that now?" he presses.

"I legit wanted to see the letters," I say, as if that is supposed to make my deception less terrible.

I hate the way he nods, like he is already two steps ahead of me. "You only asked to see them because you knew this was there too."

I drop my eyes and try to avoid the diary, but he holds it in front of him so there is no way I can miss it.

I step away. "Listen, I know this looks kinda weird, but—"

"Kinda?"

"I just wanted to see if there was anything in there that could get me closer to understanding what happened to my mom."

He stays on my heels as I head back into the main living space. "You thought reading my mother's diary could get you to who killed your mom?"

I turn to him. "It can't be a coincidence that my mom was gutted and stuffed in a trash bag right before her baby would've started showing."

He looks genuinely flabbergasted. "What are you saying?"

"A baby that was probably your dad's."

I see it click on his face, and he makes a disgusted sound through his nose. "Now you're saying my *dad* had something to do with what happened to her?"

I don't deny but don't confirm either.

"Is that what you're saying, Simone?"

I flinch at the way he says my name, so cold. He wants a verbal response from me, but I put more distance between us. He follows me until his pocket buzzes. He glances at the caller ID before setting the diary down and lifting his phone to his ear.

"Hey, man." He listens and holds back a groan. "Sure, let me check and see if I still have the files on my desktop. I'll call you back in fifteen." He ends his call and glances at the door.

I stare at the wall.

"My dad had nothing to do with what happened to your mom," he says, his voice so low I can barely make out the words. He doesn't look back at me before stepping toward the door. "I'm out."

My heart continues to pound even after he's gone until I realize he left the diary on the arm of my couch.

23

AFTER HUNTER IS GONE, his words still reverberate in my head.

Family over everything.

Over love?

Even if Scott had actually fallen in love with my mom, it didn't mean much when it came down to him possibly losing his wife, his family. He sacrificed love because he couldn't risk his wife leaving him. He killed my mom and her unborn child so he could continue to play Happily Ever After with the mother of the son he already had.

Dad is right. Love don't mean shit. Love is cheap as fuck.

Most people want to know how a person can cheat on someone they love, but what I want to know is how you kill someone you love. What kind of diseased love is that?

I don't know what is bothering me more, that Hunter was looking in my drawers for a condom or that he invaded my privacy the moment I turned my back. Other than the diary, there is nothing in there I'm ashamed of, but it still feels like I have been violated knowing someone has been poking around in my personal space. To be fair, I invaded his mother's privacy and stole her diary, which is technically a double invasion, but my mind keeps drifting to what would have happened if he hadn't noticed the diary.

Reggie and I stopped using protection months ago after we both got tested, and I went through the specifics of what I would do to his balls if he gave me herpes. So what would Hunter have done when he realized I didn't have one? Would he have given up on the prospect of getting laid and instead settled for grabbing a fistful of my clean panties and inhaling their scent? Had he already done that before I stepped out and caught him?

I send a text to Reggie saying I need to see him tonight. I don't tell him it is because I need help figuring out my next move now that Hunter knows I stole his mother's diary and am onto his dad. I keep it vague so maybe he thinks I am being sexy. He doesn't get right back, so I pull up my TBR spreadsheet. I am slightly off track with all the new and upcoming releases, but none of the blurbs I skim over from the list sound particularly intriguing.

Come on, Simone. I know you.

Hunter's words repeat in my head, and I suddenly feel naked.

A few minutes later, there is a blank Word document saved as CLOSURE, and I can't even remember creating it when I blink it back into focus. So many thoughts swarm my head, but I don't work up the courage to type a single word before my phone starts to buzz.

"What you doing?" Reggie asks once I answer his FaceTime call.

"Nothing. Just…" I glance at the time and see I've been stalling under the guise of brainstorming for almost two hours. "Just reading." It comes out before I process that it's a lie.

"I can be there in fifteen if you'll still be up," he says, and I tell him the door will be open.

He gets here in twenty, and I've already filled him in on everything Hunter said during dinner by the time he has stripped down to his boxer briefs. There is usually something so erotic about watching him peel out of his suit, pulling his shirt from the waistband of his pants, unzipping the fly, but I haven't noticed tonight. It is like I blinked, and now he is one motion away from being naked.

"What do you mean *what if he's right?*" I pull my glasses off and stare at him. "He's not."

"Just because dude thinks the baby could've been his dad's too doesn't mean his pops actually did it. It's correlation, not causation."

"The other day you agreed that—"

"How much time are you gonna be spending with this dude anyway?"

I look at Reggie and snap my laptop shut. It is a fair enough question, but his tone isn't.

"I wasn't *spending time* with him. I was doing recon."

He gives me a look. "You sure?"

"What does that mean?"

"Just asking if you're sure you know what you're doing."

Of course I don't know what I'm doing. At least I am *doing* something. But I know Reggie isn't concerned with how I am going about solving my mom's cold murder case. He is still talking about the one-on-one time I've been spending with Hunter. Obviously, I omitted the part about the condom. I was vague and just said he found the diary in my room while I ran to the bathroom.

"I'm trying to figure out what happened to my mom," I say, trying not to sound as irritated as I feel. "If the police gave a shit back in the day, I wouldn't have to."

"Okay," he says with a shrug, and I want to scream because he doesn't sound like he's *okay.*

Reggie shuts the door behind him when he steps into the bathroom. He doesn't want me to follow him. He wants a whole-ass partition between us. I've bruised his ego. I've fucked this up. I push in anyway, and when I do, he is already completely undressed, adjusting the temperature of the water in the shower.

When he sees me, he relinquishes his hold on the hot water knob and ducks in behind the curtain. He snatches it shut with force and something reflexive in me makes me snatch it right back open. He glares at me as he reaches for my coconut-scented bar of soap.

"There's nothing going on," I say, cutting to the chase.

I don't want to fight with Reggie. I only have so much emotional bandwidth, and trying to prove that Scott Bishop killed my mother is dominating most of it right now.

"I said *okay.*" He pulls the curtain shut again. I yank it back open. "What are you doing?"

"You're mad at me," I say, softly.

He blows out air through his nose. "Can I just wipe the sweat from my balls in peace, please?"

My eyes drop down reflexively when he says the word, but I jerk my gaze back up, feeling weird about looking at his genitals like this, exposed and vulnerable against his thigh while he stands under a lukewarm downpour, already so vulnerable. This time when he shuts the curtain, I keep my hands at my sides and back away. He adjusts the hot water to his usual near-scalding temperature and shame floods my cheeks for being so petulant.

When he is done, we don't have sex. It might be the most uneventful night we have ever spent in my bed together, aside from the time when he came back to the city with a stomach virus after going home to see his family in Philly.

I roll over on my side under the covers in my matching satin bralette and shorts, facing his broad bare back. "Reg..."

He never sleeps on his side. I refuse to believe he has fallen so deeply asleep so fast, but I don't call his name again. He has already responded loud and clear.

It hurts when other people hurt you, but it doesn't compare to the pain of knowing you've hurt someone else. I flip on my stomach and push my hands under my pillow. I try to brainstorm a book concept that doesn't suck until my dreams take over.

24

"YOU *KNEW* MOM was having an affair that whole time?"

I'm thirty minutes into my morning commute, which means I'm only one block away from the office, but considering Matt's warning, I circle the block when I get to the corner instead of heading inside. As I pass a magazine stand, I remember how the media OJ Simpson'd Dad's mug shot before releasing it to the local news outlets. The same doctored images were used when Mom's murder made national news. I barely recognized him, thought it was my grandfather's face on the screen, a man I'd only met once or twice. They had augmented his soft toffee complexion to be considerably darker in order to keep their narrative straight that the true predators in suburbia are dark-skinned Black men.

I still cannot believe this, that my father wasn't in the dark about Mom's affair all those years like I was. "Dad."

I don't know what he's thinking or if he's simply stalling because he's waiting for one of his fellow inmates to pass by or something, but the wait is driving me insane.

"Of course I knew," he says, and I almost stutter to a complete stop, which I'm sure the gale of pedestrians walking behind me would not appreciate. "I knew *her*. She couldn't hide anything from me."

He says it like I should have known better, should have known this about him, but I slip under the dark green awning to a pub, truly stunned. I expect him to ask me how I know about the affair, but he just asks me if I'm almost at my job like everything is fine, like this doesn't change everything.

Sadness strikes me with a pang in the pit of my stomach, but the fury quickly dominates. I've watched my father suffer for the past thirteen years, mourning and grieving the death of his wife, the mother of his child, behind bars. My mother has made my father suffer in death but also in life, and I am not sure how to handle this. I'm sure my dad was no angel in their relationship, but if she never would have had an affair with Scott, my dad never would have had to identify her mutilated cadaver, attend her funeral, break down on the stand when giving his testimony, his last plea to the jury that he was an innocent man. I can only judge how good of a husband my dad was from the outside, but no matter his flaws, he was faithful. He was committed. He kept his vows.

I look down at my feet and my stomach roils, this surge of rage devouring my body whole. I've never felt this repulsed by my mother, and I don't know what this says of me, if this is allowed, to be furious with the dead. Is it okay when the dead is the reason you had to watch your father lose his job, get blackballed from the financial industry, humiliated and strip-searched and thrown in a cage like he was an apex predator? I don't understand this. My parents rarely fought. I knew they weren't having sex, but they were still emotionally intimate at the breakfast table, in the car on a long drive. How could he have known and stayed so silent? How could I have not only missed the signs of my mother's yearslong affair, but also my father's pain?

"How's Reggie?" Dad asks, and I realize my fingers are tangled in Mom's necklace around my neck. "You should call with him on the line sometimes."

I shake my head, trying to remember Reggie's schedule. "He has this big presentation at work tomorrow. Gonna be prepping for it all day."

My eyes are on the traffic going by each way, but all I see is his heartbroken face when I have to tell him about the documentary Pia is making. I've spared him the news to keep him from spiraling, to keep the sliver of hope alive in his heart that I'm losing my grip on. Eventually, I'll have to tell him, prepare him for how the reception of the film could derail our next petition. I just don't know how I'm going to say the words.

"How come you never...did anything? Said anything?"

"Denial was easier," he says, so simply, so detached. He drifts off in thought, and it's painfully quiet on his end until he says, "But then it was right there in my face when we got the autopsy back. Couldn't deny it anymore."

"The baby could have been yours," I offer, hoping he'll agree with me.

It is hopeless, but anything is possible.

Dad snorts. "Evelyn hadn't let me touch her in years."

I turn the corner and am one more turn away from where I began, which is a few minutes from the entrance to my office building. "So the baby was definitely Scott's?"

There's no immediate response. I wish I could decipher Dad's silence, or at least be across from him so I can read his expression.

I know this is probably the last thing he wants to talk about, but I can't stop there. "I knew they had—"

"*Scott's?*"

I nearly lurch back at his bellow. I try to justify his outrage, but I am only more confused.

"Yeah, you just said..." I pause, the alarm in his silence clear now, and my hand covers my mouth. "You didn't know who—"

Dad sounds like he jumps to his feet and drops the receiver. I wonder if this is it for our call today, if he'll pick it back up so we can continue. There are so many emotions he must be feeling all at once.

"Evelyn was sleeping with *Bishop*?" he snarls into the receiver. His mouth is much too close to it at the volume he speaks in, but I'm just relieved he didn't leave me hanging.

He said her name. A rarity. But I don't like the way he said it.

I imagine him mentally pacing since he can't move freely when he is on the phone. I want to ask what difference it makes if it was Scott she was cheating with or some other man, but I can't because I know it is like asking the difference between a star and a planet. They look the same to the naked eye twinkling in the night sky, but one generates its own energy through nuclear reactions and the other does not.

There is a tempest in the pit of my gut as I accept it is time to renege on a promise I made a long time ago.

"I saw them," I say, a tremor in my voice, but I'm sure he doesn't hear it over the sound of an ambulance blaring by.

"What?"

"Me and Hunter..." My voice is loud enough to compete with the loud street sounds, but still just above a whisper. "We saw them together in the kitchen."

It takes him a few moments to respond. "When was this?"

"I was eight."

I expect another eruption, at least a spurt of derision, but nothing. He doesn't react at all.

"When did you realize?" I ask, the silence strangling me.

"Not too long after that." He sounds depleted already. "I think you were in fourth grade."

I don't know what to say, don't know how to get past this as a family. Together. The last time we had to get through something this devastating, I was a child who listened, followed, obeyed. Now we are both adults, and I can see this is the age when child starts to morph into caregiver.

I can't see him right now, but when I imagine being face-to-face with him this weekend, I know it will be through a new filter. I know he is an easygoing man, but I wouldn't have ever pegged him as the kind of man who stays with his wife fully aware that she is sleeping with another man. I'm stunned at this revelation, not only because of what it says about my father but also that Aunt Patrice was right. Partly. She insisted that Dad knew. But she's wrong about his discovery of the affair being the trigger that made him go and kill Mom. He'd known about the affair nearly from its inception. He wouldn't just snap one day after putting up with it for so many years.

He wouldn't. Couldn't.

And it wasn't as if it was the baby that pushed him over the edge, because he didn't learn she was pregnant until the autopsy. He said so himself. He couldn't deny it any longer. It was right in his face.

I have almost strung a few words together to offer my dad some solace amid this shitstorm when he bursts out laughing. Laughing. I know this kind of laughter, the kind where his mouth is open wide and his belly is contracting. I squint, thinking my mind is malfunctioning or the phone line is translating the sounds of him crying incorrectly, but when I pause at the door to the building, he is definitely laughing and I don't like it.

Now I really don't know what to say. "What could possibly be fu—"

"Evelyn was sleeping with Bishop," he roars, cutting me off. "That's good. Oh, that's *real* fucking good." He howls some more. Then his laughter abruptly stops and his voice is deeply serious.

"Tell Reggie I said hi." His voice is no longer boisterous but solemn, resigned. "I've got chores to do."

And then he is gone and the operator is loud and annoying in my ear.

Even though I am blocking one of the glass doors, I can't move, this emotional whiplash highly debilitating.

I thought getting confirmation would feel a lot less shitty, but all I want to do is bury my head in the sand like an ostrich checking on her fertilized eggs. Correlation, causation, my ass. Dad wasn't the father of Mom's unborn baby. That leaves only one person who could have gotten her pregnant. And according to Hunter, Scott absolutely would have done anything he had to do in order to keep the peace inside his own home.

Family over everything.

When I get to my desk, I take out Kate's diary, and in between shooting off emails and keeping a lookout for Matt, I reread her diary from the beginning.

After work, I'm so drained I refuse to wait for food to come to me, so I stop at Subway and eat half of my dinner on the train next to a guy sleeping horizontally across three seats. As soon as I walk into my apartment, I can tell something is off. At first it's sort of a hazy sense and I figure maybe I'm just tired and need a nap. But then I walk into my bedroom and flick my eyes across the room and see a few things out of place: the right edge of my mattress noticeably off-center, the bottom drawer of my nightstand slightly ajar. I feel a breeze and my head jerks toward the window. I take slow steps toward it, and once I'm close enough, I see that it has been lifted about three inches or so. I never open this window, not even a little bit, because it's ancient and impossible to shut. My heart starts to speed up as

I try to remember this morning, if maybe I opened it and just don't remember.

I look around the room again, but everything else seems exactly how I left it. I pull out my phone and call Reggie, and when he tells me he hasn't come by today, I'm shocked into a temporary silence because it hits me that someone has broken into my apartment. Just the thought of that seems preposterous, but I can come up with no other reasonable explanation.

25

I HAVE THE unpopular opinion that Fridays are overrated. By the time the end of the week comes along, you are so tired of all the code-switching and there is just no more energy to shuck and jive, but this Tuesday feels as rough as a typical Friday. I barely slept last night.

When Reggie got to my apartment I had calmed down drastically, but I still needed to be held in his solid arms and told that everything was okay, I was safe and sound now that he was here. And that's exactly what he did. He even climbed in bed with me and listened to me drivel about my monotonous day at the office. I eventually got to relaying the conversation I had with my dad this morning, which completely drained me, yet Reggie still managed to fall asleep before me.

It's a unique violation, a specific breed of uneasiness that is born when someone violates your physical space, the place where you masturbate, fuck, eat, piss, all the basic human behaviors that are also all extremely personal. As a woman, I've gone through scenarios in my head of having my body violated by a stranger or someone close to me, and though in reality I would probably go limp to avoid being clobbered, in most of my imaginings I not only fight back, but fight them off and get away. Still, I've never imagined having my home invaded, and though it is not as terrifying or traumatic as being physically assaulted, I feel particularly vulnerable this morning.

My neighborhood is pretty gentrified, and true, crime can happen anywhere, but I thought you could pretty much price yourself out of such random acts of violence. Actually, even considering this eerie feeling I can't let go of, *violence* seems to be a stretch because nothing was taken, or even touched, really. Reggie did a sleepy, but careful sweep before getting into bed with me last night and again this morning before heading to work to see if anything was missing, and aside from a few books I can't seem to find, nothing appears to have been swiped. All we've been able to conclude is whoever was inside my place hadn't had enough time before my arrival to find what they were looking for. That seems like the most logical explanation: they were on the hunt for something specific—Reggie thinks my MacBook, which I had in my tote, or some other kind of expensive tech that can be resold for a good amount of money, or even valuable jewelry, which I don't have, aside from my mom's necklace, and that never comes off my neck—and once they realized it was a bust, they fled through the fire escape.

Between yawns, I asked Reggie if we should still file a police report, but he pointed out that whoever my intruder was, they were good. So good he couldn't detect any signs of forced entry at the door, which he promises me is made to look much easier on TV than it is in real life. We both decided for that reason—the lack of anything being taken—and because the NYPD generally sucks, that it would be pointless to give them a call. I did text my building manager asking if a chain lock could be installed on my front door and have yet to hear back.

Hope you're on the pill.

Upon my reread, I make sure of it—Kate's diary never mentions my mother's name, but my mind keeps flitting back to that night after dinner when she cornered me in the hallway.

Wouldn't want my son to end up pressuring you into getting an abortion.

Maybe Hunter is wrong and Kate *did* know Scott was sleeping with Mom and maybe she's the one who got Scott to pressure her into ending her pregnancy. Then when Mom stood her ground, Kate threatened to leave him, went as far as getting her attorney to draw up the papers to show she wasn't bluffing. And that's when Scott made his decision. End of drama. Drop the curtain.

I stare at my computer screen, at the new manuscript I am supposed to be reading so that I can turn in my review on time, which is due by the end of the day, but instead I pull out my cell and call Reggie.

"I was thinking about writing something. A book." I wait, but he doesn't react. "Like my own."

"For what?"

He sounds genuinely baffled, like I've just told him I want to leave New York to go live in a lesbian commune in Wyoming.

I shrug. "For me."

"But you're so good at what you do."

"That doesn't mean it's what I *want* to do. The book reviewing thing was supposed to be temporary. Just a side hustle."

"I feel you, but you're kicking ass. A book will get in the way. You have to focus on one goal at a time."

"This freelancing is what's in my way. I'm a writer." It's been so long since I've said this, the words feel odd coming out of my mouth, but also it feels good, because I am a writer and should absolutely fucking say it. "That was always my dream, not to help make other people's dreams come true for the rest of my life."

"Fine. Do what you gotta do to satisfy this itch, but don't lose focus on what's really important."

I want to ask him what he thinks that is, but I don't have the energy, and I want to see if I can get in another five hundred words before my boss clogs my inbox with more menial shit.

"Nothing is more important than getting my dad out of prison," I say, my voice low but firm. "If I didn't blow my chances at getting this promotion, I can still write in my downtime. Those checks will be enough to cover my overhead and save up for the retainer and I won't even have to freelance anymore."

"What do you mean *blow your chances*?"

After I realize I completely forgot to tell Reggie about the promotion, I catch him up to speed, then let out a sigh. "And even if I still get this raise, it'll still be all for nothing if I can't convince Pia to make the film about Dad's innocence or can it altogether. Preferably I can get her to do the former. It would help the petition."

"Didn't she say she was handing over the footage to her editor tomorrow?"

"Hence why I'm over here freaking out." I glance around to make sure Matt is still inside his office. I catch eyes with Jasmine across the way and give her a little wave, which she returns. "Everything I have is still only theoretical."

"Maybe there's nothing, you know?"

"What?

"Think about it. If it was easy to find, your dad wouldn't be the one in prison right now."

That's debatable considering the shitty job the GHPD did with Ford Fitzpatrick at the helm.

"So I just give up?" I ask, my adrenaline going now. "I just keep visiting my dad in prison for the next twenty, thirty years knowing he's innocent and the man who murdered my mother in cold blood is living easy inside the same four walls he probably impregnated her in?"

"I'm not saying that..." It's all Reggie offers, and I wonder if he's trying to figure out a way to articulate his next thought or if he's just distracted by something on his computer's screen.

"If that documentary spreads the lies all over again, we're completely fucked," I tell him. "I have to stop her."

There's another pause. I wait, expecting Reggie to jump in and tell me I got this. I'm going to figure something out before tonight, before Pia sends her footage to be pieced together in a narrative that couldn't be farther from the truth. Maybe he's exhausted from last night too or maybe he thinks I'm delusional to believe I can prove my father's innocence thirteen years after the murder.

"How late are you staying at the office today?" I ask, eager to end this call as quickly as possible.

"Should've brought my sleeping bag," he says, sounding stressed, and I feel bad that I've been so preoccupied with my own shit that I've completely forgotten how much pressure he's under with his new demanding position. "Probably won't make it to your place tonight."

I tell Reggie it's fine and end the call, my mind whirring and crunching. I respond to an email, the last in my unread folder, then sit back in my chair. My mind goes back to Kate. To that house. I grab my phone and walk to the restroom.

"I took your advice," I say when Hunter answers. "I started writing again."

I hear loud footsteps, the sound of a printer and a few muffled voices like he is not at his desk.

"Cool," he finally says, and I wait for him to continue, but that is all I get.

"It's been flowing pretty well," I say. "I'm already a few chapters in and it's not *complete* garbage. Biased opinion, but still."

"Cool."

His bluntness feels like an attack. "Well, then. I will promptly go fuck myself. Thanks for the not-so-subtle hint."

"What do you want me to say, Simone?" he asks, exasperated like our brief exchange has somehow already exhausted him.

I sigh. "Look, I'm sorry I wasn't honest with you, but I—"

"It's not about that. The diary thing, that's fucking weird."

I take a breath. Swallow. Soften my voice. "I was just curious. You have no idea how bad I want answers."

"I get it, but you can't want answers so bad you stop caring about the truth."

I frown. "I *do* care about the truth. I'm just trying to figure out who could've had a reason to want my mom dead."

"You're looking in the wrong place."

He sounds so sure. But I guess if someone said something like this about my dad, I'd tell them to fuck off too.

I take another breath. "Sorry I tricked you."

"Yeah. Fine. It's…" I can't read his pause. "I'm actually pretty busy, so I'm going to—"

"Wait."

There is a small sigh, but I ignore it. "Yeah?"

"Was my mom the only woman your father cheated with?"

"That I know of."

"And you're sure your mom didn't know it was her?"

Hunter scoffs. "There's no way Kate would have let your mom continue to come over every day if she knew it was her," he says, and the clarity in his voice stings.

It did make my theory slightly more interesting if Kate had been the one to pressure Scott into forcing the abortion onto Mom, but as much as I hate to admit it, Hunter is right, and so is Reggie. I have to stick with the facts, not embellish them to create a more compelling narrative to fit my own bias.

"Why?" Hunter asks, something sharp in his tone again. "Do you still think my dad had something to do with—"

"No." But I say it too fast. "No, I was just…" I struggle for a moment. Then the lie comes to me so easily, it's scary. "This new thing I'm writing is gonna be loosely based on their affair. You're right. I feel like it'll help me process it all."

"Cool," he says, and before I can respond, the call drops in my ear, and I know at this moment that getting information from Hunter is a dead end. He doesn't trust me anymore, and while I understand why, I don't have the time to try to earn it back.

As I head back to my desk, I know what I need to do if I'm ever going to get to the bottom of this. I need to go directly to the source no matter how daunting it seems.

I need to go back to Asher Lane.

26

I PARK TWELVE houses away, at the beginning of the serpentine curve that once was my residence but never my home. As I get closer, I pass several missing-dog signs that say *Answers to Cooper*, and my heart thumps. There is practically one in front of every house. They've banded together in solidarity.

There are more signs alerting people of a missing cocker spaniel than there were of my mom's disappearance.

I reach my old house and surprisingly I feel nothing. It is like everything inside of me has stopped. And then the memories come rushing back all at once. I don't look away. I refuse to look away as Dad pushes out of the front door with Mom, happy and glowing, holding my tiny hand in hers the way she always did.

And then I hear the sirens.

I blink a few times, and they are still blaring. I glance around, see the cop car passing behind me, and when I look back at the house, the man smiles at me and so does his wife, their daughter running toward their car, laughing and giddy, her blond hair whipping behind her.

I look away when it hits me that they are the new family living in the house I grew up in. I close my eyes for a moment, trying to hold it all still, then wipe the tears from my cheeks and head next door.

There is a sign with Fitzpatrick's photo on the front lawn. Soliciting votes. Disrupting the sublime verdancy. I roll my eyes and push the doorbell. As I wait, I slip a hand into my jacket pocket, shift my fingers until I feel the smooth metal of the pocketknife I took from the drawer Reggie keeps all his miscellaneous things in. I blow out a breath and realize I'm trembling. I think of bolting across the street and renege on this entire plan. What the hell was I thinking, facing him alone, the man who slaughtered my mother with his own hands? But then it's too late.

The man who pulls open one of the matching wrought iron doors is generically handsome with a taut, lean body similar to his son's. He is not that grizzled, paunchy image that comes to mind when you hear the word *judge*. He has a symmetrical face with the kind of cheekbones and lips that would have made a beautiful daughter. His skin has been reddened by the sun and is clean-shaven, which seems both odd and stylish, but the density of his wolfish brows and full head of silver hair balances out his bare chin and jawline.

Scott doesn't look much older than I remember him looking a decade ago. I don't know if it's because he has been taking it easy the past few years or if my worsening astigmatism is to blame and I just can't make out the new wrinkles and deeper fine lines. He is also not what pops into your head when you think *murderer*. There is something too clean, too pristine about him. And maybe that is the problem.

"Since when do you come in through the…?" Scott pauses,

then draws back the stack of mail he almost pushed in my hands as his eyes widen in shock. "Jesus. You look just like your mother. Thought I was…"

Hallucinating, probably.

Dreaming, maybe.

I expect his gaze to drop, for him to fully check me out, to compare my tits with the ones he used to touch, to compare the spread of my hips to the ones he used to hold, but his eyes stay locked on mine.

I fight to keep his gaze, my heart already pounding against my chest. *Breathe*, I tell myself.

"Mr. Bishop." I force the smile, hoping he can't smell fear like a bloodhound. "Hi."

"Simone." He drops my name like a load he has been carrying uphill for miles. "What are you doing here?"

Without his robe, his presence is less regal, but there is still this impenetrable quality to his stance that nearly forces you to bow down to him. And then it hits me that I am close enough to kill the man who murdered my mother. Close enough for him to murder me with a swift movement of his hands.

"Sorry for showing up unannounced," I say, fighting through the shakiness I hear in my own voice. I take a breath, firm my words. "I don't come out this way too much anymore. I live in the city now, but was meeting a friend at the mall who sorta stood me up, so I just figured I'd stop by and see if Hunter was here."

"No, uh…" He smiles and beams with paternal pride. "Hunter's in the city too now. At Sachs & Marston, naturally."

I almost fuck everything up and correct him. "Oh. Yeah. Of course he is."

The house is immense and immaculate, everything I remember it to be, but also nothing at all. Inside, it still smells the same and I wonder if he still employs the thin, chatty housekeeper who was fond of amber-scented potpourri.

I wait on the sofa, my leg bouncing, while Scott drifts into the kitchen that spans the entire width of the house, which was the final selling point for my mom when we toured the carbon copy next door. I run my fingers against the cold metal of the knife again, just for reassurance, my eyes never leaving the doorway.

Scott slips back into the living room, pushing one of two mugs forward. "Coffee?"

I give a polite smile. "No caffeine for me."

"Vodka?"

I'm not sure if he is joking or not and it hits me that I don't really know this man other than the perceptions I have of him based on scrutinizing his career moves and hearing about him through Hunter's eyes. This is the first time I've ever been totally alone with him. There were times when I was over visiting Hunter and I'd be left alone with his father for a few minutes, but Hunter was always on his way back, Kate probably hovering somewhere in the house too. But this time we are *alone* alone.

Anything can happen.

No one knows I'm here.

I don't know if I should force myself to joke back because that is actually water in the other mug, not alcohol, or if he's genuinely asking me if I want a glass of vodka before noon in earnest.

"I have to drive home," I say, even though it takes much more than a few ounces to get me drunk.

He accepts that with a bit of a shrug, but doesn't push or challenge me. He sits across from me in one of the deep blue velvet armchairs, elegantly crossing a leg over the other, and pours the clear liquid into the mug that is lightly steaming. I watch his face as he sips, and though he does not grimace, it is definitely vodka.

"Do you still think of her?" I ask, willing myself to push through this, all the tough questions I have prepared.

His head tilts slightly. "Who?"

I hate the way he looks at me. It is not a casual glance. It is an intense stare as if he is studying, constantly watching the way a predator does, waiting for the right moment to pounce.

I think about saying her name, but I don't. I can't. "My mom."

Scott sits back and thinks for a long moment, giving me no indication that I have blindsided him. My ears ring as I watch him tip his mug back again. The lump in his throat bobs when he swallows, and finally he blinks.

"She was so good to my mother."

His words come slowly and his eyes are slightly out of focus. It seems as if he has traveled far in the last few moments, as if the slightest mention of his former affair serves as a portal for the past, and I already have the answer to my question. He does. He thinks of her often.

Maybe her bloody corpse haunts him in his dreams. Maybe her screams reverberate in his head every time he closes his eyes. I still wait patiently for his response even though I want to hawk spit straight into both of his eyes in rapid succession and rip the mug from his grasp, slam it into the side of his skull until the ceramic cracks and there is blood raining down his face, soaking the carpet.

"I don't think I would have been able to get through those last few years with my sanity intact if it wasn't for her," he says with the faintest smile, and I want to rip it from his face. "She was like an angel."

The fucking gall of this motherfucker, the one who brokered her halo, the one who commissioned her wings.

"Look, I love my mom…" I pause for effect, to see if he flinches. He doesn't. "But you and I both know she was far from angelic."

His expression doesn't change, but he tilts his head the tiniest notch, just enough to let me know he did not expect that and does not fully get the subtext.

"Kate hated my mother living with us," he insists. "Evelyn gave her some good last years and saved my marriage."

"That's a little ironic, isn't it? Most people would consider my mom to be a home-wrecker."

And now he gets it. He knows I know about the affair.

He is so uncomfortable, he scratches at his temple and chuckles. "Simone, I—"

"I'm not here to judge you or my mom," I say, and it is true. I've already judged them thoroughly. "There's just this one thing."

He wants me to stop. He wants me to go back to where I came from. He regrets opening his door without checking his security camera first.

But he glances at her name in gold around my neck and asks, "What's that?"

"Did you force my mom to get an abortion?"

"What?" he asks, outraged but quietly so, and it almost makes it seem like it is a genuine reaction.

But I know who Scott Bishop really is. I once walked in on him watching an old clip of himself in court when he was still a prosecutor. The way he courted the jurors with such eloquence and sold them a perfectly crafted story. The drama of every pause, every modulation. It was all a performance. Scott Bishop is a master of manipulation. He is fooling no one.

I push up to my feet, speak through my teeth with periods after each word. *"Did you ever force my—"*

"Absolutely not," he says, squeezing his eyes shut like he can't even bear to hear me say the words again. "Where's this coming—"

"She was pregnant when she died. Three months."

Scott does not run. He does not bark at me. Does not bare his teeth. He simply nods. "I...I saw that on the news."

"Was it yours?"

His eyes drift to the left. "I don't know."

I roll my eyes, my patience as thin as vaporized breath in the cold. "Did you use con—"

"Simone, with all due respect, I don't feel comfortable having this conversation with you."

Scott uncrosses his leg and looms over me when he stands. I flinch backward, preparing for the hit, the attack, but I quickly see I've read him wrong. I blink and hope that he didn't notice it, the way I cowered beneath him. But the way his expression switches from anger to a sort of disgusted outrage, I know he did.

"What if it was yours?" I ask, slipping my hand into my pocket. Just in case. *Just in case.*

"I certainly wouldn't have forced her to get rid of it," he says, and I can hear the recoil in his voice, the revulsion. "I cared about your mother." He pauses. "I know it's probably strange to hear this now, but I did. I—"

"So you cared about her, but not your marriage?"

He blanches, eyes widening. "Of course I did. I—"

"You don't think your wife would've left you if she found out you had a love child with the next-door neighbor?"

Scott is trapped. He stares at me, his eyes revealing absolutely nothing for a long moment, then glances in the direction of the foyer. "I'm getting the feeling that there's no friend who stood you up."

His eyes come back to me and they suddenly appear less blue. They are full of steel.

I see no point in coming clean. I move on with my line of questioning. "Scott—"

"Mr. Bishop," he corrects, and my blood boils. The fucking nerve of him to demand respect from me.

"*Scott.*"

We flinch in unison at the third voice. My eyes jump to his, but he is busy glancing toward the rear wall of the house that is lined with glass accordion doors. He seems as alarmed as I am that Kate is here in the house.

"Are you home?" she calls again, and it is my turn to blanch.

I can't let her see me here. This would look so weird, and if they start talking, if Kate mentions having seen me and Hunter recently, the lie I told to Scott will detonate in my face. He knows I did not show up to see Hunter, but if he finds out that we've been in contact recently, things will just get unnecessarily messy, especially since Hunter isn't exactly feeling me right now.

Scott's eyes come back to mine. "I think we're done here."

He motions to the foyer with his hand and heads off. My heart knocks so hard against my chest, I almost answer it.

"Where's my mail?" Kate asks, her voice faint now as he's probably already made it to the back of the house. "I told you to have it organized when I got here. I'm late to see Dr. Lasser."

My eyes dart to the pile of mail on the small end table by the door. Scott was carrying it earlier. He thought I was Kate when he opened the door for me.

I eye the staircase. I know this house and everything that awaits me beyond the landing.

I'm gone by the time Scott returns to pass through the living space. I check my phone to make sure the voice memo is still actively recording, then push into the master suite at the crown of the corridor.

27

I OPEN DRAWER after drawer as quickly and as quietly as I can. Clothes. Underwear. Then I get to the bottom drawer and there is a stack of DVDs beneath a pile of socks, vintage ebony porn. Pretty soft stuff. Beneath the stack is a Polaroid of my mother. On the back, there is a date. November 9, 1999. I recognize the picture; I remember it. It's one Dad took of her outside the house when I was seven. I flip the photo back around, and as I slowly run a finger over my necklace, I realize that Mom is wearing the same one in the photo and that I am breathing through my mouth.

"What are you doing in here?"

I jump and look up to see Scott inching inside the room.

"Sorry. Bathroom," I say, slipping the Polaroid into the back pocket of my jeans. "Long drive ahead."

"You know there's one on the first level and two in the hall," he says, flipping on the light.

Of course I do. The layout is identical to my old house. "Yeah, I just… Is your wife gone?"

"*Ex*-wife."

"Is she—"

"We're alone."

"Good," I say, and a very particular kind of silence envelops us, heavy and full of the things neither of us wants to say.

Scott moves a few steps toward me, narrowing the gap between us, and I try my best to look calm, though my chest is pounding.

When he speaks, his voice is a tight whisper. "Listen, I'm not sure how you expected me to react to seeing you in my bedroom, but this is uncomfortable for me on multiple levels. I'd like it if you left."

And then I realize how this looks, like I am propositioning him for sex. I shake my head. I am disgusted for a moment, that his mind would even go there. Then I take a breath and work up the courage to speak, to not back away now that I've come so far.

"If you cared about my mom, if you cared about her at all, why didn't you leave your wife?"

He takes a moment. "You ask that like it was so simple. Splitting up your family. Flipping your entire life upside down."

I briefly wonder if the complications he's thinking of are the financial kind. It is hard to believe a man like Scott, grandson of a real-estate magnate, would marry Kate without a prenup, but it's even harder to imagine that it is truly hard for him to break up his family because of some kind of guilt or any other human emotion.

"Did my mom tell you she was pregnant?" I ask, not actually expecting the truth, just curious to see his reaction. He is sharp. He is quick. I have no doubt he has already caught on to the path I am dragging him down.

I find the pause he takes interesting. I find the way his eyes

rove me, top to bottom and back to top, just as interesting. I
don't expect the sigh of defeat that follows his vacant once-
over. I was expecting anger. Fury. Rage.

"Did she?" I snap, compensating for his lack of emotion.

He balks. Then there is a faint nod, and I almost scream.
"I...I found out about a week before she disappeared."

"A week," I parrot, but I don't hear my own words. A low-
frequency hum has muted all sounds. I am in a tunnel and falling too fast to breathe.

I think of Kate's last diary entry. Picture the date scribbled in
her barely-legible handwriting. She wrote that entry exactly one
week before the night Mom never came home. It all checks out.

I should probably leave while I still have a chance. I should
probably not further provoke a man who has committed murder against a pregnant woman he claims to have cared about, a
claim his son wholeheartedly backs him up on. I already know
the ugly this man is capable of. But something bolts my soles
to the floor and I look directly into Scott's eyes.

"Just enough time to mastermind her murder so well, you
got away scot-free, pun intended."

He looks at me like I've just lit my head on fire. "Are you
insinuating that I—"

"Oh, I'm doing more than insinuating."

I just want him to say it, to finally admit it after all of these
years. Nothing will ever bring her back. Justice will never be
served for my mother or my family, but maybe knowing Scott
Bishop will be rotting in a dirty cell for the rest of his life will
help me sleep at night. Maybe I can finally move on.

Scott's mouth opens, but no words come out. There are a
myriad of sharp, serrated things I wish I could shove down his
throat.

"It was yours," I say, hoping he can't see me shaking as I
step closer to him. "My dad said he and my mom hadn't been
intimate in years."

Scott shifts, and for a second I think he is bolting, but he moves back and forth, paces with his head down like a captive animal. I watch him, truly impressed by his aptitude. He is acting like it is news that he is the one who got my mom pregnant. It is all an extension of the performance, but it doesn't make sense why he is trying so hard to convince me that he is stunned when moments ago he was so honest with me.

He knows. He has figured out where I've led him and now realizes he's said too much. That is why he has to pretend he didn't know the baby was his. Or maybe he feels no regret, maybe he is humoring himself and is already two steps ahead of me. Maybe he really wants to get all this off his chest, this truth that has been eating away at him all these years, and the prospective relief from finally coming clean is too tempting for him to resist.

"Your wife was fed up with your cheating," I say, and I barely recognize the sound of my own voice. "She threatened to file for divorce. You were desperate to keep her from leaving you. Maybe all of your other mistresses were fine with getting an abortion, but my mom wouldn't—"

"There were no other mistresses," he snaps, and I find it strange that this is what he chooses to clarify.

I also find it telling.

"Did she refuse to get rid of the baby? Is that why you killed her?"

"Get out." He blows air out of his nostrils. *"Get the hell out of my house."*

Scott did not answer my question, but I have the answer I was looking for.

I shut my laptop and toss it to the other side of the bed. I've been trying to write for over an hour to distract myself from the glaring reality that I've failed to come up with something that will inspire Pia to reconsider turning in her footage to her editor tomorrow, but nothing is coming. I let out a yawn, then look over at Reggie, still working as usual.

"You okay?" he asks, sensing my eyes on him.

I nod, realizing that my migraine from earlier has completely gone away. "How does the Advil know where to go?"

Reggie chuckles, his eyes pinned on his screen again. "It doesn't go anywhere. It shuts off your pain receptors."

I watch him work for a minute, and my mind goes back to the moment that he told Dad he could see himself marrying me, and I seriously consider if I am the marrying type as I try to imagine our lives together. I open my laptop again and pull up a bunch of web pages, every news article written about my mom's disappearance that I have bookmarked. Nothing sticks out. I click back into the first article and stare at Ford Fitzpatrick's name and contact info at the bottom of the page.

Asshole.

Reggie gets up to go to the bathroom, and I turn to look at his ass, then slide my phone out from underneath my pillow.

Pia answers on the fourth ring, and once I hear her voice come through, I bulldoze past her attempt at small talk. "I need another week. Please."

"Simone, it's—"

"I spoke to Scott Bishop. He admitted that he found out about my mom's pregnancy a week before she was killed. *One* week. When I asked him if the reason he killed her was because she refused to get an abortion, he flipped and threw me out of his house. He knows I'm onto him. I just..." I sigh. "Sorry for bugging you so late. Just give me a few more days to prove it. Promise I won't be wasting your time. It's Scott. It has to be."

"I spoke to Scott too. On camera."

"What did he say? What did you ask?"

"It's confidential."

"Oh, come on. I—"

"But," she says, clearly not appreciative of me interjecting,

"I can tell you he definitely told me some interesting things. None which match your theory."

"Can you just give me until end of day Friday? If I have nothing solid by then, you're free to—"

"I already sent my editor the hard drives an hour ago."

I can't even react right away. "Don't you think you should have led with that?"

"Simone, I get this story is personal for you, and I'm truly sorry about what happened to your mom. But putting the blame on Scott Bishop because maybe that's easier to digest than it being your dad won't change the fact that she's gone."

I knew I was justified in not liking this woman. I scoff. "Are you—"

"I know you feel it's exploitative because of how close you are to the subject, but in reality, it's enlightening. Think about it this way. This can help other women who are currently married to abusive and violent men and inspire them to get—"

"Fuck you," I spit and end the call.

I pace the full available square footage of my room more times than I can count, thankful that Reggie is still in the shower so he doesn't have to witness my tears of frustration.

No one knows who my father really is. No one. He wasn't abusive or vio—

I pause and blink the fountain pen down by my foot into full focus. I've never seen this before, and when I angle it in front of my face, there's only one name that comes to mind.

"Reg!"

He doesn't hear me, so I push inside the bathroom, pull the shower curtain back and push the pen forward for appraisal. "Is this yours?"

"What?" He looks from the pen to me, confusion contorting his wet face. "Damn, girl, you scared me. You came in here like you found a thong or some shit."

"That's not funny."

He gets serious. "That's not mine."

"You sure?"

"Positive."

"Well, it's not mine either." He takes it with his dripping hand and examines it closer. When he shakes his head, I say, "It was by the window. Next to the fire escape."

I don't have to explain any further. He understands the importance and shuts off the water. The person who burgled their way into my apartment dropped this just as they climbed out of the window and fled.

We're both in bed chasing separate thoughts a few minutes later when I just say it.

"Don't you think a guy like Scott would use a pen like this? Looks expensive."

He nods. "Like a collector's edition. But why would he break into your place?"

I rack my brain for the longest time until finally it saunters right into my frontal lobe. "Shit."

"What?"

"The diary." I turn to him, mouth open. "He wanted the diary back. He knows I'm onto him."

"But why would he let you in his place earlier today if he already knew you were onto his ass?"

"He had to play it off. Think about it. Who else wouldn't want me to figure out the truth?"

He actually thinks about it. "Hunter."

"Hunter?" I'm appalled. "What are you talking about?"

Reggie shrugs. "He's the one who for sure knows you have it. You're assuming he told his pops."

Reggie is…right. I am assuming. But he's wrong about Hunter. Hunter would never violate me like this. He would have just called me and told me to hand it over and I would've complied. There's no way he climbed out my fire escape and dropped this pen.

No way.

I pull the comforter back and jump out of bed.

"What are you doing?" Reggie asks.

I grab my phone and kiss him on the forehead. "I'm fine. Go to sleep."

I ease onto the other side of my bookshelves and am so relieved when Reggie turns off the lamp on my nightstand. I dial the precinct and speak in a whisper when I ask for Detective Quinn, the woman who took Fitzpatrick's position once he was promoted to sheriff.

When Detective Quinn answers, asking how she can help, I freeze. I'm not sure what I expected, but I guess I didn't think she would answer on the first ring so late in the evening. I introduce myself, stumbling over my words at first, then ask if she is familiar with a murder case involving a woman named Evelyn Watson. She says it was before she joined the force but that everyone at GHPD knows about this case. I tell her an abridged version of my theory about Scott, about the diary, and she is quiet on the line for a while.

"I hear you, Simone, but the case has been dead for—"

"Ten minutes," I snap, then soften my voice again. "That's all I need, I promise."

28

THE INTENSITY OF the police station is a lot to take in at once. I've been offered water and some generic brand of instant coffee out of a paper cup, but declined both. I can't keep anything down when my nerves are this shot. It boggles my mind every time I hear a white person describe a feeling of safety in the presence of the police, but then again, it must be nice to have an entire militia on your side.

I expected Detective Quinn to take me into her office, but she unceremoniously gestured to a cluttered desk toward the back of the bullpen. But she is pint-sized and soft-spoken, her skin pale and freckled, nothing like the seemingly devoid of emotion Fitzpatrick when he asked me a few generic questions about my mom's last whereabouts thirteen years ago. Kate's diary has been between us since I sat down in the uncomfortable folding chair next to it. She has only flipped it open once to skim the last entry under my direction.

It is obvious by her constant yawning and glances at her

phone that she thinks I am wasting her time. She doesn't trust me either.

At least the feeling is mutual.

"I thought Kate could have pressured Scott into doing it," I say, but she is still looking down at her phone. "She didn't know who Scott was cheating on her with, but she definitely knew about the affair and clearly wanted it to end."

"You think Kate Bishop conspired to have her husband murder his mistress after she found out he'd gotten her pregnant... instead of just packing up her things and leaving him?"

Detective Quinn looks at me like she is stifling a sneer. She is not taking me seriously. I was so confident when I stepped inside the precinct, but now I am insecure about everything I say.

"I don't picture someone like Kate actually planning on getting a divorce, but I can see her using it as a threat." I think it over for a second. "I don't think she had to be specific. She could have told Scott something general like *get rid of the problem or I'm leaving*, and he went about it in his own way. Maybe it wasn't premeditated and it just escalated. Kate mentioned something to me about men like Scott forcing women to have abortions. Maybe that's what he intended to do, convince my mom to get rid of the baby. But maybe my mom threatened to tell Kate, and he snapped, grabbed a knife and..."

I can't say the rest. I don't need to say the rest.

Detective Quinn jots down a few fragments because none of her notes are written in complete sentences, but she gives me no indication that I am being in any way convincing. She yawns audibly, and even though she has not excused herself any of the prior times, I can't help but expect her to this time.

She valued the aesthetic too much. As long as they looked happy to everyone else...

"It's not as wild as it sounds," I continue. "Kate wanted a picture-perfect life. That was her number one priority, according to Hunter, which included having the head of the household present. As long as it looked pretty from the outside. And who knows? Maybe he had her locked in an ironclad prenup and it was better for her to not leave. Maybe the lifestyle was more important to her than him being faithful. All I know is that mixed baby would have ruined the picture."

I glance up from my hands but Detective Quinn's expression is inscrutable, her eyes still full of doubt. She's a lot younger than Fitzpatrick, at least half his age, but I can tell she's already seen some things that give her a slightly older vibe.

"But I can't back that part up," I add, quietly. "And I might be biased because…"

I stop because I don't know how to tactfully tell a white woman about another white woman's racist tendencies. I have no idea whose side the one inches away from me will take. This is my second time running through all this anyway. Now I am adding in unnecessary details.

"Remind me how we know Kate was aware of the pregnancy," she says after a moment, her pen poised to begin her perfunctory scribbling again, which assures me I am not flat-out wasting my time here tonight.

I struggle long enough for her eyes to lift from her pad and meet mine. "We don't, I guess. I'm just assuming Scott told her after he found out and that's when she got the divorce papers drawn up and gave him that ultimatum."

She nods and sips her black coffee that is either decaf or not working. "You're assuming a lot."

I take a breath. I didn't think this would be so hard.

"But Scott definitely said my mom told him she was pregnant a week before she went missing," I remind her. "One week passes and then she vanishes? That's not a coincidence. Maybe Kate wasn't involved at all, but Scott knew for sure and did what he had to do in order to not lose her."

Detective Quinn lifts a hand up, letting me know she wants to finish jotting down her note, but also needs to interject. I've lost track of how many times she has done this, but it is amazing how much you can learn about a person's mannerisms in such a short amount of time.

"Earlier you said Scott found out a week before Evelyn went missing," she says, cocking her head to the side.

I nod. "That's what I just said."

"No. You just told me Scott was told a week before your mother disappeared. Which one is it? Did Evelyn *tell him* or did he *find out?*"

"How else could he have found out if my mom didn't tell him?"

Detective Quinn nods, not in agreement, in a way that tells me she is done hearing my take and jots down her own. Her handwriting is atrocious, so I can barely make out any of the words.

"Quinn."

Before I even glance over my shoulder, I know who just barked her name.

This time when I meet eyes with Ford Fitzpatrick, he doesn't smile or wave. He doesn't so much as acknowledge my presence before gesturing to Quinn, who immediately excuses herself and follows him into his office.

I can't resist. I turn and watch them over my shoulder. No surprise that he shuts the door completely, but there are two rather large picture windows that allow me to maintain a relatively clear picture of their brief meeting. The glass panes are thick enough to seal away all sounds, but it's obvious Fitzpatrick has a bone to pick with his subordinate. Fitzpatrick is of below-average height for a man—five-eight would be generous of me—so he is by no means of intimidating stature, but Quinn looks reverent as he clearly talks hard at her. I don't need reverberations of their exchange to see that he's pissed about something, and when his eyes come to me through the glass, I nearly squirm in my chair. He's got those thin, villainous lips and sunken cheeks that give his resting face this odious quality.

I look away first, and it's only a moment or two later when Quinn is sitting opposite me again.

"Sorry about that. Where were we?"

"I was telling you about—"

"Oh, right," she says, before I even have the chance to remind her, and she sighs. "Simone, I see where you're going with this. Okay, it makes perfect sense that Scott would be the first person—maybe even the *only* person—Evelyn would have told about her condition. That way they could figure out what they were going to do considering their individual marriages."

"Exactly."

"Doesn't mean that's what happened."

I stare at her. She seems different now. Less open, more impatient. I glance back toward Fitzpatrick's office and see that he's sitting behind his desk, shuffling through some paperwork.

My eyes shift back to Detective Quinn. "So you're saying you don't think—"

"I'm not saying anything," she says, and to me, she sounds defensive. "I'm hearing you out like you asked. I don't have to do this, you know. I have other active cases with a lot more heat than this that I could be trying to solve right now."

She is not shy about maintaining eye contact when I am speaking, but when she talks, her eyes never meet mine. Not since she left Fitzpatrick's office.

I wonder if that's what he told her, to focus on her current cases instead of me. Motherfucker.

I cross and uncross my legs and make sure I sound calmer as I try another angle. "Scott lied to me the first time I asked him if he knew about the pregnancy. His instinct was to hide the fact that he knew about it before she died. That means something. He knows it makes him look suspicious. Gives him motive."

"Which would explain why he wouldn't want to share that with you, doesn't it?"

I wasn't expecting her to make a decent point. "But—"

"You know what I've found in the nine years I've been on the force, Simone?" She tilts her head and waits for some indicator that I am anticipating her response, but I give her nothing. "An innocent person wants to steer clear of implicating themselves no less than a guilty person. Especially an intelligent, educated person who is aware of how the justice system works."

It is like we are on opposing teams. I didn't come here for her to play devil's advocate. I came for her to confirm that I'm on the right track and assist me.

I was foolish.

"Scott couldn't convince my mom to abort the baby, so he came up with his own solution to get rid of it," I say, desperate now. "Maybe I'm slightly off in the details, maybe it was an accident. But it's all there. You just have to see it."

Detective Quinn doesn't look swayed a bit. She looks like she is just humoring me at this point, scribbling down illegible notes just so I don't call up her boss and complain. She thinks I am a fucking joke.

"It's because he's a judge," I mumble.

"What was that?" Her tone is sharp, defensive, and I know she heard every word I said.

I fold my arms across my chest and cross my legs. "Nothing."

Detective Quinn glances toward Fitzpatrick's office, then makes a show of reviewing the notes she has taken so far, dragging the tip of her pen up and down the page as she skims the chicken scratch. "Did anyone else know about their affair besides you?"

Her eyes drop a few inches from my face, and I realize my fingers are tangled up in my necklace. I let the chain go and consider her question. "Pretty sure Hunter and I were the only ones."

"Hunter." She scribbles his name down. "That's…"

"Scott's son. He was my friend back then. Well, he's still…"

"And how did you two find out?"

"We walked in on them one time when we were kids," I say. "I thought it was just the one incident all this time, but the diary…"

I stop because I've already told her this part.

"What about Hunter?" Detective Quinn asks.

I wasn't expecting that. "What about him?"

Detective Quinn lets out an impatient sigh. "Did he also think it was an isolated incident?"

I shake my head. "He knew it went on for years. He was… He's older. He probably noticed things I was too young to pick up on."

Detective Quinn nods, showing no indication as to where she is headed with this, and jots something down. "And how old was he at the time of your mother's death?"

"Um…seventeen."

"Still a minor, but…"

I wait for her to finish, but she just lets that hang in the air. I can hear the echo of the word she didn't say.

Capable.

"But what?" I press, not sure if my tone has betrayed how offended I am. It's like what Reggie did before, throwing Hunter's name in the hat like it's even in the realm of possibility that he is the one who murdered my mom.

Detective Quinn looks me square in the face, and I notice the gray at her roots for the first time. I want to ask if she thinks Hunter is a suspect just so I can then assure her that he is the wrong tree to bark up, but she cuts in before I get a full word out.

"And what about your father?" she asks with the same tone, which throws me off slightly.

I wait until she glances up from her notepad to respond because this will be my first and last time saying this. "My dad is innocent. That's why I'm here."

Quinn cocks her head and I instantly regret my last words. "I thought you were here because you had a strong reason to believe Scott Bishop was responsible for your mother's death?"

"Two things can be true, can't they?"

Quinn doesn't react to the way my voice rises. She remains psychopathically calm. "Did your father know of Evelyn's pregnancy?"

"He knew she was having an affair, but the autopsy completely blindsided him."

Another scribble. It takes so much out of me to resist the urge to snatch up her pad and cross out the last couple of notes. Whatever she has written about my dad doesn't need to be there.

"Simone, I appreciate you coming down here, but there's not much I can do with what you've given me."

Again, she glances over my head toward Fitzpatrick's office before shutting her notepad. I uncross my legs in panic.

"What do you mean?" I ask.

"You've got a lot of interesting speculation going on here. I can't do anything with postulation and certainly not thirteen years post hoc. My job is to follow the evidence, not a finely-tuned narrative."

"What if it's more than that? Just because I can't prove it doesn't mean it's not true."

"Welcome to the shitty part of being an investigator." She moves to her feet in dismissal. "If we ran our investigations on hunches based on narrative appeal, we would be in even more debt than we are in now." She nods and heads off with her lukewarm cup of coffee.

"You can't even bring him in for questioning?" I ask.

She pauses for a beat. "Bring me something else and maybe we can have a different conversation."

I almost step away. But first I have to ask, "Doesn't it eat at you?"

She swings back around. "What?"

I look at her, hating that I've borrowed the phrase Matt used right before his hurtful words. "Of course it doesn't. My mom wasn't a helpless innocent white woman. She was just another casualty to you all."

I see the way my words hit Detective Quinn, her eyes softening just the slightest bit, but she doesn't say anything to me as I move past her, and because my heart is racing and my hands are shaking, I don't wait for her to speak. I leave her cubicle and feel her eyes on my back like an insult.

Before I make it out of the precinct, I am gobsmacked to see all six feet of Pia waltz into the station right past me, her eyes down on the screen of her phone. She's too busy either texting or emailing someone to see me. I watch her head straight to the back of the station. She stops right in front of Fitzpatrick's office. She taps on the door, and when he looks up, her hand rises. She waves a few times, smiling warmly as she does it. Then he gestures for her to come in, which she does, shutting the door softly behind herself. Fitzpatrick crosses the small space and opens his arms. My mouth opens when she hugs him back, her embrace so easy and casual. They aren't strangers. They've met before.

I've been played.

29

I WAIT AN entire hour for Pia to come back out of the precinct. When she emerges, the bulky bag holding her camera equipment is hauled over her shoulder just like it was when she went inside Fitzpatrick's office.

"I know you don't like me, but I thought I at least earned your respect."

"Simone..." Pia looks so thrown, her stride coming to a halt as she takes me in. "What are you—"

"I don't know why I'm so shocked. Since when were journalists honest, stand-up people?"

"Okay, you want to talk, we can talk, but if you're just going to call me names—"

"All I did was state straight facts, but trust me, there are a lot of names I can call you."

She takes a beat to look me over. My stance, my temperament. "What are you doing, following me?"

"Don't flatter yourself," I say, stepping to her. "I saw you inside."

"You saw me speaking to—"

"I saw you go into Fitzpatrick's office to interview him, which is really strange because you told me you'd sent all your footage to your editor earlier tonight."

"You think…" She laughs a little, as if she's just now catching up to where I am. "I didn't lie. My editor did get my footage. Unless you know something I don't."

"Did you call my job?"

"What?"

"My boss suddenly knows about my dad, the case, my mom—everything. And you're one of the only people—"

"I have no idea what you're talking about."

I pause. She seems to be telling the truth. Granted, I don't know her that well, but I don't see any tells. "You didn't call asking to speak to me or anything?"

"Why would I call your job when I have your cell? And why would I be trying to get to you? You're the one who needs *me* now, remember?"

I need a minute to think, but Pia circles around me, heading for her car.

"Wait."

I'm surprised she slows her stride as quickly as she does. "What now? You still haven't explained why you're following me."

"I came here to see Detective Quinn."

She shrugs. "Then why were you waiting for me in the parking lot?"

"Whatever footage you just got…" I look at her camera bag and suddenly feel out of breath. "Please don't use it. Fitzpatrick is not the guy everybody around here thinks he is."

"No?" She tilts her head, curious and challenging at the same time. "Oh, yeah, because you know everything, right?"

"Believe me about Scott Bishop or don't. But one thing I know for sure is Fitzpatrick is a dishonest prick who made it his mission to get my dad convicted of a crime he didn't do, all because he wanted to be seen as the godlike hero everyone thinks he is today. My father's freedom was nothing more than a pawn to him and my mother's death was just an opportunity to start his bid for mayor."

Pia nods, but I can tell she doesn't agree with me. "He sees things pretty differently."

"Of course he…" I pause, realizing what she's just confirmed. "So you *did* interview him, then?"

"A few weeks ago."

I glance at her bag. She's a lot taller than me, but I'm pretty fast. I could probably wrestle the drive from her. If it came down to it.

"So what was this?" I ask. "Needed a reshoot to make sure his lies were consistent? Convincing enough?"

Pia smirks, and I can't help but get the feeling that she thinks she is a step ahead of me. "I didn't film him tonight."

I hope it's just her arrogance.

"Then what's the camera for?" I ask.

Pia unzips her bag and opens it to show me her Nikon point-and-shoot. I was expecting something much more sophisticated and complicated, at least a DSLR of some kind.

"Was just showing him some shots I got at Grandpa's funeral last month," she says.

I shake my head, not getting what this has to do with anything. "What?"

"He got pulled into something and missed the burial. Took them so he could properly see his father being put to rest. I've been so bogged down by the film, I haven't had a chance to stop by yet."

"His father? His father is your grand…"

I can't believe this. I am almost stunned enough to laugh. "No wonder you don't want to hear me out. He's your uncle."

"If you're insinuating that I am unable to be impartial in my film because I'm related to one of the participants, you're wrong."

"Prove it. Tell your editor to take a minute before beginning their cut."

Pia scoffs. "We're already weeks behind schedule."

"Did your uncle put you up to this?"

"No."

"Then why touch it? You don't see the glaring conflict of interest?"

Pia steps closer to me, making sure I hear every word loud and clear. "I know it's easier to blame everyone else, but all Uncle Ford did was his job, getting a dangerous man who killed his wife off the streets. This murder rocked the entire town. All I heard growing up was what happened in Asher Lane and I lived eight entire miles away. There's questions that have never been answered. From you, your father, neighbors and, yes, law enforcement. All I'm doing is getting to the truth."

"Then how come you haven't talked to the Bishops? Mainly it's Scott you need to hear from, but you might as well get everyone's perspective, right? Talk to them and maybe I'll consider telling my dad about this."

I head to my own car hoping she stops me.

"I told you, my editor need—"

"Your editor needs the full story if your project is going to be anything close to the truth." I'm not sure if I have her yet, but she looks like she's breaking. I stop and say, "Three days. That's all I'm asking for."

Pia scoffs, but then drifts off into thought. She's considering my proposition.

Then she does something I don't expect.

She turns and heads off toward her car.

30

I STOP SHORT when I see him and now I will have to stop judging all the deer who are stricken with sudden paralysis when blinding headlights appear out of nowhere.

While my brain tries to compute the image before my eyes, some guy calls me out of my name as he steps around me, which is so uncalled-for, but I still don't move or react. I am so distracted by the sight of Hunter waiting at the crown of the steps leading into the subway station I use to get home from work that I don't even stop to consider how he knew where to find me. He looks like he hasn't shaved in a few days too long, which makes him look older and also less like his father. When we're within a couple of feet of each other, I see the depth of his anger glowing in his blues.

"Why would my dad want your mom dead?" he asks, obviously pissed but still in control.

I shuffle my brain back to our last conversation. So much has happened in the few days since then. It is mostly fuzzy, but

I know I told him I was writing a novel and that I no longer thought his dad had anything to do with my mom's death. I figured I wasn't all that convincing, but I thought he believed me, or at least couldn't care less either way. I don't understand why he has tracked me down and accosted me like this.

"Hunter." I thrust the saliva collecting in my mouth down my throat. "What are you—"

"He *loved* her."

"No, Hunter," I say, glancing over his shoulder to the steps that lead into the station. "He was fucking her. That doesn't mean he felt anything. Doesn't mean he car—"

"He cared. I could tell he did."

"Well, you know what he cared about more?" I release a wry laugh. "Keeping your mom from filing for divorce. He didn't want to have to explain my mom's mixed baby to your mom. He knew she'd finally divorce—"

"Shut up, okay? None of that makes any fucking sense."

The rest of my words scramble off my tongue. Hunter has never talked to me like this. He is the one who is standing in my way, and he is telling *me* to shut up?

"That was the one thing that would ruin *the picture*," I say, noticing his hands are now in loose fists at his sides. "It would've been the scandal of the decade on Asher Lane. Kate couldn't risk that, so she threatened to leave. That's when your dad did what he had to do to get rid of their little problem."

I step around him and jog into the station. Once I get mixed in with the dense foot traffic, I let out a breath. I just told Hunter everything. I don't know how I feel about this. I never intended to let him in on my theory, and now that he is aware, I hope he doesn't try to stop me.

After sliding my card through the turnstile, I glance back and see him digging into his pocket for his wallet as he huddles up to one of the TAP vending machines. Of course he doesn't have a MetroCard. There is no line ahead of him, so I pick up my pace and take the stairs to the southbound platform as fast as I can. I push through larger, heavier bodies, but as soon as I get to the top of the stairs, the doors squeeze shut, and I see a guy who tried to keep them open with his bare hands force himself in only to get the majority of his jacket caught in the doors, and am grateful I wasn't that desperate.

I look up at the digital monitor and see that the next train is scheduled to arrive in six minutes. A lot can happen in six minutes. I look around to see if Hunter has followed me up to this level and am relieved to see I've lost him. I reach into my pocket to text Reggie about him popping up out of nowhere, and I realize I don't even know how to explain this. I don't know how Hunter knew where to find me.

"We don't even know if the baby was my dad's."

I don't look over my shoulder. Hunter circles me and now we are face-to-face again.

"My dad and my mom hadn't had sex in years," I say, opening up a random app on my phone so I appear occupied even if my ruse is completely transparent.

"So maybe your mom was fucking some other guy on the block too."

That pauses me. I look at Hunter in a way I've never looked at him before. It is clear from his expression that he not only loves his father, he will go to battle for him, maybe even kill for him, and while part of me understands this level of devotion and loyalty, it's hard to comprehend how anyone can side with a murderer.

"Don't do that," I snap. "Don't talk about my mother like that."

"And you can talk shit about my dad all you want?"

"Leave me alone, Hunter."

I step off and head down the platform to where the middle of the train will arrive even though I prefer to be in the last few cars. Hunter grabs my forearm, forcing me to stop. It is the second time he has touched me since we were kids, the first time since angling my arm to read my tattoo. His grip is so much stronger than I remember. It would be so easy for him to toss me in front of a train if he wanted to.

"My dad knew your mom was pregnant, all right?" he says. "But he didn't know it was his baby. He had no reason to hurt her."

Hurt her.

As if she was just hurt. As if she wasn't fucking slaughtered and dumped like trash.

I scoff. "That's what he told you, huh?"

I snatch my arm free and head down the platform. As soon as I stop, Hunter sidles up next to me.

"He didn't know," he says, overemphasizing each word. "But you know who probably did? Your father."

My blood goes cold. "What?"

"You said so yourself. Your parents hadn't had sex in years. My dad knew it was rocky between them. It was obviously why she kept coming to see him. But he didn't know it was obsolete. Your dad? Oh, he knew. He fucking knew." Hunter steps closer. "So you know what actually happened, Simone? Your dad is the one who found out she was pregnant, knew it wasn't his and handled the situation."

I shake my head. "Dad didn't know Mom was pregnant until the autopsy results came back."

"That's what he told you, huh?" he asks, mimicking my voice, and I want to lift up to the tips of my toes and backhand him.

This confrontation, this aggression—this is not the Hunter I know. But maybe he has always felt like this, that my father killed my mom, and has been holding it in for so long that this is the only way for it to come out, explosive.

Hunter continues. "Your dad knew the baby wasn't his and he blacked out, grabbed that butcher knife and—"

"You're just as bad as him." I can't stop my head from shaking. "You're just as fucked up as your father."

"Whatever. At least *my* dad isn't the one who's a murderer."

Hunter steps off, and instead of relief washing over me, a surge of adrenaline courses through my veins.

"Well, you sound *real* sure."

That pauses him more than I expected it to. "Trust me, you don't want to mess with my dad."

I only smile because his words actually terrify me a little. There's a tremble in my core that I hope isn't detectable in my voice when I say, "So now you're threatening me?"

"Stop running your mouth to that detective."

So that's what this is about. I don't get how he could possibly know about my visit to see Detective Quinn a few days ago. Unless he or Scott heard from her. I thought I would never hear from her again and she'd move on to other cases like our little meeting never happened, but something I said must have gotten through to her because clearly she made some calls. I wonder if she contacted Scott even though she claimed she didn't have enough to officially bring him in for questioning.

Then I think of Fitzpatrick.

Of course.

My train of thought is derailed by the loud scraping of the literal incoming train and the swell of anticipation as everyone waiting on my side of the platform inches closer to the yellow line. I am about to make a beeline for the empty space by one of the doors on the opposite side of the track, but my mind zips back to the series of questions Detective Quinn slung at me in the precinct when she was making the distinction between Scott finding out if Mom was pregnant or being told she was pregnant. Then I jump to how she followed up that sequence with questions centering on Hunter. Now I see what was going on in her head and it renders me inert among a sea of people stuffing themselves inside the string of underground cars.

I blink and see that the train is practically filled to the brim and spot Hunter about to reach the stairs that will take him to ground level and out of the station.

I think of the terrible smells of this rush hour–dense train, the people who put on tailored office attire yet didn't brush their teeth this morning, the men who rub their semi-erect dicks against your ass under the guise of trying to get by the tight, crowded space, and I jog away from the opening doors.

I catch up to Hunter at the top of the stairs. "The only way you can be a hundred percent sure your dad didn't do it is if you know who *did*."

He stops, lines between his brows like a mini tiger clawed him there. "That's horseshit. My dad—"

"Maybe you do know who did it, Hunter." I hear myself speak, but I have no idea what I am saying, where I am taking this. "Maybe you know this person even better than you know your dad."

He rolls his eyes. "I had a long day. Just keep my dad's name out of your mouth if you go see that detective again."

"Fine. Should I give her yours, then?"

He stops only having gotten a few steps away. I wait as people rush past him, bumping his shoulder and barking for him to *move out the fucking way.* Then I realize I could be standing inches from the person who was there for my mother's last breath. The station is bustling with people. I spotted a pair of uniformed guards on my way in, but where they are now, I have no idea. They could be tied up with something, too busy to help me if this got hostile. This was stupid. Even though there was a time when Hunter made me feel nothing less than safe and protected, I should have bolted when I had the chance.

Hunter could have been the person who told Scott about Mom's pregnancy. I have no idea how he could have found out, but now that I realize it is possible, I am freaking out. It is such a stretch, it almost feels preposterous to even consider, but

Hunter knew which topiary planter I kept my spare key in. He could have walked around my house looking for me and walked in on my mother talking to her doctor on the phone. He could have found out that Mom was pregnant somehow, and since he actually knew about the affair, he would have gone to Scott to warn him. It seems crazy to think that Hunter wouldn't have come straight to me, but if he was thinking ahead and thinking like his father…

Family over everything.

There is so much I still don't know. So I stick with what I do know. I know Hunter has always felt this immense pressure to please his father. Maybe a few years ago he managed to find the courage to rebel against the law firm he wanted him to work at, but back then, back on Asher Lane, Hunter was much less defiant. He was living under Scott's roof, Scott's law.

And then the fighting. I think of how bad it must have gotten between Scott and Kate for it to affect Hunter the way that it has. Could Hunter have wanted the fighting to stop badly enough to murder my mom?

I don't think they were thinking about me that much back then.

Maybe Hunter overheard Mom telling Scott she was pregnant with his baby and decided to take it into his own hands.

Maybe it was an accident. Maybe he's the one—not Scott—who confronted Mom with the intention to convince her to get rid of it because he knew the baby would ruin his already strained relationship with his parents. Maybe it escalated. Maybe it got out of control and he made a mistake.

Maybe Scott went to talk to the DA while my dad was locked away in his holding cell because he was afraid his son's future would be shot.

Maybe Hunter agreed to escort me to his mother's house because he knew it would be better to keep me close. Maybe we are enemies. Maybe Hunter has been playing me the whole time I've been playing him.

Maybe I should have left the past in the past.

It's a little too late for that now.

"You must have hated her," I say, relief flooding me when one of the guards I saw earlier edges into my periphery. I know I shouldn't provoke him, but seeing security so close by gives me the illusion of a shield. "She tore your parents' marriage apart. She's the reason your mom became a raging drunk. Must not have been that hard for you to slice and dice—"

"Are you fucking out of your mind?"

Hunter takes a step forward, suddenly so tall and massive, and I curse myself for never listening to Reggie, who has been trying to convince me to carry a vial of Mace on my key chain pretty much since we met. I never thought I'd have to use it, definitely not on someone like Hunter. But then again, I've never seen Hunter this angry. I reach into my pocket, feeling for Reggie's knife, but then I realize I left it in my other jacket.

I take a breath and swallow hard. "You had to get rid of the baby so your mom wouldn't leave your dad."

"I *wanted* my parents to get divorced." He sounds furious and amused at the same time and it discombobulates me. "I begged my dad to leave her a hundred times so the fighting at three a.m. would stop."

"And you got tired of waiting. Took it into your own hands. Got rid of what made them fight."

It was just a dig at first. A way to get under his skin. To show him how blind he is to his father's obvious actions. But the more I milk this, the more it seems like it could be true. Maybe I've been barking up the wrong tree this whole time. Maybe I've been pinning my mom's murder on the wrong Bishop.

The only difference is that if I have to see this one behind bars, my heart would be shattered.

The man who slams into me at the foot of the stairs has to be at least two hundred and fifty pounds. Before I can even process the fall, I am on my bare hands and knees, but the pain from the impact isn't even enough to distract me from the piss and bacteria I am now covered in. I am still trying to pull myself together when I see his bloated hand reaching out for me. Hunter says something to him that makes him draw back. Then I see Hunter reaching down for me too, but I refuse his gallantry and struggle back to standing on my own. Who knows if he would have just let me go when I was back on my feet? Maybe he would have grabbed me up, dragged me out of the station and delivered me a fate similar to the one he delivered to my mother.

"I'd never hurt your mom," he says as I straighten out my top and dust off my jeans. "You know why? Because I'd never hurt *you*."

I look away because he sounds so earnest, and I don't know what to believe anymore. Hunter's jaw flexes like he is about to say something else, but then he heads off. Before he gets a few steps away, he flips back around. "You know someone who was so used to being hurt, so used to being heartbroken, that maybe he just snapped one day?"

I push past him. "Leave my dad out of this."

"Oh, yeah? Like you're doing with my dad?"

I ignore him and head back to the platform. He jumps on my heels. I grind my jaw.

"Your father sat back while his wife got fucked by another man for years. You don't think that—"

"Leave me alone, Hunter," I snap, feeling anger snake through my entire body like fire.

"Think about it. He hadn't touched your mom in years. You know what that does to a man's psyche? No wonder he snapped."

"I said, leave me—"

"It's always the husband, right?"

"You're such a fucking asshole." I push him off and use a crowd of tourists to put some distance between us.

He loses me for a second, then catches up. This time he doesn't have to grab my arm to hold me in place. He just stares down into my eyes and my soles are pinned to the ground.

"You're wrong," he whispers, and the ground beneath my feet quakes and it is not only because another train is arriving.

"I'm going to prove it," I say with as much conviction as I can manage.

"No, you won't. Because you don't want the truth." His head is shaking in disappointment or disbelief or something, but it looks like his anger has dissipated. "Not if it hurts."

"You don't know anything about what I want."

"You want to investigate, fine. But you can't just craft a narrative that'll make a juicy plot for a fucking *New York Times* bestseller and try to fit everything into it. If you want to be creative, then write, but you can't just fucking ignore the obvious just so you can still eat chocolate and drink Coke with your father every Sunday."

"Get the fuck away from me," I hiss, tears prickling in the corners of my eyes.

I break away from him and make it to the platform just before the doors shut. Seven stops in, I realize I am on the wrong train. But at least I'm alone. Hunter didn't follow me.

31

I TOLD HUNTER the name of the temp agency I used to get my job at the PR firm. This hits me as I try out a new font in Word for the measly two thousand words I have drafted so far.

He could have contacted them and found out my assignment, but that has to violate some kind of privacy law. He could have done some hefty research to find out the offices the agency sends candidates to and called around until he found the one where I work, but the time commitment that would warrant seems unreasonable.

He also could have followed me.

Hunter could have stalked me from my building in Brooklyn onto the R and continued by foot once I got off in Manhattan.

The truth is, I don't know who Hunter is anymore. We were neighbors. Best friends. But that was over a decade ago. We are history. Bygone.

It is way later than I am supposed to stay up in order to get eight hours of sleep before my alarm goes off in the morning, but I can't stop the cacophony of thoughts that have been buzzing around in my head since I spoke to Detective Quinn, which have multiplied tenfold since bumping into Hunter. My mind goes back to the idea that Hunter somehow orchestrated that first run-in at Reggie's firm's building. It is still weird that they are working at the exact same firm, but there is nothing to support that he purposefully ran into me that afternoon.

I was supposed to be writing the first draft of whatever this manuscript I've started is going to be, but I haven't gotten more than a couple hundred words in today. I am in my bathroom, brushing my teeth, thinking about how militant my father used to be about brushing twice a day, when that laugh he let out after I told him it was Scott Bishop who was sleeping with Mom all those years reverberates in my head.

I need some air. I rinse and slip on a chunky pair of ASICS. Then I remember it's past midnight on a Thursday and I have to clock into work in less than seven hours. I kick them off and tuck myself into my bed, repeating what I know to be true over and over in my head.

Scott Bishop knew my mother was pregnant. He never ended the affair.

Kate knew about the affair but never knew it was with my mom.

My dad knew about the affair but never knew it was with Scott. He had no idea about the baby.

Hunter knew about the affair, knew it had gone on for years. *Family over everything.*

Part of me wants to believe Hunter was only trying to convince me that Dad is the one who murdered Mom because he has to take the heat off himself somehow. Or off his father. I can't tell anymore.

Then I hear the echo of my father's laughing again, and I can't help but wonder which part he found ironic. Maybe my father was only pretending to be surprised to learn that it was

Scott. Maybe he found out thirteen years ago and went into a blind rage and killed her, and the fact the man Mom was pregnant by was the judge next door makes it even sweeter.

Or maybe laughing was the only thing he could do at that moment to keep from completely breaking down.

I don't know who or what to trust anymore. My father is my only family. My loyalty defaults to him.

But I still need answers.

32

Before
Saturday, May 9, 2009

THE DAY YOUR mother died you came straight to me. You showed up at my home unannounced in the afternoon, my husband still at work, and before you could even get out the words, I knew. It was all over your face, the grief, the anger. I made you a negroni and you slumped down on the couch. You reminisced for a while, telling me story after story of you and your mom, moments you cherished from your idyllic childhood. The way she'd show up for every one of your Little League games even though she hated baseball. Something about your eighth birthday party. You smiled as you talked, but you kept your head down. I only half listened, my mind elsewhere, rubbing your back and patting you gently as you cried in my arms. You told me your wife wouldn't even leave work to visit your mom in the hospital before she passed, to be there for you. You were pissed. I'd never seen you this angry. I stopped listening completely then. I could only think of your wife at that point. I'd seen you with her and your son plenty of times. Talking. Laughing. You all looked perfect together. Like a still from a Kohl's commercial. You seemed to have everything figured out. Your home was gorgeous, you even vacationed together twice a year. If I hadn't known the truth, I would have thought she was the perfect wife. She always looked so elegant, so well put together. She was pretty and thin and blonde. She looked the part, kept herself in pristine shape. Routine facials and highlights and Botox. Bergdorf's and Barneys and high-end designer sample sales on the Lower East Side. I'd often see her at the supermarket dressed in her head-to-toe black spandex, straight from whatever trendy workout class she was into at the moment. Her smile always seemed genuine, wide and symmetrical. To be honest, there were times when I envied her. I understood her dedication to her job—I was the same way before I left—but what she'd done to you was just cruel. I was not perfect, but even I was not that bad.

You kissed the back of my hand and told me you were so grateful to have me in your life, that every night before you fell asleep you wished you'd met me first. You were always saying things like this to me, but this time they felt painfully sincere, your eyes dark and urgent as you spoke. I ran my hand over yours and told you to keep talking, to talk all you needed if it would make you feel better.

We sat there on the couch until we both were a little too drunk, then drifted into the kitchen. I fixed you a plate of the pot roast that I'd cooked for dinner, and you smiled at me from across the table at something I said. I watched you eat, then put the rest back in the oven as you ignored a phone call from your wife.

"Fuck her," you snarled and tossed the phone on the counter. Your anger was palpable even from across the room. I made my way over to where you stood, slid a hand up your leg, and you used both of your hands to lift me onto the counter. You kept your shoes and pants on, only undid them as much as you needed to and pushed into me like that, shallow at first and then deeper. I wrapped my arms around your neck and you whispered my name. You rarely made me come, but this time was different, and it wasn't until after you came inside me that I realized we hadn't used a condom. You seemed to be just as shocked as me after I pointed it out, that after all this time, we both had let it slip so casually. You apologized profusely like that would do anything now. I left the room to shower, and as soon as I came back out of the bathroom, I told you I was pregnant. You laughed, sort of, and said that was absurd, there was no way for me to know that, then reminded me of your vasectomy.

"It's impossible anyway," you said, your yawn full of satisfaction. "I can't get you pregnant."

Of course, it wasn't actually impossible. I was not on birth control. I'd stopped taking the pill a year before I got pregnant and never started back up. Vasectomies, I knew, also were not 100 percent. It was possible.

I had a feeling. A sickening, atrocious feeling.

When my husband finally came home that night, I half expected him to walk through the door, take one look at me and call me a whore. To say he knew my secret. He knew I was pregnant with another man's baby.

But he did nothing like that. Instead, when he saw me, washing dishes in the kitchen sink, he ducked slightly under the threshold and smiled across the room at me.

"Sorry I'm so late," he said. "Left you a message. Did you get it?"

"Yeah," I said. I hadn't checked my phone.

He came closer and hugged me from behind. I felt the warmth of his body against mine, his hands slipping around my waist, over my belly, and my stomach turned. All I could think of was the potential lump of cells starting to form, growing in my womb with every second. I also couldn't figure out why he was in such a good mood. Something must have happened at work, a promotion, maybe? It was the only time he seemed to want to have sex.

He must have felt me tighten, because he kissed the back of my neck and then pulled away slowly. "What's wrong?" he asked, and I could tell by the way his voice dropped that the question was genuine.

"Nothing. I'm just tired. I'm going to bed," I said, cutting off the water and turning for the door. I felt like shit. I rushed upstairs to the guest bathroom and locked the door, but by the time I knelt down on the cold tile, the urge to vomit had passed.

33

I WATCH DAD across from me in his usual slump nursing his Coke, probably wishing it was something stronger. He hasn't unwrapped his Snickers in the fifteen minutes I've been here. I didn't let him know I was coming because I didn't want him to have time to prep in anticipation of my arrival.

"But it had to drive you crazy," I say, furiously eyeing the bottle of Coke as he takes another casual swig. "Another man screwing your wife all those years?"

"Watch your mouth, Simone," he snaps, glancing at the couple on the other side of the space.

"Having sex. Whatever. Didn't that get to you after a while?"

"What do you want me to say? I was angry? Okay, I was angry." But his voice stays level and remains devoid of any emotion. "I just wanted your mother to be happy."

"Happy with another man?"

He doesn't look at me. Doesn't blink. Doesn't take another swig. He has gone completely catatonic.

I fold my arms in front of my chest. "So how come you never left her?"

He takes a moment. "I didn't want you growing up only seeing me two days a week."

Now he looks at me and a shiver goes down my spine. So often people in this world make it impossible to believe in the kind of nobility he describes. He stayed silent, knowing about her affair, because he didn't want to lose me. He stayed for me, not my mom. That means he might not have loved her anymore. Maybe after he found out she was sleeping with another man, he started to hate her.

And one day he snapped.

Like Hunter said. Like Aunt Patrice has been trying to get me to believe all this time.

My stomach clenches before my next obligatory question. "Did you know she was pregnant before the autopsy?"

"Simone, you better watch your tone," he says, speaking with his jaw clenched. "Who the hell do you think you're questioning like this? Don't you think I've had enough of people questioning me?"

He didn't answer. He is avoiding the question.

"You said she couldn't hide anything from you," I say, leaning in and lowering my voice. "So how'd she manage to hide a growing baby from you?"

Dad finishes off his soda, then looks me right in the eyes. "I told her to get rid of it."

Another lie. Not only did he know Mom was cheating on him all those years, but he also knew she was pregnant. Pregnant with another man's baby. How could my father have kept this from me all these years? If he is capable of hiding this, what else is he capable of?

Before I can come up with possibilities, Dad makes a gesture to one of the guards, which is a signal that he's ready to head back. We still have forty minutes left until my visit is over. The fact that he would rather be locked in a cell than across from me is a statement in and of itself.

I give the guard a gesture of my own and he pauses, looking to my dad to see if he's changed his mind. He nods and the guard heads back to his post. But Dad doesn't sit back down.

"But she didn't do it," I say, and I can't believe the chasm my thoughts have fallen into. "She didn't get rid of it."

Dad glances at the unopened Snickers bar and shrugs. "Her body, her choice. She said she was keeping it and leaving me."

"So why'd you pretend...?" I swallow. I can barely look up at him. "When we got the autopsy results, you acted like you were surprised that she was pregnant."

"I was under a police investigation. I had to act like I didn't know."

"Sure, with them, but with *me*?"

"It was easier to stick to one story."

I was right. My mom was being forced to have an abortion, but maybe I've had the wrong perpetrator in my head this whole time.

Mom and Dad never fought. So much animosity must have been brewing inside Dad. Maybe one day he just couldn't take it anymore. Maybe she told him she would not abort the baby, and he blacked out.

I can't do it. I can't stay in this place, the place where I've cried gallons of tears for my mother, while my father acts like it is no big deal that he has lied to me all these years.

Dad calls my name a few times, but I don't look up to meet his eyes. I'm afraid of what I might find there. Before I can object, the guard is back and escorting him back to his cell.

An affair and love child don't justify murder, but if my dad killed my mother, I will have to mourn another parent, the only one I have left.

My phone buzzes in my hand while I'm slipping my key into my car's ignition. It's Reggie asking me if I will meet him for dinner at a restaurant in Park Slope at seven. I just found out my father might have actually murdered my mom and Reggie is asking me out on a date like we've boomeranged back to the beginning of our relationship. I'm too in shock to do anything else but give him an ETA and I can't help thinking that maybe he was right.

Maybe there's nothing I can do to get my dad exonerated because he is the one who murdered my mom.

Maybe closure isn't all it is cracked up to be.

34

I'VE ALREADY FENDED off a handful of oily men in their fifties looking to cheat or lure and curbed my anxiety with two shots of gin by the time Reggie slinks up behind me at the bar looking more appetizing in his disheveled suit than anything I've spied on the menu. There is another short wait until we're seated in a booth toward the back of the restaurant. Reggie sits next to me and rubs my arm as he reminds me that even if my dad knew my mom was pregnant with another man's baby, it doesn't necessarily mean he killed her. Feeling my goose bumps, he drapes his suit jacket over my bare arms and brings up the correlation versus causation thing again, and weirdly I am way more receptive to his critique of my thought process this time.

I know my dad. I know he is not a killer.

Reggie also makes sense of what my dad could have meant by just wanting Mom to be happy. He says maybe Dad truly did just want my mom to be happy even if that happiness was found with another man and meant he had to sacrifice his own happiness. It still makes sense that he would have told her to get rid of the baby because the baby would inevitably split up our family. He could have made the suggestion out of love as an attempt to protect me.

I ask Reggie if this means I was right, that it is either Hunter or his dad who murdered Mom and then tossed her into the river like garbage. Reggie is still reluctant to come to a conclusion with such shoddy evidence, but he eventually picks Hunter, and I can tell it is his own bias creeping in there. It's obvious that he is still sour about the fact that we've been spending so much time together, so I take his opinion with a huge heaping of salt.

Three glasses of wine later, I shrug off Reggie's jacket, our laughter helping warm me up from the inside, though I barely know what Reggie is saying at this point.

"That wasn't even that funny," he says, reaching for my untouched water glass. "You drunk?"

I smile and don't answer his question. "I miss just being with you. No phone. No emails. No laptop. Just us."

I touch his knee. He gives me a smile, all mouth and eyes. My hand slips up to his thigh and his lips part like that one touch was enough to make his heart pound, and now I am smiling back, all teeth.

"Look at us," he whispers, tucking my curls behind my shoulder. "Vibing. Smiling…" He leans in, angling his face, and my breath hitches. "Kissing…"

I expect a lingering peck, but Reggie kisses me with an open mouth and it makes me moan as embarrassment immediately flushes my cheeks. I can't remember the last time we were actually inebriated out in public like this and therefore able to put on such a bold public display of affection. I don't object when he slips me his tongue or worry that anyone can see how wide my legs are spread under this table. I kiss him back like this is the first and last chance I will ever have and I'm aware that the whole restaurant now knows what's going down as soon as we get out of here, but I don't care. Let them watch.

Our server sidles up to the table twice before we part for air. This time our food is here and steamy. We are warned to be careful with the piping hot plates, but we don't even get to our food until it has cooled off considerably, which is perfect since we both love us some lukewarm pasta.

I can't remember what I expected Reggie to taste like the first time I went down on him, but I remember being surprised by how pleasant and subtle it was, and also how silky his flesh felt on my tongue. The heat of him stunned me too. I guess that part should have been obvious, but I didn't expect the sensory experience to be pleasurable on my end too.

"You're so cute when you're concentrating," he whispers, fisting a handful of my curls so he has an unobstructed view of the hard work I am putting in.

Sometimes he gets a little too into it, and I have to remind him that I am not one of those lank-haired white girls he used to fuck in college, but right now the slight pain his grip causes at my scalp feels invigorating.

I push off my knees with a smile that makes him grin, and he grabs my hand to help me balance as I straddle his lap. All twenty of our fingers are interlocked when I align us and push down so he breaks through me all at once. Rarely is there not reciprocal foreplay, but sometimes I need this raw, slightly abrasive feeling of being impaled without manual preparation or premeditation. I don't move right away. I am emotional and I have no idea where this is coming from, but it is like a vortex. My buzz has almost entirely worn off, but I feel like I could burst into tears if he looks at me the wrong way. Or the right way.

"You okay?"

I nod because words are too difficult right now and because he knows I am not okay. I am disintegrating. Useless. I am his, all his.

Reggie releases his grip on my hands and loops my arms around his neck. He takes my waist in both palms and guides me the way he did when he was teaching me what he likes. Again, it feels like we've ricocheted back in time, like we are back at the genesis of our love story.

If it wasn't for the two polite knocks that arrive at my front door, I would have come in a few more strokes, probably on the brink of tears.

"Expecting somebody?" he asks, as I come to a complete stop.

I thought I was the only one who heard it. I glance at the door, alarmed, then back at Reggie, who looks totally calm, only mildly irritated, and I remember how men can go through life not fearing random knocks on their doors at night.

"No," I say, suddenly feeling cold and exposed, though his hands are still very warm against my bare skin.

"Might be a neighbor. Locked out or something." He looks around for his pants. "I'll get it."

He lifts me off with such care, I feel more tears tingle in the corners of my eyes. I reach for my blanket as he jumps back into his suit pants. His erection is still very visible against the top of his thigh, but I don't say anything in case he is right and it is one of my neighbors who are both straight women living alone. If they are locked out, it is the least I can do to lift their spirits.

I creep to the edge of my bookcase and watch Reggie look through the peephole. He draws back, just stands there for a beat, then looks back at me, confusion on his face.

"Who is it?" I mouth.

Reggie eases away from the door as quietly as he can and hastily finds his shirt on the floor, then throws his arms into the sleeves. "It's the dude who works at the firm with me. The one I've been helping."

"With the extra work?" He nods, rushing to button his oxford. "How'd he know you—"

"No idea. Be right back."

Reggie is already jogging to the front door before I can tell him he has buttoned his shirt lopsided. He opens the door and steps out in the hall, but holds his arm between the door so he doesn't lock himself out.

I head back to my bed, thinking I am just going to pull the sheets back and get comfy until he gets back, but stop short when I realize there is only one person who works at Reggie's firm who would know my address.

Hunter.

I hurry to pull on the first sweat suit I find in my drawer, but I already know there is no salvaging this. I'm just going to have to watch it burn, maybe find some beauty in the flames.

35

I CAN'T BREATHE. Can't move. Can't blink. I consider bolting over to the other side of the bookcase and shoving the door shut right in Hunter's face before he realizes—

It doesn't matter. Hunter knows this is my building. He's been here before, knows exactly which floor I live on and exactly where to find my unit.

All I can do is hold my breath as I imagine Hunter taking in Reggie in his lopsided shirt. I didn't even notice if he zipped up his fly. I don't even know why I'm hiding like this. Reggie has missed a button on his shirt and is barefoot. Hunter can probably smell me on him. He knows I am here. He knows I've lied and deceived him. Not just about the diary. He knows I lied to him when we were snuggled up in the attic, when I willingly let him believe I was single.

"You came to see my girlfriend?" Reggie asks.

It is not so much of a question as it is an accusation.

I lean against the bookcase, but I can only hear what Reggie says, Hunter's softer voice not making it through both partitions.

I grab my stomach. I can't believe it is coming to this. I want to charge toward Hunter and curse him out for showing up at my place uninvited. I want to sling a *how dare you* and a *who do you think you are* his way, but the other part of me is indifferent to Hunter. Fuck Hunter and his feelings. Fuck that he now knows I am a liar. For all I know, he murdered my mom. Reggie is the one who is totally blindsided here. He is the one who has to be reeling right now, not only to see some random dude showing up at my place at midnight, but for this random dude to not be random and actually one of his colleagues. And not just any colleague—the one he has been assisting, trying so hard to impress.

I've really fucked this one up.

I hear Hunter say something, his voice louder now as if he wants me to hear.

"Bro, no disrespect, but I offered to help you with work," Reggie says. "Not to share my girl with you."

I pace and dig my hands into my scalp. I want to rip out my curls. I want to scream.

"Your...what?" Hunter asks, and I almost start ripping books from the shelves and tossing them around the room.

I can't take this. Why won't Hunter just leave? He is the type who can always think on his feet. So why won't he just make up something stupid but reasonable about him needing him to do some lawyer thing by the morning and he stopped by to see if I could relay the message to him since his phone died and he was in the area?

"Wait. You're talking about..."

There is a pause. Reggie is putting it together.

Shit. He is there. He knows.

I'm fucked.

"You two grew up in Jersey, right?" Reggie asks.

It sounds like Hunter confirms this. The next few things Reggie says back to him are swallowed up by the distance. Then I hear the front door click shut, and I clench my belly, bracing myself for what is to come. I don't know what kind of tempest to expect. I don't know what to say.

Reggie doesn't storm in. He doesn't toss around my furniture or punch a wall, but I notice his fists are clenched tight when I creep to the other side of the shelves. He opens the refrigerator and shifts things around only to shut it, gently. He is not hungry, I know this. We just polished off restaurant-sized plates of pasta less than an hour ago. He is stalling. He is working through the noise in his head.

"It never came up," I say, almost in a whisper.

"It never came up," he repeats with a nod.

Then his eyes slowly come to me, and I have never felt more exposed in my entire life. I can't tell if it is distrust or disgust in the slight squint his eyes hold, but it makes me wobble.

"I'm just so glad I never went through with the consultation."

I rack my brain and come up with nothing. "What consultation?"

"You clearly have other priorities," he says.

"I don't know what you're talking about."

He doesn't answer. He comes toward me, and I squirm, not because I think he will hurt me or anything close. Because I am afraid of hearing what he really thinks of me.

Reggie brushes past me, eyes averted, and disappears on the other side of the bookcase. I give him a minute and gather my words, then step on the other side with him. He is looking for his shoes.

"Reg, I know this feels—"

"Really? Your girl started talking to some other dude behind your back too?"

"I just thought it would be easier to get him to do what I wanted if he thought he had a chance with me." I slide a hand up his arm just as he reaches for his second shoe. "But come on, Reg. He never *actually* had a chance. I was just—"

"You know I have to work with him, right?"

He glares at me and shrugs me off. I can't tell which hurts more, the disdain in his voice or his apparent aversion to my touch.

"That's the thing," I say, trying to keep my voice as level as possible. "I didn't realize he worked at your firm until—"

"You could've given me a heads-up as soon as you found out. But you didn't. That's telling."

"No, it isn't. It was right after he realized I stole the diary."

He shrugs. "What does that have to do with me?"

"I thought you'd use it as an excuse to tell me to stay away from him. But I couldn't. I figured I might need him again."

I try to take the shoes out of his grasp, but he doesn't let me.

"He's mad at me now anyway," I say. "Probably won't be seeing him anymore."

He scoffs. "Probably?"

I pause and give him a strong look. "What, are you giving me an ultimatum?"

Reggie shakes his head, not in response to my question but in exasperation, and sits on an edge of my bed. I think he is going to calm down and we will be able to talk this out rationally, but then he reaches for his socks and slides them on, shaking his head again.

"I've been doing this white man's work while he's been trying to fuck you. Been calling him *bro* when I should've just called him *master*."

"Reg."

He ignores me and finds his phone on the bed. I follow him into the main area and he shrugs into his suit jacket even though the humidity is in the high eighties tonight.

I get it. His ego is crushed. But this is a little dramatic. And I still have no idea what consultation he was talking about.

"It's been a lot lately." Reggie looks at me, a softness in his eyes for the first time since Hunter interrupted our night. "My schedule. Your dad being in prison. Your mom being murdered. You just now telling me about all this shit."

His voice is softer too, so soft it is scaring me. There is a note of finality in his tone and it makes me want to scream loud enough to bust the screen of the TV the way that mermaid did in *Splash*.

"What are you saying?" I ask, feigning nonchalance the best I can, but I don't think the tiny crack at the end was any bit convincing.

"Maybe we should take a break," he says, and the suggestion steals my breath, but I don't look up at him and give him the satisfaction of seeing the shock in my eyes. I can't bear to see how he is looking at me right now either.

Breaks are what men suggest when they want to test the waters and see if there is anything better swimming beneath the surface. Men don't book weekly therapy sessions or use the extra free time to start that old hobby back up when they are on a break. They go into full bachelor mode, filling any orifice they can with as much as they can. To them, a break is temporary freedom, a kaleidoscope.

A break to me would be internment, a black hole.

Because this is all my fault. I should have been honest. With Reggie. With Hunter.

But I already knew that. I just thought Reggie would understand how important it is that I find out what happened to my mother after so many years of wanting answers. Closure. My dad out of prison where he belongs.

Clearly he doesn't. Or he still thinks my investigation is tainted by my creative mind and obsession with literature. I don't know which is worse.

I barely recognize my voice when I manage, "For how lo—"

"Indefinitely," he says with no hesitation, and I think of the way Reggie kissed me earlier tonight, how he held my face and kissed me like no one else existed in that restaurant, on the planet, in the universe. How quickly things can change.

Reggie doesn't wait for me to respond or accept. He ducks out of my apartment without looking back, doesn't text me when he gets home or when he wakes up. I don't text or call either. He has his ego. I have my pride.

I realize what consultation he was referring to when I am plucking out the one long chin hair that grows back thicker every month, everything making sense now.

Reggie was going to buy me a ring.

36

MY FINGERS FLY across the keyboard as I finish up my second chapter of the day. I have not stopped writing since I sat down at my desk this morning. If I stop I'll think of last night and I really don't want to think of last night. Not anymore. I glance at an incoming email and decide that it can wait until after my lunch break, then click back into my story.

"Do you wash your hair *every* day?"

I pause, my fingers still hovering over the keyboard, an unfinished sentence beckoning me to add the few words it needs to be complete. First I place the voice, which is vaguely familiar in this context, then replay the absurd question. I almost laugh, but I don't want to be insulting. I've been writing my chapters in the body of an email draft, so I hit Send, sending it to myself, and play it cool with the woman who interviewed me for this gig, like I haven't been doing personal work during company time. But when I swivel around to face Lindsay, one of the senior assistants whose main responsibility is to keep the summer interns in check and a Chloe eau de parfum enthusiast, my cool is obliterated when I see the man being escorted into the suite by one of the said interns.

Hunter is here.

Like literally strutting inside the bullpen at the place where I work. He has already tracked me down at home. Now he is at my job.

Of all the times to find out what it is truly like to be a gazelle, to be hunted and never see it coming. Last night, I was so tangled up in my chaotic emotions about Reggie wanting to take a break and not even giving me a chance to object that I never even considered why Hunter had come over. But it's all I can think about now. What does Hunter Bishop want with me? Is he here to try to silence me somehow? Why would he show up at *my job*?

"Simone?"

I blink Lindsay back into view, her nipple-length, dark-rooted, silky blond hair that she definitely washed, blew out and manually curled this morning.

"Lindsay," I say, wishing I could pop her smile. "You know I'm Black, right?"

Her smile gets even wider, but it's strained now. "What? Of course."

I expect her to get it, but by the way she laughs and playfully pushes me on the shoulder, I can tell she couldn't be farther from understanding. She has no idea why it would be follicle suicide for me to wash my hair every day because she lives in a society where she doesn't have to know the proper maintenance of any hair texture different than hers. I want to explain, but Hunter is here, and I am pretty sure I just saw the intern point in my general direction out of the corner of my eye. Luckily, Lindsay is standing right in front of me, blocking most of my body.

She also doesn't get the hint. "Me and all the other assistants were just having this huge debate downstairs about girls washing their hair every day. I mean, in a perfect world we all would, but—"

"Sorry. I have to…"

Hunter has spotted me.

I stand and slip my feet into my sandals. Lindsay glances over her shoulder, and following my sight line, she sees Hunter studying me.

"Oh, I see," she croons as I grab my purse. "He's hot. Get it, sis!"

I am so stunned by her audacity that I come to a full stop.

If Hunter wasn't waiting for me, I would school her so good, she would never, ever call another Black girl her *sis* again unless they were legit adoptive sisters or something, but I am rushing toward the exit before my anger can even detonate.

It is raining when Hunter and I make it outside. We stand close under the scaffold with all the smokers, and I do my best to remain calm.

"I'm just trying to understand," Hunter says. "You throw me out, then turn around and try to hook up with my dad?"

I catch the *gross* on the tip of my tongue before it rolls out of my mouth and shake my head. "It wasn't like that."

"I guess you have some other reason why you were waiting for him in his bedroom, then."

I roll my eyes. I am fucking tired of his sarcasm already. "It's not like I was waiting naked."

He steps closer, and I almost back away. "Why the hell were you even at the house? What kind of twisted game are you playing?"

"I'm not playing—"

"She wants it back."

I frown. "Wants what back?"

"The diary. Kate wants it back."

And there it is. "That's why you came over last night?"

He looks away, running a hand through his hair. "What difference does it make?"

"You showed up at my apartment *and* my job just to get your mom, who you don't even fuck with like that, her diary back?"

Just saying the words makes me tingle. There must be something inside those pages that she doesn't want anyone, namely me, to see. Something I must have missed.

"I told her why you stole it. How you think Dad killed your mom." He stops, waiting for my reaction, but I give him nothing, pretend to be totally unconcerned with Kate's reaction even though I am dying to hear the details.

"Then I had to tell her why," he continues. "You know what it's like to watch your mother's heart break right in front of your face?"

"You know what it's like to attend your mother's closed-casket funeral?"

Hunter's mouth opens, closes. He turns and watches a few people walk by, two with toddlers in strollers that are too small for them, one guy in navy scrubs talking loud into the mic of his earbuds to combat the traffic zooming by.

Then he looks at me again, eyes hard and direct. "She had no idea it was your mother. She respected her. She was her best friend."

I scoff. "She asked her to use the back entrance whenever she had guests over."

"It was easier to get to Nana's suite that way."

"Wow," I say, too floored by his willful ignorance to even come back with something quick enough. I just hope it is only his emotions making him dense right now, and he isn't truly this blind.

I am only allowed fifteen minutes on my morning break, which is only halfway done, but I have to empty my bladder, so I try to step around him to head back inside the building.

He blocks me like he was anticipating my next move, like we are in a ring.

"You and I were the only ones who knew what was going on between them and you know what? It should have stayed that way. All this shit should have stayed in the past. Everybody's moved on except you."

As if there is a way to move on without any proper answers. Without closure. With my dad rotting in his cell despite his innocence.

Fucking asshole.

"Did she cry? Did Kate cry when you told her it was my mom?"

He knows what I am asking. His eyes lock on to mine as he shakes his head. "Not one tear."

I break the eye contact, this moment feeling overwhelming and intense, though it has brought nothing new to the table. Kate and her bland-looking fried chicken had nothing to do with my mom's death, but I could still be standing within arm's reach of the person who was there for her last breath.

"It's her personal property," Hunter says, impatient, nothing like the guy I hopped into that elevator with or the one who drove me to Jersey or the one who wanted to kiss me after we talked about my *Charlotte's Web* tattoo. "She wants it back."

"Fine. I don't need it anymore. Already read it cover to cover."

I sidestep him again, but Mr. Consistent doesn't miss a beat. He squares his stance. "I'll send a courier over tonight. Eight okay?"

"It's like that?"

He firms his voice. "Will you be home at eight?"

"I'll give it to your courier." He starts to back off, and I can't help but add, "Unless Reggie comes over and is busy fucking my brains into the wall."

Maybe that was too much, especially since I technically did

steal property from his mother's home, but even as I watch his face contort with the sting of those words, I am finding it hard to feel an ounce of remorse. Of course, Reggie won't be coming over tonight, but Hunter doesn't know that.

He grinds his teeth and shakes his head. I expect him to storm off, but he inches closer to me. "When we ran into each other a few weeks ago, I was so excited. I thought it was fate and I don't even believe in that shit. All these years, worrying about you, hoping you were okay. Got all excited like some stupid kid thinking it could be the way it used to be." His laugh is wry, empty. "But it can't, right, Simone? What, did your boyfriend tell you where I worked? Then you tracked me down and tricked me into telling you about the diary? Everything's going to plan, huh?"

"Yup," I say, giving him a taste of his own sardonic medicine. "You've got it all figured out."

He speaks through his teeth, jaw clenched. "Don't call me. Don't text me. And leave my fucking family alone. I'm a lawyer, remember? Don't try me."

Hunter turns away and gets swallowed up by the foot traffic before making it to the corner.

I don't know who that was. That wasn't the Hunter I grew up with.

Family over everything.

Reggie obviously didn't track him down and I obviously didn't follow him into that elevator only to get him to talk about his mother's diary, a diary I had no idea even existed, and I can even see in hindsight how it could look like I brilliantly orchestrated the whole con. If only I were that good and there wasn't a glaring glitch. Like Hunter said, no one knew about what we had seen when we walked in on our parents in that kitchen but us. I thought it was a onetime thing. It was finding out about the extensive affair that sent my Spidey senses off.

I know what Hunter is trying to do. He is trying to reverse

psychology me or some other twisted lawyer tactic or some-thing. He is trying to paint himself as the innocent one, like he really has no idea what is going on. He is trying to throw me off track.

It won't work.

I pull my phone out from my back pocket hoping, foolishly, to see a text or missed call from Reggie. It is my umpteenth time playing myself today because there is nothing but noti-fications of a few robocalls and junk emails waiting for me.

I am halfway through the lobby when it buzzes in my hand. I lift it up so fast, just knowing Reggie's face will be there, but there is no face. It is a 212 number, which makes me consider it for another two rings. It can still be spam—they are getting really clever nowadays—but I have nothing to lose, so I tap to join the call.

"This diary you gave me was useless like I figured."

I freeze. Then it rushes toward me. I recognize the voice. Detective Quinn. She sounds a bit different on the phone, a little raspier, like maybe she has just come off a smoke break.

I think she is done until she says, "Except one thing."

I pause. "What thing?"

"Would be better to do this at the station," she says, and I tell her I will be there as soon as possible.

37

I HUSTLE TO Jersey right after I get off work. Rush hour traffic is horrendous, but Detective Quinn is still at the station when I arrive. I take a seat adjacent to her desk and she pulls out Kate's diary.

"Sterling & Birch." She pauses, pointing to a specific entry. "She mentioned she was up for a big promotion there, but wasn't sure if she wanted to take it because she'd be away from the house more, blah, blah, blah."

"Okay."

"She ended up turning it down and resigned a few months later after Scott was appointed."

I nod. I remember skimming over these mundane entries she is referencing.

"I did some research," she continues, as if she has done me a favor instead of her job. "The bags your mother's body was found in were made of industrial-weight polyethylene. But there's multiple kinds."

I have no idea why this is significant, so I shrug. "Okay."

"I know what you're thinking. I had the same thought. *That's a long shot.* I thought it was nothing…until I saw that that model went out of production. Two years before she went missing."

I lean in. "What?"

"Stay with me here. About twelve years ago S&B went from making their bags with a plastic that used low-density polyethylene resins to one that used linear low-density polyethylene resins."

"What's the difference?"

"LLDPEs are substantially stronger than LDPEs. It's the standard now."

I nod, even though I am still not sure what this is leading to. "Okay."

"They're different, but what they have in common is they're the only plastics that have a lower density than water, which means these resins will float." She pauses, catching my eye. "Remember a piece of the trash bag your mom was stuffed in floated to the surface? It had traces of her blood on it. That's how her body was eventually located."

I remember.

The divers were out there for hours. That's what I had been told.

Detective Quinn glances at something she jotted down on a page of her notepad. "There aren't many companies who manufacture LDPE bags anymore, not even ten years ago. I made a few calls. I found a guy who's been at S&B for almost thirty years who was able to identify the bags from the photos we have."

Detective Quinn reaches for a folder I hadn't even noticed. Her eyes come to me. "You okay to…?"

"Yeah. I'm good," I say, though I'm not sure if I am.

Detective Quinn shows me the photos of Mom's body in the black plastic she has been describing to me. Looking at them now isn't as gruesome as I remember. Her face and body are completely covered, only the outline of her body visible beneath the thick plastic, and even that makes my stomach tighten.

Detective Quinn pulls out another photo. The same shot but blown up and slightly pixelated. "See this emblem?"

I nod.

"Of course, I can't prove who put your mother's body in those trash bags. But now that we know these particular bags were out of production for years at the time of her murder, it means the person who used them didn't get them from their local Lowe's. They had a stockpile. Could be anyone, sure. But considering the proximity..." She shrugs. "Well. I've never been the type to believe in coincidences, but I guess I'd suck as a cop if I did."

I say nothing, am very aware of how hard I am breathing through my nose, my jaw clenched, pandemonium inside my head. I could scream, I could sob, I could flip this table.

I could have had the answers to what happened to my mother thirteen years ago.

First, there is the guilt. For even considering my father could have killed my mom. He loved her. He wanted her to be happy no matter what it cost him. He wanted to die with her. Somewhere, somehow, I always knew that.

Then an image. I picture the inside of the Bishops' three-car garage, the way Hunter would always hang out in there to get away from his parents' fighting, and I am pretty sure it is where Kate kept her stash of trash bags.

"It's been thirteen years and this is the first thing you've found," I say, and my voice sounds robotic and remote, even to my own ears.

All this time, all I've wanted was any sign of a commitment to finding her, any proof that her life mattered, that the years she graced this planet meant something, that my dad and I were worthy of finding out the truth.

Detective Quinn will never understand how deeply her colleagues' cavalier investigation ruined me. I didn't just lose my mother when I was twelve. I lost all the illusions about how the world saw girls like me that I took for granted.

"Simone—"

I don't look at her. I can't. "When a white girl goes missing, you pull all-nighters and exhaust every means to find her. When a Black woman goes missing, you assholes go home and get a full night's sleep."

"Listen, I understand your—"

"You don't understand shit about me," I snap, staring her in the eyes. "Fitzpatrick was so eager to put this on my dad just so he didn't have to spend what it would take to do a proper investigation. Black death isn't worth a fucking dime to you."

"There's no reason to make this about race or get angry. Now—"

"Don't you think it's a little late for that?"

She sighs and reaches for her smelly cup of caffeine. "Simone."

"You guys are the ones who made it about race when you decided my mother's disappearance wasn't worthy of this state's resources because she didn't pass the brown paper bag test."

"Simone, let's—"

"No reason to get angry?" My laugh burns with fury. "You wouldn't be *angry* if your mother disappeared and the people who are supposed to protect and serve convict your innocent father instead of her killer, who lives right *next fucking door*?"

She takes a breath and waits until I calm down. "Are you gonna let me do my job?"

I let my exaggerated eye roll and the folding of my arms be my answer, but I can't seem to stop my head from shaking.

"Listen, Simone. We had no grounds to investigate the Bishops. There were no leads. The evidence was all moot. We couldn't have searched their home without a warrant. If we would've known about the affair, it would've been a different story. I believe Fitzpatrick questioned you, didn't he?"

"Don't do that." I shake my head harder, aware of but also

indifferent to how petulant I must look. "I was *twelve*. I didn't know what I saw mattered."

Detective Quinn sips her coffee and sighs again. "How about we leave the past in the past and focus on what we have now?"

I shrug, so over this woman. "Fine."

And we both ignore the single tear that leaks out of my left eye.

Detective Quinn leans in and tells me more about the trash bags. She also informs me of how she stayed at the office eighteen hours straight trying to get to the bottom of it. And while the trail of intel she has navigated seems impressive, I daze out before she wraps up her soliloquy, the details going fuzzy in my head as soon as they pass through my ears, my anger too strong for rational thought.

When she's done, I say, "She wants the diary back, by the way."

"Kate?"

"She sent Hunter after me."

Detective Quinn shrugs and glances at the time. "It's evidence now."

"And there's nothing you can do?"

"No, I'm sorry. It's…"

Her words trail off when she sees that Fitzpatrick has sidled up next to her desk.

"Sir," she says, regarding him with the level of respect I could never muster just for the sake of my dignity.

I avert my eyes and play with my cuticles while Fitzpatrick pulls Quinn out of earshot to give her an update on another case, I assume.

Then he stops and says loud enough for me to hear, "Why aren't you writing this down?"

She hustles to grab her notepad and realizes she doesn't have a pen within reach. He rolls his eyes as she moves things around her crowded desk to find something to write with. Then, irritation clearly building, he reaches into his back pocket, but comes up empty too. Quinn eventually finds one under a stack of paperwork on her desk and hands it to him. She apologizes when she remembers the pen was for herself. While Fitzpatrick rolls his eyes again, unable to hide his aggravation, I feel a pang of realization in my gut.

Fitzpatrick is generally a lovable, charming guy. He's good at presenting the best sides of himself to the public. It's obvious there's something about my presence that causes him to lose all candor, most of his tact. He wasn't happy when he saw Quinn talking to me a few days ago and I can only imagine seeing me again in such a tight time frame has his nerves shot. He wouldn't want me poking around. No, he absolutely wouldn't want the daughter of the man he convicted of the most heinous crime potentially uncovering the truth.

Especially not when he's running for political office.

"Does he have anything to do with it?" I ask softly once he's out of earshot, back in his office. Quinn looks like she's still recovering from embarrassment, so I refresh her. "The diary. Not being able to get it out of evidence."

"This is standard procedure. What would Fitzpatrick have to do with it?"

I'm not sure I buy that, but I have no choice but to take her word. "He doesn't want you helping me, does he?"

"Simone, I'm not at liberty to discuss that."

"Is that usual for him? To not have a pen on him?"

"Is what unusual?"

"You guys take a lot of notes. I would think you'd always carry around a pen. And not just like a basic ballpoint one. Like the good kind. I don't know, like one of those fancy fountain pens."

"Fountain pens use a liquid-based ink. Takes longer to dry. Not good for note taking," she says, totally and completely crushing my theory that it was him who burgled his way into my apartment. I feel deflated, like every time I make prog-

ress, I'm shucked right back to my starting point. But then
Quinn says, "I used to transcribe his notes because they're always smudged. Used to be so annoying. He treated me like I
was his assistant until I made detective."

Holy shit. How fast things can turn around.

Now all I have to do is figure out why he would want the
diary. How did he even know it existed and was in my possession?

I get my answer only a few minutes later once I'm in the
driver's seat of my car, key in the ignition. I've been scrolling
online for only minutes and I've already come across multiple
friendly images of Scott and Fitzpatrick together. There's even
one with Kate where she's standing between the two men, angled slightly more toward Fitzpatrick.

Of course, it's not surprising that these two are—or at least
were—good friends. Cops and prosecutors are fighting the same
fight, on the same side. I recognize Kate's dress, a blue-and-white
sleeveless sheath with a print that reminds me of fourteenth-
century china. I remember my mom complimenting her on it.
Kate said it was new, which dates this photo to around a year or
so before we left Asher Lane.

It's kind of incredible. White men always look out for white
men. Fitzpatrick is protecting Scott.

I wonder if this means he knows what he did.

All these years I've thought of Fitzpatrick as merely a lazy
idiot at best, an egotistical, narcissistic maniac at worst. But I
never considered he was as corrupt as this.

At least now I can rest knowing my father is innocent, any
lingering doubt now annihilated.

38

"FITZPATRICK KNOWS SOMETHING," I say to Pia as she heads out of the coffee shop with her matcha iced latte.

"What?"

She agreed to meet me for coffee again this morning, but there was train traffic, so I was nine minutes later than I promised. I try to keep up with her fast clip as she joins the flow of the herd of pedestrians on their way to work, a near-impossible task with her long legs. "If all your uncle did was his job, then why was he in my apartment snooping around?"

She stops in front of an opened cellar and glares at me over her shoulder. "What are you talking about?"

"He picked the lock to my front door and tried to find Kate's diary, but I had it on me, so he fled through the fire escape and left this behind." I reach into my pocket and hand her the weighty fountain pen Quinn all but confirmed belongs to him. "He clearly doesn't want me to know the truth. Why? Because he knows he flubbed? Because he doesn't want the truth to come out before the votes are in?"

For the first time, Pia is speechless. There's no sarcasm, no rebuttal. She just stares at the ink-filled vessel in her hand, and by the way her lips fall open, I know she recognizes it.

She's either thinking of a rebuttal or reeling in shock, I can't tell, but she doesn't speak or blink long enough for me to question whether her respiratory system is still functioning.

"Prove it," I say in a whisper, and her eyes slowly shift to mine. "Prove your mission is to find the truth. Talk to your uncle for real this time. Ask the hard questions. Ask the questions you don't want the answers to."

I don't give her a chance to respond. I step around her and let the crowds swallow me whole.

When I get home, I undress on the way to the bathroom, then order food. I stand at the edge of my peninsula and eat mostly with my hands. The courier shows up at eight on the dot. I ignore the knocking and go into the bathroom to wash my face.

In the morning, Hunter calls me at 6:00 a.m., wanting to know why I didn't send the diary back with the courier. I tell him I can't give it to him and end the call.

Later, just as I am about to head outside for my lunch break, an email pops up in my inbox. I read it quickly, as it is only one sentence, and immediately grab my cell and head for the elevator bank.

Hunter picks up after only two rings, and I speak before he can. "You're wasting your time."

"Am I?" he asks, and he sounds so different from the man I know, the boy I grew up with, like I mean nothing to him, and I can't say anything because deep down I know I've given him every reason to feel this way.

"You think I don't know about Reggie's past?"

"A felon working for a law firm. I believe that's irony, Ms. Writer, isn't it?"

"There's no law that prevents an ex-con from being an attorney. This was supposed to be expunged anyway."

"It was. I had my dad pull a few strings to dig it up. Figured it would be worth the effort."

And then I get where he is going with this. I swallow, feeling sick to my stomach, a wave of dread and inevitability washing over me in sections.

My head shakes even though I know he can't see me. This can't be happening.

"What, am I supposed to dump Reg now and come running into your arms?" I snap.

"This isn't about me. This is the part where you stop talking to that detective about my family unless you want me to show this to the partners. Do you know how fast they'll drop a Black guy with a felony drug possession charge on his rap sheet? They're just waiting to say *they're all the same.*"

I don't say anything for the longest moment, and when I do, there is a hitch in my voice. "Hunter. You... This isn't even you."

His breathing quickens through the phone. "I'm not the one who made it get to this."

"Do you know how hard Reg worked to clean his life up? No, of course you don't. Everything's been handed to you on a silver platter with gold trim. You have no idea what it means to struggle, to do what you have to do. All you had to do was be born."

That doesn't pause him. "Get me the diary back or I forward that to the partners."

The call drops in my ear, and I stare at my phone, my brain still trying to process what just fucking happened.

"Hey."

I don't know how long it's been since I was downstairs on

the phone with Hunter, but when I look up to the voice, I see Jasmine standing in my cubicle, zero memory of riding the elevator back up to the suite. "Yeah?"

"The conference room is all clear," she tells me, and I can see concern flicker in her gaze but am grateful she doesn't speak on it or badger me with the kind of questions I am not in the mood to answer. "You can go set up now."

I shake my head and remember the meeting I am supposed to be setting up for at 2:00 p.m. I grab my phone and glance at the time. I have ten minutes to set up. I head to the second floor and flip the lights on in the conference room. It is a mess from the last meeting. I restart all of the computers and bring up Outlook and PowerPoint. I check the fridge, and while there is plenty of water, there is barely anything else, so I head to the break room and steal some LaCroix. When I get back, I still need to wipe down the table and chairs and make fresh coffee, but I check my phone again and Reggie still has not texted me.

Call me back.

I wait a couple of minutes, but don't get a "read" receipt. So I send another.

Please. Need to tell you something!

When I am done setting up, a guy in Marketing shows up early and greets me at the door. I smile and say good afternoon even though there's nothing good about this particular afternoon, and when I glance down at my phone again, there is still no response.

By the time my phone finally rings, I'm on the toilet. I reach for it midhover, lactic acid building in my quads, and pause when I see that it's Pia and not Reggie. I don't even leave the stall before tapping to answer.

"Okay, first of all, my uncle is not a dishonest prick." This is her greeting. "You might not like the outcome of the trial, but he did his job the best he could. Your mother's murder was not just a stepping stone for his career." She pauses, then starts up again just as I open my mouth to object. "But maybe he was wrong."

That changes everything I was about to say. I take a beat to regroup my thoughts. "Like an honest mistake?"

"They happen."

Sure, they do. I'm not convinced the laughably weak evidence Fitzpatrick and the rest of his department gathered and presented against my dad to the grand jury was a simple mistake, though. But at least I have Pia's ear.

"So you agr—"

"I said *maybe*," she interjects.

"Okay. *Maybe* is something."

I wash and dry my hands as I wait for her to continue.

I even have time to check to see if the puffiness under my eyes has receded before she says, "I spoke to my uncle again last night. Off camera. Asked him a bunch of straightforward questions."

"And?"

"He gave no straightforward answers." There is another pause and I desperately wish I could hear inside her head. "I'm not saying he's lying. I'm not saying you're right. I'm saying...you have two days."

And that's the end of the call.

When I slip out of the bathroom, I see that Matt has just stepped out of his office and is heading my way.

At least he rips the Band-Aid off fast and lets me know that I'm being let go without making me sit through ten minutes of awkward small talk. Matt calmly explains that he just got off the phone with an irate client who was determined to rip him a new asshole because of a ball I dropped earlier this week. He also cites the multiple times I've fucked up the past few days, including earlier when I left my post to take that call with Hunter, and honestly, I'm shocked at how bad of an employee I've been. If I'm honest, I've been slowly getting to the point where I can't give a shit about this job. Pia's documentary and the anniversary of Mom's death have only been exacerbating factors. The only reason I haven't quit was because of the salary boost I'd get if Matt gave me Katrina's old office.

On my way out of Matt's office, I ask who will be getting her accounts and he says he's still undecided. When I'm halfway through clearing out my desk, I see Jasmine heading toward me wearing a just-swallowed-a-canary smile, and it hits me that Matt lied. Jasmine was the one who told Matt about my past, my dad's conviction. She intentionally sabotaged me so that she would get the promotion instead of me. I slide the pieces together just in time, and when she makes a beeline toward the break room, I follow her inside. The room is empty except for a guy who works in Marketing washing out his mug in the sink. I wait until he slips out the door to sidle up next to her, my arms folded across my chest.

"You told him, didn't you? About my mom? What happened to my dad?" I ask, doing my best not to raise my voice and draw any of my coworkers' attention away from their desks, but Jasmine barely reacts. "How did you even know any of that?"

"Heard you. In the bathroom."

I shake my head in confusion. "You…"

And then it rushes back. When I took that call with Pia. I could have sworn the bathroom was empty. Obviously it wasn't.

"Listen, it wasn't like that." She pauses, her hand cradling the refrigerator door handle, but doesn't meet my narrowed gaze. "It just slipped out one day and…"

"How does something like that just slip out?"

"It's not like I plotted this whole thing from the jump, if that's what you're thinking. Don't take it so personally. It's not that deep."

A wry laugh slips from my throat. "*You just got me fired.* I'm now unemployed in the most expensive city in the country. My mom's dead. My dad's in prison. I have no backup plan. No cushion. No sponsor. What part of this am I not supposed to take personally?"

She pulls out a small blue-topped Tupperware container and shuts the door, her expression resigned when she finally looks at me. "I actually thought you'd be thanking me right now," she says, completely calm, and it's her nonchalance that is making my blood boil more than the actual betrayal.

"Are you...?" I flex and unflex my jaw; it's taking everything inside me not to toss her lunch out one of the large windows behind me. "I can't believe this."

I back away from her and pace away, my arms akimbo, a cacophony between my ears. I can't lose it here. I can't say what I really want to say to her.

Before I get my thoughts together, she says, "You don't want this job, Simone."

"What do you mean *I don't want this job?*" I snap, snatching around to face her again before I even truly consider her words. "I have bills. I have shit to take care of. I *need* this job."

"I know you—"

"No. You don't know me like that. You don't know everything I'm dealing with."

She places her food in the microwave, setting the timer for two minutes. "You don't need this job. You have options. You have talent." She studies me for a second over her shoulder. "It might take a while, but at some point you'll realize I did you a favor."

I scoff. "You think hijacking my main source of income is doing me a favor? What are you, delusional or—"

"Simone, listen—"

"I trusted you," I say, cutting her off and instantly realizing I am no longer using my office-appropriate inside voice. "I thought we had each other's backs here."

She nods and breaks our eye contact for a beat, then sighs and says, "Okay, I know this feels fucked up right now, but aren't you always talking about how much you hate this place and how you wish you could be working on your own dreams instead of someone else's? Well, this is your chance. Go write. Tell the stories you need to tell." I think she's done, but then she adds, "Nothing's stopping you now but you."

And it's hard to find my voice for a few seconds. Her words hit me right where it already hurts. My head shakes. "It's not that easy. I don't—"

"Who said any of this was supposed to be easy? Girl, all you do is make excuses. That's your problem. You take so much shit for granted and you don't even realize it. I know you've been through some shit, but now you have it so good. You're pretty as hell, healthy, you have a rent-controlled apartment in a decent neighborhood and a good man. Do you know what I would do if I had someone like Reggie on my arm?" Something inside me lurches at the sound of his name. "He's smart, sexy as hell—the man is a motherfucking attorney. You basically won the lottery, but that's not enough for you. And I get it. You want more. But this is all I have. I'm not like you. I don't have a backup plan either, Simone. I don't have anything to fall back on. You know what that means? I'm gonna be here for a while. So yeah, I did what I had to do to avoid spinning my wheels in a junior position for years. Now I'm moving up and you're...free."

I almost blurt that Reggie and I aren't even on the greatest terms right now, get so close to going into how our relationship isn't as perfect as it may seem on the outside, but it feels feeble at this point. It doesn't matter. She's wrong for what she did, but she's right too. I hate that part.

"You're gonna be fine, Simone," she says, giving me meaningful eye contact, her voice so sincere, I almost believe her. "I'll look out for that 'thank you' email to pop up in my inbox and I promise no hard feelings as long as you do too."

She grabs her food out the microwave and I let her go, the weight of her words still sinking in, and I realize I'm more pissed that I didn't see any of this coming than actually getting fired. Jasmine betrayed me for a salary and title bump, and while this is one of the lowest things I can imagine, at least she used her vindictiveness to compete with another woman for a promotion and not over a man. In some ways, what happened is fair. In others, it's complete bullshit. Another iteration in what feels like a never-ending cycle of progress and regression that is my life. There's no such thing as me catching a break. I've been doomed since my mother was senselessly slaughtered. It's like the universe doesn't want the world to know the truth, and all I can think standing in the subway car back to Brooklyn is this has all been for nothing.

39

THE NEXT TIME my phone rings, it is about to die and it's still not Reggie. I put Detective Quinn on speakerphone and sit on the edge of my bed as I unpack my things from the cardboard box HR gave me on my way out of the office.

"I went to see Kate," she says, jumping straight into it, and I try to sound cool, like I am not falling apart over my recent unemployed status.

"What happened?"

"I went to apologize for the diary thing, but I snuck in a few questions." She pauses. "She was pretty hammered."

I nod even though she can't see me. "That's kind of her MO."

"Just booze or pills too?"

"I've only seen her drink," I say, though it wouldn't surprise me if she was also taking some combo of designer antidepressants.

"Well, the most interesting part was when I asked her if it was possible that Scott murdered Evelyn."

"You flat-out asked her?"

"I'm a detective. That's what I do. I ask questions. She wasn't obligated to answer."

"Did she?"

"Anything is possible, isn't it, Detective?"

"Anything is possible," I parrot in disbelief. "She said that?"

"Verbatim."

I'm staggered for a moment, then shake my head. "But why would she even open that door?"

"Maybe it was the alcohol."

"I know they're divorced now," I say, picturing Scott in my head, the look on his face when he caught me in his bedroom. "But does divorce mean your loyalty ends?"

I'm not really expecting a response. It feels good just to air out my thoughts.

But then Quinn says, "Well, his loyalty ended when he began his extramarital activities, didn't it?"

True. But I am still shocked. It's almost like Kate wanted to give Quinn a reason to suspect him. Could she hate him that much? It would help if I knew why they actually got divorced. I pace as my mind whirs to Hunter. I can't help but think of how everything is ruined between us. Then it slams into me.

Kate might have been inebriated when Quinn questioned her, but she was still sharp enough to protect her own. Now it makes sense. She was in mama bear mode when she said *anything is possible.* That was her purposefully leading Quinn to Scott because she knows Hunter is really the one who killed my mom, the one who never crossed my mind. Kate is just doing what she has to do to protect her only son at the sacrifice of her lying, cheating ex-husband.

"Other than that little slip, she was..." Detective Quinn is judicious in the time she takes to search for the word she wants to use. "Tight. Patronizing. Passive-aggressive."

"That's just Kate Bishop."

"You *did* steal from her," Quinn points out.

I shrug even though she can't see me. "It was worth it, wasn't it?"

"It robbed me of the leverage I normally have. She evaded most of my questions. She knew I was standing on shaky ground."

"You're saying she was more resistant to being grilled because I stole from her?"

"Precisely."

I go quiet, thinking of ways to rectify this. "So there's really no way we can just give it back?"

"Not until this investigation is over," she says. "It's the only piece of evidence we've got."

I pull at my hair. "Can't you just make copies or something?"

"It's out of my hands."

Again, I want to ask if that means this is up to Fitzpatrick, but decide against it when I get a new idea. "What if I apologize for taking it?"

"You want to apologize to her?"

"Maybe it'll loosen her up and she'll be willing to cooperate."

Detective Quinn weighs that for a moment. "I won't stop you."

"And what about Scott?" I ask, hoping I like her next response just as much.

"What about him?"

"I tried talking to him. He gave me nothing."

"I'll give it a go, but as with Kate, he won't be obligated to talk unless he's under arrest."

Again, I nod to myself only, and suck in a breath. There have been times I've doubted my instincts, times I almost bought into what Reggie was saying about me caring about having an answer more than I cared about uncovering the truth. I even almost considered my dad killed my mother, the love of his life. I'd almost thought of him as a bloodless murderer. I may have been wrong about Scott, but I had the right family from the start.

Hunter.

My best friend.

We were so close, nearly inseparable during my most formative years.

But I guess that's why I never noticed. Maybe I never really knew him. Or maybe I only knew a part of him, the part he wanted me to know, the lovable, sweet part of him I clung to when I was a kid, felt protected by, believed in.

"What would we need for you to arrest him?" I ask, popping back into the moment.

"A warrant."

"How do we get a warrant?"

."We're far from it," Quinn says with a sigh. "Let's just take this one step at a time, all right?"

I tap my thumb and hang up the phone, everything spinning in my head, terrifying and exhilarating all at once, round and round like a vortex.

An image of us in the attic fills my mind. Hunter leaning on me, so close, my smell, his smell, one smell, and all the while he's been the last one to see my mother alive all these horrific years ago, had momentarily appointed himself a god and took her life from us, from me. All her dreams, her plans, her love in his hands. Then gone, just gone.

I push inside my bathroom and immediately vomit. I haven't had lunch yet and skipped breakfast too, so nothing of substance comes out. I flush the toilet, wash my hands in a robotic stupor, then finally work up the courage to face my reflection.

I don't take in my features, don't pick apart what I don't like, don't admire the things I am pleased with. I go back and forth a few times, trying to weigh the consequences of each decision. And then I realize that I have to do it. Dad has been suffering behind bars for ten years. I can't let this go on any longer, not when I'm so close.

If I have to talk to Kate, I will talk to Kate.

40

I MAKE IT over to Reggie's apartment in less than a half hour, though the sun has already gone down. He still hasn't answered my texts or called me back. When I knock on his door, I get no answer. I tighten my fist and knock harder, not giving a shit about his neighbors, knowing the likelihood that he's inside and ignoring is extremely low, but I'm also unable to contain the sour energy inside me that's been compounding since my call with Detective Quinn. I want to take it out on him, especially because he's been ghosting me, but in the interim, his door gets the brunt of my frustration.

I bam out one more text to him, and as I hit Send, the elevator dings. I hear the bass of his voice before I see him and take a breath, still trying to find the right words to explain all of this. I know the last name he wants to hear come out of my mouth is Hunter's. I run my hand over my hair and brace myself, though as I wait for him to turn the corner and see me waiting in front of his door, I hear a soft voice, which throws me off because I assumed he was on the phone.

"Don't worry about going easy on me." It's the voice, a female voice, slightly distorted under an exaggerated vocal fry and an obvious slur. "I actually have insurance."

"What?" he asks, and I can tell he is also drunk, which is off-putting because he never drinks an ounce past his limit, not when we go out, not when he's out with colleagues or his boys from college.

"In case you rupture my cervix," the girl says a little too loud, laughing, and I imagine her teeth are cappuccino-stained and crooked in that uninteresting, slightly grotesque European way, though I know she is probably beautiful. A few things run through my mind. She could be from his office, but I can't match her voice to the kind of woman who wears Ann Taylor suits and conservative, low-heeled Banana Republic heels to work every day. I wonder how close she's standing as they head my way, where her hands are, where his eyes are. Then I remind myself we're on a break, but never did we discuss fully ending things.

I clench my teeth.

"Who says I'm that big?" Reggie asks, and I feel my head shaking, the walls closing in, the ceiling dropping, the rage burgeoning.

"Um, you're Black and you're like six-two."

She laughs again, and then I hear them kissing, loud and sloppy. It's hard to visualize. It sounds gross, porny, almost like they're both too twisted to latch on to each other's lips, forget about finding a rhythm. My fist tightens at my side. I lean off the door in silent fury and step around into the main hallway. He's got her shoved up against the wall, face buried into the curve of her neck, his pelvis pushed into hers.

"At least now I know why you've been too busy to call me back," I say unceremoniously, and Reggie's eyes pop open so fast, it looks like he's been stabbed in his lumbar vertebrae.

"Simone." Staggering toward me, he can barely formulate words, much less process me standing before him witnessing his transgression. "What are you—"

"You've been ghosting me for the past couple of days. My dumb ass thought maybe something was wrong."

I almost laugh at myself, at the level of humiliation.

The girl turns to me, her bouncy box-blond hair falling over her shoulder in one smooth motion. "Hey, I didn't know—"

"This is between me and Reg. Or actually, there's nothing between us anymore. I don't even know why I'm still here." I meet his eyes. "The break is over."

I brush past him, knocking his arm with my shoulder, and head to the elevator.

"Simone," he calls after me, but I don't stop. I can't stop. There aren't enough words in the Oxford English Dictionary for me to express the way I feel right now. I was worried and he was moving on? Entertaining himself?

I barely wait for the elevator doors to part before storming through them and head out of the building. As soon as I step off the curb to cross the street, Reggie cuts me off, slightly out of breath. I glance over my shoulder and realize he must've jogged down the emergency stairwell.

"Babe, wait—"

I move around him, my face stone. "Don't waste your time."

"She doesn't mean anything to me."

"How does that make it better?"

"Will you slow down for a sec?"

I stop short and take a breath. He wasn't expecting me to come around so fast and collides with me from behind. It's a clumsy few moments, but then we're both standing facing each other, adrenaline going haywire.

"Reg, I want to write," I say, before I can talk myself out of it.

"We're on a break. I tho— What?"

I look away, then meet his eyes again and force some conviction in my voice. "I want to be a published author."

"What does that have to do with—"

"You obviously think I should just keep chasing checks with my day job. I want to be with someone who gets my dream."

It's clear by his expression he has no idea what to say. "I…"

It's not totally his fault. I should have come clean about this a while ago. Not just to him. To myself.

"And you know what else?" I say, on a roll, not ready to stop. "Our schedules are incompatible."

He's shaking his head now, maybe detecting the note of finality in my voice. "For now. Once I get settled in, it'll be different."

"Well, you know what's never gonna change? I don't want to get married. Ever. Obviously that's something you see yourself doing and who am I to keep you from that?" I blow out a breath, and it is like everything that I've been holding in comes out all at once. "It's not just our schedules that don't work. *We* don't work anymore."

Something flashes in Reggie's eyes, but I can't tell what it is, and before he can try to change my mind or talk me into staying, I turn away and head back to the station because the look on his face is too much to bear.

41

I PACE OUTSIDE Hunter's office building, ignoring the blisters that have started throbbing along my soles, and I check the time for the third time. Finally, when I look up from my phone, I see Hunter strutting out of the revolving doors. It's still hard to see him as my mother's killer, a duplicitous monster, even in the flesh, even with all that I now know. But it's still there, still true even if my brain refuses to see it.

"Real petty," I say, grabbing his attention right away. "Getting security to block me?"

His eyes immediately drop down to my hand. "Where's the di— What do you want?"

"If you want to out Reg to the partners, go ahead. Ruin his career all you want. I don't care."

"All of a sudden you don't care?"

"Not anymore. We're done."

He scoffs, thinks I'm bluffing. "You expect me to believe he broke up with you because I showed up at your apartment?"

"No, I just broke up with him because he's fucking some fucking white girl."

He shifts his weight from one leg back to two, firm stance, square. "How is her being white relevant?"

I bulldoze past his question and step close to him. "You can't silence me, Hunter. I'm gonna get the person responsible for my mom's murder behind bars and I don't care what it takes or who it is."

I pause for a moment, making sure he feels the subtle threat I just tossed his way. I expect his eyes to bug out like I've just thrown a lasso around his neck, but oddly, he doesn't even seem fazed.

"Simone," he calls as I step away. *"Simone."*

I slip my AirPods in and refuse to give him the satisfaction of seeing me look back.

Even when I am halfway to Jersey, I can still hear his voice, the way he shouted my name, and as much as I want to fully revel in my anger toward him, I can't, not completely, because even as I walked away, he sounded like he cared.

I make it to Kate's impeccably manicured home and everything is the same as the last time I was here, the lawn perfectly trimmed, her white Range Rover parked in the driveway, offensively bright in the dark. I push the doorbell, and as the double chime reverberates, I have the illogical yet demanding urge to run before she answers, but then I remember why I'm here and force myself to root my soles to the ground like a tree's roots. I think of Reggie and his face before I left, how hurt he looked, betrayed even when he was the one doing the betraying. I know I told Hunter I didn't care, but I do, at least a part of me does. What we shared was real and real doesn't die just because lies are born. I will not let him lose his job over me, and if this is what it takes, then so be it.

After a few anxiety-inducing moments, I finally hear Kate's

staccato walk to the door, and I have no idea who she was expecting but it definitely wasn't me. In pretty but sensible heels, she stares at me as if she has gone mute, her mouth open but no words slipping past her overplumped lips. Her lipstick is faint. Most of it probably smudged onto the rim of her wineglass, and without the veneer, it's awkwardly obvious her last injection was a bit overzealous.

"Do you have a minute?" I ask before it gets too awkward.

"Simone. Come in," she says with the perfect closed-mouth smile, but really she means fuck off, because by the flat look in her eyes, she clearly does not want me anywhere near her pristine sanctuary.

I feel like a mosquito as I follow behind her slow-moving hips as she leads me into the kitchen. There is something cooking on the stove, one large pot. She checks a burner, then flips around and asks if I'm hungry. Since I can smell the scent of dead, burning flesh already, I decline as politely as I can and take a seat at the island. The seats are high enough for my feet to not touch the ground and just this makes me feel vulnerable.

Kate looks slightly offended by my rejection, but recovers quickly and elegantly, murmuring something to herself that I can't make out. She grabs a bottle of wine out of the fridge and two cabernet glasses from a cabinet by the stems, then extends one my way.

I shake my head. "No, thanks. I'm fine."

Something flashes in her eyes, a sort of mild panic. "You're not..."

"I'm not what?"

"You're not pregnant, are you?" she asks, and maybe she sees the look on my face, because her eyes flutter, and then she waves her hand, dismissing her own question. "Oh, of course. I forgot you don't drink."

"I'm not staying. I just wanted to apologize." I take a breath and will myself to just spit out the words in the most gracious way I can manage. "I shouldn't have invaded your privacy."

Her eyes don't blink. "You stole from me. I could press charges, you know."

I look away from her stare, the intensity too much to bear. "I just thought—"

"It's okay, Simone," she says, getting rid of the cork in the bottle as effortlessly as a magician shuffles a deck of cards. "I haven't filed a report and I have no plans to. We all know how things can end up with people like you when the police are involved."

She tips the bottle over, filling the glass, but holds my gaze until the liquid nearly spills over the edge. Cougar pour.

I'm not sure how to take that. Somehow, it sounds more like she is threatening me than doing me a favor, and I am still stuck on the way she says *people like you*. There is something mildly intimidating in the way that she stares at me from across the table, which makes me wonder if she is fucking with me. If she is, in fact, covertly telling me to stay away from her ex-husband and son, because she knows it was one of them. It's not something I've considered, how much Kate has known all these years.

I clear my throat. "Just wanted you to know that I tried to get your diary back, but Detective Quinn—"

"She stopped by, you know," she says matter-of-factly, and I'm still trying to read her as she takes indulgent sips of her ox-blood-hued beverage. "Had a lot of questions."

She punctuates everything with a friendly quirk of her lips and disguises her irritation in this syrupy, benign tone, but it's all aesthetic. Artificial. I still pick up on the accusation in her words. I'm working her nerves. I wish I could thoroughly enjoy it.

"I heard," I say and carefully choose my next words. "Do you really think it's possible that Scott—"

"I was just trying to annoy her."

All I can do is watch her drain her glass with steady, consistent gulps. "What?"

"For asking such a ludicrous question."

I shake my head, try to understand. "So it was a joke?"

"*Sarcasm* is probably more accurate."

"My mom is actually dead, no joke," I say, and I swear I am trying to keep my cool but this white woman is pushing me to the edge. "I'm just trying to figure out what happened to her. I didn't mean to make you feel violated in any way. I'm sure you can understand."

"Of course I understand. You have no idea how much I miss her."

She reaches across the table and squeezes my hand, which feels like something she has practiced too often. No energy transfers from her hand to mine. Hers feels dead. A fish head with a hook in it.

"God, it must still be hard for you to not have any closure with that whole situation. You were still so young when it happened. It had to be traumatizing to have all those people in your house, looking for answers that weren't there." She pauses, and I look up, waiting with bated breath for her to finish. "Kind of what you did reading my diary."

She's pissed, deeply, but she's still wearing a faint smile.

My jaw tightens and I force myself to stop considering the corkscrew next to the bottle of cabernet sauvignon, how with one well-engineered swipe it could drain perfectly crimson blood from her neck and artfully disrupt the snow whiteness of her outfit. Instead of taking my brewing anger for her son out on her, I stare at an empty space on the wall. There is no point in arguing with her. She is always the victim. It doesn't matter who is actually hurting, it doesn't matter who is at fault, she is the victim. She has made that clear. Our home gets raided and my father gets unjustly arrested, then thrown behind rusty iron bars, and she is still the one who has suffered more egregiously.

"Yeah, it was rough" is all I manage as I straighten out to my feet.

I head back to the foyer, and though I hear her start to follow a few steps behind, I don't slow down. I came, I did, I'm done.

"And the way she was butchered," she says from behind me, with a pitiful shake of her head, I imagine.

I stop and part my mouth to stop her, because I don't have it in me to go there tonight, to that night my mother took her last breath, without me, without her mother or her husband or her daughter. Because I can't listen to the mother of my mother's murderer speak of my slain matriarch and not reconsider that corkscrew. Or the many knives in the wooden block on that marble countertop too. Even the half-filled wine bottle would do it.

But she goes on before I can get a word out. "Why couldn't they just push her in the river or something? Why did they have to be so gruesome? Stabbing her God knows how many times, then drowning the poor thing. I could barely watch the local news. For weeks I couldn't even turn on the TV."

I pause, my fingers curled around the door handle. I replay her words over and over. Over and over until pandemonium erupts inside my head.

The trauma of the days and weeks following my mother's death bubbles right back to the surface. The smells. The questions. The endless people in our house. Having to sleep in a foreign bed until the forensics teams got what they needed, all for the police to do nothing. Watching my dad nod along as the coroner explained how it might have happened, silent tears streaming down his neck. Picking out the casket design. Choosing between lilies and roses. Screaming as they took my dad away from me in handcuffs. Being orphaned. Moving in with Aunt Patrice. Waking up from dreams, or perhaps nightmares, of hugging her. Forgetting midday that she wouldn't be home, or next door, when I climbed off the bus after school. Receiving the autopsy. That inconclusive report starting it all over again. More questions. More confusion. More salt into an unhealable wound.

Crushed by relief, paralyzed by shock, my grip on the door handle goes lax and I slowly glance at her over my shoulder. I barely hear my own words as they slip off my tongue, barely feel gravity pinning me to the ground. "That's not what happened."

"What?"

I scramble for the rest of my voice. "My mom wasn't drowned."

"I saw it on one of the reports. She had all those stab wounds, but that's not what killed her. They said she died from asphyxiation." She shrugs. "I just assumed…"

I fully face her, and now when I see that crimson raining down over her white outfit, I don't try to stop the images from coming. Multiplying.

"It was from the blood," I tell her, resenting with each word that she's forced me to relive the very moment I learned of this, still too young to fully process it. "She choked on her blood and stopped breathing. That's when she was dumped in the river. That's what the autopsy results showed. They were inconclusive, but the medical examiner said that would be his best guess."

"Oh."

This time Kate forgets for a split second to manufacture a smile and I think of the smallest knife I spied in that wooden block in the kitchen, how with the right grip on the hilt, I could effortlessly carve her the perfect substitute smile in the bottom of her face, red and permanent like a clown's.

"You know how they always get things wrong in the initial reports," she says in explanation, but part of me suspects she knows it's too late and her words are moot. "I had to stop watching the coverage after a while. I was having nightmares. Kept thinking 'What if the sicko that did this comes after me next?' Jesus."

Kate visibly shivers. I watch her for a moment, then just stand there, replaying her words until I feel Kate charging at me. I jump back, my heart skipping a beat, my fists curling into usable weapons.

"What's wrong?" Kate asks, clearly taken aback by my reaction, and then as her arms open I realize she was trying to give me a hug. A hug. She wasn't trying to attack me.

I force myself to calm down and thrust back the saliva I have the urge to hawk into her eye. "Nothing. Sorry, I was just..."

Kate wraps her arms around me and pulls me close. I barely reciprocate. Everything feels still inside me. The muscles in my legs feel tight and strange. And I don't know what to do with my hands. I don't know what to say. I don't understand what the fuck is happening right now.

"Sweetie, I know we've lost touch over the years after everything," she whispers, her wine-stained lips so close to my ears, I shiver. "But my son has always loved you. So I do too. I hate that you've had to relive all this. At least Evelyn is at peace now, right?"

I say nothing, just go helplessly limp like a kitten being carried by its scruff, and when she finally pulls back, my hands are shaking.

42

"HAVE YOU TAKEN a test yet?" It was the first thing you said after I told you I'd missed my period for the third week in a row.

"Not yet. But I never miss my period."

You shrugged. You weren't the least bit worked up like I was. "It has to be a fluke. Unless…"

"Unless what?" My voice was flat.

"What if it's not mine?"

But I hadn't been with my husband in the last three months. You knew that. We'd talked about it.

"We don't even know if I'm pregnant yet," I said, trying to be sensible about this, to not let my emotions get me too close to the edge.

"What if you are?" you asked, quietly, as if you were afraid of the answer.

I looked right into your eyes. "I'll get an abortion."

"Just like that? You're not even going to consider keeping it?"

Your reaction didn't make any sense to me. You were such a rational, levelheaded person in every regard, yet when it came to this, you'd suddenly lost all your acumen.

I shook my head, confused. "How can I keep it?"

You sat on the edge of the bed, your elbows on your knees. I could tell by the way you bounced your leg that you wanted a cigarette. Your voice dropped. "You say that like it would be the worst thing in the world."

"Of course it would. What are you saying?"

"I'm just saying we could try to work it out."

"Really? How would we work it out?"

You rose to your feet. "Look, I'm not saying it would be ideal—"

"I'm not having your goddamn baby," I snapped.

Your eyes widened. You couldn't believe that I'd just sworn at you. You swallowed hard and looked away. You looked like a petulant child. I didn't feel bad. I wanted to slap some fucking sense into your head. You were not thinking of your family. Your career. Of me. This baby would ruin everything and there was no way I would let it.

You didn't talk to me for weeks after that.

You called me insensitive. Callous. I thought that was a bit dramatic since you were the one who stormed out and stopped talking to me completely.

Of course, I took a pregnancy test two days after our fight, three in fact, and they all came back negative. My period came seven days later and I forgot about the whole thing. Around the four-week mark, you called me, said you missed my company, and I agreed to meet up with you.

For the most part, everything went back to normal. We met up. You vented. We fucked. We let time pass and did it all over again. It was great. It was exactly what we both needed. I was the ear you so desperately needed and you were there for me when I needed you most—and I definitely *needed* you.

I didn't see the end coming; I thought we had more time. In retrospect, I should have known that something was off the day everything went wrong because you were twenty minutes late arriving at the hotel and you were never late. When you saw me, you told me you'd left your wife and that it was over for good. You laughed, an ugly, hateful laugh, and recounted the whole thing to me, minute by minute, though I never asked.

You didn't even come right out and say the words. You got drunk. You slammed the papers down on the kitchen table while the woman was eating dinner. You called her lazy and selfish and a horrible mother. You went nuclear. You said she cried as you spoke, huge crocodile tears. She even got on her knees and begged you to stop, to come back when you were sober and talk about all of this rationally. She even suggested therapy, but you insisted that you meant everything you said. It was over. It was fucking over. You stormed out of the house and spent the night in a hotel. Our room at the Marriott. You slept naked for the first time in over ten years. You masturbated to porn with the sound on and left the toilet seat up in the bathroom. You ignored your phone, twenty-three missed calls, turned it off. You knew it would hurt her, that it would push her over the edge, but you needed her to get your message, to know how serious you were. There was no turning back, no apology that could fix the damage you'd done.

After you told me all of this, I could feel your expectation. You wanted me to pat you on the back for finally being a man and standing up for yourself and what you wanted. To tell you that you did the right thing.

But this was not what I wanted.

This was *never* what I wanted.

You were still drunk. I could still smell the gin on you, sour and stale. Your hair was a mess. It looked like you hadn't slept all night, like you hadn't even brushed the plaque from your teeth. I was disgusted. I wanted you to leave. I wondered what I'd ever found attractive about you, about this.

"I want to spend more time with you," you said, wistfully, reaching over and taking my hand into yours as if this was the ending to some fucking fairy tale. You'd never seemed so small to me before, so infantile.

Suddenly, I knew without a doubt, this was the end.

I had been dreading it from the start, the inevitable moment where you would make this more than the escape, more than what it was, and we could never go back to that happy, peaceful state.

"You know that's not possible," I said, pulling my arm away.

"Why not?" You sounded offended. Hurt.

I scoffed, incredulous. "Because I'm *married*."

"Well, you're going to leave him, aren't you?"

"No."

"No?" You looked shocked. You sounded utterly betrayed. "What do you mean *no*?"

I walked away from your glare and slipped on my shoes in the corner.

Thank God there had been no baby beginning to gestate in my uterus. Thank God I got my period a few days after we'd seen each other that day. You would have put up another fight and I would have had to terminate it behind your back and lie about what had happened.

"You said he doesn't pay you any attention. He barely notices you anymore. You're going to stay with this man and be miserable for the rest of your life? Is that what you want?"

I rolled my eyes at that. "You have no idea what I want," I said, but really I wanted to tell you that you were not special, you were just there. It could have been anybody, really, but you were the most convenient. Always dropping by like it was nothing, masking your frequent visits as if you were interested in my husband, though the entire time you couldn't keep your eyes off me. You also had the most to lose.

"Come on, Kate. He doesn't care about you. Not like I do."

I hated the way you said my name.

I never told you I was going to leave Scott. This was never about feelings. This was never about love. You didn't love me, you just loved the idea of me. You weren't thinking straight. You were scared of being alone, maybe, but that was not my fault.

"I'm leaving," I said, grabbing my bag off the side table and heading for the door. I felt you moving close behind.

"Kate—"

"Don't follow me."

"Will you just talk to me? Please. I did all of this for you, dammit, and you're just going to walk away like this?" you said, and the way you grabbed my wrist, the meaning behind your words was unmistakable. You weren't only talking about leaving your wife. You were talking about before, things we agreed to never speak about again.

"For me?" I laughed. I knew it would hurt you. "I didn't ask you to do any of this."

You rolled your eyes and let go of my arm. "For Christ's sake, Kate, you didn't have to *ask*."

You wanted me to apologize, but there was nothing I was sorry for. I spoke carefully through my clenched teeth, making sure you understood that I meant every word. "I didn't ask you to divorce your wife. I didn't ask you to do what you did for me. You did all of that yourself."

"Bullshit. I wouldn't have done any of it if it weren't for you. Everything I've sacrificed—my career, my entire *fucking* life. It was all for you—for *us*."

To be honest, I didn't think you had the balls. I thought you would crack. You had told me I didn't need to worry, you would keep me safe. You stuck to your word. I had to give you that, I guess.

You leaned closer to me and softened your voice, but I could only see the speck of spit above your lip from shouting so hard. "I know you're scared. You said you were waiting for the right time. Well, I'll tell you this—there's never going to be a right time. You just have to *do* it."

I huffed out a breath and looked you in the eyes so directly it was painful. "I have a good life. I'm not giving that up."

My words hit you hard. I could see it in your face. You were finally starting to understand.

I turned to leave.

"After everything he did to you, to your family. You're just going to accept that? Don't you want better? You're worth so much more than that, Kate."

I really hated when you talked like that. You sounded trite, like one of those stupid books you were always reading.

"It was all a lie, wasn't it?" you said as I started to open the door.

"What?" I flipped back around, my hand still on the door handle. We were nose to nose. I could feel you breathing on me, hard and uneven.

Your eyes drifted away, then came back, harder. "You told me it was self-defense. Was that a lie too?"

"Of course it was self-defense. You *know* what happened, Ford."

There was a pause. "I know what you told me."

"I told you the truth."

It was the last thing I said to you.

I expected you to say something else, but you never did. You took a few steps back and let me open the door. I left the room and never looked back.

43

I DON'T REMEMBER texting Hunter for his address. I don't remember the traffic-heavy drive back into the city. But I am standing in front of him and he is staring at me in the hallway with his jaw flexed.

It breaks my heart, this unyielding look he gives me. Only weeks ago seeing me made him smile in such an unrestrained way, and when we were kids, he would never, ever look at me with such vitriol, not even after we bickered. I am not sure if it is my guilt for thinking he could have done something so heinous, so unspeakable, or if it is relief that I will not have to mourn another loss, the loss of my childhood hero, but I lower my eyes and tuck my chin so he can't see the stupid tears that gush from my eyes all at once. So many emotions attack me, narrowing in from multiple angles like raptors.

"Hey," he says after a moment.

It is more of a grunt than a greeting, more like a *what do you want* than a *hey*. There is a question in it, like why the fuck did

I ask to come over like this with no notice, sounding urgent as fuck with the all caps and multiple exclamation points. There is also a note of impatience, like now he's seen my "emergency" was quite hyperbolic considering all my limbs are still attached and I am not covered in blood.

But I can't look up, can't see him seeing me like this. I cried the whole way here, hiccups and gasps and swallows, and all because even though there are still unanswered questions like *why* and *where*, the *who* is no longer pending. I can't even imagine what my face looks like, but I figure it's something similar to someone who has just crawled out of a coffin.

I was wrong. I was so wrong.

"Simone."

I gasp at my name and I hate myself for it. I've never felt this kind of shame before. This kind of unbridled need.

Reggie should be here. Reggie should be holding me as I break, catching all of the pieces in his palms so I can put myself back together soon. But he is not. He has moved on, so all I want is for Hunter to touch me, to pull me in tight and softly ask me why I needed to see him tonight. But he doesn't, and I don't know what feels worse, his ambivalence or my unrequited neediness.

"You should…" He transfers his weight from one foot to the other and nods toward his living space, which I can tell without a tape measure could fit two of my studios. "Do you want to sit down for a sec?"

All I can do is nod.

Hunter steps aside and shuts his door after me. There's a soft, still satisfying click. I sniffle and the expensive smell of his place invades my nostrils. It is not like the cologne he used to douse himself in once his voice changed and he started trying too hard to impress easy-to-impress high school girls. It must be a candle burning, but I glance around and don't find a flame.

I lower myself to a couch that is too beautiful to be this comfortable. I wish for it to swallow me whole, but nothing happens. He takes the chaise section so we are not within touching distance and is quiet until his patience wears thin.

"What are you doing here, Simone?" he asks, his voice soft, but edged with exasperation.

I wipe my face with both palms, then my sleeve. Then I sniffle obnoxiously loud. "Thanks for letting me in. I know I'm not your favorite person right now. I'm probably the last person you wanted to see tonight, huh?"

"Pretty much."

It was a rhetorical question, but I accept his response with a tight nod.

I still haven't lifted my gaze from the floor and now I notice his bare feet. They look nice. As nice and as clean as his cookie dough hands, probably just as soft.

"I'm glad you're starting to look like your dad," I say, relieved that most of my voice is intact.

I don't know why I just said that. I don't know how to do this, how to walk this tightrope. It doesn't help that Hunter just looks at me as if he is waiting for me to get to my point, to the reason I'm here, so he can as quickly get rid of me.

"I..." He shakes his head and shrugs. "Okay."

"Because if you looked like her, I couldn't look at you anymore."

I watch his expression morph from slight irritation to total befuddlement.

"What's the real reason you hate your mom?" I ask.

I could just say it. But this is Hunter, this is someone I used to love, someone I used to make plans with, big plans. Even with the birth of a new hate, an old love doesn't just detonate to its exquisite death like a star.

"What?" he asks, but I know he heard me. He has no idea where this is going; I can see it on his face. He is afraid. Of me. Of saying the wrong thing. Of where I might lead him.

I keep my voice even, aloof. "Why do you hate her?"

He frowns, focusing on his thoughts, maybe a memory, for a moment. "I don't really hate her. I just…"

"Just what? Spit it out."

The veil of concentration on his face falls away and his features contort into an expression that is somewhere between confusion and fury. I instantly regret rushing him.

"Simone, what is this?" he asks, his forehead creasing again. "Why are you here?"

I let the new tears roll down without disturbing their flow. "I know why you hate her."

He doesn't say anything, just looks away. I know it is because he hates to see me cry. It makes me feel better, to know he doesn't actually hate me, that I didn't completely ruin us.

"You hate her because of what she did."

He pauses. "What are you talking about?"

"What do you think I'm talking about?" My voice is almost a whisper now. I can barely project.

"Why can't you just say whatever it is you think she did?"

"Because I don't want to say it. If I say it, it'll make it too real."

The tears come in sheets now. I jump back to my feet. I need to walk off this rush of emotions. I can't just sit here and let him watch me break in two. I pace over to the door and then back to the couch. I take a breath and look at him. His face is open, not deceptive, but then again, wouldn't a deceptive face look open for it to be effective?

"So you really don't know?" I ask in a whisper.

"Know what? Why are you being so weird?"

I stare at him, not sure what I am even looking for. I open my mouth and start to speak, but then stop myself. "God, I hate this. You were the one person I could trust back in Asher Lane. You were…and now…"

"Trust? You stole from me and I'm the one who can't be trusted?"

I meet his eyes. "I had a good reason to take the diary. And I didn't steal from you. I stole from Kate."

"Simone." Hunter is on his feet now too. "You just showed up to my place tonight, all right? Just fucking showed up. What do you want?"

"I'm sorry."

I fall back against the wall behind me and hold back a sob.

He's frowning so hard I can count the lines in his forehead. "You came here to say you're sorry?"

I can't tell if it's his disbelief that sounds like surprise or surprise that sounds like disbelief.

I shake my head. "For insinuating that you or your dad killed my mom," I say, my voice flickering in and out.

"You did a little more than that."

"I fucking said I was sorry, Hunter," I snap, and so many hot tears rush down my face.

I can't take him seeing me like this. I stagger over to the island in his kitchen and hold on to the edge of the marble until the tears release their hold on my voice.

"Fuck." I can barely hear myself. "Sorry. I didn't mean to yell at you. I'm just a mess right now. I'm sorry."

A pause. Then, "It's okay."

The dismissive words sound reluctant, but I appreciate them.

"Did something happen?" he asks, crossing the space to get closer to me. "What made you come around?"

"I just realized…" I suck in a shaky breath. "Realized who did it."

"Did Quinn find something?"

"No. I did."

"What?"

He sidles up next to me. Doesn't say anything else. He waits, then glances at me, not impatient this time. Concerned. "Simone, you can trust me."

I look at his hand on the counter not too far from mine, the hand I used to hold when he was struggling to read. His phone buzzes and he checks the caller ID. He glances at it, but doesn't tap to answer.

I wipe my face. "Just get it."

"It's…my mom."

The look we exchange is the same from both ends, surprise and slightly weirded out because we were just talking about her.

He accepts the call. They exchange greetings and then I hear him giving her the room number to his apartment and my blood goes cold.

He hangs up his phone and looks at me. "She's on her way up."

"She's *here*? Why?"

"I don't know. She's never even been to my place."

I don't say anything else, just turn and head toward the bathroom.

"What are you doing?" Hunter asks.

I swing back around and keep my voice low. "I know you think I'm a little crazy right now, but your mom killed my mom."

He rolls his eyes. "Here we go again."

"That's what I was trying to tell you. I'm sure this time."

"That's… She didn't even know it was your mom Dad was sleeping with. Why would she—"

"She knew."

"She freaked when I told her."

I shake my head. "It was bullshit. You didn't break her heart. She was playing you."

He thinks for a beat, but still can't accept what I am saying. "But she…"

Hunter just shakes his head over and over. No words. Only disbelief. Absolute refusal.

"She knew," I say. "She fucking knew it was my mom. That's why she killed her. Everybody on Asher Lane would have known your parents' marriage was a sham if my mom kept the baby. And she was going to keep it. My dad asked her to get rid of it, but she stood her ground."

Hunter paces, as if he is trying to make sense of all this. "Where are you getting this from?"

"I went to her house tonight to apologize for taking her diary, and she told me exactly how Mom died."

"So what? It was all over the news."

I shake my head. "Not the part she knew."

"Anyone can look up an autopsy. When are you going to give this up and accept that your father isn't who you think he is?"

Hunter snatches away from me, fire in his steps now. He's panicking. I get it. But I need him to listen.

"What she told me wasn't in the fucking autopsy," I say. "She knows what *really* happened."

He stops and runs a hand through his hair. "Simone, you have to—"

"The medical examiner told us that they had to fill in gaps because of how long it took to find my mom's body. They knew asphyxiation was her cause of death. The best they could come up with is that she choked on her own blood." Again, I wait for him to meet my eyes. "So why did your mother just tell me she drowned?"

Hunter looks like he is going to crush something. Maybe me.

But then a knock at the door slices through the silence and we both jump.

"I'm not here," I whisper, darting toward his unlit hallway in the back.

"Maybe she read that somewhere," he says, his voice as soft

and as breathy as mine. "Or heard it from one of the neighbors. You know how fast gossip travels on Asher Lane."

I do. It's like an inferno.

I stop in front of what I assume is his bathroom. "I promise I'll explain more later. Just don't tell her I'm here. Please."

I can almost feel him tense, wondering if he can trust me, if I am still worth protecting. He pushes out a breath, shaking his head, and then heads for the door. I hold my breath.

44

"WHAT ARE YOU doing here?" Hunter asks, and I impatiently wait for her response, unable to pace through my anticipation.

"I hate this furniture," she says, sounding indignant. "It's so cold."

Of course she avoids his question. Of course she criticizes him before even acknowledging his presence.

"It came like this," he says, on the edge of sounding annoyed.

Her heels clack loudly on the floor. Then they come to an abrupt stop. "I don't want you seeing that girl anymore."

It's a snap. A command.

Hunter doesn't say anything. I can practically hear his mind whirring, maybe picturing me in his bathroom among his private grooming tools and toiletries, probably hoping I don't make a sound.

"She came by my house."

"I know," he says, then quickly adds, "I mean, she told me earlier that she was going to stop by."

"You need to cut ties with her. She knows too much."

"What's there to know?"

She pauses for so long I almost think she won't respond. "She knows Scott killed her mother."

My mouth opens. I was right? I was right this whole time and no one would believe me. So many emotions move through me at once. There is shock and anger, but there is also confusion. Kate knew she was drowned, water is how she asphyxiated, not her own blood.

"What?" he asks, sounding as staggered as I feel.

"I was supposed to take that to my grave. Now you have to take it to yours." A moment passes, my heart thumping against my chest. "Should have burned it."

"Burned what?"

"That diary," she says, and it's almost a scream. And then she lowers her voice again. "I thought it got lost during the move. Thought it was gone."

The room falls silent again. I think about taking out my phone and recording this for Detective Quinn, but that would probably make too much noise, and these high-quality walls are so thick that I decide against it and just listen.

"Dad wouldn't…" Hunter sounds so confused, so betrayed. "He loved—"

"He didn't love her, Hunter. He was *fucking* her. She was a goddamn whore like the rest of them."

I almost push out of the bathroom, but somehow I keep my cool, though my entire body is trembling and I literally feel like I am going to detonate. I want to kill her. I want to kill this fake bitch. She was never really my mom's friend. Their relationship wasn't superficial. It was artificial.

Like the rest of them.

I glance at myself in the mirror, telling myself to stay calm, but then I see a razor on the counter and I imagine cutting this bitch's face with it. I force myself to start counting backward from one hundred.

"I thought you said you never knew who Dad was sleeping with," Hunter says.

There is another long pause, and my fingers are now on the razor. "I only pretended I didn't know because it was less embarrassing for you to think I was stupid than to think I was weak."

I grip the razor, tighter, harder. She knew this whole time. She knew that her husband killed my mother. She did nothing. All this time.

I hear Kate's heels crossing the room and inch back toward the door so I can hear again. A minute passes.

"You can't smoke in here," Hunter says. "The building is…"

But he gives up. I hear the flick of a lighter and then there is more silence.

"Why did he do it?" Hunter's voice is shaking. "Why would Dad—"

"Because I filed for divorce. It scared him. I just couldn't stay with him after that. After the baby."

"So you knew Evelyn was pregnant too?"

"When I told Scott, I gave him two options," she says. "Have the baby and lose me. Or lose the baby and keep me. I expected him to pay her off to get an abortion and keep quiet. When she went missing, I was just as shocked as everyone else on Asher Lane."

"Did you ever ask him if he did it?"

"I was scared to. At first. Scared to know the truth."

"So you never asked? He never actually said he did it?"

"Not directly."

"But you knew he killed her?"

"I put two and two together," she says impatiently, and I grip the razor again, so hard, the plastic digs into my skin. "He didn't mean for it to get so out of hand that night. It just…happened."

That is such bullshit. She wouldn't stay with him because he got another woman pregnant, but she was willing to stay after she found out he murdered someone? Nothing she is saying makes sense.

Hunter is quiet for so long, I can't tell what is happening on the other side of the wall.

"Isn't that something? It was easier for him to slice her up than keep his hands off her." Kate pauses again, I assume to take a pull on her cigarette. "I didn't want her dead. I just wanted the baby gone."

The silence goes on for even longer this time. I let go of the razor and stare at the red mark on my hand.

"That doesn't make sense. Dad wouldn't..." Hunter struggles for a moment. "He's not even a violent person. He would never—"

"I know this is all shocking, Hunter, but people are complicated," Kate says, and I can picture the kind of smile she presents him with perfectly. "Especially fathers. I'm sorry yours isn't the man you thought he was."

I hear more footsteps moving farther and farther away. She is near the door.

"Your friend has that detective showing up asking questions," she says. "Just thought I'd let you know. She seems like she's onto your father. You might want to spend some quality time with him while you can."

Her words are so cold and detached it seems like she is joking. And then I get it. She is lying. This time I'm not going to fall for it.

A few seconds later, the front door closes. I step out from the bathroom, and Hunter is already reaching for his phone.

45

"WHAT ARE YOU DOING?" I ask, crossing the room.

He doesn't look up. "Calling my dad."

"Don't tell me you believe her."

"I don't..." Hunter blows out a breath like he's truly conflicted. "Look, I'm not saying I believe her. I don't know what to fucking believe. It doesn't make sense... None of that shit she said makes sense. I just need to hear his side."

I lunge toward him and take the phone from his hand just as it starts ringing. I end the call and cock my head. "He kills for her, then divorces her?"

Hunter glares at me, but not with disdain. "What?"

"Your dad was willing to kill for her to save their marriage, but not willing to be faithful to her in order to save it?" I wait for him to give me an indication that he sees how incongruous that is, but it's like his brain has stalled. "You know that was all bullshit, right?"

"Why would she come here and lie about this?"

"Because she knows how close we've been lately and that I've been talking to Detective Quinn. She needs to make sure you're on her side. Think about it. She's got to still be bitter about Scott leaving her after all she did to *save their marriage.* I bet she'd love to see him go down for murder even if he had nothing to do with it."

Hunter starts to pace again. His head shakes like he is conflicted, like he is battling with both sides of his brain at once.

I grab a hold of him, force him to meet my eyes. "Hunter, you *know* your dad."

He just keeps shaking his head. "He'd never..."

"But would *she*?"

Hunter can't even go there. I see it on his face. He turns away and plops down on the couch. I sit next to him and can feel him shaking.

"I don't..." He pulls his lip in, his leg bouncing. "I..."

And then he is back on his feet, pacing like a captive tiger. I tell him about the specific trash bag Kate used, everything Detective Quinn and I discussed, and watch the wheels turn in his head. I fill him in on Fitzpatrick, about him leaving his pen in my apartment after he tried to steal the diary. Hunter hears me out, then confirms my suspicion—Fitzpatrick and his dad were friends. When I ask him if he thinks Fitzpatrick could have felt any allegiance to Kate back then, he nods, and then I ask if he thinks it could have been enough for him to orchestrate my dad's arrest to protect her. This time he struggles for a moment.

"Fuck." His eyes finally meet mine in apology. "How...?" He shakes his head, starts over. "Simone, you know if I knew I would have..."

"Would've what?"

"I would have done the right thing," he says, the tremor in his voice betraying how much my question offended him. "I would have helped you. Told somebody. I will help you. Whatever you need. I'll help you get your dad out of—"

I shake my head. "But she's your mother."

"In a euphemistic way."

Chills run down my spine.

It takes me a moment to fully process what he's really saying. Hunter isn't willing to fight for his mother the way he's been fighting for his father, and I wonder what a woman could have done to make her son this way. She was hard on him, even cruel sometimes, but clearly his scars run deeper than that. I can only imagine how angry she became after she killed my mom. Holding that secret in for so many years and then for Scott to divorce her. It must have driven her crazy, to be so utterly powerless.

I reach out to Hunter and stop him from pacing. "Hunter, calm down," I say, his skin warm beneath my palm. "Let's just get through tonight, okay?"

He stops and studies me for the longest moment, and all I can think of is how profoundly wrong I was. Scott Bishop did love my mom. And maybe she loved him back, but that love cost her her life.

My father loved my mother too.

I don't know how to feel. I don't know what to think. It's all too much to deal with right now.

"You're right," Hunter says, like he's still trying to convince himself. "You're right."

I watch him run his hands through his hair, and suddenly, I feel cold. I sit on the couch, pull my legs to my chest and wrap my arms around them, holding myself together, trying to ride out the chaos, the sadness and the anger and the grief. By the time he sits down next to me, my tears have already begun to fall down my cheeks.

"Hey," Hunter whispers. "You okay?"

"I'm fine," I manage to croak out before my voice breaks off.

But Hunter doesn't move away. He scoots in closer, and I shudder when I feel the heat of him, just the smallest bit. "Sorry, I…"

"Don't apologize." He sounds almost offended by my attempt. "Please. It's just gonna make me feel shittier."

I wipe my face, but the tears keep coming, and when he leans in more, my head falls forward onto his strong chest.

"I was never going to do it," Hunter says after a while, his hand easing up my lower back now, strong and warm, and it feels so good, so soothing, I close my eyes for a second.

I angle my face toward his. "Do what?"

"Show the partners your boyfriend's rap sheet. I was just…"

"Protecting your dad at all costs. I get it. I'd do the same for mine. And it's *ex*-boyfriend."

"But this was different. I hurt you. I'm sorry."

I can practically feel his shame rock me.

I break eye contact and my gaze lands on the tops of my thighs. "All this time I thought you were one of the good ones. Thought I could trust you."

"I am. You can." His voice trembles and at least it makes me feel less alone. And then he stands from the couch. "Look, I'm not perfect, all right? I know I have things to learn. Unlearn. I'm always getting on my mom and then I threatened to do the same fucking thing. I hate that I said that to you. I didn't mean it. You don't have to accept that, but it's the truth. I was just scared."

I look up at him, his eyes shining bright in the dim light, and I feel myself teetering on a sharp edge.

"Not that fear is an excuse," he says, panicking. "I know—"

"Hunter, you ever been with a Black girl before?"

He just stares down at me, thrown by the inquiry. I'm not sure if he knows what I'm asking until he swallows so hard, I hear the sound.

"I've dated all kinds of girls," he says.

I study his face, hoping he can see how much I need him right now in a way I've never needed, or even wanted, him. "Not what I asked."

He shakes his head, like he is done racking his brain but can't come up with anything to say. I reach over and run my hand up his leg. He tenses, his entire body going stiff at that small touch, and this time when I smile at him, he mirrors my expression, though I'm sure he looks more beautiful.

"I'm on the pill, but…"

"Uh…" He glances back toward his bedroom. "I—I have some in my drawer…in my room."

But he doesn't move. I get off the couch and slip into his bedroom. He follows me inside, his steps slow and quiet, and I find a loose condom in the top drawer of his nightstand and wave it in the air. He slips it from my grasp, but doesn't immediately tear it open like I anticipate.

"Are you sure?" he whispers.

I nod, appreciative of that, but he doesn't look convinced. He doesn't reach out and touch me.

I reach for the hem of my sweatshirt. Actions speak louder than words.

But then he says, "You're not just sad, are you?"

I shake my head, and it is the quietest, most subtle lie I've ever told.

I don't want to have to feel anything else tonight. I want his hardness, his warmth, his honesty. I want to be swept up in the moment, no more dwelling on the past. I don't want to think. I look up into his eyes. Soft and blue and filled with questions. My fingers curl, gripping the bottom of my top again. I'm prepared to lift it off and be naked for him in one motion, ready to see me through his eyes, no critique, just admiration. And I don't know what happens, but as soon as his lips touch mine, his hands take my face, and I am paralyzed from the chin down. The feel of his lips against mine, even softer than his palms, renders all four of my limbs useless and the thick cotton of my sweatshirt remains between us. He doesn't even open his mouth. He just holds me close and destroys what is left of my strength with slow, soft kisses.

And now I see how Hunter truly sees me.

I can't handle this. I don't want to take this slow. I don't want him to be precious with me tonight, not because of our history, not because it is our first time together. I don't want to matter so much to him until after we both come. I wish he would just fuck me, use my body and help me keep my feelings dormant until after my dreams.

I open my mouth. I kiss him harder, faster. I offer my tongue. Harder, faster. I reach for his drawstring waistband.

Before I can make contact with his flesh, before I can size him up with my palm, his eyes flutter open, and so I open mine too, feeling his long lashes dance against my skin. He pulls back just enough to watch me for a beat, surprised, excited, scared, nervous, I can't tell.

He takes a breath, his eyes on my mouth. "If we do this…"

"I know."

"Can't ever take it back."

My eyes fall down his body, then back up, and I feel a pull in me like gravity. "I know what I want."

Hunter studies my face for another moment, then takes me by the small of my back, pulls me to my tiptoes and kisses me for real. I like the way his mouth tastes. Clean. Almost neutral. Hunter squeezes both his arms around my back, hugs me tight and kisses me deep like he can't get enough, and it's like a cello has just started playing in the background.

Hunter knows I have attempted to deceive him. He knows I am a pathetic, sad little thing right now who wants nothing more than to go numb. Maybe he is trying to punish me. That is why he is torturing me like this, doing everything he can to make me feel every inch of my body, every degree of my humanity. It is why he is kissing me the way a man kisses a woman he is trying to make fall in love with him.

I can't fall in love with the son of the woman who killed my mother.

I don't need love tonight.

I don't want love tonight.

"It's okay," I whisper. "I don't need..."

"Shh," he whispers back, and it makes me want to slap him as much as it makes me want to reach inside his pants.

I don't think I've ever been kissed like this before. With so much care, so much depth. Each one feels like our first. Each one makes me want another. I feel buried thousands of miles beneath the earth and at the same time I feel like I am soaring.

Hunter's hands move down my body and he lifts my shirt over my shoulders. He smiles and it feels so good to be taken in like this, to be admired in this way by him.

"Don't pull my hair," I tell him, stepping out of my jeans. When he nods, I add, "And I don't like it rough."

He makes a little face like he doesn't understand why I pointed that out. Then he kisses me again. I grip his hair at the roots and pull him deeper, like *please can we fuck now*. He pulls away and peels off his clothes, and when he is done I am standing there with my mouth hanging open and I don't even try to play it off.

"You don't have to look so surprised," he says with a grin, and it's not even that, I just can't believe this is actually happening, but also, yes, I was not expecting the enormity of his dick, so thick and fully swollen already.

We make it onto the bed, and when he shifts on top of me, I almost forget to breathe. He's so beautiful that I almost tell him to stop, almost push him away. I know he wouldn't try to coerce me into continuing, I know he would never force me, and maybe that is why I keep my arms limp at my sides while he reaches between our bodies and aligns us. I trust him.

"Did you really think of me all these years?"

The throaty words slip out just as he is about to push into me. I watch his mind rewind to when he admitted this to me, and his smile is perfect.

"You were the only one who really got me when we were kids," he says, and the way he looks at me makes me wish we could stop and he could just hold me until I fall asleep, until I forget once again that I'll never see my mother's face again.

"Yeah," I whisper, nervous to let him inside all of a sudden, because now I am thinking of after, of what this all will mean in the morning, when the sun is above the horizon again. "Same."

I don't know if what I attempt comes off as a smile, but I reach between us and guide him in. If we draw this out any longer, I'm going to start crying again. Hunter is careful and patient, but I still have to do a significant amount of down-playing until he fully breaks through me. Every thrust is slow and measured. His eyes don't look, they marvel.

I try not to ugly cry because I don't want him to stop, and when the first tears roll down my temples I can't tell if they are from pleasure or pain or both. Hunter whispers something in my ear, and I tell him not to stop. He breaks the rhythm anyway, and I'm mortified, worried that I've scared him off, until I realize it is so he can shift us around some, and as he adjusts my legs, it feels like kindness because now we are both on our sides, and I can cry with dignity. I don't know how he knows this is exactly what I need, him inside me to quiet all the thoughts, but that fucking eye-to-eye would be too humiliating. I come as soon as he kisses me on the nape of my neck and I don't think I stop until he puts me on my back again. This time he grips my wrists, my arms bent above my head, and I silently hope this position makes my boobs look cuter, but he is too busy looking in my eyes to notice.

I clamp mine shut, so close to the edge again, and I hear him saying something, but the words get lost under a low-frequency hum. I don't open them for a while, and when I do, it is just in time to see his features get stolen by the beautiful agony he has put me through countless times already. I have never seen anyone look so pretty making such ugly faces. He is quiet, his shallow breathing the only sound in the room as he moves inside me slowly, and I watch in awe of his elegance. He hovers above me for a few moments, catching his breath and rubbing his nose into the curve of my neck. Then he releases my arms and draws his hips back. I squeeze my eyes shut to keep from yelping, but a desperate sound escapes my throat and I am so embarrassed by the distress this has caused me that I keep them shut.

"Sorry," he whispers, and pangs of guilt detonate in my gut for making him feel like he needs to atone. "Did I—"

"No, it wasn't…" I reflexively glance down toward the culprit, that curve near the tip of his still very firm erection, and go mum. I refuse to let him know he has hurt me because I know he didn't mean to. It was only the shocking kind of pain, not the kind that does any damage.

Hunter looks like he doesn't quite know what to say, so he kisses me, and it is so slow, it's like he is silently begging for absolution, and so I silently commend him. A man who kisses a woman after sex, like really kisses her, that is a different kind of man. That is the kind of man I am sharing a bed with tonight. For a moment as he's pulling away, he stares at me, flushed and happy, the look in his eyes bright and unmistakable. Once he is on his back, I notice how much he filled the condom, and it hits me.

It's done. We can never go back.

His mother killed my mother.

I stare at Hunter as he peels the latex off, and the vulnerability of his body is almost too much to take. He looks so young right now, sweat dampening his full hairline. I don't think I ever look like that. So carefree and unconcerned. There is a constellation aglow in his eyes when they meet mine, and for a moment I think I still love him, that maybe I never stopped.

"Gonna go pee," I say, shifting off the bed. "Want me to flush that?"

Hunter has drifted off by the time I come back out of the bathroom. The covers are up to his waist, his mouth is closed, and there is no snoring because of course he is perfect like that. He looks a little lonely, but also so beautiful in the unlit space that I find it more obscene than attractive.

I am meticulous about the way I slip back into bed, making absolutely certain our bodies don't touch because I think if they do, I will cry noisily. I have one of those eerie dreams that I'm slipping off a cliff right before I fall completely asleep.

46

WHEN I WAKE UP, Hunter is moving around the room looking for his phone. He is still completely naked, and for a minute I watch him, the way his muscles gleam in the hazy morning light as he pulls back sheets and turns over pillows, his phone buzzing somewhere beneath the mess we made last night.

He finds it on the floor and answers, sitting on the edge of the bed, and while this is all happening, I am wondering if it's too early to call Quinn and update her on what Kate said to me.

If it means giving this up, I don't want to ever go back.

"Is he okay?" Hunter asks with a pained urgency, and I sit all the way up, my smile fading. "Where is he?"

He listens for a minute, then jumps off the bed. He scans the room for his clothes and then finds his jeans and shirt. He whips them on, not a word to me. I check my phone and see that it is only five thirty, but before I can put it down, Hunter turns to me and tells me that his father has suffered multiple stab wounds and is in the emergency room and asks if I can drive him to Jersey.

I stare at him for so long he has to repeat himself before I hustle out of his bed. I throw on my clothes from yesterday and grab my shoes on the way out the door. We rush downstairs and into the garage without another word.

I hop behind the wheel and grip it with both hands. We make it onto the interstate within minutes and a wave of relief runs down my back because it is practically empty.

"How many?" I finally ask, glancing at him.

"Six," he says, his voice seeming to come from far away. "In his chest."

"And he's still in critical condition?"

"They said he's lost a lot of blood, but he's stable for now."

Hunter doesn't look at me. He is staring out the window, his jaw working nonstop. I try to think of something else to say but nothing I come up with sounds right, so I remain silent, thinking of what he has told me, of everything that has led up to this point.

"You know what I was thinking?" I pause, running through it in my head one more time. "How did your mom find out my mom was pregnant?"

Hunter glances at me, but doesn't respond. A minute passes, but I can't let it go.

"She said she's the one who told Scott," I remind him. "When she was in your apartment. She said—"

"I can't think right now," Hunter snaps, his leg bouncing hard, ramming into the dashboard over and over. "Can you just drive?"

"Right. Sorry."

I grip the wheel tighter and focus on steering through the sparse early-morning southbound traffic, but seeing Hunter like this, hearing the acute pain and worry in his voice, is making my heart break.

★ ★ ★

We make it to the hospital in thirty minutes flat. Hunter heads straight back while I give our information to the front desk. By the time I am let in the back, Hunter is on his knees by his father's side. Scott's entire torso is bandaged up. He is still unconscious.

"Come on, Dad. I'm here. Wake up." His voice breaks on those last words as tears drop from his eyes. "Fuck."

I shift toward him, wanting to comfort him, but as I move I see Kate turn down the hall through the small window. I watch her for a second, then notice Detective Quinn a few paces behind her.

Kate bursts in the room, fire blazing in her eyes. "I told you to stay away from her."

"What?"

"They found her necklace in Scott's bed!"

Hunter jumps up to his feet and turns to me, confusion and anger making lines in his face. My hand lifts almost against my own will, and when I go to touch my "Evelyn" necklace, it isn't there.

"My…"

But I can't get another word out. I can't remember the last time I took it off. I never take it off. Of course, it could have slipped off somewhere, but that is so unlikely and that still wouldn't explain how it managed to get into Scott's bed. I've worn the necklace every day since I snuck into his bedroom at Asher Lane, so I couldn't have lost it that day. This doesn't make any sense.

"Simone," Detective Quinn says as she slips into the room, eyes on me. "I need you to come with me."

I want to object but of course I remember where I am and our respective places in society, that she is a white woman in an authoritative position and I am not as fortunate, and stand up from my chair. I follow after her in a robotic stupor, realizing what this all means. That I am now a suspect for having tried to stab Scott to death. I look to Hunter before turning out of the room, but he avoids my eyes. He doesn't say anything, doesn't speak up for me, just looks deeply confused, and a part of me doesn't blame him.

I follow her out to the parking lot, everything a blur as I try to work through my overlapping thoughts. How could my necklace end up in Scott's bed? I rack my brain but nothing comes. All I know is that bitch is lying. I was with Hunter all night. Someone else had to plant it there and I know it was Kate. But how could she have gotten my necklace?

Once we are out of earshot of anyone nearby, Detective Quinn whips around, her eyes hard and direct. "I thought you wanted justice, not vengeance," she says, squaring off with me.

"I was with Hunter all night. He can corroborate that."

"Simone, I'm going to have to take you in for…"

Detective Quinn's voice fades as my mind races, trying to remember the last time I saw the necklace. I had it on when I went to see Kate. I remember. And then it comes to me in a flash. I slow the memory down, remembering how Kate had thrown her arms around my neck to hug me as I was leaving her house. The whole thing was weird, and now I realize why. Kate has never hugged me before. I can't remember ever seeing her hug anyone, not my mom, not even her own son. The slick bitch was two steps ahead of me.

It had to be her.

It had to be.

"Hey," Detective Quinn says, pulling me out of my trance. She looks pissed. "Are you listening to me? I can only help you if you—"

"She hugged me before I left," I say, everything so clear now.

"What?"

"It was quick, but it was weird. She must have taken it then."

Detective Quinn frowns, impatient. "Taken what? And who are we talking about?"

Before I can answer, I feel a soft hand tighten around my arm and I am being yanked across the asphalt. "What are you—"

"Arrest her!" Kate screams, and it's obvious she is accustomed to having her every demand met instantaneously.

Detective Quinn reaches for her. "Ma'am, release her. You—"

"*Arrest her right fucking now!* She tried to kill my husband."

I scoff, snatching my arm from her. "*Ex*-husband."

"Oh, fuck you and your fucking whore mother too."

Kate lunges at me, and before I realize what is happening, I am on the ground, on my back. I kick her skinny ass away as Detective Quinn does her best to hold her back. As I make it back to my feet, another officer in uniform jogs up to my side, holding me in place.

"I need you to calm down," he says, his voice rough in my ear.

"*Me?* She's the one—" I stop myself. My heart is pounding. I take a deep breath, force myself to calm down. I know how this looks. "I didn't try to kill anyone. She's the one who drowned my mother when the stab wounds didn't work fast enough and stuffed her in a plastic bag like a pile of trash."

"Stop lying, you little cun—"

Kate charges at me again and Detective Quinn pulls her back before she can make contact.

She glares at me. "Scott killed your whore mother because he didn't want me to find out she was pregnant."

"You're lying." I turn to Detective Quinn. "She's lying."

"Scott stabbed your mother to death and now you stab him to death," Kate says, screaming now. "An eye for an eye, right? Well, you should've been more careful instead of leaving the evidence right there in his bed."

"That's such bullshit." I turn to face the officers. "She's the one who found out my mom was pregnant. *She's* the one who told Scott."

The cops exchange a glance, then look at me like they don't understand why this is important. I don't know how to explain all of this right here, right now, like this, so I turn back to Kate, my blood like lava as it courses through my veins.

"You should've just gone for an artery this time," I hiss. "Much more effective."

"What?"

"My mom never woke up because you fucking drowned her. But when Scott wakes up, it's all over for you."

Detective Quinn exchanges a glance with the other officer.

Kate snarls and struggles against Detective Quinn. "Let me go. She's demented."

Eventually they do let her go and Detective Quinn takes me to the precinct to get my side of the story. I tell her everything. I tell her my theory on what happened last night, that Kate must have stolen my necklace when I went to see her that evening. I tell her about the hug, how awkward and out of place it was. I tell her about my alibi, that I was with Hunter all night and Kate was the only one who could have attempted to kill Scott. I tell her about the strange look on her face when I told her my mother wasn't drowned, that this must have been the moment when Kate realized she'd slipped up and that I knew too much. I tell her about the way she'd come to Hunter's apartment and confessed that it was Scott all along, that he is the one who killed my mother. Kate knew she would need someone on her side to back up her story about Simone wanting retribution for her mother's death. But she fucked up because she didn't realize that I was hiding out in the bathroom while she was there. I explain that if she would have known I was there on the other side of the wall and had a solid alibi, she wouldn't have tried to kill Scott and planted the necklace in his bed last night. She would have chosen another night to kill him if she knew there was no way to pin it on me.

Detective Quinn writes all of this down, and when I'm done, she looks up and asks me if I'm okay. I don't answer. I honestly don't know.

47

I JERK AWAKE to the sound of my phone buzzing on the coffee table. I sit up and it takes me a moment to remember where I am. My dad's furniture comes into focus a little at a time. I'm on the couch. I crashed once I got here after leaving the hospital.

My phone is still ringing when I finally pick it up.

I clear my throat. "Hey."

"He's awake," Hunter says. "Sorry. Clearly you weren't."

"No, it's fine. So he's gonna be okay?"

"Yeah. I talked to him for a sec, but he's resting now. I just…"

Hunter's voice trails off into nothing. I wait for him to speak again, but he never does.

"What?" I ask, as gently as I can.

"You were there. With me. All night."

"I know."

"You were in my bed *all night*."

"Before I left your mom's house, she gave me this weird hug. She took my necklace."

He makes a pained sound. "Fuck."

"She planted it there in his bed," I say, whispering now. "She's trying to frame me."

"I never doubted you. It all happened so fast," he says, and I can hear the struggle in his voice, like he doesn't know how to process all this now that it's spelled out right in front of his face, but also, he can't deny it anymore.

I understand, but still, it hurts. I wish he would have stood up for me in that hospital room. I wish he hadn't just left me hanging when I needed him the most.

"You're lucky she failed this time," I say, the meaning behind my words unmistakable, and the silence from Hunter's line is so heavy I feel it like a weight on my shoulders.

"I told the cops," he says after a minute. "They have your alibi now, but we can't prove she planted the necklace. We definitely don't have enough to prove she killed your mom."

"Don't you think this at least helps? I mean, why else would she try to kill your dad? She needed to silence him and get rid of me at the same time. Two birds, one stone. No one ever doubts her story because if she can make it look like I killed Scott, it looks like he killed Mom and I was just out to avenge her death. It's fucking brilliant."

I can almost hear him nod. "If we can prove she tried to kill Dad last night, it helps us prove she killed your mom."

"Exactly."

"But how do we do that?"

"You're asking me? You're the one who knows how this all works."

"You're the one who reads all those books. I swear this is like straight out of some fucking novel."

I blow out a breath and start to pace across the room. I still don't understand why Kate told Scott about the baby and it didn't happen the other way around. I need to know how she found out. Then everything will make sense. It will have to.

"Can I see your dad tomorrow?" I ask, fully aware that I am asking a lot. "There's something I need to ask him."

"Sure. I just left, but I'll be here first thing in the morning," he says, and then he stops. "Shit."

"What?"

"Hold on. It's the hospital calling again."

The line drops and I stare at my phone until it starts to vibrate again. When I answer Hunter tells me that Scott's vitals have plummeted suddenly and he can barely get the words out. He says he is on his way back to the hospital, and I run down the stairs, pushing my arms into my jacket.

Twenty minutes later, I find Hunter pacing outside his father's room, his head in his palms.

"What happened?" I ask.

He looks up, his eyes bloodshot. "His IV line was disconnected."

I glance at the room, then back at Hunter. "Was she here?"

It takes him a moment to catch what I am saying, but when he does, I see the revelation move across his face. "You think…"

"She didn't want him to wake up," I say with big gaps between the words, remembering the last thing I said to her, that once Scott woke up, this would all be over. "She didn't want him to remember what happened."

Hunter is quiet, stunned, like this is all just too much for him, and I want to hold him. "You were right," he whispers, no longer in disbelief, but acceptance. "About everything."

48

THE NEXT MORNING, I head straight to the hospital, and when I get there, Hunter is already at Scott's side. I smile at him and he tries to smile back, but it fails.

I give him a kiss on his forehead and hand him the Starbucks bag in my hand. "You have to eat something."

He nods and takes it. I watch him bite into a muffin and then let him know I'm going to the restroom. When I get back, the doctor is in the room and Scott is awake and stable.

Hunter is holding his hand and it is all so pure I start to cry, my tears hot against my skin. The doctor ducks out of the room to help another patient and tells us a nurse will be in shortly. Hunter excuses himself, saying that he needs more caffeine, and I smile at him before he leaves the room.

Once we are alone, I lean in to Scott, as close as I can. "I just wanted to say sorry. I mean, this is all my fault."

He frowns, looking truly confused. "How is any of this your fault?"

"Well, Kate never would've tried to…hurt you if I hadn't told Detective Quinn that I thought you killed my mom. She was going with the narrative I created. That I tried to kill you as an act of vengeance."

"It's no one's fault but my own," he says with a sigh, as if just speaking is an effort, and pangs of guilt detonate in the pit of my stomach. "If I wouldn't have waited so long to leave her, none of this ever would've happened."

I try to swallow my thoughts, but I just have to know. "What broke the camel's back? Why did you divorce her?"

There's a long pause before he opens his mouth again. "I left Kate when I realized she killed Evelyn."

His eyes come to mine in apology, but I can't look at him. It's like everything stops at once.

Somehow, I find my voice. "You knew? All this time…"

He sighs and coughs a couple of times, throat dry. I look around for the paper cup I saw the nurse bring him and hand it to him just as he starts coughing again. "It came out during one of her drunken fits."

My head shakes. This makes no sense.

"You left her, but you still protected her?" I ask, but Scott doesn't answer. I'm not surprised. White women get to move through the world knowing that white men will protect them at all costs. There is no one to protect Black women, especially in a country where the Black men are being mass incarcerated and murdered in plain sight by the people designated to serve and protect.

For years, Scott knew Kate killed my mom and said nothing while my dad's been locked in a cell. The anger that creeps up my spine is unprecedented and I'm not even sure what to do with it. So many people. It took so many people for this to all go wrong, for my dad to do ten years of prison time for a crime he didn't commit. Scott. Kate. Fitzpatrick. The witnesses that testified against my dad. The judge. All twelve members of the jury. So. Many. People. So. Much. Anger.

"How did Kate know my mom was pregnant?" I ask after a moment. I've got most of the answers, but I will not sleep again until I get them all. It's the least I deserve.

"Your mother was over at the house one afternoon." He pauses for a moment, I assume picturing the memory, letting it play out in his head like a vintage silent film. "Kate offered her a glass of wine. Evelyn politely declined, but it was the only time she'd ever done that. So Kate invited her over a few days later and she declined again. She had her suspicion, but she wanted to know for sure, so she made her some lemonade. When Evelyn used the bathroom, the toilet wouldn't flush. Kate had clogged up the flapper before Evelyn had gotten there."

I grit my teeth. "So she used her…"

He nods. "The tests all came back positive. She told me. Gave me an ultimatum."

I roll my eyes. "Yeah, option one—you keep the baby, you lose her. Option two—you lose the baby and keep her."

"Guess it's obvious which one I picked."

"Option one."

"Kate couldn't handle it," he says. "Guess she thought I'd go for the other one. And she was especially sensitive about the baby."

I nod this time. "Because of the picture," I say, but Scott turns to me, confused. "Everyone in Asher Lane would know you two were having problems if my mom had your baby."

"Oh. Right. Sure. But we'd been trying to have a second child for years. Evelyn was able to give me what she couldn't. It wasn't planned, but it happened. Kate couldn't handle that."

The door opens, but I don't look up. Hunter steps in with fresh lattes, but I decline. He sets the coffee down and leans in to kiss Scott on the cheek.

A few minutes later, he turns to me. "Hey. You okay?"

I nod quickly and take out my phone, then step out of the room. Detective Quinn answers on the first ring.

"It was Kate," I say before she can speak.

"I tracked down her credit card records. She purchased three pregnancy tests nine days before Evelyn's disappearance."

"Nine days before?"

"If she'd gotten Evelyn to take one somehow, she would've been the first to know about her pregnancy."

"Exactly. That's her motive. She knew Scott would leave her for my mom and the baby."

"That's where I'm at too."

The adrenaline is pumping so wild. "So you're going to arrest her?"

"I'm bringing her in for questioning as we speak."

"Well, what about...what about Scott? She tried to kill him too. I know it was her."

"We just got security footage of Kate entering the hospital minutes before Scott's vitals took a plunge," she says, and that's all I need to know.

I end the call, and when Hunter slips out of Scott's room to use the restroom, I wave to him. I slip back in the room and inch close to Scott again. He looks tired, badly in need of more rest. But there is one last thing I need to know before I reach out to Pia.

"There's one more thing," I say, and my voice is barely audible even to myself.

"Sure."

"My dad has been in prison for ten years." I pause, and he nods but averts his eyes. I wait for him to say something, but clearly he's incapable of coming up with anything. I go on, hoping my fury isn't overflowing as greatly as it feels. "Those witnesses lied. The whole trial was a sham. Fitzpatrick. It's all his fault. Isn't it?"

Scott blinks a few times. "I can't speak for—"

"He was your friend. I saw the photos of you three. You could have told him after you found out the truth. You could have done something. My dad could be free right now."

Scott meets my eyes and I hate how much I see Hunter in them. He lets out a sigh. "You're right. We used to be friends."

"What happened?"

"We had a falling-out a few years ago."

I hate how vague he's being. It has to be intentional. There's got to be something else he's hiding.

I do some quick math while he reaches for a paper cup filled with tap water. Scott also divorced Kate a few years ago. I want to know if there is any correlation, or possible causation.

"Was this before or after you left Kate?" I ask, and I know I'm onto something when he flinches at the question.

I step even closer to him. "Did Fitzpatrick know Kate murdered my mom when he arrested my dad? Did he know this whole time? Was he covering for her because you were his friend?"

Scott clears his throat before he parts his dry lips again to answer me. "Fitzpatrick was only my friend so he could get close to Kate."

49

I PACE OUTSIDE the precinct for a while, waiting for Pia to show up. When she finally does, she looks annoyed.

"Whatever you have couldn't have been a phone call?"

I don't answer her. "Is your uncle here?"

"He's in his office. What's the emergency?"

By the time I catch her up on everything, I am breathless and she is mute. I don't know how I expected her to react, but I wasn't anticipating absolute silence. I almost ask her if she's still breathing when she locks eyes with me.

"That can't be true," she finally whispers.

I have no idea which part she's referring to, but her head is shaking like a bobblehead. "Quinn just brought Kate in for questioning a few minutes ago," I tell her. "It's over."

Just saying the words makes it feel like a thousand pounds have been lifted from my shoulders. I can see it. The moment I get to tell Dad that our fight is over. He's coming home. We're going to get his record expunged and pick up where we left off.

Maybe we're different people now. Maybe who we've become would be unrecognizable to the people we left in Asher Lane. But we are going to do this. We are going to go on living our lives looking forward, not backward. No matter how long it takes, we are both going to be happy again.

"So what do you want with me?" Pia asks, backing away from me like I have something contagious.

"I need your help."

"With what?"

"I want the truth. From Fitzpatrick's mouth."

Pia glances at the entrance of the station like she's never been inside, then just stares at me in disbelief.

I break away from her. Head inside. "You coming?" I ask, pausing at the door.

I wait a beat, but her long limbs don't budge.

"For someone who claims to value the truth, you look pretty scared," I tell her.

"I'll have to start over." She shakes her head, like this is all too much to process. "Everything I've shot…"

"Isn't starting over better than perpetuating lies?" I wait, but she is catatonic. "Please. This is more than a film. This is my father's freedom. His life. My life."

I stop and turn back around because I don't want to cry. Not here, not in front of Pia. Not before I have to face Fitzpatrick.

I head inside, my pace slow. If I said I wasn't also scared, I'd be lying. Just when I think I'm in this alone, I glance over my shoulder and Pia is only a few paces behind me.

50

Three months later

WHEN HUNTER SNAPS on his seat belt, I follow suit and ask him where he's taking me. He tells me it's a surprise, and after we pull up in front of the massive brick building, I have to admit I wasn't expecting this, though thinking about it now, I totally should have guessed that out of all places, this is where Hunter would take me.

He knows the me I sometimes forget myself.

"Still looks the same," I say, staring at the library we used to go to when we were kids, so many memories rushing to the surface at once.

"Yeah."

He nods toward the entrance doors. "Want to walk around?"

I smile, because this feels special, like he saved this just for me. "Sure."

We get out of the car and step inside, a smile on both of our faces. We head straight to the history section and look around like it's our first time. I pull out a leather-bound book and sniff it. Hunter smiles and does the same with another.

"I told my dad about working at G&W," he says after a while.

I look at him but he keeps his gaze straight ahead. "You did? What did he say?"

He pulls another book from the top shelf and flips through it. "He said…he's proud that I'm doing what I feel is important work."

"Wow. Big change of heart."

"Guess almost dying will do that to you." Hunter smiles with half his face, but I can still hear the hurt in his voice.

I smile back and then we're quiet for a while.

"Are you happy?" I ask.

Hunter turns and stares at me for the longest time, eyes moving over my face before locking on mine. "I think so."

Heat covers my face and my eyes close before his do, and then I feel his face so close to mine. He kisses me soft, so slow at first, and it feels like being swept away, beautiful and overwhelming and completely terrifying at the same time.

I smile against his mouth and pull back. "You should come over for dinner tomorrow night at my dad's place."

Hunter looks away. "I don't think I should."

"It was his idea."

He raises a brow. "Is that good or bad?"

I smile and kiss him again. "It's just gumbo."

Dad refused my help and insisted on preparing all the food himself. I set the kitchen table, which is much smaller than the one in the dining room, but right now the latter provides a prime view of all the unsightly camera, lighting and sound equipment that Pia's crew left behind for tomorrow's final recording session. I was there for most of it, though it was hard to watch him have to relive the darkest moments of his existence. I kept whispering for him to speak slowly, to take his time. Pia allowed him as many breaks as he needed, and on a few of them we took a circle around the block, watching the birds and squirrels do whatever seems to keep birds and squirrels so busy. I think it's been therapeutic for him in a way, to voice things he's been too scared or ashamed to admit. I've also scheduled a consultation with a board-certified therapist for him next week.

I was there for every moment he spoke about Mom. Hearing him say her name so many times, it was like she was there...*here* again, even if only for the moment. I don't know which one of us went through more tissues, but tonight there have been no tears. All six of our legs are a tangle under the small table, and I can feel the bulk of Dad's ankle bracelet against my shin.

So much has changed. So much.

But so much is still the same.

"You know what this reminds me of?" Dad asks, his voice slightly hoarse from the hours of talking he did earlier. I glance at Hunter, then back at Dad, no idea what story he's about to tell. "Evelyn hated me at first. Man, that woman despised me. But I made her laugh. And I was persistent. Never knock persistence. This one night she came over for dinner. I cooked this exact gumbo. When we sat down to eat, she stopped me from swatting this spider trying to get into my pot. I said, 'It's *only* a spider.' She goes, 'You think it thinks that?' That's when I knew I'd marry her. She'd carry my child. I'd protect and provide for her the best I could. We'd make a life together. For better or for worse. Our marriage was far from perfect, but I meant that. 'Till death do us part.' That's why I never left."

His eyes come to mine on the last few words and I don't have enough time to brush away the tears that have already started easing from my eyes, slow and hot. Under the table, Hunter rubs my leg as I wipe my cheeks. I want to tell him I'm okay, but I don't want him to move his hand.

"You did, Dad," I whisper. "You did all those things."

I nod with my words, hoping he will too, but he blinks a couple of times, then sips his drink, unconvinced. A part of him will always blame himself, I know that, but it kills me.

Hunter clears his throat. "Mr. Watson, for what it's worth, I'm really sor—"

"No apology will bring Evelyn back. So let's all just move on, all right?"

Dad meets my eyes and gives me a small smile. I nod at him, and we continue eating, though his words repeat over and over in my head, and for the first time in my life, I feel like I truly understand my father.

"I'm getting more," Dad says, standing up from the table. "Y'all want seconds?"

"No, we're good," I say, as he heads for the stove. I frown at Hunter's plate. "You actually like asparagus? I only like the tips."

He raises a brow. "Just the tip? That's not what you were saying last night."

I grin hard, feeling my whole face flush, and I hate him and adore him at the same time. I lift my plate and scrape the stalks onto his as Dad makes it back to the table.

"What?" he asks, because I am still blushing like an idiot when his eyes find mine.

My head shakes. "Nothing."

Dad smiles at me anyway like he just knows. I've missed that smile. I wish he would smile at everything I say for the rest of my life.

It's not over. There are still hills to climb, one last hearing before Dad's official exoneration, lots more calls and meetings to take with his new attorney, a shark we were able to get to come on board pro bono with Hunter's help. It's not over, but for the first time in thirteen years, there's hope, a bright, majestic kind of hope.

At some point between cleaning off the table and washing the dishes, Dad pulls Hunter aside and I pretend to not listen as they talk in the living room.

"What do you want?" Dad asks, his voice firm but kind, and I can almost feel Hunter tense up.

"I'm not sure I under—"

"Do you think if you're nice to Simone it somehow makes up for what your parents did to my marriage? My career? My livelihood? My wife?"

"No, Mr. Watson, but I do genuinely care about her."

There's a pause. "As what?"

"As a friend," Hunter says, and I swallow hard, because while I appreciate his tact, I also wonder if that's true, if there is any possibility of us ever being more than that. More than just friends.

"That's all?"

Hunter doesn't answer. I glance back over my shoulder and his head is down.

"Listen, here," Dad says. "If you think you're going to swoop in and save the day, you're wrong."

"With all due respect, I don't think Simone is the kind of girl who—"

"Woman."

"*Woman* who needs saving."

"You're damn right she doesn't. And if she did, I would be the one to rescue her. You hear me?"

"Yes, sir," Hunter says, his voice full of resignation, and it is almost funny, the way my father seems to intimidate him, but mostly it's endearing.

"If you do anything to hurt my—"

"I won't," Hunter says, his conviction palpable.

I cut off the faucet and pat my hands dry with a towel. I hear Dad step away, but when I peek over my shoulder, he is turning around, and I hold my breath.

"She was with this other kid not too long ago," he says to Hunter, and the fact that he is bringing up Reggie makes my heart stop and beat faster at the same time. "Black. Educated. Good on paper. The exact kind of guy I always dreamed she'd choose. But she was missing this thing when she looked at him. This thing in her eyes that's there when she looks at you."

I step into the living room, shrugging into my jacket. They both go quiet and turn to me.

I look at Hunter, unable to hold back my smile. "Hey. Ready to go?"

51

I HEAR HUNTER finishing up in the bathroom just as I'm finishing up the last chapter of *Closure*, the initial draft of my now-completed manuscript. I scroll to the top of the document and skim through the beginning, though I am at that point where I hate everything I wrote.

"Hey," he says, climbing on the bed next to me. "Writing?"

"Just finishing up something."

He glances at the screen. "Can I read it?"

My heart flutters in my chest at the thought of him reading my words. "It's not done. Just the first draft."

"Oh, come on. I'm sure it's good. Let me see."

I take a breath, then slide him my laptop. He takes it, adjusts the color and size of the text so it's easier for him to read and starts to read out loud. Some passages are a struggle to get through, but he relaxes whenever I rub his arm. By the time he gets through the first five pages, my heart is about to beat out of my chest, and then he says, "You need to try to get this published."

I stare at him. "You think it's good enough?"

"Yeah. Seriously. I'm gripped already."

I smile and then he smiles and then we are kissing, soft and slow, like we have all the time in the world.

I shut my laptop and stare down at it for a while, my thoughts catching up to me.

"You okay?" Hunter whispers, running his fingers through my hair.

"Just thought it would feel different."

"What?"

"Knowing what happened. Why. I don't know." I shrug. "Closure isn't all it's cracked up to be, I guess."

"I think we all romanticize knowing the truth."

We're both quiet for a while. When I look up, Hunter is staring at me, his eyes so bright and soft. "I think I'll go back to therapy. At least try one more time. Maybe with Dad. Maybe alone too."

Hunter nods. "It's a lot to process," he says, and I immediately think about how wrong I was to think that he could never truly understand me.

I sit up so I'm on my knees. "Let's play Simone Says."

"Am I going to regret this?"

"Simone says—" my eyes go down his body, then back up "—take off your shirt."

He grins, happy to oblige, and the way he pulls his shirt over his shoulders and then looks at me like *what else you got?* makes me immediately want to sit on his face.

"Simone says...take off your pants."

Hunter pushes off the bed, still smiling, and makes a show out of pulling off his pants. He moves slowly, allows me to indulge, then kicks the unnecessary material off and tosses them across the floor.

I look up into his eyes. "Underwear too."

He moves his hand to the waistband, tugs slightly, then instantly realizes his mistake.

"I win," I say, laughing at his expression, and it feels like old times, back when everything was so much easier, the world so much smaller and bigger at the same time, and I realize I am happy. Like really, actually happy.

"Oh, yeah? What do you win?"

"Simone says—" I bite down on my lower lip "—get on your knees."

No hesitation, Hunter lowers down into a kneel to claim his prize, and I watch him, seeing only the future, no longer burdened by the secrets or darkness of the past.

★ ★ ★ ★ ★

Praise for *Someone Had to Do It*

"A disturbing peek into the world of privilege. *Someone Had to Do It* is a tense page-turner that had me yelling out loud at the characters."

—Lucinda Berry, bestselling author of *The Secrets of Us*

"A juicy, brilliant treat of a thriller that combines sexy fashion-world glamour with salient points about privilege, racism, and the corrosive effects of extreme wealth. Somehow, *Someone Had to Do It* manages to be both a scathing critique of our late-stage capitalist hellscape, and the perfect mental escape from it. I couldn't put it down!"

—Layne Fargo, author of *They Never Learn*

"*Someone Had To Do It* has everything. A dark and riveting page turner that has the allure of pulling off the perfect crime with an intelligent twist."

—Nadine Matheson, author of *The Jigsaw Man*